Praise for *The Indian Clerk*

'Accomplished, informed and very dramatic in its quiet way' Edmund White, *TLS*

'A lovingly researched and vivid account' *Financial Times*

'Leavitt's descriptions of the excitement of mathematical chase, the tussles with proof, inspiration, the frustrations of algebraic rigour and the thrill of revelation are better than in any other novel involving mathematics that I've read' *Spectator*

'Richly imagined' *New York Times*

'An insightful presentation of the entrancing, obsessive strangeness and beauty of pure mathematics . . . A memorable feat' George Steiner, *TLS*

'Mathematics and its paradoxes provide a deep vein of metaphor that Leavitt uses to superb effect, demonstrating how the most meaningful relationships can defy both logic and imagination' *New Yorker*

'Intelligent, ambitious' *Washington Post*

'An intriguing blend of fact and fiction . . . Leavitt beautifully captures the fragility of human relationships . . . a brilliant evocation of a bygone era shot through with warmth and wit; a deeply satisfying read' *Attitude*

The Indian Clerk

David Leavitt

BLOOMSBURY

First published in Great Britain 2007
This paperback edition published 2008

Copyright © 2007 by David Leavitt

The moral right of the author has been asserted

Bloomsbury Publishing Plc
36 Soho Square
London W1D 3QY

www.bloomsbury.com

Bloomsbury Publishing, London, New York and Berlin

A CIP catalogue record for this book is available from the British Library

ISBN 9780747596325

10 9 8 7 6 5 4 3 2 1

All papers used by Bloomsbury Publishing are natural,
recyclable products made from wood grown in well-managed
forests. The manufacturing processes conform to the
environmental regulations of the country of origin.

Archimedes will be remembered when Aeschylus is forgotten, because languages die and mathematical ideas do not. "Immortality" may be a silly word, but probably a mathematician has the best chance of whatever it may mean.

—G. H. Hardy, *A Mathematician's Apology*

PART ONE
The Kite in the Fog

I

T HE MAN SITTING next to the podium appeared to be very old, at least in the eyes of the members of his audience, most of whom were very young. In fact he was not yet sixty. The curse of men who look younger than they are, Hardy often thought, is that at some moment in their lives they cross a line and start to look older than they are. As an undergraduate at Cambridge, he had regularly been mistaken for a schoolboy up for a visit. As a don, he had regularly been mistaken for an undergraduate. Now age had caught up with him and then outrun him, and he seemed the very embodiment of the elderly mathematician whom progress has left behind. "Mathematics is a young man's game"—he himself would write these words in a few years time—and he had had a better run of it than most. Ramanujan had died at thirty-three. These days admirers smitten with Ramanujan's legend speculated as to what he might have achieved had he lived longer, but it was Hardy's private opinion that he wouldn't have achieved much. He had died with his best work behind him.

This was at Harvard, in New Lecture Hall, on the last day of August, 1936. Hardy was one of a mass of scholars reeled in from around the world to receive honorary degrees on the occasion of the university's tercentenary. Unlike most of the visitors, however, he was not here—nor, he sensed, had he been invited—to speak about his own work or his own life. That would have disappointed his listeners. They wanted to hear about Ramanujan.

While the smell of the room was in some ways familiar to Hardy—a smell of chalk and wood and stale cigarette smoke—its sounds struck him as peculiarly American. How much more noise these young men made than their British counterparts! As they rummaged in their briefcases, their chairs squeaked. They murmured and laughed with

3

one another. They did not wear gowns but rather jackets and ties—some of them bow ties. Then the professor who had been given the task of introducing him—a youth himself, whom Hardy had never heard of and to whom he had been introduced just minutes before—stood at the dais and cleared his throat, at which signal the audience quieted. Hardy made certain to show no reaction as he listened to his own history, the awards and honorary degrees that authorized his renown. It was a litany he had become used to, and which sparked in him neither pride nor vanity, only weariness: to hear listed all he had achieved meant nothing to him, because these achievements belonged to the past, and therefore, in some sense, no longer belonged to him. All that had ever belonged to him was what he was doing. And now he was doing very little.

Applause broke out and he ascended to the dais. The crowd was larger than he had thought at first. Not only was the room full, there were students sitting on the floor and standing against the back wall. Many of them had notebooks open on their laps, held pencils poised to write.

(Well, well. And what would Ramanujan think of this?)

"I have set for myself," he began, "a task in these lectures which is genuinely difficult and which, if I were determined to begin by making every excuse for failure, I might represent as almost impossible. I have to form myself, as I have never really formed before, and to try to help you to form, some sort of reasoned estimate of the most romantic figure in the recent history of mathematics . . ."

Romantic. A word rarely heard in his discipline. He had chosen the word with care, and planned to use it again.

"Ramanujan was my discovery. I did not invent him—like other great men, he invented himself—but I was the first really competent person who had the chance to see some of his work, and I can still remember with satisfaction that I could recognize at once what a treasure I had found." Yes, a treasure. Nothing wrong with that. "And I suppose that I still know more of Ramanujan than anyone else, and am still the first authority on this particular subject." Well, some might dispute that. Eric Neville, for one. Or, more to the point, Alice Neville.

"I saw him and talked with him almost every day for several years, and above all I actually collaborated with him. I owe more to him than

4

to anyone else in the world with one exception, and my association with him is the one romantic incident in my life." He looked at the crowd. Did that ruffle some feathers? He hoped so. Some of the young men glanced up from their note taking, met his gaze with furrowed brows. One or two, he felt sure, gave him looks of empathy. They understood. Even the "one exception" they understood.

"The difficulty for me then is not that I do not know enough about him, but that I know and feel too much and cannot be impartial."

Well, he had said it. That word. Although, of course, neither was in the room—one was dead, with the other he had been out of touch for decades—from the back row, Gaye and Alice met his gaze. Gaye looked, for once, approving. But Alice shook her head. She did not believe him.

Feel.

2

THE LETTER ARRIVES the last Tuesday in January 1913. At thirty-five, Hardy is a man of habit. Every morning he eats his breakfast, then takes a walk through the Trinity grounds— a solitary walk, during which he kicks at the gravel on the paths as he tries to untangle the details of the proof he's working on. If the weather is fine, he thinks to himself, *Dear God, please let it rain, because I don't really want sun pouring through my windows today; I want gloom and shadows so that I can work by lamplight.* If the weather is bad, he thinks, *Dear God, please don't bring back the sun as it will interfere with my ability to work, which requires gloom and shadow and lamplight.*

The weather is fine. After half an hour, he goes back to his rooms, which are good ones, befitting his eminence. Built over one of the archways that lead into New Court, they have mullioned windows through which he can watch the undergraduates passing beneath him on their way to the backs. As always, his gyp has left his letters stacked on the little rosewood table by the front door. Not much of interest today, or so it appears: some bills, a note from his sister, Gertrude, a postcard from his collaborator, Littlewood, with whom he shares the odd habit of communicating almost exclusively by postcard, even though Littlewood lives just on the next court. And then—conspicuous amid this stack of discreet, even tedious correspondence, lumbering and outsize and none too clean, like an immigrant just stepped off the boat after a very long third-class journey—there is the letter. The envelope is brown, and covered with an array of unfamiliar stamps. At first he wonders if it has been misdelivered, but the name written across the front in a precise hand, the sort of hand that would please a schoolmistress, that would please his sister, is his own: G. H. Hardy, Trinity College, Cambridge.

Because he is a few minutes ahead of schedule—he has already read the newspapers at breakfast, checked the Australian cricket scores, shaken his fist at an article glorifying the advent of the automobile—Hardy sits down, opens the envelope, and removes the sheaf of papers that it contains. From some niche in which she has been hiding, Hermione, his white cat, emerges to settle on his lap. He strokes her neck as he begins to read, and she digs her claws into his legs.

Dear Sir,
    I beg to introduce myself to you as a clerk in the Accounts Department of the Port Trust Office at Madras on a salary of only £20 per annum. I am now about 23 years of age. I have had no University education but I have undergone the ordinary school course. After leaving school I have been employing the spare time at my disposal to work at Mathematics. I have not trodden the conventional regular course which is followed in a University course, but I am striking out a new path for myself. I have made a special investigation of divergent series in general and the results I get are termed by the local mathematicians as "startling."

He skips to the end of the letter—"S. Ramanujan" is the author's name—then goes back and reads the rest. "Startling," he decides, does not begin to describe the claims the youth has made, among them this: "Very recently I came across a tract by you styled *Orders of Infinity* in page 36 of which I find a statement that no definite expression has been as yet found for the number of prime numbers less than any given number. I have found an expression which very nearly approximates to the real result, the error being negligible." Well, if that's the case, it means that the boy has done what none of the great mathematicians of the past sixty years has managed to do. It means that he's improved on the prime number theorem. Which *would* be startling.

    I would request you to go through the enclosed papers. Being poor, if you are convinced that there is anything of value I would like to have my theorems published. I have not given the actual investigations nor the expressions that I get but I have indicated the lines on which I proceed. Being inexperienced I would very highly value any advice you give me. Requesting to be excused for the trouble I give you.

The trouble I give you! Hardy nudges Hermione, much to her annoyance, off his lap, then gets up and moves to his windows. Beneath him, two gowned undergraduates stroll arm in arm toward the arch-way. Watching them, he thinks of asymptotes, values converging as they near a sum they will never reach: a half foot closer, then a quarter foot, then an eighth . . . One moment he can almost reach out and touch them, the next—whoosh!—they're gone, sucked up by infinity. The envelope from India has left a curious smell on his fingers, of soot and what he thinks might be curry. The paper is cheap. In two places the ink has run.

This is not the first time that Hardy had received letters from strangers. For all its remoteness from the ordinary world, pure mathematics holds a mysterious attraction for cranks of all stripes. Some of the men who have written to Hardy are genuine lunatics, claiming to have in their hands formulae pointing to the location of the lost continent of Atlantis, or to have discovered cryptograms in the plays of Shakespeare indicating a Jewish conspiracy to defraud England. Most, though, are merely amateurs whom mathematics has fooled into believing that they have found solutions to the most famous unsolved problems. *I have completed the long-sought proof to Goldbach's Conjecture*—Goldbach's Conjecture, stating simply that any even number greater than two can be expressed as the sum of two primes. *Needless to say I am loath to send my actual proof, lest it fall into the hands of one who might publish it as his own* . . . Experience suggests that this Ramanujan falls into the latter category. *Being poor*—as if mathematics has ever made anyone rich! *I have not given the actual investigations nor the expressions that I get*—as if all the dons of Cambridge are waiting with bated breath to receive them!

Nine dense pages of mathematics accompany the letter. Sitting down again, Hardy looks them over. At first glance, the complex array of numbers, letters, and symbols suggests a passing familiarity with, if not a fluency in, the language of his discipline. Yet there is something off about the way the Indian uses that language. What he is reading, Hardy thinks, is the equivalent of English spoken by a foreigner who has taught the tongue to himself.

He looks at the clock. Quarter past nine. He's fifteen minutes behind schedule. So he puts the letter aside, answers another letter (this one from his friend Harald Bohr in Copenhagen), reads the latest issue of *Cricket*, completes all the puzzles on the "Perplexities" page of the *Strand* (this takes him—he times it—four minutes), works on the draft of a paper he is writing with Littlewood, and, at one precisely, puts on his blue gown and walks over to Hall for lunch. God, as he hoped, has disregarded his prayer. The sun is glorious today, warming his face even as he must shove his hands into his pockets. (How he loves cold, bright days!) Then he steps inside Hall, and its gloom muffles the sun so thoroughly his eyes don't have time to adjust. Mounted on a platform above the roar of two hundred undergraduates, watched over by portraits of Byron and Newton and other illustrious old Trinitarians, twenty or so dons sit at high table, muttering to one another. A smell of soured wine and old meat hovers.

There is an empty seat to Bertrand Russell's left, and Hardy takes it, Russell nodding at him in greeting. Then a prayer is read in Latin; benches scrape, waiters pour wine, the undergraduates begin to eat lustily. Littlewood, across the table from him and five places to the left, has become caught up in conversation with Jackson, an elderly classics don—a pity, as Hardy wants to talk with him about the letter. But perhaps it's just as well. Given some time to think, he might realize it's all nonsense, and spare himself coming off as an idiot.

Although the Trinity menu is written in French, the food is decidedly English: poached turbot, followed by a lamb cutlet, turnips and cauliflower, and a steamed pudding of some sort in a curdling custard sauce. Hardy eats little of it. He has very strong opinions about food, of which the strongest is a detestation of roast mutton that dates back to his days at Winchester, when it seemed that there was never anything else on the menu. And turbot, in his opinion, is the roast mutton of the fish world.

Russell seems to have no problem with the turbot. Although they are good friends, they don't much like each other—a condition of friendship Hardy finds to be much more usual than is usually supposed. For the first few years that he knew him, Russell wore a bushy mustache that, as Littlewood noted, lent to his face a deceptively dim and mild expression. Then he shaved it off, and his face, as it were, caught up with his personality. Now thick brows, darker than

9

the hair on his head, shade eyes that are at once intensely focused and remote. The mouth is sharp and slightly dangerous looking, as if it might bite. Women adore him—in addition to a wife he has a clutch of mistresses—which surprises Hardy, as another of Russell's distinctive features is acute halitosis. The breadth of his intellect and its vigor—his determination not merely to be the greatest logician of his time, but to diagnose human nature, to write philosophy, to enter into politics—impresses and also irritates Hardy, for the voraciousness of such a mind can sometimes look like capriciousness. For instance, in the last couple of years, he has published not only the third volume of his mammoth *Principia Mathematica*, but also a monograph entitled *The Problems of Philosophy*. And yet today it is neither the principles of mathematics nor the problems of philosophy of which he is speaking. Instead he is amusing himself (and not amusing Hardy) by laying out—complete with diagrams sketched on a pad—his translation into logical symbolism of the Deceased Wife's Sister Act, which legalizes the marriage of a widower to his wife's sister; Hardy all the while keeping his face averted so as not to have to take in Russell's acrid breath. When Russell finishes (at last!), Hardy changes the subject to cricket: off-spinners and short legs, hooking mechanisms, the injudicious strategies that, in his opinion, cost Oxford its last game against Cambridge. Russell, as bored by cricket as Hardy is by the Deceased Wife's Sister Act, helps himself to another cutlet. He asks if there are any new players for the university whom Hardy admires, and Hardy mentions an Indian, Chatterjee of Corpus Christi. The summer before, Hardy watched him play in the freshman's match and thought him very good. (Also very handsome—though he does not say this.) Russell eats his *gateau avec crème anglaise*. It is a considerable relief when at long last the proctor utters the final grace, freeing Hardy to escape logical symbolism and walk over to Grange Road for his daily game of indoor tennis. As it happens, his partner this afternoon is a geneticist called Punnett, with whom he also sometimes plays cricket. And what does Punnett think of Chatterjee? he asks. "Perfectly fine," Punnett says. "They take their cricket seriously over there, you know. When I was in Calcutta, I spent hours on the maidan. We'd watch the young men play and eat the strangest stuff—a sort of puffed rice with a sticky sauce poured over it."

Recollections of Calcutta distract Punnett, and Hardy beats him easily. They shake hands, and he returns to his rooms, wondering whether it's Chatterjee's playing or his handsomeness—a very European handsomeness that the contrasting dark skin only renders all the more unexpected—that has really drawn his attention. Meanwhile Hermione is yowling. The bedder has forgotten to feed her. He mixes tinned sardines, cold boiled rice, and milk in her dish, while she rubs her cheek against his leg. Glancing at the little rosewood table, he sees that the gyp has delivered another postcard from Littlewood, which he ignores as he did the last, not because he doesn't care to read it, but because one of the tenets that governs their partnership is that neither should ever feel obliged to postpone more pressing matters in order to answer the other's correspondence. By adhering to this rule, and others like it, they have established one of the few successful collaborations in the history of their solitary discipline, leading Bohr to quip, "Today, England can boast three great mathematicians: Hardy, Littlewood, and Hardy-Littlewood."

As for the letter, it sits where he had left it, on the table next to his battered rattan reading chair. Hardy picks it up. Is he wasting his time? Better, perhaps, just to toss it in the fire. No doubt others have done so. His is probably just one name on a list, possibly alphabetical, of famous British mathematicians to whom the Indian has sent the letter, one after the other. And if the others tossed the letter in the fire, why shouldn't he? He's a busy man. G. H. Hardy hardly (*Hardy hardly*) has time to examine the jottings of an obscure Indian clerk . . . as he finds himself doing now, rather against his will. Or so it feels.

No details. No proofs. Just formulae and sketches. Most of it loses him completely—that is to say, if it's wrong, he has no idea how to determine that it's wrong. It resembles no mathematics he'd ever seen. There are assertions that baffle him completely. What, for instance, is one to make of this?

$$1 + 2 + 3 + 4 + 5 + \ldots = -\frac{1}{12}$$

Such a statement is pure lunacy. And yet, here and there amid the incomprehensible equations, the wild theorems unsupported by proof, there are also these bits that made sense—enough of them to keep him going. Some of the infinite series, for instance, he recognizes. Bauer published the first one, famous for its simplicity and beauty, in 1859.

$$1 - 5\left(\tfrac{1}{2}\right)^3 + 9\left(\tfrac{1\cdot 3}{2\cdot 4}\right)^3 - 13\left(\tfrac{1\cdot 3\cdot 5}{2\cdot 4\cdot 6}\right)^3 + \ldots = \tfrac{2}{\pi}$$

But how likely is it that the uneducated clerk Ramanujan claims to be would ever have come across this series? Is it possible that he discovered it on his own? And then there is one series that Hardy has never seen before in his life. It reads to him like a kind of poetry:

$$1 + 9\cdot\left(\tfrac{1}{4}\right)^4 + 17\cdot\left(\tfrac{1\cdot 5}{4\cdot 8}\right)^4 + 25\cdot\left(\tfrac{1\cdot 5\cdot 9}{4\cdot 8\cdot 12}\right)^4 + \ldots = \frac{2\sqrt{2}}{\sqrt{\pi}\left\{\Gamma\left(\tfrac{3}{4}\right)\right\}^2}$$

What sort of imagination could come up with *that*? And the most miraculous thing—on his blackboard Hardy tests it, to the degree that he can test it—it appears to be correct.

Hardy lights his pipe and begins pacing. In a matter of moments his exasperation has given way to amazement, his amazement to enthusiasm. What miracle has the post brought to him today? Something he's never dreamed of seeing. Genius in the raw? A crude way of putting it. Still . . .

By his own admission, Hardy has been lucky. As he is perfectly happy to tell anyone, he comes from humble people. One of his grandfathers was a laborer and foundryman, the other the turnkey at Northampton County Gaol. (He lived on Fetter Street.) Later this grandfather, the maternal one, apprenticed as a baker. And Hardy— he really is perfectly happy to tell anyone this—would probably be a baker himself today, had his parents not made the wise decision to become teachers. Around the time of his birth Isaac Hardy was named bursar at Cranleigh School in Surrey, and it was to Cranleigh that Hardy was sent. From Cranleigh he went on to Winchester, from Winchester to Trinity, slipped through doors that would normally have been shut to him because men and women like his parents held the keys. After that, nothing impeded his ascent to exactly the position he dreamed of occupying years ago, and which he deserves to occupy, because he is talented and has worked hard. And now here is a young man, living somewhere in the depths of a city the squalor and racket of which Hardy can scarcely imagine, who appears to have fostered his gift entirely on his own, in the absence of either schooling or encouragement. Genius Hardy has encountered before. Littlewood possesses it, he believes, as does Bohr. In both their cases, though, discipline and knowledge were provided from early on, giving genius a recognizable shape. Ramanujan's is wild and incoherent, like a climbing rose that should have been trained to wind up a trellis but instead runs riot.

A memory assails him. Years before, when he was a child, his school held a pageant, an "Indian bazaar," in which he played the role of a maiden draped in jewels and wrapped in some Cranleigh school version of a sari. A friend of his, Avery, was a knife-wielding Gurkha who threatened him . . . Odd, he hasn't thought of that pageant in ages, yet now, as he remembers it, he realizes that this paste and colored-paper facsimile of the exotic east, in which brave Englishmen battled natives for the cause of empire, is the image his mind summons up every time India is mentioned to him. He can't deny it: he has a terrible weakness for the gimcrack. A bad novel determined his career. In the ordinary course of things, Wykehamists (as Winchester men are called) went to New College, Oxford, with which Winchester had close alliances. But then Hardy read *A Fellow of Trinity,* the author of which, "Alan St. Aubyn" (really Mrs. Frances Marshall), described the careers of two friends, Flowers and Brown, both undergraduates at Trinity College, Cambridge. Together, they negotiate a host of tribulations, until, at the end of their tenure, the virtuous Flowers wins a fellowship, while the wastrel Brown, having succumbed to drink and ruined his parents, is banished from the academy and becomes a missionary. In the last chapter, Flowers thinks wistfully of Brown, out among the savages, as he drinks port and eats walnuts after supper in the senior combination room.

It was that moment in particular—the port and the walnuts—that Hardy relished. Yet even as he told himself that he hoped to become Flowers, the one he dreamed of—the one who lay close to him in his bed in dreams—was Brown.

And of course, here is the joke: now that he lives at Trinity, the real Trinity, a Trinity that resembles not in the least "Alan St. Aubyn's" fantasy, he never goes after supper to the senior combination room. He never takes port and walnuts. He loathes port and walnuts. All that is much more Littlewood's thing. Reality has a way of erasing the idea of a place that the imagination musters in anticipation of seeing it—a truth that saddens Hardy, who knows that if ever he traveled to Madras, steeped himself in whatever brew the real Madras really is, then that pageant stage at Cranleigh, bedecked with pinks and blue banners and careful children's drawings of goddesses with waving multiple arms, would be erased. Avery, swaggering toward him with his paper sword, would be erased. And so for this moment only can he take pleasure in imagining Ramanujan, dressed rather as Avery was dressed, writing out his infinite series amidst Oriental splendors, even though he suspects that in fact the young man wastes his days sorting and stamping documents, probably in a windowless room in a building the English gloom of which not even the brilliant sun of the east can melt away.

There is nothing else to do. He must consult Littlewood. And not, this time, by postcard. No, he will go and see Littlewood. Carrying the envelope, he will make the walk—all forty paces of it—to D staircase, Nevile's Court, and knock on Littlewood's door.

3

EVERY CORNER OF Trinity has a story to tell. D staircase of Nevile's Court is where Lord Byron once resided, and kept his pet bear, Bruin, whom he walked on a lead in protest of the college rule against keeping dogs.

Now Littlewood lives here—perhaps (Hardy isn't sure) in the very rooms where Bruin once romped. First floor. It is nine o'clock in the evening—after dinner, after soup and Dover sole and pheasant and cheese and port—and Hardy is sitting on a stiff settee before a guttering fire, watching as Littlewood pushes his wheeled wooden chair from his desk and rolls himself across the floor, without once averting his eyes from the Indian's manuscript. Will he crash into a wall? No: he comes to a halt at a spot near the front door and crosses his legs at the ankles. Socks, no shoes. His glasses are tipped low on his nose, from which little snorts of breath escape, stirring the hairs of a mustache that, in Hardy's view, does little for his face. (*Little for Littlewood*.) But he would never say so, even if asked, which he never would be. Although they have been collaborating for several years now, this is only the third time that Hardy has ever visited Littlewood in his rooms.

" 'I have found a function which exactly represents the number of prime numbers less than x,' " Littlewood reads aloud. "Too bad he doesn't give it."

"I rather think he's hoping that by not giving it, he'll be able to entice me to write back to him. Dangling the carrot."

"And will you?"

"I'm inclined to, yes."

"I would." Littlewood puts down the letter. "Look, what's he asking for? Help in publishing his stuff. Well, if it turns out there's something there, we can—and should—help him. Providing he gives us more details."

"And some proofs."

"What do you think of the infinite series, by the way?"

"Either they came to him in a dream or he's keeping some much more general theorem up his sleeve."

With his stockinged foot, Littlewood rolls himself back to his desk. Outside the window, elm branches rustle. It's the hour when, even on a comparatively mild day like this, winter reasserts itself, sending little incursions of wind round the corners, up through the cracks in the floorboards, under the doors. Hardy wishes that Littlewood would get up and stoke the fire. Instead he keeps reading. He is twenty-seven years old, and though he is not tall, he gives an impression of bulk, of breadth—evidence of the years he spent doing gymnastics. Hardy, by contrast, is fine-boned and thin, his athleticism more the wiry cricketer's than the agile gymnast's. Though many people, men as well as women, have told him that he is handsome, he considers himself hideous, which is why, in his rooms, there is not a single mirror. When he stays in hotels, he tells people, he covers the mirrors with cloth.

Littlewood is in his way a Byronic figure, Hardy thinks, or at least as Byronic as it is possible for a mathematician to be. For instance, every warm morning he strolls through New Court with only a towel wrapped around his waist to bathe in the Cam. This habit caused something of a scandal back in 1905, when he was nineteen, and newly arrived at Trinity. Soon word of his dishabille had spread as far as King's, with the result that Oscar Browning and Goldie Dickinson started coming round in the mornings—though neither had a reputation for being an early riser. "Don't you love the springtime?" O. B. would ask Goldie, as Littlewood gave them a wave.

Both O. B. and Goldie, of course, are Apostles. So are Russell and Lytton Strachey. And John Maynard Keynes. And Hardy himself. Today the Society's secrecy is something of a joke, thanks mostly to the recent publication of a rather inaccurate history of its early years. Now anyone who cares to know knows that at their Saturday evening meetings, the "brethren"—each of whom has a number—eat "whales" (sardines on toast), and that one of them delivers a philosophical paper while standing on a ceremonial "hearthrug," and that these papers are stored in an old cedarwood trunk called the "Ark." It is also common knowledge that most of the members of "that" society are "that" way. The question is, does Littlewood know? And if so, does he care?

Now he stands from his chair and walks, in that determined way of his, to the fire. Flames rise from the coals as he stokes them. The cold has got to Hardy, who in any case feels ill at ease in this room, with its mirrors and the Broadwood piano and that smell that permeates the air, of cigars and blotting paper and, above all, of Littlewood—a smell of clean linens and wood smoke and something else, something human, biological, that Hardy hesitates to identify. This is one of the reasons that they communicate by postcard. You can speak of Riemann's zeta function in terms of the "mountains" and "valleys" where its values, when charted on a graph, rise and fall, yet if you start actually imagining the climb, tasting the air, searching for water, you will be lost. Smells—of Littlewood, of the Indian's letter—interfere with the ability to navigate the mathematical landscape, which is why, quite suddenly, Hardy finds himself feeling ill, anxious to return to the safety of his own rooms. Indeed, he has already got up and is about to say goodbye when Littlewood rests his hot hand on his shoulder. "Don't go just yet," he says, sitting Hardy down again. "I want to play you something." And he puts a record on the gramophone.

Hardy does as he is told. Noise issues forth from the gramophone. That's all it is to him. He can ascertain rhythm and patterns, a succession of triplets and some sort of narrative, but it gives him no pleasure. He hears no beauty. Perhaps this is due to some deficiency in his brain. It frustrates him, his inability to appreciate an art in which his friend takes such satisfaction. Likewise dogs. Let others natter on about their sterling virtues, their intelligence and loyalty. To him they are smelly and annoying. Littlewood, on the other hand, loves dogs, as did Byron. He loves music. Indeed, as the stylus makes its screechy progress across the record, he seems to enter into a sort of concentrated rapture, closing his eyes, raising his hands, playing the air with his fingers.

At last the record finishes. "Do you know what that was?" Littlewood asks, lifting the needle.

Hardy shakes his head.

"Beethoven. First movement of the 'Moonlight Sonata.'"

"Lovely."

"I'm teaching myself to play, you know. Of course I'm no Mark Hambourg, and never will be." He sits down again, next to Hardy this time. "You know who it was who first introduced me to Beethoven,

17

don't you? Old O. B. When I was an undergraduate, he was always inviting me to his rooms. Maybe it was the glamour of my being senior wrangler. He had a pianola, and he played me the 'Waldstein' on it."

"Yes, I knew he was musical."

"Peculiar character, O. B. Did you hear about the time a party of ladies interrupted him after his bathe? All he had was a handkerchief, but instead of covering his privates, he covered his face. 'Anyone in Cambridge would recognize my *face*,' he said."

Hardy laughs. Even though he's heard the story a hundred times, he doesn't want to take away from Littlewood the pleasure of thinking that he is telling it to him for the first time. Cambridge is full of stories about O. B. that begin just this way. "Did you hear about the time O. B. dined with the king of Greece?" "Did you hear about the time O. B. went to Bayreuth?" "Did you hear about the time O. B. was on a corridor train with thirty Winchester boys?" (The last of these Hardy doubts that Littlewood has heard.)

"Anyway, ever since then, it's been Beethoven, Bach, and Mozart for me. Once I learn, they're the only composers I'll play."

He gets up again, removes the record from the gramophone and returns it to its sleeve.

Dear God, please let him take out another record and put it on the gramophone. I'm in the mood for music, hours and hours of music.

The ruse works. Littlewood looks at his watch. Maybe he wants to work, or write to Mrs. Chase.

Hardy is just reaching for Ramanujan's letter when Littlewood says, "Do you mind if I keep that tonight? I'd like to look it over more carefully."

"Of course."

"Then perhaps we can talk in the morning. Or I'll send you a note. I rather imagine I'll be up most of the night with it."

"As you please."

"Hardy—in all seriousness, maybe we should think about bringing him over. Make some enquiries, at least. I know I may sound as if I'm jumping the gun . . ."

"No, I was thinking the same thing. I could write to the India Office, see if they've got any money for this sort of thing."

"He may be the man to prove the Riemann hypothesis."

Hardy raises his eyebrows. "Really?"

"Who knows? Because if he's done all this on his own, it might mean he's free to move in directions we haven't thought of. Well, goodnight, Hardy."

"Goodnight."

They shake hands. Shutting the door behind him, Hardy hurries down the steps of D staircase, crosses Nevile's Court to New Court, ascends to his rooms. Forty-three paces. His gyp has kept his fire going; in front of it Hermione now lies curled atop her favorite ottoman, the buttoned blue velvet one. "*Capitonné*," Gaye, who knew about such things, called the buttoning. He even had a special cover made for the ottoman, so that Hermione could scratch at it without damaging the velvet. Gaye adored Hermione; spoke, in the days before he died, of commissioning her portrait—a feline Odalisque, nude but for an immense emerald hung round her neck on a satin ribbon. Now the cover itself is in tatters.

Should they bring the Indian to England? As he mulls over the idea, Hardy's heart starts to beat faster. He cannot deny that it excites him, the prospect of rescuing a young genius from poverty and obscurity and watching him flourish . . . Or perhaps what excites him is the vision he has conjured up, in spite of himself, of Ramanujan: a young Gurkha, brandishing a sword. A young cricketer.

Outside his window, the moon rises. Soon, he knows, the gyp will arrive with his evening whiskey. He will drink it by himself tonight, with a book. Curious, the room feels emptier than usual—so whose presence is he missing? Gaye's? Littlewood's? An odd sensation, this loneliness that, so far as he can tell, has no object, at the other end of which no mirage of a face shimmers, no voice summons. And then he realizes what it is that he misses. It is the letter.

4

H E TRIES TO remember when it started. Certainly before he knew anything. Before he learned it was one of the great problems, if not the greatest of them all. He was eleven, maybe twelve. It started with fog.

The Cranleigh vicar had taken him for a walk—at his mother's request, because he seemed not to be paying attention at church. It was foggy out; now he can imagine the gears shifting in the vicar's brain as he landed upon the idea of using the fog to explain faith. The fog, and something a boy would like. A kite.

"If you fly a kite in the fog, you cannot see the kite flying. Still, you feel the tug of the string."

"But in the fog," Harold said, "there is no wind. So how could you fly a kite?"

The vicar moved slightly ahead. In the humid stillness, his torso blurred and wavered like a ghost's. It was true, there was not a touch of wind.

"I use an analogy," he said. "You are, I trust, familiar with the concept."

Harold did not answer. He hoped the vicar would mistake his silence for pious contemplation, when in fact the young man had just eradicated any last shred of faith that the boy held. For the facts of nature could not be denied. In fog there was no wind. No kite could fly.

They returned to his house. His sister, Gertrude, was sitting in the drawing room, practicing reading. She had only had the glass eye a month.

Mrs. Hardy made tea for the vicar, who was perhaps twenty-five, with black hair and thin fingers. "As I have been trying to explain to your son," the vicar said, "belief must be cultivated as tenaciously as any science. We must not allow ourselves to be reasoned out of it. Nature is part of God's miracle, and when we explore her domain, it must be with the intention of better comprehending His glory."

"Harold is very good at mathematics," his mother said. "At three he could already write figures into the millions."

"To calculate the magnitude of God's glory, or the intensity of hell's agonies, one must write out figures far larger than that."

"How large?" Harold asked.

"Larger than you could work out in a million lifetimes."

"That's not very large, mathematically speaking," Harold said. "Nothing's very large, when you consider infinity."

The vicar helped himself to some cake. Despite his emaciated figure, he ate with relish, making Mrs. Hardy wonder if he had a tapeworm.

"Your child is gifted," he said, once he had swallowed. "He is also impudent." Then he turned to Harold and said, "God is infinity."

That Sunday, as on every Sunday, Mr. and Mrs. Hardy took Harold and Gertrude to church. They were believers, but more importantly, Mr. Hardy was the bursar at Cranleigh School; it mattered that the parents of his pupils see him in the pews. To distract himself from the drone of the vicar's sermon, Harold broke the numbers of the hymns down into their prime factors. 68 gave $17 \times 2 \times 2$, 345 gave $23 \times 5 \times 3$. On the slate behind his eyelids, he wrote out the primes, tried to see if there was reason to their ordering: 2, 3, 5, 7, 11, 13, 17, 19 . . . It seemed there was none. Yet there had to be order, because numbers, by their very nature, conferred order. Numbers *meant* order. Even if the order was hidden, invisible.

The question was easy enough to pose. But that did not mean that the answer would be easy to find. As he was quickly learning, often the simplest theorems to state were the most difficult to prove. Take Fermat's Last Theorem, which held that for the equation $x^n + y^n = z^n$, there could be no whole number solutions greater than 2. You could feed numbers into the equation for the rest of your life, and show that for the first million n's not one n contradicted the rule—perhaps if you had a million lifetimes, you could show that for the first billion n's, not one contradicted the rule—and still, you would have shown nothing. For who was to say that far, far down the number line, far past the magnitude of God's glory and the intensity of hell's agonies, there wasn't that one *n* that did contradict the rule? Who was to say there weren't an infinite number of *n*'s that contradicted the rule? Proof was what was needed—immutable, incontrovertible. Yet once you started looking, how complicated the mathematics got!

He remained preoccupied with the primes. Up to 100—he counted—there were 25. How many were there up to 1000? Again he counted—168—but it took a long time. At Cranleigh he had replicated, on his own, Euclid's astonishingly simple proof that there was an infinity of primes. Yet when he asked his maths master at Winchester if there was a formula for calculating the number of primes up to a given number *n*, the master didn't know. Even at Trinity, seat of British mathematics, no one seemed to know. He nosed around, and eventually found out from Love, one of the Trinity fellows, that in fact the German mathematician Karl Gauss had come up with such a formula in 1792, when he was fifteen, but had been unable to provide a proof. Later, Love said, another German, Riemann, *had* proven the formula's validity, but Love was hazy on the details. What he did know was that the formula was inexact. Inevitably it overestimated the number of primes. For instance, if you counted the primes from 1 to 2,000,000, you would discover that there were 148,933. But if you fed the number 2,000,000 into the formula, it would tell you that the number was 149,055. In this case, the formula overestimated the total by 122.

Hardy wanted to learn more. Might there be a means, at the very least, of improving upon Gauss's formula? Of lessening the margin of error? Alas, as he was discovering, Cambridge wasn't much interested in such questions, which fell under the rather disgraced heading of pure mathematics. Instead it put its emphasis on applied mathematics—the trajectory of planets hurtling through space, astronomical predictions, optics, waves and tides. Newton loomed as a kind of God. A century and a half earlier, he had waged an acrimonious battle with Gottfried Leibniz over which had first discovered the calculus, and though in America and on the continent it had long since been agreed that Leibniz had made the discovery first, but that Newton had made it independently, at Cambridge the battle raged as bitterly as if it were fresh. To deny Newton's claim of precedence was to speak sacrilege. Indeed, so steadfast was the university's loyalty to its famous son that even at the turn of the new century it still compelled its mathematics students, when working with the calculus, to employ his antiquated dot notation, his vocabulary of fluxions and fluons, rather than the simpler system—derived from Leibniz—that was favored in the rest of Europe. And why? Because Leibniz was German, and Newton was English, and England was England. Jingoism, it seemed, mattered more than truth, even in the one arena in which truth was supposed to be absolute.

It was all very disheartening. Among his friends, Hardy wondered loudly if he should have gone to Oxford. He wondered if he should give up mathematics altogether and switch to history. At Winchester he had written a paper on Harold, son of Godwin, whose death in 1066 in the Battle of Hastings was portrayed in the Bayeux tapestries. The subject of the paper was the complicated matter of Harold's promise to William the Conqueror not to seek the throne, yet what really fascinated Hardy was that in the battle Harold took an arrow in the eye. This was, after all, just a few years after Gertrude's accident, and he had a morbid obsession with eyes being put out. Of course, there was also the coincidence of the name. In any case Fearon, his headmaster, admired the paper enough to pass it on to the Trinity examiners, one of whom later told Hardy that he could just as easily have got a scholarship in history as in mathematics. He kept this in the back of his mind throughout his undergraduate years.

His first two years at Cambridge, he led a bifurcated life. On the one hand, there was the mathematical tripos. On the other, there were the Apostles. The former was an examination, the latter a society. Only a few members of the society took the examination; still, the life they led within the rooms in which they held their meetings undermined its very foundations.

The Apostles first. Election was highly secretive, and, once "born," the "embryo," as he was called, was made to swear that he would never speak of the society to outsiders. Meetings took place every Saturday evening. As an active member—as one of the brethren—you were obliged to attend every meeting during term so long as you were in residence. Eventually, each member "took wings" and became an "angel," at which point he would attend only those meetings he chose to.

Hardy was elected to the society in 1898. He was number 233. His sponsor, or "father," was the philosopher G. E. Moore (no. 229). At this point the active members of the Society, in addition to Moore, were R. C. and G. M. Trevelyan (nos. 226 and 230), Ralph Wedgwood (no. 227), Eddie Marsh (no. 228), Desmond McCarthy (no. 231), and Austin Smyth (no. 232). The angels most likely to be in attendance were O. B. (no. 142), Goldie Dickinson (no. 209), Jack McTaggart (no. 212), Alfred North Whitehead (no. 208), and Bertrand Russell (no. 224), who had taken wings only the year before. Nearly all were from King's or Trinity, and of them, only two— Whitehead and Russell—had taken the mathematical tripos.

And what was the mathematical tripos? Reduced to its skeleton, it was the exam that all mathematics students at Cambridge were obliged to take, and had been obliged to take since the late eighteenth century. The word itself referred to the three-legged stool on which, in olden times, the contestants would sit as they and their examiners "wrangled" over points of logic. Now a century and a half had gone by, and still the tripos tested the applied mathematics that had been current in 1782. The highest scorers on the exam were still classed as "wranglers," then ranked by score, the very highest being deemed the "senior wrangler." After the wranglers came the "senior optimes" and the "junior optimes." Much ceremony attended the ritual reading of the names and scores, the honors list, which took place annually at the Senate House on the second Tuesday in June. To have any future in mathematics at Cambridge, you had to score among the top ten wranglers. To be named senior wrangler guaranteed you a fellowship or, if you chose not to pursue an academic career, a lucrative post in government or law. Whitehead in his year had been fourth wrangler, Russell seventh.

The tripos had something of the quality of a sporting event. Wagers preceded it, revels followed it. The third week in June, no man in Cambridge was as famous as the senior wrangler, whose photograph street vendors and newsagents sold, and whom undergraduate aspirants and girls followed through the streets, asking for his autograph. Starting in the 1880s, women were allowed to take the examination, though their scores didn't count, and when, in 1890, a woman beat the senior wrangler, no less worthy an organ than the *New York Times* reported on her astonishing victory.

Some, generally those who had no personal experience of it, thought the tripos rather fun. O. B., for instance. A historian by inclination and profession, he adored pomp of any kind, and therefore could not understand why Hardy should object so vociferously to what was for him just a nice bit of Cambridge pageantry. In particular—and this was typical of O. B.—he loved the wooden spoon. Each year on degree day, when the poor fellow who had got the lowest score of all—the last of the junior optimes—knelt before the vice-chancellor, his friends would lower down to him from the Senate House roof an immense spoon, five feet long, elaborately hued and emblazoned with the insignia of his college as well as bits of comic verse in Greek along the lines of:

> In Honours Mathematical
> None in Glory this shall equal.
> Senior Wrangler, shed a tear
> That you this Spoon shall never bear!

The fellow would then carry the spoon off with him into the distance with as much pathos and equanimity as he could muster. For the rest of his life, he would be known as that year's wooden spoon.

Once, in the mingling hour that followed an Apostles meeting, O. B. said to Hardy, "What's he supposed to do with it, stir his tea?"

"Who?" Hardy asked.

"The wooden spoon."

Hardy did not want to talk about the wooden spoon. Already he despised the tripos, the preparations for which he considered an undue burden, pulling him away from those matters to which he would have preferred to devote his energy, such as the prime numbers. For him, the tripos was an exercise in archaism. When taking it, you had not just to employ Newton's out-of-date vocabulary, but to recite the lemmas of his *Principia Mathematica* just upon being given their numbers, as if they were psalms. Because few dons lectured on this mathematics, a cottage industry of private tripos coaches had sprung up, their fees proportionate to the number of senior wranglers they "produced." These coaches were in many ways more famous than their counterparts, the dons. Webb was the most famous of all, and it was to Webb that Hardy was sent.

These are not days that he remembers with any fondness. Three times a week, during the term and also during the long vacation, at precisely 8:15 in the morning, he would be sat down with five other young men in a room that was damp in summer and freezing in winter. The room was in Webb's house, and Webb spent the entirety of every day in it, hour after hour, coaching successive groups of six until dusk fell, while Mrs. Webb, dour and silent, hovered in the kitchen, filling and refilling the tea urn. The routine never varied. Half the meeting was devoted to rote memorization, the other half to practice against the clock. Hardy thought it a colossal waste of time, yet what made his suffering all the worse was the conviction that he was alone in experiencing it. Ambition seemed to have blinded the other men to the folly of what they were doing. He didn't know then that in Germany the professors made a game of mocking the questions on the exam: "On an elastic bridge stands an elephant of negligible mass; on his trunk sits a mosquito of mass m. Calculate the vibrations of the bridge when the elephant moves the mosquito by roaring his trunk." Yet this was exactly the sort of question in which the tripos specialized, and for the sake of which generations of Cambridge men had given up the chance to have a real education, just at the moment when their minds were ripest for discovery.

Later, he tried to explain all this to O. B. Through the Apostles they had become, in a peculiar way, friends. Although O. B. never made his famously salacious jokes to Hardy, or tried to touch him, he did have a habit of dropping by Hardy's rooms unexpectedly in the afternoons. Often he would speak of Oscar Wilde, who had been his friend and whom he greatly admired. "Just before he died I saw him in Paris," O. B. said. "I was driving in a cab and passed him before I realized who he was. But he recognized me. Oh, the pain in his eyes . . ."

At this stage in his life, Hardy knew little of Wilde beyond what rumors had managed to slip through the fortifications that his Winchester masters had erected to protect their charges from news of the trials. Now he asked O. B. to tell him the whole story, and O. B. obliged: the glory days, Bosie's perfidy, the notorious testimony of the hotel maids . . . Even today, only a few years after Wilde's death, the scandal was still fresh enough that one dared not risk being seen carrying a copy of one of his books. Still, O. B. loaned Hardy *The Decay of Lying*. When Hardy touched the covers, heat seemed to rise off them, as off an iron. He devoured the book, and afterward copied out, in his elegant hand, a passage that had made a particularly strong impression on him:

Art never expresses anything but itself. It has an independent life, just as Thought has, and develops purely on its own lines. It is not necessarily realistic in an age of realism, nor spiritual in an age of faith. So far from being the creation of its time, it is usually in direct opposition to it, and the only history that it preserves for us is the history of its own progress.

So of art, he decided, of mathematics. Its pursuit should be tainted neither by religion nor by utility. Indeed, its uselessness was its majesty. Suppose, for instance, that you proved Fermat's Last Theorem. What would you have contributed to the good of the world? Absolutely nothing. Advances in chemistry aided the cotton mills in developing new dyeing processes. Physics could be applied to ballistics and gunnery. But mathematics? It could never serve any practical or warlike purpose. In Wilde's words, it "developed purely on its own lines." Far from a limitation, its uselessness was evidence of its limitlessness.

The bother was, whenever he tried to articulate this to O. B., he got tied up in knots—such as on the evening when he complained that the mathematics tested on the tripos was pointless.

"I don't understand you," O. B. said to him. "One day you're carrying on about how gloriously useless mathematics is, the next you're grumbling that the mathematics that the tripos tests is useless. Which of you am I to believe?"

"I don't mean it the same way," Hardy said. "The stuff on the tripos isn't useless the way pure mathematics is useless. It's not a question of applicability. If anything, the tripos stuff is eminently applicable . . . just antiquated."

"Latin and Greek are antiquated. So should we give those up?"

Hardy tried to put his position in a language O. B. would understand. "All right, look," he said. "Imagine you're taking an exam in the history of English literature. Only for the purposes of the exam, you have to write your answers in Middle English. It doesn't matter that you'll never be called to write an exam, or anything else for that matter, in Middle English ever again, you still have to write your answers in Middle English. And not only that, the questions you have to answer—they're not about major writers, they're not about Chaucer and Milton and Pope, they're about, I don't know, some obscure poets no one's ever heard of. And you have to memorize every word that the poets wrote. And these poets wrote hundreds of thousands of terribly boring poems. And on top of that, you have to memorize twelve sixteenth-century treatises on the nature of melancholy and be prepared to recite any chapter upon being told its number. If you can imagine that, then perhaps you can imagine what it's like to take the tripos."

"It sounds as if it would be rather fun," O. B. said. "Anyway, I still think you're making an artificial distinction. One kind of uselessness you glorify because you enjoy it, the other kind you condemn because you find it dull. But it comes to the same thing."

Hardy was silent. It was obvious that O. B. didn't understand, would never understand. Only a mathematician could. O. B. didn't know what it felt like to be dragged away from something in which you believed passionately and forced to fix your attention on something you despised. Nor did he understand the injustice of being obliged to devote years of effort to the acquisition of skills that, once the tripos was over and done with, you would never again be called upon to employ. More and more O. B. lived for spectacle: the petits-fours served and the music played at his "at homes," where sailors mingled with dons. He did not care about ideas or ideals. His fellowship, so far as Hardy could tell, mattered to him only because it allowed him to remain forever ensconced within the safe confines of King's College. By nature he was a creature of the college. Most of the Apostles were. A few years earlier McTaggart had written of heaven: "It might be said of a College with as much truth as it has been said of the Absolute, that it is a unity, that is a unity of spirit, and that none of that spirit exists except as personal." But of course "the Absolute is a far more perfect unity than a College." With such a sentiment O. B. would not likely have been in agreement, as for him King's was the perfect unity.

O. B., Hardy knew, did not much care for McTaggart. Nor did he appreciate McTaggart's "religion," a sort of anti-Christian Christianity in which Platonic souls ascended to a paradise without a God. Hardy felt the same way. One of McTaggart's many behavioral oddities was that he walked sideways—a habit cultivated during his school days, when he had had to keep close to walls in order to avoid being kicked. He suffered from a slight curvature of the spine, and navigated the streets of Cambridge on a lumbering antique tricycle. Years before, he had delivered a paper to the Society entitled "Violets or Orange-Blossom?" in which he put forward an eloquent defense of love between men, which he believed to be superior to love between men and women, so long as a clear distinction was drawn between the "lower sodomy" and the "higher sodomy." When he first gave his paper, McTaggart firmly allied himself with the higher sodomy, and still did, despite his recent marriage to a robust New Zealand girl, Daisy Bird, whom he proudly described as being "not the least bit feminine" and with whom, he told the brethren, he shared everything, including a passion for schoolboys.

All told, Hardy found G. E. Moore more (*Moore, more*) congenial. They met during Hardy's first year at Trinity. The father was five years older than the embryo, but looked the same age or even younger, which came as a relief. Already Hardy was growing tired of people mistaking him for a schoolboy. Although Moore was not handsome in a conventional sense, he radiated a childlike gloom that made you want to protect him and slap him, to tousle the hair creeping out over the wide forehead, and fondle the ears, which had no lobes, and kiss the look of perpetual surprise off his mouth. Not that Hardy ever had the chance to kiss away that look. The only intimacy Moore conceded was hand-holding. He was churlish on matters of sex—surprisingly so, given that one of the principal tenets of his own philosophy (a sort of simultaneous extension and refutation of McTaggart's) was the belief that pleasure is the highest good in life. Almost from the moment of his birth into the Apostles, he had been acknowledged as a genius, a savior sent down from the heaven of the angels to awaken the brethren from the torpor of the *fin de siècle*. Walking through the meadows of Grantchester with Hardy, his small hand somehow limp and at the same moment grasping, he would speak of "goodness." For him, goodness was indefinable, yet also fundamental, the only soil in which a theory of ethics could take root. And where did goodness lie? In love and beauty. Perhaps unwittingly, Moore was offering the Apostles moral justification for the pursuit of activities at which most of them were already proficient: the cultivation of beautiful boys and the acquisition of beautiful objects. Later, out of his whole magnum opus, *Principia Ethica*, the reverent Bloomsbury set extracted a single phrase, placed it on a pedestal, and called it Moore's philosophy: ". . . personal affections and aesthetic enjoyments include *all* the greatest, and *by far* the greatest, goods we can imagine . . ."

Affection, enjoyment: on those walks in Grantchester, Hardy tried, and failed, to get Moore, by means of his own words, onto the grass. When their tussles concluded, as they inevitably did, in frustration and the brushing of dandelions off trousers, Moore would turn the conversation to mathematics. He would assure Hardy that he was absolutely right to want to pursue pure instead of applied mathematics. Prime numbers, for Moore, were part of the realm of goodness in a way that sex never could be.

All first loves may be fated to leave one feeling deluded. Hardy's and Moore's only lasted through the first year of Hardy's membership in the Society. Then Moore met Alfred Ainsworth. They paid their first visit to Ainsworth's rooms together on a winter evening, to see if Ainsworth might be embryo material. Ainsworth had fresh cheeks and smoky breath. As he talked, he flicked lit matches at the carpet. Afterward, as he and Moore were leaving, Hardy noticed the tiny burn marks that dotted the rug, growing in density until they formed a charred circle near the chair on which Ainsworth did his reading.

It was the first and only time in his life that anyone left him for someone else. Within a few weeks Moore's fondness for Ainsworth had developed into a full-fledged passion, though, as with Hardy, the affair never progressed beyond the hand-holding stage. This was in part because Ainsworth, unlike Hardy, regarded physical intimacy between men with distaste. Yet surely someone else—someone like John Maynard Keynes—could have nudged or badgered him into it. Once again, Moore's priggishness was the sticking point. When, at a gathering of the Society, Moore was asked to sing Schubert lieder (he had a lovely tenor voice), he attacked the music with gusto, all the while gazing at Ainsworth dreamily. But then he read a paper on whether it was possible to fall in love with someone purely on the basis of "mental qualities." The knots he tied himself into! "Though, therefore, we may admit that the appreciation of a person's attitude towards other persons, or, to take one instance, the love of love, is far the most valuable good we know, and far more valuable than the mere love of beauty, yet we can only admit this if the first be understood to *include* the latter, in various degrees of directness." Which was basically a way of saying that he could never fall in love with someone who was ugly.

Had Hardy not considered himself ugly—and had Moore not left him for Ainsworth (whom he, too, thought beautiful)—he might have greeted the betrayal with outrage or amusement. Instead he observed with dispassion the sorry spectacle of Moore undermining his own desire. Moore adored Ainsworth, he wanted obviously to sleep with Ainsworth, yet even as he went so far as to move to Edinburgh in order to live with Ainsworth, who was teaching there, he wouldn't admit it. Then Ainsworth married Moore's sister, and Moore returned to Cambridge. Hardy didn't know what to say to him when they first ran into each other. Congratulations on your sister's marriage to your great love? I'm sorry that he left you? It's what you deserve?

It didn't matter. He had learned something important from Moore: to go his own way. His name, he often thought, was providential. By nature Hardy was fibrous, pertinacious. He stuck to his guns. If the Apostles could overlook Christianity, convention, "the rules," then he could just as easily cast his attention, as it were, *across* the stupidity of England, even across the obtuseness that fancied itself imperiousness and the ignorance that fancied itself superiority; across the emblematic channel itself. And where did that attention, once it had begun this tremendous journey, finally land? In Lower Saxony, in the small city of Göttingen, acknowledged capital of pure mathematics, city of Gauss and Riemann. Göttingen, which he had never visited, was Hardy's ideal. Whereas in Cambridge newsagents sold photographs of the senior wrangler, in Göttingen the shops sold picture postcards bearing signed photographs of the great professors. Photographs of the city itself revealed it to be beautiful and ancient and ornate. From the *rathaus* with its gothic arches and noble spire, cobbled streets extended, small brick houses winking over them like grandmothers, their white balconies leaning out like aproned stomachs. In one of these houses, two centuries ago, the Göttingen Seven, two of whom were the brothers Grimm, had rebelled against the sovereignty of the kings of Hanover, while in another the great mathematician George Friedrich Bernhard Riemann had conjured—out of what? out of the ether?—a famous hypothesis concerning the distribution of the prime

31

numbers. Yes, the Riemann hypothesis, which Hardy once made the mistake of trying to explain to the brethren. Still unproven. That was how he began his talk. "It is probably the most important unproven hypothesis in mathematics," he said from the hearthrug, which sent a ripple of comment through the audience. Then he tried to lead them through the series of steps by which Riemann established a link between the seemingly arbitrary distribution of the primes and something called the "zeta function." First he explained the prime number theorem, Gauss's method for calculating the number of primes up to a certain number n. Then, by way of indicating how far Cambridge had fallen behind the continent, he told the story of how, upon his arrival at Trinity, he had asked Love whether the theorem had been proven, and Love had said, yes, it had been proven, by Riemann—when in fact it had been proven only years after Riemann's death, independently, by Hadamard and de la Vallée Poussin. "You see," he said, "we were that provincial." At this Lytton Strachey, a recent birth (no. 239), gave a high-pitched, snorting laugh.

The problem was what Hardy called the error term. The theorem inevitably overestimated the number of primes up to n. And though Riemann and others had come up with formulae to lessen the error term, no one had been able to get rid of it altogether.

This was where the zeta function came in. Hardy wrote it out on a blackboard:

$$\zeta(x) = \tfrac{1}{1^x} + \tfrac{1}{2^x} + \tfrac{1}{3^x} + \ldots \tfrac{1}{n^x}$$

The function, when fed with an ordinary integer, was fairly straightforward. But what if you fed it with an imaginary number? And what was an imaginary number? He had to backtrack. "We all know that 1 × 1 = 1," he said. "And what does −1 × −1 equal?"

"Also 1," Strachey said.

"Correct. So by definition, the square root of −1 doesn't exist. Yet it's a very useful number."

He wrote it in on the blackboard: $\sqrt{-1}$. "We call this number i."

He knew where this was going to lead: a long argument about the phenomenal and the real. If outside this room, Strachey said, outside this Saturday evening, i was imaginary, then in this room, on this Saturday evening, i must be real. And why? Because in the world that was not this room, this Saturday evening, the opposite was true. For the brethren, only the life of the meetings was real. Everything else was "phenomenal." Thus the Apostles embraced i without having the faintest idea what it meant.

After the talk was over, O. B. patted him on the back. "God willing, you'll be the man to prove it," he said, which was deliberate provocation: O. B. knew as well as any of them that Hardy had long since renounced God, going so far as to ask the dean of Trinity for permission not to attend chapel, and then, at the dean's insistence, writing to inform his parents that he was no longer a believer. Gertrude pretended to weep, Mrs. Hardy wept, Isaac Hardy refused to speak to his son. A few months later, his father contracted pneumonia, and Hardy's mother begged him to reconsider his choice. To placate her, he agreed to meet with the vicar—the same, thin-fingered vicar by whom, years before, he'd been taken on a walk in the fog to discuss the kite. While they talked, the vicar ate chocolates from a tray. At a certain point Hardy noticed that the vicar was glancing, not very subtly, at his trousers. *Well, well,* he thought.

His father died the next evening. From that day on, Hardy never again set foot inside a Cambridge chapel. Even when some formal protocol required him to go into a chapel, he refused. Eventually Trinity had to issue a special dispensation on his behalf. By then, though, the college was more pliable. After all, Hardy was a don. And Oxford had sent out lures.

Occasionally, when he was working on the hypothesis, he'd remember his walk with the vicar. Looking for a proof, he'd think—*that's* like groping in a fog, feeling for a tug on the string. Somewhere high above you truth hovered—absolute, indisputable. When you felt the tug, it meant that you'd found the proof.

God had nothing to do with it. Proof was what connected you to the truth.

And what of the tripos?

Halfway through his first year Hardy went to Butler, the master of Trinity, and announced that he was giving up mathematics. He would rather change over to history, he said, return to Harold and the Battle of Hastings, than waste another minute in the gloom of Webb's ugly house.

Butler had a gift for quick thinking. He rotated his wedding ring a quarter turn (this was his habit) and sent Hardy off to talk to Love. Love, though an applied mathematician himself, recognized the source of Hardy's passion, and gave him a copy of Camille Jordan's three-volume *Cours d'analyse de l'Ecole Polytechnique*. This was the book, he later said, that changed his life, that taught him what it really meant to be a mathematician. Love also persuaded Hardy that if he quit mathematics just to avoid the tripos, he would be submitting to its tyranny far more completely than if he simply buckled down and took the thing.

The *Cours d'analyse*, Hardy told Littlewood, made the difference. The mere fact of knowing it awaited him on his shelf made it possible for him to endure Webb's coaching. So he resumed the protocol of memorization, practice, memorization, and when June came, he went to take the tripos with the first volume of the *Cours d'analyse* secreted in his coat pocket, as a talisman, and came out fourth wrangler.

For years afterward, naysayers grumbled that Hardy's subsequent determination to destroy the tripos was sour grapes, that it owed entirely to his not being named senior wrangler. This he denied vociferously. Nor, he insisted, did his not being named senior wrangler have anything to do with his decision, a month or so later, to leave Cambridge for Oxford. Had he been named senior wrangler, or twenty-seventh wrangler, or wooden spoon, he would have done the same. For the grudge he bore was not against the men who had scored higher than he had: it was against the tripos itself, and more generally, Cambridge, the insularity of which the tripos embodied, and more generally still, England, its rigidity and smug, unquestioning belief in its own superiority. In the end it took Moore to persuade him to stay. England, Moore told him, he could not remake. But perhaps he could remake the tripos.

From then on, tripos reform became his crusade. He waged a campaign that was passionate, intelligent, and unrelenting, and eventually, in 1910, he won: not only was the tripos modernized, the reading of the honors list was terminated. No longer would wranglers and optimes stroll the avenues of Cambridge in June. No longer would wooden spoons be handed down from the Senate House roof. Instead the tripos would be just another exam. None of which, he maintained, with just a hint of vexation in his voice, had anything to do with his having been named fourth wrangler. After all, Bertrand Russell had been seventh wrangler, and he was—well, Bertrand Russell. Had Hardy been senior wrangler, he would have felt the same way. Done the same thing. It was important to him that strangers understood and believed this.

5

F OR A WEEK, Hardy and Littlewood study the math. They sit together, either in Hardy's rooms or in Littlewood's, with the pages of the Indian's letter spread out before them, copying out the figures on a blackboard or on sheets of the expensive, creamy, eighty-pound paper that Hardy uses exclusively for what he calls "scribbling." As they work, they drink tea or whiskey—all this a deviation from their usual routine of postcards and letters, but one that the situation seems to demand.

There are clashes, and when they occur, it seems to Hardy that they are the clashes of spouses, not collaborators. "You always have to finish the night so damn cheerful," Littlewood says one night as he's putting on his coat.

"What's wrong with that?"

"It's unrealistic, that's what. We work and work, we have to stop sometime, and you always make sure we stop when we think we've untangled something."

"So? I like to go to bed feeling I've got something to look forward to in the morning."

"But what if in the morning we find out we've made a blunder? That we're wrong? Half the time we are."

"Then we'll work it out in the morning."

"I'd rather go to bed knowing the worst."

"Right, then. We'll stop when we're stuck. That way you can leave unhappy. Despairing. Gloomy. Is that what you'd prefer?"

"I do. Hope for the best, expect the worst, that's my philosophy."

Most nights they're up past one. They pick over Ramanujan's results, make sense of some, fail to make sense of others, and, in the end, divide them into three rough categories: those that are either already known or easily deducible from known theorems; those that

36

are new, but interesting only because they are curious or difficult; and those that are new, interesting, and important.

All of it adds to their conviction that they are dealing with genius on a scale neither has ever imagined, much less encountered. What Ramanujan has not been taught he has, using his own peculiar language, reinvented. Better yet, building on this foundation, he has constructed an edifice of astonishing complexity, originality, and strangeness. Little of which Hardy indicates in his reply, which he tries to keep as understated as he can manage. So far as the first group of results goes, he forgoes confessing his amazement and offers only consolation, telling Ramanujan: "I need not say that if what you say about your lack of training is to be taken literally, the fact that you should have rediscovered such interesting results is all to your credit. But you should be prepared for a certain amount of disappointment of this kind." To the second and third groups, he devotes more attention. "It is of course possible that some of the results I have classed under (2) are really important, as examples of general methods. You always state your results in such particular forms that it is difficult to be sure about this."

They worked hard, he and Littlewood, on that last sentence. First Hardy wrote "peculiar" before "forms," but worried that the word might put Ramanujan off. Then he crossed out "peculiar" and wrote "odd," which was worse. It was Littlewood who came up with "particular," the slightly arch connotation of which (Hardy imagined Lytton Strachey saying it) he doubted that Ramanujan would pick up on.

"It is essential that I should see proofs of some of your assertions," he writes next. "*Everything* depends on rigorous exactitude of proof."

His conclusion mixes encouragement with caution. "It seems to me quite likely that you have done a good deal of work worth publication; and, if you can produce satisfactory demonstrations, I should be very glad to do what I can to secure it." Then he signs his name, puts the letter in an envelope, addresses it, has it stamped, and on the morning of February 9th—the day after his thirty-sixth birthday—slips it into the mouth of the postbox outside the Trinity College gates. For a time in his childhood he believed that all the postboxes in the world were connected by a system of underground tubes; that when you mailed a letter, it actually sprouted legs and ran to its destination. Now he imagines his letter to Ramanujan scuttling along the passageways underlying England, crossing the Mediterranean and the Suez Canal, tirelessly trudging forward until it reaches an address he can hardly visualize: Accounts Department, Port Trust, Madras, India.

And now he only has to wait.

6

New Lecture Hall, Harvard University

ON THE LAST DAY of August, 1936, Hardy wrote on the blackboard behind him:

$$1 - \frac{3!}{\left(1!2!\right)^3}X^2 + \frac{6!}{\left(2!4!\right)^3}X^4 - \ldots = \left(1 + \frac{X}{\left(1!\right)^3} + \frac{X^2}{\left(2!\right)^3} + \ldots\right)\left(1 - \frac{X}{\left(1!\right)^3} + \frac{X^2}{\left(2!\right)^3} - \ldots\right)$$

"I am sure that Ramanujan was no mystic," he said as he wrote, "and that religion, except in a strictly material sense, played no important part in his life. He was an orthodox high-caste Hindu, and always adhered (indeed with a severity most unusual in Indian residents of England) to all the observances of his caste."

Even as he spoke, though, he was doubting himself. He was giving, he knew, the script: the authorized version of his own opinion, already at odds with other versions of Ramanujan's story, in particular those circulating in India, where the youth's piety and devotion to the goddess Namagiri were situated at the dramatic heart of his mathematical discoveries.

Hardy did not—could not—believe this. His atheism was not merely part of his official identity; it was part of his being, and had been since his childhood. Still, even as he uttered them, he had to admit that his words simplified considerably not just the real situation but his own feelings about it.

He would have liked to put down his chalk at that moment, turn to his audience, and say something else. Something along the lines of:

I don't know. I used to think I did. But as I get older it seems that I know less and less rather than more and more.

I used to believe that I could explain anything. Once, at Gertrude's request, I attempted to explain the Riemann hypothesis to some girls at St. Catherine's School. This was during the early spring of 1913, when we were still awaiting Ramanujan's reply to the first letter. I really thought that leading these girls through the steps of the Riemann hypothesis would be easy, that I would awaken in them a fascination that would last them the rest of their lives. And so, while Gertrude stood attendance with Miss Trotter, the maths mistress, a pale-faced young woman whose hair, though she could not have been more than thirty, was already white, I lectured those girls in their starched pinafores. They gazed up at me with eyes that were either love-struck or vacant or contemptuous. One chewed her hair. The Riemann hypothesis might be the most important unsolved problem in mathematics, but that did not make it a subject of interest to twelve-year-old girls.

"Imagine," I said, "a graph, like any ordinary graph, with an x axis and a y axis. Let us say that the x axis is the ordinary number line, with all the ordinary numbers lined up in succession, and that the y axis is the *imaginary* number line, with all the multiples of i lined up in succession: $2i$, $3.47i$, $4,678,939i$, and so on. On such a graph, as on any graph, you can draw a point, and then connect the point, with lines, to points on the two axes. In this case, the numbers that correspond to these points on the plane are called *complex numbers* because each one has a real part and an imaginary part. You write them like this: $2i+1$. Or $4.6i + 1736.34289$ or $3i + 0$. The part with the i is the imaginary part, and corresponds to a point on the imaginary axis, while the other part is the real part and corresponds to a point on the real axis.

"So this is the Riemann hypothesis: you take the zeta function and you feed it with complex numbers. And then you look at your answers, and you see at which points the function takes the value of zero. According to the hypothesis, at every point where the function takes the value of zero, the real part will have a value of $\frac{1}{2}$; or, to put it another way, all the points at which the function takes the value of zero will line up along the line of $\frac{1}{2}$ on the x axis, which is called the *critical line*.

"To prove the hypothesis, you must prove that not a single zeta zero will ever be off the critical line. But if you can find just one zeta zero off the line—just one zeta zero where the real part of the imaginary number *isn't* $\frac{1}{2}$ —then you'll have *disproved* the Riemann hypothesis.

So half the job is looking for a proof—something airtight, theoretical—but half the job is hunting for zeros. Counting zeros. Seeing if there are any that are off the critical line. And counting zeros involves some pretty knotty math.

"And what will you have done, if you find the proof? You'll have eliminated the error term in Gauss's formula. You'll have revealed the secret order of the primes."

That was it, more or less. Of course there was a lot that I left out: the so-called trivial zeros of the zeta function; and the need, when exploring the zeta function landscape, to think in terms of four dimensions; and most crucially, the complex series of steps that leads from the zeta function to the primes and their calculation. Here, if I had tried to explain, I would have foundered. For there is a language that mathematicians can speak only among themselves.

After the lecture, the students applauded politely. Not for very long, but politely. I inspected their faces. They wore expressions of boredom and relief. Already, it was obvious, they were thinking ahead: to hockey practice, or Gertrude's art class, or a secret rendezvous with a boy. "Are there any questions?" Miss Trotter asked, her voice as colorless and icy as her hair, and when no girl spoke, she filled in the void with her own words. "Do you believe, Mr. Hardy, in your heart of hearts, that the Riemann hypothesis is true?"

I thought about it. Then I said, "Sometimes I do, sometimes I don't. There are days when I wake convinced that it's just a question of counting zeros. Somewhere there must be a zero off the line. Then there are days when a stab of insight slices right through me and I think I've made a step toward a proof."

"Could you give us an example?"

"Well, a few weeks ago, when I was taking my morning walk—I take a walk every morning—it suddenly occurred to me how I might prove that there is an infinite number of zeros along the critical line. I hurried straight home and wrote down my ideas, and now I'm very close to completing the proof."

"But that means you've proven the Riemann hypothesis," Miss Trotter said.

"Far from it," I said. "All I'll have proven is that there is an infinite number of zeros along the critical line. But that does not mean that there is not an infinite number of zeros not along the critical line."

I watched her as she tried to untangle the triple negative. Then I looked at Gertrude. It was clear that she had got the point before I'd even made it.

Afterward, when we were walking home together, I said to my sister, "This is why the Indian's letter interests me so much. If, as he claims, he's significantly reduced the error term, then he may be on to Riemann."

"Yes," Gertrude said. "He may even be the man to prove Riemann. How would you feel if he did?"

"I'd be delighted," I said. She smirked. Of course she doubted—and was right to—my pose of selflessness. We stepped into the house, where what seemed an infinity of maids was in the throes of an orgy of cleaning, Mother supervising their activities. One swabbed the floor, another scrubbed the windows, a third was beating pillows. Suddenly I saw the maids as zeros of the zeta function. I imagined them lining up, drawn as if by magnets along the critical line. There is a secret history through which a monstrous housekeeper strides, destroying all she touches. According to O. B., a famous musician went deaf after taking his housekeeper's advice that he treat an earache by stuffing cotton dipped in ether in his ears. And of course there was Riemann's legendary housekeeper, who, upon learning of his death (if the story is to be believed), threw all of his papers—including a reputed proof of the hypothesis—into the fire. How clearly I can envision that scene! The summer of 1866, warm weather, and this vigorous woman—in many ways the most important figure in the history of mathematics—methodically feeding the pages into the stove's stinking maw. Feeding and feeding, scrawled sheet after scrawled sheet, until, as legend has it, Riemann's Göttingen colleagues arrive in a mob. Cry out for her to stop. Patiently they sort through what they have salvaged, praying that the proof will have survived her reign of terror, while in the background . . . what does she do? Does she weep? Probably not. I see her as plump, methodical. Energy without imagination. No doubt she goes about her business. Scrubbing down floors. Washing pots.

The irony, of course, is that Riemann wasn't even there. He didn't witness, even in death, the conflagration. He had gone to Italy, hoping the balmier weather would improve his health. He was thirty-nine when he died. Consumption.

And do you think his housekeeper imagined that somehow the papers themselves might be tainted?

People understood so little about contagion in those days.

I can't stop thinking about this woman. What I find most monstrous about her is her efficiency. It has a bloodthirsty edge. In my mind I try to place myself at the scene in Göttingen. I try to explain to her, after the fact, the importance of the documents she has destroyed. In response she simply gazes at me, as if I'm a perfectly benign idiot. Her belief in her own rectitude is impregnable. This is the side of the German character that I preferred, before the war, not to contemplate, because I could not reconcile it with my dream image of the German university town down the cobbled streets of which Gauss and Hilbert strolled arm in arm, in defiance of fact, in defiance even of time. Ideas and ideals have a homey smell, rather like coffee. And yet in the background there always lurks this housekeeper with her ammonia and her matches.

7

SATURDAY EVENING, he goes to the weekly meeting of the Apostles, which is held on this occasion at King's, in the rooms of Jack Sheppard, classicist. He goes mostly out of boredom, because he is impatient to receive Ramanujan's reply, and hopes that the meeting will distract him from trying to guess at its content. In his coat pocket he carries the first page of Ramanujan's original letter, as, when he took the tripos, he carried the first volume of Jordan's *Cours d'analyse*.

It is his habit to arrive exactly twenty minutes late to the meetings, thereby avoiding both the awkwardness of being the first to arrive and the ostentation of being the last. Fifteen or so men between the ages of nineteen and fifty stand gathered on Sheppard's Oriental carpet, trying to look as if they're smart enough to deserve to belong to such an elite society. Although some are active undergraduate members, most are angels. (The Society's stock is rather low at the moment.) But what angels! Bertrand Russell, John Maynard Keynes, G. E. Moore: himself excepted, Hardy thinks, these are the men who will determine England's future. And why should he be excepted? Because he is merely a mathematician. Russell has political aspirations, Keynes wants to rebuild the British economy from the ground up, Moore has published *Principia Ethica*, a work that many of the younger Apostles regard as a kind of Bible. Hardy's ambition, on the other hand, is merely to prove or disprove a hypothesis that perhaps a hundred people in the world even understand. It's a distinction in which he takes some pride.

He counts the other angels in the room. Jack McTaggart is here, pressed up against the wall, as always, like a fly. So is suave little Eddie Marsh, who, in addition to serving as Winston Churchill's private secretary, has recently established a reputation as a connoisseur of poetry. Indeed, he has just published an anthology entitled *Georgian Poetry*, to which one of the major contributors is Rupert Brooke (no. 247), whom everyone thinks very handsome and whom, at the moment, Marsh is chatting up. Of the more significant angels, only Moore and Strachey are missing, and Strachey, Sheppard tells Hardy, is due any minute on the train from London. For this is no ordinary meeting. Tonight two new Apostles are to be born into the society. One of the "twins," Francis Kennard Bliss, has good looks and a talent for playing the clarinet to recommend him. The other, Ludwig Wittgenstein, is a new arrival from Austria via Manchester, where he went to learn to fly an aeroplane. Russell says he's a metaphysical genius.

To distract and amuse himself, Hardy plays a game. He pretends that he has not, in fact, come alone to the meeting, but that he has brought along a friend. No matter that such a thing would never be done, or that the "friend," though he answers to the name Ramanujan, bears an uncanny physical likeness to Chatterjee, the cricketer: so far as the game goes, the young man standing next to him is the author of the letter in his pocket, fresh off the boat from India and eager to learn Cambridge ways. He wears flannel trousers that ripple when he walks, like water touched by a breeze. A shadow of beard darkens his already dark cheeks. Yes, Hardy has studied Chatterjee with care.

He takes his friend on a tour of the rooms. Until recently, they belonged to O. B., who kept them filled with visiting royals, Louis XIV furniture, *Voi che sapete*, and handsome representatives of the Royal Naval Service. But then O. B., much to his dismay, was forced into superannuation and Italian retirement, and Sheppard took the rooms over. His sordid motley of domestic possessions looks forlorn and miserly in a space so accustomed to grandiose gestures. A portrait of his mother, stout and contemptuous, gazes across the Hamlet chair at a pianola that doesn't work. On the wall are some photographs of Greek statues, all of them nude, several missing limbs, none, Hardy notes, missing the dainty penis-and-balls set that the Greeks considered so elegant, especially when compared to those huger, crasser appendages that figured so prominently in O. B.'s badinage, and continue to figure prominently in Keynes's. And what does his friend from India think of Keynes? At the moment, the rising star of British economics is lecturing a rapt audience of undergraduates on the comparative size of "cock-stands" in Brazil and Bavaria. Wittgenstein

45

is standing alone in a corner, staring at one of the photographs. Russell is directing at Sheppard a foul-odored expatiation on the liar's paradox from which poor Sheppard has intermittently to turn away, if only to catch his breath.

"Imagine a barber who each day shaves every man in his town who doesn't shave himself. Does the barber shave himself?"

"I should think so."

"All right, then the barber's one of the men who doesn't shave himself."

"Fine."

"But you just said he did shave himself."

"I did?"

"Yes. I said the barber shaved every man who didn't shave himself. If he does shave himself, then he doesn't shave himself."

"All right, then he doesn't shave himself."

"But you just said he did!"

"Hardy, come save me," Sheppard says. "Russell is tying me to a spit and is about to roast me."

"Ah, Hardy," Russell says. "Yesterday Littlewood was telling me about your Indian, and I must say, it sounds quite exciting. On the brink of proving Riemann! Tell me, when will you be bringing him over?"

Hardy is rather taken aback to learn that Littlewood has been talking Ramanujan up. "I'm not sure we will," he says.

"Oh yes, I've heard about the fellow," Sheppard says. "Living in a mud hut and scribbling equations on the walls with a stick, isn't that right?"

"Not exactly."

"But Hardy, couldn't this be someone's idea of a joke? Mightn't your Indian be, I don't know, some bored Cambridge man trapped in an observatory in the wilds of Tamil Nadu, trying to while away the hours by having you on?"

"If so, the man's a genius," Hardy says.

"Or you're a fool," Russell says.

"Isn't there a point, though, where it comes to the same thing? Because if you're clever enough to construct something this brilliant as a joke . . . well, you've defeated your own intention, haven't you? You've proven yourself a genius in spite of yourself."

Sheppard laughs—a wheezy, girlish laugh. "A puzzle worthy of

Bertie!" he says. "And speaking of puzzles, Wittgenstein ought to be a client of your maddening barber, Bertie. Look at the cuts on his chin."

They look. There are indeed cuts; fairly pronounced ones. "Excuse me, will you?" Russell says, then walks over to join his protégé, with whom he confers in a quiet voice.

"Thick as thieves," Sheppard says, leaning in closer to Hardy.

"So it seems."

"You know, of course, that Bertie fought against his election."

"Wittgenstein's? But I thought Bertie was his champion."

"He is. He says he's worried that Wittgenstein's so brilliant he'll find us all puerile and shallow, and resign as soon as he's elected. Of course we assumed the truth was that Bertie wanted him all to himself, but now I'm beginning to think he might be right. Look how he's staring at us!" He mimics a stage shudder. "As if we're a bunch of silly dilettantes. And who's to say we're not, what with our Keynes carrying on about Bulgarian cocks and what have you? Did you hear that, by the way? I'm sure *he* did."

"From what I've been told, there's no reason that talk of cock-stands would offend him."

"Oh, but he's very sensitive on such matters. For instance, he absolutely loathes Count Békássy."

"Who's Count Békássy?"

"Count Ferenc István Dénes Gyula Békássy. Hungarian. Born last year. You should come to more meetings, Hardy."

"Which one?"

Sheppard points to a tall youth with dark eyes, a thin mustache, heavy Tartar lips that lend to his expression a quality at once doubting and lewd. At present he is talking to Bliss, the clarinetist. He has one hand on Bliss's shoulder, and with the other is stroking his hair.

"Most of us find him charming," Sheppard says. "Even Rupert Brooke finds him charming, which is generous, as rumor has it he's after Brooke's girlfriend. As well as Bliss."

"Evidence to back that up. Still, it doesn't explain why Wittgenstein loathes him."

"Perhaps it's some old Austro-Hungarian rivalry simmering to the surface. Or he's jealous. I've heard the Witter-Gitter man's rather keen on Bliss himself."

G. E. Moore comes into the room. Arguably he is the most influential

Apostle in the Society's history. Nonetheless he comes through the door shyly. He is fat, with a frank, friendly, childlike face. With gingerly self-effacement, he inserts himself between Wittgenstein and Russell. He speaks, and as he does, he looks at Hardy and nods.

Although he's a few years younger than Hardy, Sheppard's hair is turning white. He has a cherubic, doughy face, a weakness for gambling, and the sort of instinct for the classics that finds a truer expression in theatrical productions than in scholarship. As an under-graduate, he was brought to Hardy's rooms for tea once, part of the complex procedure through which the Society replenishes its stock. Sheppard's hair, in those days, was still blond. He had no idea that he was an embryo. None of them did. The assessment and the courting had to take place without the embryo ever realizing that he was being assessed or courted, his "father" given the difficult task of ushering his charge through a series of interviews that the charge was never to recognize as such. If the embryo failed to pass muster, he would be an "abortion," and—in theory, at least—never learn that he had been in the running. If, on the other hand, he did pass muster, then his discovery of the Society's existence—again, at least in theory—would be simultaneous with his invitation to join.

Now Sheppard sits on a small, spindly, upholstered chair—no, Hardy thinks, he *doesn't* sit. He roosts. There is something distinctly henlike about Sheppard. These days he is the fulcrum on which the Society's doings turn, not because he brandishes, as Moore does, vast intellectual influence—intellectually he contributes nothing—but because he can be counted on to order the whales, and arrange the tea cart, and, most importantly, to look after the Ark, which is really just a cedarwood trunk presented years before to the Society by O. B., and now filled to the brim with the papers that the members have given over the course of countless Saturday nights, going back to the early days when Tennyson (no. 70) and his fellows debated such topics as "Have Shelley's Poems an Immoral Tendency?" (Tennyson, the record shows, voted no.) Part of the initiation for any new Apostle is being given the chance to rifle through the papers in the Ark; to peruse "Is Self-Abuse Bad as an End?" (Moore), and "Should a Picture be Intelligible?" (Roger Fry, no. 214), and "Does Absence Make the Heart Grow Fonder?" (Strachey). And, of course, McTaggart's "Violets or Orange-Blossom?"

48

Sheppard is talking to Moore now. Over his head, Moore looks at Hardy, and Sheppard takes out his watch. "Oh dear, oh dear," he says—and all at once Hardy realizes who it is that he reminds him of: it's the White Rabbit in *Alice in Wonderland*. The white head, the twitching nose . . . "Oh, where is Strachey?" he says, gazing at the watch. "He's late, he's late! I'm afraid we'll have to start without him."

By now the room has grown crowded. Hardy counts nine angels and six active brethren. Abandoning cock-stands for the time being, Keynes joins Sheppard and Moore by the Ark, where the three of them lay out the hearthrug, which is in fact an old piece of kilim. The men go quiet, and Hardy takes a seat on Sheppard's rather uncomfortable velvet sofa. He wants his charge to have a good view of the reading of the curse.

The curse is an old Apostolic tradition. Decades before, an Apostle named Henry John Roby (no. 134) declared one Saturday evening that he was sorry but he was just too busy to go on attending the weekly meetings. His flouting of the rules, not to mention his supercilious tone, outraged the brethren, who banished him from the Society, and declared that forever after his name would be spelled with lowercase letters.

Now the curse is issued as a warning at every birth. Usually the father does the issuing, but since this is a twin birth, the duty has been handed over to Keynes. While the other Apostles watch in ruminative silence, Keynes stands before the embryos, Wittgenstein a head taller than the broad-shouldered, pink-cheeked Bliss. "May you know that the vow you are about to take is sacred," he warns. "Never shall you reveal to any outsider the existence of the Society, for should you do so, your soul shall writhe forever in torment."

This aspect of the curse has always puzzled Hardy. What has secrecy to do with Roby (or roby)? *He* didn't reveal the Society's existence to anyone. Instead he committed a different sin: that of failing to treat the Society with the deference it felt was its due. In subsequent years more Apostles than Hardy can name have broken their vow of secrecy, writing about the Society in memoirs and letters and speaking of it at luncheon parties. None, however, has committed the apparently more grievous offense of pooh-poohing his membership. Until now.

As Keynes reads the curse, the twins listen in silence, Wittgenstein without expression, Bliss with a look of solemnity behind which Hardy can detect a suppressed impulse to laugh. Then Keynes backs away and the brethren, bursting into applause, stand to give the new members (nos. 252 and 253) their official welcome.

It is in many ways a beautiful moment, and, as with most beautiful moments, it is interrupted by a knock on the door. Sheppard answers, and Strachey comes bounding in, accompanied by Harry Norton (no. 246). "There's your mathematician," Sheppard says to Hardy, which is what he always says to Hardy when Norton enters a room. Generally speaking, the Society spurns scientists, unless, as Sheppard once put it, the scientist in question is "a very nice scientist."

"My dears, we had an absolutely beastly journey," Strachey says, shaking out his umbrella. "The train was stuck for *hours* near Bishops Stortford. A body on the track, they said. Can you think of anything more ghastly? If I hadn't had dear Norton to entertain me, I might have had a fit. Now tell me, what have we missed?"

"The reading of the curse," Sheppard says. "We couldn't wait."

"Oh, what a pity. But not the paper, I hope."

"No."

"Good. Who's on the hearthrug tonight?"

"It was supposed to be Taylor but he couldn't get his written."

"Thank heavens for that," Norton murmurs. The decision as to who should read is made by drawing lots; whenever an Apostle arrives at a meeting without his paper (something very much frowned upon), an angel is asked to read in his stead one of his old papers, ferreted out of the Ark. More often than not McTaggart reads "Violets or Orange-Blossom?" and tonight he looks as if he would be glad to do so again. Keynes and Moore, however, appear to have other ideas, for they are even now digging through the Ark-ive.

Norton says, "They're probably trying to figure out how to take advantage of Madam Cecil's withdrawal to make a better impression on Wittgenstein. You know they're all terrified of him."

"Are they?"

He nods. Like Sheppard, Norton makes it his business to stay in the know. As Sheppard likes to point out, Norton is a mathematician—or used to be, until mathematics drove him "to the point of nervous collapse," after which he pretty much gave up his academic career and started spending most of his time in London, trying to ingratiate himself with the Bloomsbury set. Now he counts among his close friends not just Strachey but the Stephen sisters and that elusive object of desire, Duncan Grant. Yet for all his literary aspirations, Norton doesn't seem to *do* anything. This is what puzzles Hardy—how he can live within the radiance of artistic men and women without exhibiting any artistic impulses of his own. Today he remains what he's always been—short, monkeyish, rich from trade; a convenient source of cash when the Bloomsberries are hard up—and yet he's also less than he used to be, because he is no longer a man with a driving passion. Hardy likes him, even had an affair with him once—but that was long ago.

As for Taylor (no. 249), he is, as the brethren put it, Sheppard's "special friend": a blandly handsome, ill-tempered, rather dim young man whose only claim to distinction, so far as Hardy can tell, is that he is the grandson of the great logician George Boole. At the moment he looks distinctly put out, as if his failure to come through with the promised paper is the Society's fault and not his own. No one understands Sheppard's passion for him. Indeed, so far as Hardy can discern, the only reason he was elected to the Society in the first place was that Sheppard made it painfully clear that he would suffer acutely—perhaps at Taylor's hands—if the election failed to go through.

Now Taylor, a cross expression on his face, watches as Moore at last retrieves the paper he was looking for from the Ark, thumbs through the pages, then stands himself on the hearthrug. McTaggart turns away. "So it's to be the man himself," Norton says to Hardy. "Well, if anyone's got a shot at impressing the Witter-Gitter man, I suppose it's him."

They sit down, once again, on the sofa. Norton sits to Hardy's right, Taylor to his left, though in his imagination Taylor evaporates, replaced by the Indian friend in the flannel trousers. Through the flimsy casing Hardy imagines that he can feel the heat of a hard leg.

Moore clears his throat and reads the paper's title: "Is conversion possible?"

"Oh, that old thing," Hardy says under his breath, for he remembers the paper from when Moore first read it, back before the turn of the century.

Actually, it's not an uninteresting paper—that is, if you have the patience to untangle Moore's convoluted syntax, which Wittgenstein may not. By conversion, Moore means not religious conversion but an experience akin to the Tolstoyan concept of new birth: a mystic transformation of the spirit that we experience regularly in childhood and then, as we grow older, less and less often, until we arrive at middle age, after which we never experience it again. The question Moore poses is whether we can will ourselves to undergo this kind of "conversion" even in adulthood. He himself believed, when he first read the paper, that he had managed to do so once, perhaps twice, which surprised Hardy: did Moore really consider it such a feat? As a mathematician, Hardy "converted" every day. Every day he trafficked in numbers that could not exist, and gazed upon dimensions that could not be envisioned, and enumerated infinities that could not be counted. Yet Moore was too much a rationalist simply to accept his own mysticism. Indeed, Hardy's private belief was that, through his relentless interrogation of his capacity to "convert," he had managed merely to shut it down.

"Finally I have only this to ask the Society," Moore reads, "whether it is not possible that any one of us might discover, tonight or at any moment, this true philosopher's stone, the true Wisdom of the Stoics, a discovery which might permanently remove for him who made it, and perhaps for others, by far the most obstructive part of the difficulties and evils with which we have to contend."

He puts the paper down. Everyone applauds except for Wittgenstein, who stares stonily at the Ark. Moore steps off the hearthrug and sits on one of Sheppard's rickety chairs. Keynes asks if anyone wishes to respond.

Hardy feels the creaking of shot springs. Taylor gets up and approaches the hearthrug. Strachey covers his eyes.

Dear God, Hardy thinks, *please let Taylor talk for a long time. I so want to hear what he has to say.*

This time the feint fails. Taylor talks. He talks and talks. Time is irrelevant. As with music, the effect of slowness remains independent of the actual number of minutes eaten up. And what does he say? Nothing. "Humanism . . . ethos . . . *cri de coeur* . . ." *If he goes on much longer*, Hardy thinks, *I'm going to have a conversion here and now*. But finally he sits down again. "Thank you, Brother Taylor," Keynes says. "And now would anyone else like to speak?"

Much to Hardy's astonishment, Wittgenstein stands. Strachey

removes his hand from his eyes. Wittgenstein does not walk to the hearthrug. Instead he stays where he is and says, in his light Viennese accent, "Very interesting, but as far as I can see, conversion consists merely in getting rid of worry. Of having the courage not to care what happens."

Then he sits down again. Norton nudges Hardy in the side.

"Thank you, Brother Wittgenstein," Keynes says. "Well, then, if that's all, why don't we bring the matter to a vote? The question is: can we turn Monday mornings into Saturday nights? All in favor, say yea."

Various hands shoot up, including Taylor's, Békássy's, and, to Hardy's surprise, Strachey's. The "nays" include Wittgenstein, Russell, Moore, and Hardy himself.

The formal part of the meeting is now over. With a clattering like the inauguration of dinner in Hall, the brethren move toward the tea cart that Sheppard's gyp, who has become accustomed to the Society's strange ways, has wheeled in unobtrusively during the reading of the curse. Marsh eyes Brooke, Békássy fondles Bliss, Wittgenstein scowls, Sheppard tries to push a whale on to Taylor, who refuses it. "Ah, the drama of it all," Norton says. "Though if I'm to be honest, I must say that I wouldn't have minded the train being kept another hour. Even nursing Strachey through the vapors would have been preferable to hearing Moore read that old paper for the umpteenth time. And then the squitter-squatter . . . squitter-squattering so. Don't you despise it?"

"Taylor does go on a bit."

"You do know what it is that keeps Sheppard so fascinated, don't you? He has three balls."

"Who?"

"Madam Taylor. It's true. At first I didn't believe it either, but then I checked a medical dictionary. *Polyorchidism* is the technical term. A rare but documented condition. Apparently Sheppard just can't keep his hands off him—them."

Hardy is unequal to the three balls. "Really," he says.

"Of course I have no idea if they're all fully functional, or even the same size, or what the effect is—you know, whereas most of us have just the two, with a sort of, well, cleavage down the middle, like a piece of fruit, are his the same, only divided in three—like a three-lobed peach, if you can imagine? Or do two of them share one of the

53

compartments? Or is the third vestigial, like a cyst? Have you ever met anyone with supernumerary nipples? I knew someone who had an extra set, below the regular ones, only they didn't look like nipples, they were just these little red spots . . . Who's that Békássy is pawing?"

Hardy's attention is not so elastic as Norton's. He's still taking in the balls.

"I believe that's the clarinetist. Bliss."

"Yes, I suspect it would be." Norton sighs. "Personally, I prefer him to Békássy. Don't you? Not that Békássy isn't good-looking, but he hardly gets me going the way he does Keynes. The other day Strachey—James, not Lytton—told me that at the last meeting, Békássy got Keynes so worked up, he wanted to 'have him on the hearthrug.' Now don't you agree, our forebrethren would have looked away in shame at that?"

"No doubt," says Hardy, who's trying to envisage—and determine his views on—Taylor's anatomical peculiarity. Given the chance, he's perfectly willing to admit that he wouldn't mind seeing the malformed testes; indeed, he wonders that Taylor, given his exhibitionistic streak, hasn't already put on a show of sorts, or made them the subject of a talk from the hearthrug. The metaphorical implications! Does one ball hang lower than the other two, like the three golden balls outside a pawnbroker's shop? Yes, perhaps this is the secret that explains Taylor, his glumness and his arrogance both. For, at some point in his youth, a family doctor must have called attention to this oddity, made him aware for the first time that he was not like other boys. Quite possibly his schoolmates were cruel. How long has he borne the burden of self-consciousness, the knowledge that what repels some is as likely to attract others? And what does it say about Sheppard that he is attracted? At the moment they are quarreling, which is not unusual. Sheppard tries to put his arm around Taylor's waist, and Taylor, in response, pushes him away. "I am not precious, I am not a boy, and I am most certainly not yours!" he says, then retreats in high dudgeon to the hearth.

Norton nudges Hardy. "Rubber squirrel," he says—an old codeword, referring to a joke Norton once told in which a Japanese tries to say "lover's quarrel."

"So I see."

"And after all these years together. It's enough to make you lose your faith in marriage."

Apparently this scene—which Sheppard ornaments by saying, "Cecil, please don't make a scene"—is more than Wittgenstein can stomach. He turns away in disgust, only to find himself faced with the equally lurid spectacle of Békássy pushing Bliss, his arms around his waist, his crotch against his behind, toward the window seat. This is apparently the last straw. Wittgenstein smashes down his cup, puts on his coat, and walks out.

A silence falls. "Excuse me," Russell says a few seconds later, then gathers up his own coat and leaves, too.

"Well, I guess that squares it," Strachey says, striding up to join Hardy and Norton. "We've lost him."

"Do you really think so?"

"I fear so. Of course, given the chance, I'll do my best to talk him out of resigning. Yet how am I to persuade him that the Society's serious and honorable with all the silly business we've had going on tonight? What a pity that Madam had to put her oar in!"

"But Strachey," Norton says, "mustn't Herr Witter-Gitter realize that Cecil's not the Society any more than Hardy is, or I am, or—well, any one person? If he can't see that, there's nothing to be done."

"Still, the current lot of undergraduates . . . they don't make what you'd call a lasting intellectual impression. That's why we need Wittgenstein. To raise the bar. Do you know what he told Keynes? He said that watching Taylor and the others talk philosophy was like watching young men at their toilets. Harmless but obscene."

"But if he resigns, won't he have to be cursed and roby-ized?"

"Nonsense. You can't roby-ize a man like Wittgenstein. If anything, he might roby-ize us." Strachey turns to Hardy. "It's not like the old days, is it? In the old days, we used to talk about what *goodness* was. Or Goldie would be on the hearthrug, disquisiting on whether we should elect God. And we voted, and I think most of us agreed—you were in the minority, of course, Hardy—that, yes, we *should* elect God. And now look who we've got instead of God. The squitter-squatter. Our best days are behind us, I fear."

Strachey appears to be correct. At the moment, the tri-testicular Taylor is fuming by the fire. Békássy and Bliss are in the window seat, petting each other's necks. Sheppard looks as if he's about to weep. Fortunately Brooke—who has an instinct for such things—picks this instant to pass around the tobacco jar. Matches snap, pipes are lit. In the past, they all would have stood about chatting and arguing until three in the morning. Tonight, though, no one seems to have the heart for it, and the meeting breaks up just after twelve. McTaggart rides off on his tricycle, while Hardy makes his way back, alone, to Trinity. It's still surprisingly warm out. Patting the letter in his pocket, he thinks of his own letter. Has it yet passed through the Suez Canal? Is it on a ship crossing the ocean? Or has it already arrived at Madras, at the Port Trust Office, where the real Ramanujan will retrieve it Monday morning?

And now, as if on cue, his mysterious friend joins him; walks with him, matching his stride step for step. If the real Ramanujan really does come to Cambridge, might he be inducted into the Apostles, as the Society's first Indian member? Hardy would be his father, of course. Only what would Ramanujan make of these clever men with their fey rituals and private language? It's difficult for Hardy to reconcile the public image of men like Keynes and Moore with this boys' school atmosphere in which they frisk each Saturday night, calling each other by pet names and eating nursery food and talking endlessly, endlessly, about sex, and then about philosophy, and then sex again. Dirty jokes, boastful hints of carnal adventuring. Yet how many of them have any real experience? Practically none, Hardy suspects. Keynes, yes. Hardy himself, though few of them would guess it. Brooke—mostly with women. Also a sticking point. Hardy thinks of McTaggart, making his creaking, three-wheeled progress back to the unfeminine, Apostolic Daisy. For this is the Society's great secret, and its lie. Most of these men will marry in the end.

He is just arriving at the Trinity gates when Norton catches up with him. "Hello, Hardy," he says—and the Indian wraith evaporates.

"Heading home?" Hardy asks.

Norton nods. "I've been walking. The meeting left me full of agitated energy. I couldn't go to bed . . . I mean, I couldn't go to sleep yet."

He winks. He is not good-looking. More and more, the older he gets, does he resemble a monkey. Still, Hardy smiles at the invitation.

"You might come up for a cup of tea," he says, ringing the bell. Norton nods assent. Then they are quiet, lost in a silence in which there lingers an embarrassed silt of compromise, of settling for what's available in the absence of what's desired. Footfalls sound in the gloom, an impish, spiteful Cupid beats a drum, and Chatterjee—the real Chatterjee, decked out in his Corpus Christi robes—comes marching down Trinity Street, his heels beating out a rhythmic tap against the pavement. As he nears, his features merge into focus: ski-slope nose, lips turned up in a subtle smile, eyebrows that nearly join, but not quite. He passes so close that Hardy can feel the rushing of his robes, breathe in their smell of wardrobes. Then he's gone. He doesn't even meet Hardy's eye. The fact is, Chatterjee has no idea who he is.

It is at this instant that the porter arrives. Thinking them two undergraduates out after hours, he starts to give them a tongue-lashing—until he recognizes Hardy. "Good evening, sir," he says, holding the gate open, his face a bit red, if truth be told. "A pleasant night out?"

"Pleasant enough, thank you. Goodnight."

"Goodnight, sir. Goodnight, Mr. Norton."

"Goodnight."

Great Court is empty at this hour, vast as a ballroom, the lawn gleaming in the moonlight. Sometimes Hardy thinks of his Cambridge life as being divided into quadrants, much like the lawn of Great Court. One quadrant is mathematics, and Littlewood, and Bohr. The second is the Apostles. The third is cricket. The fourth . . . In truth, this is the quadrant he is most reluctant to define, not from squeamishness—on the contrary, he has little patience for the attempts that Moore and others make to dress the matter up in philosophical vestments—but because he doesn't know what words to use. When McTaggart speaks of the higher sodomy, he tries to draw a veil over the physical, about which Hardy feels no shame. No, the bother is when the quadrants touch—as they are touching now, Norton at his side, the two of them heading toward New Court surreptitiously even though there is nothing outwardly suspect in his inviting a friend to his room for a cup of tea that he knows will never be brewed.

They climb the stairs and he opens the door. Rising from Gaye's blue ottoman, Hermione arches her back, raises her tail in greeting. "Hello, puss," Norton says, bending over to stroke Hermione, as Hardy presses his fingers against his neck, trying to remember the last time he stroked human skin, and not a cat's fur. He tries to remember, and he can't.

8

WHEN LITTLEWOOD disappears from Cambridge, which he frequently does, it is usually to go down to Treen, in Cornwall, where he stays with the Chase family, or, more precisely, with Mrs. Chase and her children. Their father—Bertie Russell's doctor—lives in London, coming down to Treen once a month or so. About the understandings Littlewood has come to with Mrs. Chase, or Dr. Chase, or both, Hardy knows better than to enquire. Certainly such arrangements are not unheard of: Russell himself appears to have arrived at one with Philip Morrell, with whose wife, Ottoline, he is having an affair he can never quite keep secret. Indeed, the only sufferer in that situation appears to be Russell's own wife.

Littlewood has no wife. Both of them are fated to die bachelors, Hardy suspects: Littlewood because Mrs. Chase will never leave her husband, Hardy for rather more obvious reasons. This, he thinks, is why they can work with each other so much more easily than either can work, say, with Bohr, who is married. It isn't only a question of the occasional, unannounced, late-night visit; they also know when to leave each other alone. The married, he has noticed, are forever trying to persuade Hardy to join their fellowship. They live to advertise that brand of conjugal domesticity to which they have pledged themselves. It wouldn't be possible to collaborate with a married man, because a married man would always be noticing—questioning—that Hardy himself isn't married.

Littlewood never questions Hardy. Nor does he mention Gaye. He is a man who has little patience with those rules that delimit what one is and isn't supposed to talk about. Even so, he has to admit that he's just as glad that Hardy prefers not to share with him what Mrs. Chase calls "the gory details." Much easier, if not to defend, than at least to

58

explain Hardy as an abstraction, especially when Jackson—the wheezy old classicist whose inexplicable fondness for him Littlewood feels as a sort of rash or eczema—puts his mouth to his ear at high table and whispers, "How can you stand working with him? A normal fellow like you."

Littlewood has a canned answer to this kind of inquiry, which he gets often. "All individuals are unique," he says, "but some are uniquer than others." He'll only go further if the inquirer is someone he trusts, someone like Bohr, to whom he describes Hardy as a "nonpracticing homosexual." Which, so far as he can ascertain, is perfectly accurate. Aside from Gaye—whose relationship with Hardy Littlewood could not begin to parse—Hardy, from what he can tell, has never had a lover of either sex; only periodic episodes of besottedness with young men, some of them his students.

Mrs. Chase—Anne—thinks Hardy tragic. "What a sad life he must lead," she said to Littlewood this past weekend in Treen. "A life without love." And though he agreed, privately Littlewood couldn't help but reflect that such a life must not be without its advantages— he, a man who often finds himself contending with a surfeit of love: Anne's, and her children's, and his parents', and his siblings'. There are moments when all this love chokes him, and during these moments he regards Hardy's solitude as an enviable alternative to the over-populated lives for which his married friends have volunteered; the abundance of wives, children, grandchildren, sons- and daughters-in-law, mothers- and fathers-in-law; the murk of demands, needs, interruptions, recriminations. Whenever he goes to visit these friends in the country, or has supper with them at their Cambridge houses, he returns to his rooms full of gratitude, that he can climb into his bed alone and wake up alone—but knowing that, come the next weekend, he will not be alone. Perhaps this is why the arrangement with Anne suits him so well. It is a thing of weekends.

The first Friday in March, as is his habit, he goes to Treen. Rain keeps him indoors most of Saturday and Sunday. On Monday it's still raining; at the station, he learns that somewhere along the line a bridge has flooded, diverting his train, which arrives two hours late. This leaves him stuck at Liverpool Street for two hours. By the time he gets back to Cambridge, it's too late for dinner, still raining, and he's been traveling all day. He curses, throws his bags down on his bedroom floor, picks up his umbrella, and heads over to the Senior Combination room. Shadowed figures lurk in the paneled gloaming. Jackson, greeting him with a nod, points with his drink to a corner of the room where, much to his surprise, he glimpses Hardy sitting upright in a Queen Anne chair, hands on his knees. At the sight of him, Hardy bolts up and hurries toward him.

"Where were you?" he asks in a hiss.

"The country. My train was delayed. What's the matter?"

"It's come."

Littlewood stops in his tracks. "When?"

"This morning. I've been looking for you all day."

"I'm sorry. Look, what does it say?"

Hardy glances toward the fire. A small group of dons has clustered there to smoke. Until Littlewood walked in, they were talking about Home Rule in Ireland. Now they're silent, ears cocked.

"Let's go to my rooms," Hardy says.

"Fine, if you'll give me a drink," Littlewood says. And they turn around and leave. The rain is coming down in sheets. Hardy has forgotten his umbrella, and Littlewood must hold his over both of them. It makes for an uncomfortable intimacy, if one that only lasts the minute or so that it takes to walk over to New Court. Opening the door to his staircase, Hardy pulls away, clearly as relieved to be separated as Littlewood is. He shakes out his umbrella and drops it in the Chinese ceramic jar that Littlewood remembers from the old days, when Hardy shared a suite with Gaye on Great Court.

"I've only got whiskey," Hardy says, leading him up the stairs.

"That will do splendidly." Hardy opens the door to his suite. "Hello, cat," Littlewood says to Hermione, but when he bends down to pat her head, she runs away.

"What's the matter with her? I was only trying to be friendly."

"You treat her as if she's a dog." Hardy pulls the letter from his pocket. "Well, at least one thing's as I suspected," he says. "I'm not the first he's written to."

"No?"

"Oh, do take off your coat. Sit down. I'll get the whiskey."

Littlewood sits. Hardy pours the whiskey into two somewhat dirty glasses, hands one to Littlewood, then reads aloud.

" 'Dear Sir, I am very much gratified on perusing your letter of the

60

8th February 1913. I was expecting a reply from you similar to the one which a Mathematics Professor at London wrote asking me to study carefully Bromwich's Infinite Series and not fall into the pitfalls of divergent series.' That's Hill, I expect. Anyway: 'I have found a friend in you who views my labours sympathetically. This is already some encouragement to me to proceed with my onward course.'"

"Good."

"Yes, but now comes the worrisome part. 'I find in many a place in your letter rigorous proofs are required and so on and you ask me to communicate the methods of proof. If I had given you my methods of proof, I am sure you will follow the London Professor. But as a fact, I did not give him any proof but made some assertions as the following under my new theory. I told him that the sum of an infinite number of terms of the series: $1 + 2 + 3 + 4 + \ldots = -\frac{1}{12}$ under my theory.'"

"Yes, that was in the last one, too."

"'If I tell you this you will at once point out to me the lunatic asylum as my goal. I dilate on this simply to convince you that you will not be able to follow my methods of proof if I indicate the lines on which I proceed in a single letter.'"

"He's hedging. Maybe he's afraid you'll try to steal his stuff."

"That's what I thought, too. But then there's this: 'So what I now want at this stage is for eminent professors like you to recognize that there is some worth in me. I am already a half-starving man. To preserve my brains I want food and this is now my first consideration.'"

"Do you think he's actually starving?" Littlewood asks.

"Who knows? What does twenty pounds a year buy in Madras? And here's how it ends: 'You may judge me hard that I am silent on the methods of proof. I have to reiterate that I may be misunderstood if I give in a short compass the lines on which I proceed. It is not on account of my unwillingness on my part but because I fear I shall not be able to explain everything in a letter. I do not mean that the methods should be buried with me. I shall have them published if my results are recognized by eminent men like you.' And then there are—what?—ten pages of mathematics."

"And?"

"Well, at least I've worked out what he's up to with the damn $1 + 2 + 3 + 4 = -\frac{1}{12}$."

"What?"

"I'll show you." With a quick sweep of the cloth, Hardy wipes his blackboard clean. "Essentially, it's a matter of notation. His is very peculiar. Let's say you decide you want to write $\frac{1}{2}$ as 2^{-1}. Perfectly valid, if a little obscurist. Well, what he's doing here is writing $\frac{1}{2^{-1}}$ as $\frac{1}{\frac{1}{2}}$, or 2. And then, along the same lines, he writes the sequence

$$1 + \frac{1}{2^{-1}} + \frac{1}{3^{-1}} + \frac{1}{4^{-1}} + \ldots \text{ as } \underset{1}{\frac{1}{\frac{1}{1}}} + \underset{2}{\frac{1}{\frac{1}{2}}} + \underset{3}{\frac{1}{\frac{1}{3}}} + \underset{4}{\frac{1}{\frac{1}{4}}} + \ldots, \text{ which is of course } 1 + 2 + 3$$

$+ 4 + \ldots$ So what he's really saying is $1 + \frac{1}{2^{-1}} + \frac{1}{3^{-1}} + \frac{1}{4^{-1}} + \ldots = -\frac{1}{12}$."

"Which is the Riemannian calculation for the zeta function fed with -1."

Hardy nods. "Only I don't think he even knows it's the zeta function. I think he came up with it on his own."

"But that's astounding. I wonder how he'll feel once he finds out Riemann did it first."

"My hunch is that he's never heard of Riemann. Out in India, how could he? They're behind England, and look how far England is behind Germany. And of course, since he's self-taught, it makes sense that his notation would be a little—well—off."

"True, except that he seems to *know* it's off. Otherwise why put in the bit about the lunatic asylum?"

"He's toying with us. He thinks he's great."

"Most great men do."

A silence falls. Gulping his whiskey, Littlewood regards Hermione. Her gaze—predatory and accusatory and bored—disconcerts him. The fact is, he's no more comfortable here, in Hardy's territory, than Hardy is in his. The cat makes him nervous, as do the bits of decorative frippery, the ottoman with its hairy fringe and the bust on the mantelpiece. Gaye, it appears.

Putting down his glass, he takes the letter from where Hardy's dropped it; stands up. "Do you mind if I follow tradition and borrow this?" he asks.

"Be my guest. Likely you'll have more luck than I have."

"I don't see why."

"You're the one who was senior wrangler."

Littlewood raises his eyebrows. *What brought that on?*

"Show it to Mercer then," he says, handing the letter back—a little surprised by his own vehemence.

Hardy looks as if he's just been slapped. But Littlewood has already turned away from him, to Hermione. "Goodbye, cat," he says.

She ignores him.

"Sometimes I think she's deaf."

"She is deaf."

"What?"

"A recessive gene. Most white cats are deaf."

"Oh, of course," Littlewood says. "Of course you'd have a deaf cat. I should have guessed."

He moves toward the door, and Hardy reaches out his hand to stop him. "I'm sorry," he says. "I didn't mean to offend, or . . . Look, just take the letter."

"I'm not offended. Just perplexed. That you should bring up a thing like that. Is it really such a sore spot? Still?"

"Of course not. I just—"

"And you can't think it matters to *me*. I hate the damn thing as much as you do."

"I know. I misspoke. A poor effort at a joke. Please, take the letter."

He holds it out like an offering. Reluctantly Littlewood accepts it. Hardy looks humbled, and Littlewood's umbrage melts. Poor fellow! "Very good, sir," he says, to show there are no hard feelings, and mimics a military salute. "Goodnight."

"Goodnight." Hardy replies, his voice chilly and wistful. He shuts the door.

Littlewood is still young enough that, when he's alone and going downstairs, he bounds, taking the steps two at a time. Right now he's thinking about Mercer—not Mercer as he is today, but as he was when they were both coaching for the tripos. Back then, Mercer only spoke when spoken to. When he was writing, his head bobbed over the paper with metronomic regularity. Littlewood will be the first to admit that Mercer's strange mode of concentration, his apparent obliviousness to everything around him, unnerved him in a way that the stunts perpetrated by his more competitive fellows—gestures *meant* to distract—never did. And what in Mercer could possibly have appealed to Hardy? Not that he wants to hear the gory details of the case, which in this instance probably aren't even details of sex, but rather of infatuation, which is somehow worse. Littlewood knows, because he's been on the receiving end of infatuation: the hours the poor devils spend trying to "read" a smile, or interpret a pat on the shoulder, or discern the secret import of the loan of a pencil. Schoolgirl nonsense. And the notes: "Although we have never spoken, and I am no doubt invisible to you, may I risk offense by remarking on the pleasure I have taken, so many mornings, watching you bathe . . ." Still, he'd be curious to hear how things started with Mercer, and why they soured.

The rain keeps up its pluvial dance. He runs all the way to Nevile's Court without opening his umbrella. He likes the feel of the beads of water sliding down his forehead, and only wishes he wasn't so hungry.

One thing to be glad for is solitude. If he chooses to, he can go straight to bed. No phantom lover will visit him in his dreams. (And of whom will Hardy dream? He shudders to think.) Or perhaps he won't go to bed at all. Perhaps he'll sit up all night, studying the Indian's letter. And if he does, there'll be no one to scold him. No shadowed figure in a nightdress, holding a candle, will beg him to come to bed. No child will call him to comfort her after a nightmare.

He steps indoors. The silence of his rooms is familiar, consoling. No two silences are alike, he thinks; each has its own contours and shadings, because inside each silence there is the absence of a sound, and in this case it is the sound of Mozart played badly on a piano, or Beethoven, played beautifully, issuing from the horn of a gramophone. He takes off his jacket, and as he does he smells Anne's scent on it—very faint now. Then he kicks off his shoes, lights his pipe, and sits down to reread the letter.

9

CLOSE TO MIDNIGHT the rain thins a little. Hardy, in his pyjamas, watches it through the window that gives on to the archway. Although of late he's got into the habit of going to bed on the early side, tonight he can't imagine sleeping. Despite his mounting excitement over Ramanujan's new letter, he's fallen into a bad humor, thanks to Littlewood's barb about Mercer. It was his own fault, of course. If he hadn't mentioned Littlewood's having been senior wrangler, Littlewood would never have brought up Mercer. The fact is, Hardy doesn't want to be reminded of Mercer, whom—he cannot pretend otherwise—he has pretty much abandoned. For instance, when Mercer returned to Cambridge last year, he sent Hardy a card inviting him to call on him and his new bride. Hardy never replied. There was no good reason for it, either, other than that Mercer was no longer at Trinity. Then again, Christ's College is hardly the other side of the world.

His new bride. What would Gaye have to say about that?

Almost automatically, Hardy glances across the room. From the mantelpiece, the bust gazes down at him (*Gaye gazes*), its aspect as reproachful as that of Sheppard's mother. It's a small bust, made when Gaye was fifteen, the expression, as always, glinting and coy. Sometimes Hardy wonders what would happen if he took the bust and smashed it to pieces, or stuffed it away in a cupboard, or presented it as a gift to Butler, who, given the circumstances, would probably stuff it in a cupboard of his own.

The answer, of course, is that it would make no difference. Gaye's hand is all over the room. Grant him this much: he had taste. He picked the Turkey carpet, and soaked the chintz curtains in a bathtub full of tea to give them their look of having hung for years in a country house. He chose the checked fabric for the cushions on Hardy's rattan chair—the very cushions Hardy is sitting on now. All this, even though Hardy was leaving him. Poor Gaye, always so drawn to martyrdom! The old painting of Saint Sebastian he kept over his bed should have been a clue. It's gone now, taken away by his brother, along with everything else that was of any value.

And why did Gaye's brother not take the bust? It's true, when he came around, Hardy made a point of standing it in a back corner of his bedroom, not the most likely place to look. But he didn't hide it. Afterward, for years, he kept expecting a letter from the family, demanding restitution of the bust. None ever came. Perhaps they were as eager to forget about Gaye as everyone else was.

Around one, he gets into bed. Still, he can't sleep. Figures swirl in his head, fragments memorized for the tripos, and oddities from Ramanujan, and the zeta function, its peaks and valleys and the spire soaring up to infinity when it takes the value of 1 . . . This often happens to him. Sometimes such insomnia bodes well, means that a breakthrough will come in the morning. More often he wakes ill-humored and unable to work. So why doesn't he share Littlewood's terror of false hope?

And then—just, it seems, as he is falling asleep (though later he will realize that he had been asleep for almost two hours)—there is a knock on the door. At another time in his life, this wouldn't have surprised him. A visitor at three in the morning would have been routine. Now, though, the knock disorients him, throws him into a panic. "Just a minute," he calls, putting on his dressing gown. "Who is it?"

"Me. Littlewood."

He opens the door. Littlewood strides in, dripping and umbrellaless. "The stuff about primes is wrong," he says.

"What?"

"Oh, sorry. Have I woken you?"

"It doesn't matter. Come in."

Without even removing his coat, Littlewood heads for the blackboard, still covered with Hardy's earlier scribblings. "I couldn't sleep so I started looking over the letter and—may I?"

"Of course."

"Right, so this is what I think he's done." He wipes the blackboard clean. "Here's his formula for calculating the number of primes less than n. Well, it's the usual Riemannian formula, except that he's left

66

out the terms coming from the zeros of the zeta function. And his results—I've tested them—are just what you'd get if the zeta function had *no* non-trivial zeros."

"Damn."

"I have a vague theory as to how the mistake came about. He's staking everything on the legitimacy of some operations he's doing on divergent series, banking on a hunch that if the first results are correct, the theorem must be true. And the first results *are* correct. Even up to a thousand the formula gives exactly the right answer. Unfortunately, he had no one around to warn him that the primes like to misbehave once they get larger."

"Still, leaving out the zeros . . . it's not an encouraging sign."

"Oh, but there I disagree, Hardy. I think it's a very encouraging sign." Littlewood steps closer. "You must realize, ordinary mathematicians don't make mistakes like this. Even very good mathematicians don't make mistakes like this. And when you consider the other stuff, the stuff on continued fractions and elliptic functions . . . I can believe he's at least a Jacobi."

Hardy raises his eyebrows. Now *this* is high praise. Since starting at Trinity, he's kept up a mental ranking of the great mathematicians, putting each in the class of a cricketer whom he admires. He judges himself the equal of Shrimp Levison-Gower, Littlewood on a par with Fry, Gauss in the category of Grace, the greatest player in the history of the game. Jacobi, the last time Hardy ranked him, was somewhere above Fry but below Grace—in the vicinity of the young and dazzling Jack Hobbs—which means that Ramanujan, if Littlewood is correct, might have the potential to be another Grace. He could well prove the Riemann hypothesis.

"What about the rest?"

"I haven't had a chance to go over these other asymptotic formulas, but at first glance, they look to be totally original. And significant."

"But no proofs."

"I don't think he really understands what a proof is, or that it's important to give one, because he's been working on his own all these years, and who knows what books, if any, he has access to. Perhaps no one's taught him. Could you teach him?"

"I've never tried to teach anyone *why* you have to give proofs. My students have always just . . . understood."

There is a moment of quiet, now, of which Hermione takes advantage by rubbing herself against Littlewood's leg. When he tries to pick her up, she runs for cover beneath the ottoman.

"A tease, that female. Come here, kitten!"

"She can't hear you. Remember?"

"Oh, of course." Littlewood regards the floor.

"And what are we to do now?" Hardy asks.

"Is there any question? Bring him to England."

"He's said nothing about wanting to come."

"Of course he wants to come. Why else would he have written? And what's he got in Madras? A clerkship."

"But if we get him here, will we know what to do with him?"

"I think the more apt question is, will he know what to do with us?" Littlewood pushes his glasses up on his nose. "Have you heard from the India Office, by the way?"

"Not yet."

"Well, if you want my advice, which you may not, there's only one course to take, and that's to get a man to Madras. And soon. I think Neville's supposed to give some lectures there in December."

"Neville?"

"Don't scoff. He's a decent chap."

"Neville is a perfectly capable mathematician who will never in his life do anything of consequence."

"The ideal emissary, then." Littlewood laughs. "Let's bring him in on it, shall we? And then, when he gets to Madras, he can see this Ramanujan, feel him out, see what he wants and if he's what we want."

"But is Neville capable of such discernment?"

"If he's not, his wife is. Have you met Alice Neville? An impressive young woman." Littlewood is already moving toward the door. "Yes, it's the best plan. What's the saying? If you can't bring Mohammed to the mountain, bring the mountain to Mohammed."

"Wrong religion," Hardy says.

"Oh, well, Vishnu then! Good God, Hardy, you can be quite a stickler." But Littlewood is laughing as he says this, laughing as he descends the stairs, laughing as, with a whistle and whoop, he steps out onto the rain-soaked paving stones of New Court.

10

New Lecture Hall, Harvard University

O N T H E L A S T D A Y of August, 1936, the great mathematician G. H. Hardy put down his chalk and returned to the dais. "The real tragedy about Ramanujan," he said, "was not his early death. It is of course a disaster that any great man should die young, but a mathematician is often comparatively old at thirty, and his death may be less of a catastrophe than it seems. Abel died at twenty-six and, although he would no doubt have added a great deal more to mathematics, he could hardly have become a greater man. The tragedy of Ramanujan was not that he died young, but that, during his five unfortunate years, his genius was misdirected, sidetracked, and to a certain extent distorted."

He paused. Did his audience understand what he meant? Might they think that he was referring to the five years Ramanujan spent in England?

No, he wanted to say, *not* his years in England. I mean the crucial years just before he came to England, when he needed education as a newborn child needs oxygen.

Or perhaps—and here, in his own mind, he stepped back—I really do mean his years in England, which in their way were also years of damage.

He would have liked to say:

So little seems certain anymore. Words that I wrote in the immediate aftermath of his death, when I read them today, strike me as rank with sentimentality. They emanate the desperation of a man trying to escape guilt and blame. I tried to make a virtue of his ignorance, to persuade myself and others that he profited from the years he spent in isolation, when in fact they were an insurmountable handicap.

Nothing ever came easily to him, and there is no way to pretend that this was to his good. He was very poor and lived in a provincial town, more than a day's journey from Madras. And though he went to school (he was of a high caste), school was not kind to him. Starting when he was fifteen, sixteen, he was treated as a pariah. The Indian educational system, in those years, was terribly rigid, far more rigid than our own, on which it was modeled. The system rewarded the nebulous ideal of "well-roundedness"; it was designed to churn out the bureaucrats and technicians who would oversee the Indian empire (under our supervision, of course). What it was not designed to do was to recognize genius—its obsessiveness and its blindness, its refusal to be anything other than what it is.

School after school failed Ramanujan because at school after school he ignored all his subjects except mathematics. Even at mathematics he was at times mediocre, because the mathematics that he was being taught bored and irritated him. From his youth—from when he was seven, eight years of age—he was following the signposts of his own imagination.

One example will suffice. When he was eleven, studying at Town High School in Kumbakonam, his maths teacher explained that if you divide any number by itself, you will get 1. If you have sixteen bananas and divided them among sixteen people, each will get one banana. If you have 10,000 bananas and divide them among 10,000 people, each will get one banana. Then Ramanujan stood up and asked what would happen if you divided no bananas among no people.

You see, even then, when he was still doing well, the troublemaker in him was starting to emerge.

I think I sensed all this from his early letters. He was a man whom the dispensers of prizes had failed to esteem properly and he resented them for it. Naturally this rejection led him to doubt his own worth; and yet from the start he also displayed a certain hubris, a faith in his genius, and took a solitary pride in knowing that he was better than his time and place. If the world in which he lived failed to value him, it was that world's fault, not his own. Why should he then cooperate? Yet this is a very lonely sort of victory.

Of course, in this regard I was his opposite. I was the boy who won all the prizes—this, though I despised prize day with an intensity that today only the sight of a church procession is likely to rouse in me. To hear my name called, and then to have to get up before the entire school to accept my prize, provoked in me such a furor of shame and self-loathing as to make my legs wobble; I would stagger onto the stage in a kind of fever, take the book or token with clammy hands, grit my teeth so as not to vomit. By the time I got to Winchester, this peculiar variant of stage fright had got so bad that I started deliberately giving the wrong answers on examinations, just in order to be spared the ordeal of the prize. But not—I must be truthful about this—often enough that I might jeopardize my future. For I craved the imprimatur of Oxford or Cambridge, the approbation that Ramanujan was denied.

Why such hatred of prizes? I think it was because I knew, even as I excelled on its greeneries, that the playing field was rigged. It was rigged to reward the rich, the well fed, the well cared for. And, as my parents made sure constantly to remind me, I was not one of these. I was lucky to be there at all. Talent would not assist the son of the miner in Wales: *he'd* spend his life in the mines, even if he had the proof for the Riemann hypothesis in his head. Always my parents told me to pray for my own good fortune, and theirs.

Perhaps it is a sign of weakness that I played by the rules. No doubt some future biographer (if I merit one) will censure me for this failure of nerve. For there is another way to look at Ramanujan: as the resolute mind whom genius permits no other course but to follow its instincts, even at its own peril.

Once I arrived at Cambridge my mistrust of prizes, rather than abating, found a new target in the tripos. The men I despised the most were the ones who, unlike me and Littlewood, viewed victory on the tripos as a goal in its own right, and made wranglerhood the object of their education. It was to stop in its tracks the system that encouraged such fevered ambitions and immoderate hungers that I set out to reform the tripos, if not abolish it outright. And the ironic result of my success was this: never was the fever for tripos victory so intense as it was in 1909, the year the last senior wrangler was to be crowned.

Which brings me to Eric Neville—the man some credit with persuading Ramanujan to come to England. Later on, we became friends, and remain friends to this day, his wife notwithstanding. In 1909, however, Neville existed for me merely in one dimension, as the man considered the favorite, that year, to be senior wrangler. As it turned out, he came in second, and I remember gloating a little bit, thinking that he would never recover from the disappointment. He wanted so desperately to go down in history as the last of the senior wranglers.

But it is not of this tripos that I am thinking tonight; no, it is of an earlier tripos, the tripos of 1905, the one tripos during which I myself (I am ashamed to admit it) played the very role I now vilify: that of coach.

The boy I coached was named Mercer. James Mercer.

How to explain my closeness to Mercer? I suppose, at first, I was drawn to him because, like me, he was an outsider. He had come to Cambridge from University College, Liverpool, and was consequently older than most of the other men. Shy of his accent. The first time he came to see me, he covered his mouth with his hand.

And now I see that I must go back further and tell you about Gaye. Yes, my narrative tonight is not so much unfolding as opening inward, like a set of Russian nesting dolls being unpacked. Well, you must trust me that we will get back to the tripos—and Ramanujan—and Mercer—in due time.

What year was that? 1904, yes—which means that Gaye and I had been sharing the suite a year; that suite of rooms through the door to which I shall never again, so long as I live, pass; beautiful rooms, overlooking Great Court.

I don't know what to call him now. When we were alone, we were Russell and Harold. But when there were other people around we were Gaye and Hardy. In those years, in our circle, men always called each other by their last names.

I met him—I forget how I met him. We simply knew each other not well, and then we knew each other well. It was like that at Cambridge. The context might have been theatrical—I recall a student production of *Twelfth Night* in which Strachey played Maria and Gaye was Malvolio and I was "the critic." I was usually the critic. And Gaye and I talking, talking. The small, soft mouth and the dark eyes, with their expression of mingled vulnerability and exasperation, made me want to be near him as much as I could, and at the same time not to let on how much I wanted to be near him; to keep enough distance not to implicate myself. For I was like him in many ways, full of wistful longing, and yet determined to gain the upper hand, which he still had in those days before both Trinity and I expelled him. Of course, this was not long after G. E. Moore had gone off with Ainsworth, and so the last thing I wanted to do was to show weakness.

I should add that I did not know then how weak Gaye himself was: weak and sly and impatient; possessed of that slashing wit that is so often the obverse of vulnerability. From his mouth there were always emerging these perfectly formed little clevernesses, like jewels or scarabs, all the more stunning for the wet innocence of the lips that uttered them.

No one thought anything of our choosing to share the suite. In Cambridge, it was common in those days for young men to be "inseparable," and to function as couples, and socialize as couples. Gaye and I were hardly the only ones. We hosted little suppers that first year, to which we invited people like O. B., who smiled upon us and gave us his blessing. Moore and Ainsworth came to supper once, the four of us before the fire, and Ainsworth putting out his cigarettes on his plate. Gaye had more to say to him than I did. I should mention that Gaye was a classicist, and a very good one, and that when Trinity let him go, Trinity did him a monstrous injustice and itself a grave disservice.

The suite consisted of a sitting room with windows overlooking Great Court and two small bedrooms, each with a window overlooking the roofs of New Court. As a rule, we kept the bedroom doors closed only when students visited, or when one of us needed quiet to work. That year Gaye was translating Aristotle's *Physics* with another classics fellow whose name, confusingly, was Hardie. So the door to his bedroom was closed more often than not, at least during the day.

Hermione was still a kitten. We had just acquired her from the sister of Mrs. Bixby, our bedmaker; she worked on a farm near Grantchester where there was always a wealth of kittens. We'd had another cat, Euclid, but he had died. We were both very busy, Gaye with his translation, me with my prize fellowships and the several undergraduates I tutored, Mercer among them. Mercer, with his sea-glass beauty—the beauty of ill health, chronic and likely to get worse. You could see it in his skin, in the rather weary way he sat in his chair. His eyes were a luminescent gray-green that Strachey, among others, remarked upon. Even today—and he is dead several years now—his eyes are what I best remember of him.

It had been six years since I myself had taken the tripos. Nothing had changed in the interval except that Herman, not Webb, was now the coach of choice. He fed the men "potted abstracts," as someone or other referred to them. In his model coliseum the would-be gladiators were still called upon to recite Newton, to solve problems against the clock, to learn everything there was to know two hundred years back about heat, lunar theory, optics.

Mercer came to see me because, like me, he couldn't stand it. I remember he wrung his hands. Literally. I don't think I'd ever seen anyone actually do that before. I thought it was something people only did in novels. There was coffee on the table, Mercer was wringing his hands, and at some point, he started weeping. I hardly knew what to say. I didn't notice it at the time, but the door that led to Gaye's bedroom must have been open, for Hermione darted in. She regarded Mercer with an air of merciless detachment. (*Mercer, merciless*. My brain does not relent from such useless wordplay. It is like a virus.)

He told me how it was. It was like hearing myself complaining to Butler, six years earlier. The tedium. The sense of energy diverted, imagination stifled. (Would Ramanujan have stood for it?) I asked him how the other men felt, and he said, "Most of them, they just look at it as what they're here to do. You know, because one's father was sixth wrangler, one's was fifth. They want to beat their fathers, and get posts as government ministers or what have you. But I'm from Bootle. My father's just an accountant."

And what of the ones who, like him, aspired to be mathematicians? He mentioned Littlewood. At this point I knew Littlewood only in passing. ("Passing on his way to the Cam," O. B. reminds me, from the grave.) I'd heard from Barnes that Littlewood was good. Quite possibly as good as me. And how did *he* feel about the tripos? "He says the whole thing's a waste of time," Mercer said, "but if he looks at it as a game—not a game he particularly enjoys, but it's the one they play at this college, so what choice does he have?—well, then he can stomach it. He'll just play with all his might, because he likes to win."

We sat there then. Mercer wrung his hands. I told him of my own experience. By then my opinion—my contempt for the tripos and desire to see it murdered—was well known, which was probably why Mercer had come to me in the first place. In the meantime the coffee

74

grew cold. I don't remember exactly how or why but at some point a surge of empathy must have seized me, for I found myself offering to coach him myself. I also lent him my copy of the *Cours d'analyse*. "For every hour we waste on the tripos," I said, "we'll spend an hour with Jordan. We will wash down the bitter pill with fine wine."

Scratching his head, Mercer went off, not having drunk his coffee and carrying with him a book written in a language he barely understood. From the window I watched him stumble over a paving stone, reading even as he walked. It was a good sign.

Then I felt a warm hand on my shoulder; shut my eyes.

"How lovely it must be to be the rescuer," Gaye said.

"So you've been listening in?"

"What choice did I have? Can I help it that Hermione nudged open the door? And then that bawling. It *dragged* me from Aristotle. I had to make sure everything was all right."

"It was nothing I couldn't manage."

"Certainly an expressive young man."

"He's suffering. He needs my help."

"Fine, and what about what you need, Harold? Your own work?" Gaye picked up Mercer's cup from the table, and drank down the cold coffee in a single gulp. "Coaching an undergraduate for the tripos. The tripos, of all things! And after all the *screeds* I've heard you deliver against the damned—"

"He won't make it otherwise."

"Is it your job to save him?"

"Someone saved me."

"But Love didn't *coach* you. He just sent you back to Webb." Gaye put the cup down. "Now if he was ugly—"

"That has nothing to do with it."

"Of course not. Yours is a more specialized erotic thrill, that of rescuing the fair damsel from the jaws of the dragon. Or do you imagine him doing what you couldn't?"

"What?"

"Taking his place as senior wrangler and then, while standing atop the carcass of the beast, denouncing the hunt."

"You sound jealous."

"I am—of the original work that will be lost by virtue of your coaching this—"

"How selfless of you."

Gaye picked up Hermione and stroked her neck. "It's your decision, of course. Don't think I'd dream of interfering."

Wriggling out of his grip, Hermione slipped back through the door that she (or Gaye) had earlier opened, the door that led to his part of the suite. A few seconds later, Gaye followed her.

Half an hour later, he popped his head out. "Shall we have supper in tonight?" he asked, then took it back immediately. "But of course not. It's Saturday. Your Saturdays are spoken for."

"You know that, Russell."

"Gosh, I wonder what they do all those Thaturday nightth, thothe very thmart young men?"

"I can't talk about this."

"No, of course not. Of course you can't."

Now I ask myself: why didn't I ever propose him for membership? At the time, I told myself that it was to spare him being made a laughing stock, another Madam Taylor. Or perhaps the truth was that I wanted to spare myself being looked upon as another Sheppard. In thrall.

The one possibility I never allowed myself to consider was that, unlike Taylor, Gaye might be considered worthy of membership in his own right. And if he had been inducted into the Society—would it have made a difference later on? I don't know. I don't know.

And where was Ramanujan then? In 1904, he had just graduated from the high school, and won a scholarship to Government College. Still in Kumbakonam; I doubt he'd even been to Madras at this stage. Later, in one of his laughing moods—this must have been during the first year of the war, for I recall that there were soldiers lying on stretchers in Nevile's Court—he told me that back then, Government College was called "the Cambridge of South India."

Things started off well enough. He took courses in physiology, in English, in Greek and Roman history. But then he got hold of a copy of Carr's *Synopsis of Pure Mathematics*, the book that he would later say meant as much to him as Jordan's *Cours d'analyse* had meant to me. As he explained, his parents, to supplement their small income, sometimes took in students as boarders, and one of the students had left the book behind. Astonishing to think that from this book he got his start. A few weeks ago, before boarding the ship that has carried me to your good country, I borrowed it from the Trinity Library, the one copy there, dusty from disuse. The *Synopsis* is more than nine hundred pages long. It was published in 1886, and no one had charged it since 1902.

What *was* it about this book? Food for a starving man. I can see Ramanujan sitting on the *pial*, that porch in front of his mother's house about which he so often waxed nostalgic; sitting in the shade while the parade of street life passed before him, and reading through pages and pages of equations, each one numbered. He told me later that he had that book memorized. Had there been a Carr tripos, he would have been prepared to recite each equation chapter and verse, merely upon being given its number. 954: "The *Nine-point* circle is the circle described through *D, E, F,* the feet of the perpendiculars on the sides of the triangle *ABC*." 5,849: "The product *pd* has the same value for all geodesics which touch the same line of curvature." In total 6,165 equations. And he memorized them all.

He became neglectful of his other subjects. Ignoring history, he entertained his friends by making what he called "magic squares":

1	2	−3
−4	0	4
3	−2	−1

Or:

9	10	5
4	8	12
11	6	7

Child's play. Each column adds up to the same number—vertically, horizontally, diagonally. The astonishing thing was that Ramanujan could construct his magic squares in a matter of seconds. During his Greek history class he would sit at his desk, apparently taking notes, when actually he was making magic squares. (He had, needless to say, got hold of a more general theorem without even realizing it.) Or he would list the prime numbers in sequence. Trying even then to find order in them.

And of course, the more he lost himself in mathematics, the less attention he paid to his other subjects. Physiology, he said, was his worst subject because he had a horror of dissections. I think the truth was that, like most mathematicians, he had a horror of the physical. (After watching his teacher chloroform some sea-frogs for dissection, he asked the teacher, "Sir, have you chosen these sea-frogs because we are all pond-frogs?" That was typical of his wit. He knew even then that Kumbakonam was a small pond.) And then he also did poorly at English, which surprises me, because when I knew him his spoken English was flawless, while his written English, if not the stuff of Shakespeare, was certainly passable. Nevertheless, at the end of the first year, he failed his English composition examination. Notwithstanding his obvious talent for mathematics, his scholarship was taken away. Policy was policy. Now he would have to pay for his schooling—or rather, his parents would have to pay for it. And his parents were poor. His father was some sort of accounts clerk, his mother took in sewing and sang at the local temple to make ends meet. Sometimes there was no food and he had to eat at the houses of his school friends.

This was the first of several times he ran away. What he did while he was gone he would not tell me—only that he went to another town, north of Madras. Visakhapatnam. Within a month he was home again.

I think I can imagine how he felt: as angry at himself as at the system—pitiless, unyielding—on which his success depended. Government College had booted him out because he would not play by the rules, and while it enraged him that he was expected to play by the rules—as Littlewood would observe, even then he knew himself to be great—he also despised himself for his own inability (or was it unwillingness?) to be the good boy he was expected to be. For who was there to assure him that his faith in his own greatness was not vanity or illusion?

And meanwhile, back in Cambridge, Mercer was coming to see me every day. I'd hold the stopwatch. I'd call out the numbers of the Newtonian lemmas, and he'd recite them. Then we'd work through the *Cours d'analyse*.

At first, those afternoons, Gaye lingered in his part of the suite. Sometimes he'd leave the door open. Then—after I got up once in the middle of a coaching session and shut it—he stopped leaving it open.

I was there for the reading of the honors list that year, standing inside the Senate House at nine in the morning, part of a vast crowd in the murk of which I could make out O. B. with Sheppard, who must have had money riding on the favorite. The gallery was reserved for ladies. Newnham and Girton girls were piled three or four deep against the rails. No doubt they were hoping, as they hoped every year, for a repeat of 1890, when Philippa Fawcett had beaten the senior wrangler and her sisters had gone into a frenzy. Since then, no woman had even come close.

Everyone was talking at once. I should mention that the likely candidates for senior wrangler weren't there. By long tradition, they stayed in their rooms during the reading of the honors list, waiting for their friends to bring them the good or bad news. Still, you could hear their names on the lips of the crowd, and in this way they were more present than they would have been had they actually been there in the flesh.

The clock of Great St. Mary's Church began to strike nine, and Dodds, the moderator, took his position at the front of the gallery. Instantly the crowd quieted. Dodds was dressed in the full regalia of his college, and clutched in his right hand the bundled honors list, the untying of which he timed to coincide exactly with the sounding of the ninth chord. With religious dignity he intoned: "Results of the mathematical tripos, Part I, 1905." A beat of silence. "Senior wrangler, J. E. Littlewood, Trinity—"

Before Dodds could finish, applause erupted from the crowd. So Littlewood had beaten Mercer! A stab of disappointment passed through me, which I tried to dull by reminding myself how much I loathed the tripos. I looked at Sheppard, who was frowning. No doubt he'd put his money on Mercer out of loyalty to me. Then Dodds said, "Please, please, silence! If I may be allowed to continue—Senior wrangler: J. E. Littlewood, Trinity, *bracketed* with J. Mercer, Trinity."

Sheppard's face, dark with dread moments before, brightened. "Bracketed" meant that Littlewood and Mercer had scored exactly the same number of points. They were tied.

In spite of myself I let out a cheer. O. B. cast at me a bemused and contemptuous glance. I shut up and listened as the rest of the wranglers and optimes were named, right down to the wooden spoon. By then most of the crowd had gone outside to watch the senior wranglers paraded about in all their glory. I followed. Not far off I saw Littlewood borne aloft by his friends. Was he ecstatic? I doubted it.

Although, at this point, I hardly knew him, I could guess that he would be phlegmatic about such a victory. Mercer I didn't see at all.

The odd thing was, from the beginning, everyone behaved as if Littlewood alone was victorious. Mercer might as well not have existed. A week or so later, for instance, I went out—rather surreptitiously, I will admit—to buy Littlewood's photograph, and discovered, much to my annoyance, that it was sold out. "But I've got plenty of Mr. Mercer, sir," the newsagent said. "In fact, I'm having rather a fire sale on Mr. Mercer."

It made perfect sense. Mercer was frail, twenty-two, from Bootle, while Littlewood was nineteen, roaring with health, and had Cambridge connections going back more than a century. Philippa Fawcett was his cousin. His father had been, in his time, ninth wrangler, his grandfather thirty-fifth.

O. B. had both photographs. "Look at the way he keeps his legs open," he said of Littlewood's. "As if he doesn't have the slightest idea that he's being provocative. And of course, that's the delicious part— he doesn't."

"Quite a bulge, too," mused Keynes, who happened to be visiting.

I tried not to look at the bulge. Instead I concentrated on the clean-shaven, oblong face. The part that ran through Littlewood's hair might have been ruled with a straightedge. He kept his thin lips tightly closed, his heavy eyebrows raised in inquiry. All told, he radiated a kind of coiled strength, as if at any moment he might jump out of his chair and do a handstand.

In *his* photograph, by contrast, Mercer looked hesitant, almost icy. He had dark patches under his eyes, and held against his forehead a finger the nail of which he had chewed down to the quick.

What can I tell you about Littlewood? Although he shunned the limelight—perhaps *because* he shunned the limelight—he had what you Americans today call "star quality." The discoveries he made could be dramatic. For instance, shortly after we started working together, he proved that at some point beyond $10^{10^{10}}$, the Prime Number Theorem, instead of overestimating the number of primes up to a certain number n, begins to underestimate them. More crucially, beyond that inconceivably distant number, the result alternates between over- and underestimation infinitely often. This was an amazing thing to prove, in that it undid an assumption most mathematicians would never have thought to question. Yet what was especially remarkable was that Littlewood's proof revealed a change in the cosmos of the primes so remote from the arena of ordinary human counting as to be virtually impossible to conceive. For the number in question—the number beyond which the primes start to be underestimated rather than overestimated—is larger than the number of atoms in the universe.

Typically, Littlewood made little fuss over the discovery. He made very little in the way of fuss about anything. He was *Little*wood. The first time he came to see me—I mean, came to see me seriously, with the idea of our collaborating—my sister was visiting. We were in the middle of lunch in my sitting room. Gertrude was art mistress at Cranleigh's sister school, St. Catherine's, where she edited the school magazine, in which she published articles and the occasional corrosive verse. She lived with our mother, whose health was declining, and for whose benefit she had to pretend to religious feelings she did not have. She was not what you would call an attractive woman; nor, so far as I could tell, did she take much interest in men. Yet from the minute Littlewood arrived she was asking him to sit down, and fetching him a plate, and spooning onto it the remaining eggs and beans that, under normal circumstances, we would have divided. Littlewood accepted without hesitation. By nature he was a social animal, inclined to assume that if someone he liked liked two people, they would like each other. Nor did it surprise me to see him forking eggs and beans *at once* into his mouth, whereas I never mixed the foods on my plate. And all the while asking Gertrude questions about her school, her students, the magazine—questions she answered with blushing, even girlish gusto. It was discomfiting to watch. My sister—usually stern, even severe—was obviously enchanted. And Littlewood—I could see instantly something one rarely observed in those days at Cambridge: he liked women more than men. He liked their company and he liked their bodies. Flirting came naturally to him, even when the woman was a homely spinster like Gertrude. And Gertrude ate it up.

All through the conversation, I wondered if Littlewood was going to notice Gertrude's glass eye and ask about it. He did, the very next day. "An accident in childhood," I said, at which, being Littlewood, he decently dropped the subject, sparing me having to explain how the accident had happened.

And what of Mercer? I think he was gone by then, back in Liverpool. He didn't return to Cambridge until 1912, and from then until his death I hardly saw him. My sense is that he accepted his own obscurity with a humility for which I must give him due credit.

Littlewood never understood why I abandoned Mercer. I suppose I didn't understand myself. Imagine a writer who, embarrassed by the callowness of a first draft, stuffs it away in a drawer. Somehow he knows that a day will come when he will write the story again, and perhaps write it better. Only he has no idea when, or how, or who will be the hero.

PART TWO

The Crow in the Dining Room

I

A LETTER ARRIVES FROM the India Office. Signed C. Mallet, Secretary for Indian Students.

Regretfully, without further documentation as to the qualifications of the student in question, and considering the limited funds at the Office's disposal, we can at present do nothing to assist in bringing said. S. Ramanujan to Trinity College, Cambridge . . .

Hardy wads the letter up in his hand. He wants to tell Littlewood, but Littlewood's gone again. Of course he's gone. The siren song of Treen. The compelling mystery called Mrs. Chase. Littlewood's always gone when a letter arrives.

Hardy goes to see the master. Henry Montagu Butler is now nearly eighty, florid, with an unkempt white beard that makes him look like Father Christmas. An Apostle himself (no. 130), he no longer attends the meetings because he so strongly disapproves of smoking. He is a devoted clergyman in the Church of England. As Hardy speaks, he rotates his wedding ring around his finger, as always, in careful motions of a quarter turn each. He listens—or appears to listen—carefully as Hardy tells him about the letters, the patient investigations that he and Littlewood have undertaken, the reply they wrote, and, finally, the possibility of bringing the Indian to Cambridge. Such interviews are torture for Hardy, who, given his druthers, would have passed the responsibility on to Littlewood. If, of course, Littlewood could be found. But Hardy knows Butler. If Littlewood had come, Butler would have said, "This is Hardy's business. If Hardy has something to say to me, let him come to see me and say it himself."

A vast oak desk divides them. From the wood, a faint odor of tobacco rises, the legacy of previous masters with more liberal attitudes toward smoking. Across the requisite inkwell and blotting pad Hardy talks into the composed silence of Butler's rotating ring, all the while hoping that Butler will take the hint, anticipate his request, and thereby spare him the ordeal of having to make it. Instead Butler gazes down at the blotting pad. Is he dozing? "Well, that's all very interesting," he says when Hardy has finished. "Now what do you want me to do about it?"

"I suppose I want you to tell me whether the college might provide funds for bringing the young man to England."

"Funds? You mean a fellowship? But from what you tell me, the chap doesn't even have the ordinary undergraduate degree."

"I don't see why that should matter. If Newton wrote to us, would we worry about whether he had the ordinary undergraduate degree?"

"Ah, but he did have it, didn't he? And as I recall, there was a time when you weren't too keen on Newton." Butler leans into the vastness of the desk. "Look, Hardy, this is all quite interesting, but where's your evidence the man's a genius? Sounds a bit dodgy to me. Could it be a hoax?"

"I very much doubt it."

"Then you're going to have to show me some hard proof. I'm not about to allow any old nigger into Trinity on the basis of a letter."

That word: why does he feel it as a slap on his own cheek? It's Ramanujan, not Hardy, whom Butler is calling a nigger.

All at once a fury rises up in Hardy. This is his way. From timorousness and reluctance, he makes the leap to anger, skipping all intermediate stages. Gaye used to tease him about it.

"I shall acquire what evidence I can," he says. "Although if you refuse to accept the judgment of two of your own fellows as sufficient, I daresay nothing else will convince you." Then he stands up. "Good God, without so much as a shred of education, and entirely on his own, the man's reinvented half the history of mathematics. Given the proper encouragement, who knows what he could do?"

Butler makes a web of his thick, elderly fingers. "An Indian Newton. What a curiosity that would be. Well, come see me when you've learned more. Because, Hardy, contrary to what you seem to have assumed, I'm not opposed a priori to the fellow. Nor, I think, should I be looked upon as a villain for my natural skepticism. After all, what have you brought me? Two letters."

"Very well."

He is about to leave when Butler says, "I assume you've contacted the India Office."

"Yes."

"Any answer?"

"They want more information. Everyone wants more information. Littlewood says he's going to go and see a chap there. An acquaintance of his brother's."

"Well, let me know when you hear back."

"Do you mean that if they say give him the go ahead, you will, too?"

"You're very determined to make me the enemy, aren't you?"

"It seems to me that there are moments when one has to take a chance."

"Granted. But bear in mind, if he comes here, and it all comes to nothing, the college will only be out some money. You're the one who'll have to contend with him, take care of him, very possibly shelter him."

"Littlewood and I are prepared to shoulder whatever responsibilities his coming entails."

"I assume you've written back to the second letter. No reply yet?" Hardy shakes his head.

"Well, let me know when you hear from him. I'm curious, in spite of myself."

"Thank you." Hardy holds out his hand, which the old man shakes. Then he goes out the door, uncertain who has made the greater concession. This is Butler's gift, and what has kept him master for close to fifty years.

A S IT TURNS OUT, C. Mallet, at the India office, is the friend of Littlewood's brother. Littlewood goes up to London on a Tuesday morning, leaving Hardy to stew and fret until his return. Of course he tries to work, to focus on the proof he's so close to cracking, that there are infinite zeros along Riemann's critical line. Today, though, it's as if a door has shut on him. Those regions of the imagination into which he must venture if he's to make any kind of progress—he can't gain access to them. He feels as stymied as Moore in that lecture he gave, the evening that Wittgenstein came to the Apostles meeting. The one evening. After that he never came back.

Because he cannot work, Hardy takes a longer than usual walk through the Trinity grounds. It's a glorious April morning, sunny and cold, the combination of weathers he likes best. Yesterday another letter arrived from India, this one in response to one that Hardy now regrets sending, in which he tried, as gently as he could, to reassure Ramanujan that he, Hardy, had no designs on Ramanujan's ideas; indeed, Hardy wrote, even if he did try to make illegitimate use of Ramanujan's results, Ramanujan would have Hardy's letters in his possession and could quite easily expose the fraud. Not, as it turned out, the wisest move. For Ramanujan seems to have interpreted this gambit as part of a vaster conspiracy to defraud him, a poor Indian, of the only thing he treasures, his intellectual birthright. By way of reply, he wrote that it "pained" him that Hardy should ever have imagined him capable of harboring such a suspicion:

> As I wrote in my last letter I have found a sympathetic friend in you and I am willing to place unreservedly in your possession what little I have. It was on account of the novelty of the method I

have used that I am a little diffident even now to communicate my own way of arriving at the expressions I have already given.

Diffidence. Is it really all that different from pride?

So Hardy paces the carefully tended pathways of Trinity College, while Littlewood, in London, goes to the tea shop in South Kensington (he did not mention this to Hardy) where, on those occasions when both of them happen to be in London, he and Mrs. Chase make it their habit to meet. Anne travels up to London only when she absolutely must. She is a creature of the seashore, not the town. As she sits across a teapot and a plate of scones from Littlewood, brushing back her dark brown hair, grains of sand fall onto the table. She is in London only at the behest of her husband. She has left the children behind, in the care of a nanny. Chase tolerates his wife's relationship with Littlewood so long as she agrees to make herself available when his career, his stature as an eminent Harley Street practitioner, requires him to go out in public with a wife on his arm. Tonight it's some sort of charity ball. "I hardly know what to wear," she tells Littlewood, as the sand grains fall from her sleeve, her hem. He can see twinklings of mica in the folds of her ears. He loves this about her, the grit of her that sometimes, on his way back from Treen to Cambridge, he feels on his tongue, in his teeth.

She is sun-browned, freckled. Chase is pallid and losing his hair. Although, where Littlewood is concerned, he assumes a posture of pained toleration, it is Littlewood's suspicion that the arrangement suits him as well as it does Anne. Better, perhaps. After all, so long as, in Treen, Littlewood keeps Anne occupied, then Chase is free, in London, to pursue amusements that the presence of a wife and children might inhibit. Amusements, Littlewood suspects, that would be more up Hardy's alley than his own.

After prattling on for a few moments about the tedious necessity of choosing a dress (presumably Anne keeps a supply of town clothes at her husband's house on Cheyne Walk), she and Littlewood lapse into a familiar and relaxed silence. There is never between them that need to fill the air with talk that seems at once to hound and to invigorate so many couples. Silence is for them a truer medium than talk. How many hours they have sat, in the drawing room in Treen, the sound of wind and waves outside the window, and the fire, and Anne knitting

patiently! Not even the voices of children upstairs. She has two
children, a boy and a girl, both unusually quiet. They call Littlewood
"Uncle John."

He looks at his watch.

"Time running out?" she asks.

"I have a few more minutes."

"Where are you off to, then?"

"The India Office. I'm supposed to meet a chap there about the
Indian, the one I was telling you about."

"Hardy's genius."

"That's right."

She gazes at the tray of scones with contemplative ease. "I wonder
that you've never brought Hardy down to Treen," she says.

Littlewood smiles. It's true, he's never brought Hardy down. He's
brought others down. Bertie Russell's been down. But never Hardy.

"I'm not sure it's quite his cup of tea," he says.

"You could still ask." She says this companionably. Their intimacy
is curiously rancorless, perhaps because they both know it will never
lead to marriage. Early on Anne made her conditions clear. She would
not leave her husband, both because he had requested it of her and
because, for reasons very much her own, she feels bound by certain
old-fashioned proprieties, even if she does not believe in them. Or
perhaps it would be more accurate to say that, even if she does not
believe in them, she respects their rational spirit, obedience to which
will insure the perpetuation of an orderly society. In certain ways
Anne is much more conservative than Littlewood—though, at home,
she never puts her hair up, and walks for hours, sometimes, along the
beach, with her shoes in her hand.

"It's very odd to me," she says, "never having met Hardy. After all,
one might say he's the most important person in your life . . . Isn't
he?"

"Is he?"

"Well—"

"Hardy's very odd. You know Harry Norton told me once—this
was maybe a year ago, a year and a half ago—that Hardy was writing
a novel, a murder novel, in which one mathematician proves the
Riemann hypothesis and then another one murders him and claims the
proof as his own. And this was the damnedest thing—Hardy gave it

up, Norton said, because apparently he was convinced that I'd recognize that the victim was based on me."

"And was Hardy the killer?"

"Norton didn't say."

Anne drinks the last of her tea. "A pity he never finished the novel. It might have been a brilliant success."

"Only if he left out all the mathematics."

"And would you have been offended if you'd been killed off?"

"On the contrary. When Norton told me, I was flattered."

It's time for them to go. Quietly they get up and walk out of the tea shop. Early on, before Anne told her husband, there was intrigue and terror, the thrill of deception and the anguish of parting. Now their affair has become, in its way, as much a part of Anne's orderly ideal as her marriage. Much is understood, if not spoken. She does not wish to marry him. And he, if he is to be totally honest about it, does not really wish to marry her. For if he were to marry her, he would have to give up his rooms at Trinity, his piano, his recordings. He would have to buy a house, as Neville has done, and decorate it, and employ a maid and a cook to run it.

Where would his work fit into such a life? Where would Hardy fit in?

They say goodbye on the street: a shaking of hands, a brief kiss on each cheek, in which there is implied no grievance or bewilderment, no sense of an uncertain future, but rather the peaceful knowledge that they will meet again, the next weekend, at Treen, with the waves sounding in the background and the children upstairs. He watches her move away from him, down the sidewalk, and as she lapses into the distance, he swears that she leaves a trail of sand in her wake.

3

THAT EVENING, Littlewood is late to dinner. At high table, Hardy guards an empty place to his right. The fish course comes. Damned turbot again. Then the meat. Saddle of venison. More tolerable. He takes a bite, wonders what on earth is keeping Littlewood. And then Littlewood hurries in, pulling on his gown, takes the seat next to Hardy's.

"Sorry I'm late," he says.

"What happened?"

A waiter brings wine, asks Littlewood if he wants his fish. "No, I'll just move on to the . . . what is it?"

"Venison."

"Fine."

"Well?"

"Trouble, I'm afraid."

"What kind of trouble?"

"I met with the fellow from the India Office, and it's no go."

"The shits. It's not as if they can't spare a few pounds—"

"Oh, it's not the money. We've miles to go before we start worrying about the money. It's the Indian chap. He doesn't want to come."

Hardy looks genuinely startled. "Why on earth not?"

"Religious scruples. It seems he's a very orthodox Brahmin, and they've got this rule against crossing the ocean."

"I've never heard of such a thing."

"Neither had I. But then Mallet—that's the fellow's name—explained. Apparently they see crossing the ocean as a form of pollution. It's like marrying a widow. You don't want to put your galoshes to dry by someone else's grate. And if you do cross the ocean, when you come back to India, you're persona non grata. Your relatives won't let you in their houses. You can't marry off your daughters or go to funerals. You're an out-caste."

"But Cambridge is full of Indians. There's that cricketer."

"Obviously he's from a different caste. Or at least he's not as orthodox as our friend Ramanujan. Probably he's rich, from Calcutta, or some other cosmopolitan city. But in the south—at least according to this Mallet—they've hung on to all sorts of outmoded traditions. Rules about everything. When to eat, what to eat. Strict vegetarianism. Remember the mutiny of 1857, when those Indian soldiers massacred the British officers because they didn't want to bite into cartridges greased with lard?"

Hardy looks at the meat on his plate with rancor, as if it's somehow to blame. "Madness, all this religion."

"Not to him, it seems."

They chew in silence, like ruminants.

"So that's that?" Hardy asks after a moment. "It's over?"

"Probably. Not necessarily."

"How do you mean?"

"You see, after we had this conversation, I thought it might not be a bad idea to invite this Mallet out for a pint. We got to talking, and he told me a bit more about the case. I asked him how he found all this out, and he said that there was an interview, in Madras, with a fellow called Davies."

"An interview with Ramanujan?"

Littlewood nods. "Ramanujan was summoned to speak to Davies, and he brought along his boss from the Port Trust Office, an old man who's apparently even more orthodox than he is. Anyway, it happens that Mallet knows this Davies rather well. The way he put it, Davies is 'one of those come-straight-to-the-point fellows.' Mallet's hunch is that Davies just blurted out the question—do you want to come to England?—and put Ramanujan on the spot. Ramanujan may well have meant it when he said no. But he also might have said no automatically. Or because the old man was with him, and he didn't want to cause offense by seeming even to consider the possibility."

"So does that mean he might be persuaded to change his mind?"

"Perhaps. Unfortunately, your good offices are working against us. Since you wrote—*because* you wrote—his situation has improved markedly. It seems that some of the British officials over there style themselves amateur mathematicians, and so when they heard you'd given him your imprimatur, as it were, they took your letter over to the university and made noises to the effect that if the university wasn't careful, India was going to lose a national treasure. And the university capitulated, at the mere mention of your name. Had you any idea that you wielded such power?"

"No idea whatsoever. And what's the result?"

"They've given him a research grant and he's quit his job at the Port Trust."

"How much?"

"Mallet didn't know. It's probably a pittance by our standards. Still, enough to keep him going. He's got a family to support. Parents, brothers, a grandmother. And, of course, the wife."

"He's married?"

Littlewood nods. "She's fourteen."

"Good heavens."

"It's normal over there."

Hardy pushes away his plate even as Littlewood continues to chew. He does not want the venison now.

"So what's next?"

"What's next," Littlewood said, "is that someone's got to go out to India to convince him. Any volunteers?"

Hardy is silent.

"In that case," Littlewood says, his mouth full of meat, "our friend Neville may be in for a much harder time than he bargained for."

4

A FTER DINNER, Hardy writes to Neville, who invites him and Littlewood to tea the following Saturday. Neville is four months married, and has just moved with his new bride into a house on Chesterton Road, near the river. His drawing room has the somewhat overscrubbed look of a space newly furnished, in this case in the aesthetic style, with William Morris wallpaper in dark purples and blues and an ebonized sideboard *à la Japonaise*. In the middle of the room sits a slat-backed oak settee with attached side tables. Voysey, probably. Hardy and Littlewood regard it warily, then opt for a pair of matching tapestry-covered armchairs that seem to shrink away from the settee like Victorian spinsters from a neo-Expressionist painting. No doubt, like the old piano pushed against the far wall, they are an inheritance.

Books sit piled on the table between them: H. G. Wells's latest novel, *Alice's Adventures in Wonderland*, something in German on elliptic functions. Through the open windows a smell of roses wafts, as well as the fumes of the occasional car making its progress down Chesterton Road.

A doughy housemaid appears. "Sir and Madam will be down shortly," she says, before tottering into the kitchen to fetch tea. As if, Hardy thinks, he and Littlewood are an old married couple come to call on the newlyweds. And why not? Circumstances being what they are, it makes sense to invite them together. Recently a porter came to him, scratching his head because he had received a letter addressed to "Professor Hardy-Littlewood, Trinity College, Cambridge."

Not, as it happens, from India. Not this time.

As they wait, they do not speak. Littlewood has his legs crossed, is turning his foot, snug in its polished shoe, clockwise in circles.

"Herbert, get inside!" a voice cries, and Hardy hears a ball drop, a child's footsteps as it runs inside.

And then, all at once, noises erupt within the house. The housemaid emerges from the kitchen, bearing the tea ensemble on a tray, and Neville and his bride descend the creaky staircase. Hardy and Little-wood stand. Hands are shaken. Then they all sit down, the Nevilles across from their guests, on the oak settee. Alice Neville's hair is reddish, frizzed, done up in a bundle and slightly damp. Loose strands flare out here and there, as if in rebellion against the restraining pins. She wears a velvet dress that does little to conceal the amplitude of her bosom, and gives off the same scent of Parma violets that Hardy's mother does.

Neville sits closer to his wife than would a man who'd been married longer. He is twenty-five, stoop-shouldered, with an oval face and a high forehead over which his hair, piled on the right side of a zigzag part, keeps falling. So nearsighted that even through his spectacles, he has to squint. As the maid hands out the cups, he flashes at Hardy a closed-lip smile that is at once detached and good-natured, sly yet utterly lacking in irony. There is this to say about him: unlike Little-wood or Bohr or, for that matter, any other great mathematician whom Hardy has known, he is happy. Almost carefree. Perhaps this is why he will never amount to anything. He does not embrace solitude, much less suffering. He loves the world too much.

"Well, I've read the letters," he says, "and I can see what's got you so excited."

"Really!" Littlewood says. "I'm so glad."

"There have been a few more developments since we last spoke," Hardy says.

"Oh? Thank you, Ethel." Neville accepts a cup.

Littlewood repeats what he learned at the India Office about the Brahmin prohibition against crossing the ocean. "Oh, yes," Mrs. Neville says. "I remember reading about that once. My grandfather was in India. Thank you, Ethel."

"Alice is coming with me to Madras," Neville announces proudly.

"I'm very excited about it. I have an aunt who was an adventuress, she went on safari in Africa and crossed China entirely on her own, with just a friend. A female friend."

"Your presence in Madras, Mrs. Neville, may prove to be invaluable," Littlewood says, bowing his head over his teacup.

96

She flushes. "Me? How? I'm not a mathematician."

"But there'll be the two of you, won't there, to act as emissaries? And if you'll pardon my saying so, a pretty face might make all the difference."

"Come, now, Littlewood, I'm not all that ugly," Neville protests.

"We'll leave the matter of your allure for the ladies to settle."

"Anyway," Hardy says, "we're not entirely sure how serious he was being when he said he couldn't come. He might be afraid of causing offense, as it were, to the elders of the tribe."

"One thing that's becoming increasingly clear is that Ramanujan is, to say the least, rather . . ."

". . . sensitive."

"Well, what can we do?"

"Meet with him. See if he's the real thing, and if he is, see if you can talk him into coming."

"But how could we? If his religion won't allow it—"

"We have reason to believe he might be more flexible on the religious question than the local authorities assume," Hardy says.

"Is he married?" Mrs. Neville asks.

"Oh, yes. His wife is fourteen."

"Fourteen!" Neville says. "But I suppose that's common in India."

"Usually the wedding takes place when the bride and groom are about nine," Mrs. Neville says. "But then the bride stays with her own family until puberty."

"What an idea!" Neville puts his arm around Alice's shoulders. "The only trouble, Alice, is that when I was nine and you were nine, I probably would have run screaming from you. From any girl."

"You would have loathed me when I was nine. I was a bundle of sticks with pigtails."

"As Littlewood was saying," Hardy says, "since I wrote to Ramanujan, his situation's improved. Even so, there's nothing there for him. He needs to be somewhere where there are men he can work with. Men on his level. Or perhaps I should say, men who approach his level."

Neville raises his eyebrows. "High praise," he says. "Well, we'll certainly do everything we can."

"Yes," Mrs. Neville says. "I'm quite looking forward to meeting Mr. Ramanujan. And perhaps even Mrs. Ramanujan."

"The mother?"

"Her too."

Neville laughs, and kisses his wife on the cheek.

"Well, do you think he can do it?" Hardy asks Littlewood, as they make their way down Magdalene Street.

"If he can't, she can."

"You keep saying that. I'm afraid I don't quite see it."

"No, you probably wouldn't."

Hardy looks at him.

"I don't really mean that," Littlewood says. "The point is, she's got a sense of herself. Stronger than Neville's. Mark my words, she's capable of persuasion."

"Neville is so very . . . nice."

"He is, rather. But that might not be a bad thing. As we've learned of late, for all his bluster, our Indian friend is easily offended. At this stage a gentler touch may be required than you or I can manage."

"You phrased that very delicately."

"I'm not saying we're brutes, or that Neville's some weakling . . . only that . . . Well, for one thing, they're more or less the same age. In the same season of life, as a friend of mine might put it."

Hardy smiles faintly. He knows he's not supposed to say he knows who "the friend" is.

They are nearing Trinity. It is the season of balls, and undergraduates in formal dress stroll about the street, some of them accompanied by young women in gowns with tight waists and trailing hems. The sun has just set, the evening is warm, dinner in Hall awaits them. But no one whom either might sit too close to, as Neville did to Alice. At least not tonight.

At the gate, they say goodbye, each returning to his own rooms. As he settles himself into his chair with Hermione, Hardy feels a shudder of alarm shoot through him.

It is Gaye. Nothing so gothic as the bust speaking. He simply appears from the shadows near the window, his hands clasped behind his back. He does this sometimes.

"Harold," he says.

"Russell," Hardy says.

Leaning over, Gaye kisses Hardy on the top of his head. He's wearing a smoking jacket and his Westminster tie. His hair looks lacquered. "So I gather the Indian fellow's not coming," he says.

"Doesn't look like it."

"And what does that make you feel? Regret? Relief?"

"Regret, of course. It's essential that he come to Cambridge."

"Oh, come on, Harold. A boy from some tiny place you've never heard of, married to a child and beholden to a religion the doctrines of which you find utterly perverse. And on top of that, you've never seen him. He could be ugly as homemade sin."

"He's a genius, Russell. And he's dying out there."

Gaye claps his hands together. "Ah, of course! That old compulsion to rescue people. It comes out trumps every time. How good it must make you feel about yourself. And yet it must be something of a burden, too." He winks. "A pity you couldn't rescue me."

Hardy stands, shaking Hermione off his lap. "Russell—"

But Gaye is gone. Hermione, discomposed, slinks toward the shadows from which her master emerged, and into which he has disappeared. In death, it seems, he is determined to have what he so rarely had in life: the last word.

5

New Lecture Hall, Harvard University

IN THE LECTURE he did not give, Hardy said:

As a child I believed in more than I do now. For one thing I believed in ghosts. This was mostly thanks to my mother, who told me when I was very young that a ghost haunted our house in Cranleigh, the ghost of a girl who had died in my bedroom of typhoid, many years before, on the eve of what would have been her wedding day. Neither Gertrude nor I ever encountered this ghost, whose behavior, according to my mother, was generally benign. Occasionally—but only when my mother was alone in the house—the ghost would play a tinkling melody on the piano that my mother did not recognize and that sounded out of tune even when the piano had just been tuned. Or the ghost stamped her foot, like a child having a tantrum. Her encounters with the ghost my mother reported dutifully to us (but never to my father); as we listened, we would affect the benevolent and condescending patience of the governess putting the restless, tale-telling child to bed. For even then, my sister and I were confirmed rationalists; and we took it for granted that our mother was a rationalist, too, that she told these stories only to amuse and bewitch us, although once I came home from school to find her white as a sheet, gazing in astonishment at the piano.

The odd part is, I think I believed in her ghost more than she did—this though I never had a single personal encounter with the creature who had died in my bedroom. Today, if I were compelled to choose between Christianity and that occult program that attributes to the dead the capacity to trouble and console the living, or to pass cryptic messages through the curtain that divides their realm from ours, or to possess the bodies of animals, or trees, or bureaus, I should still plump for ghosts. The idea that a spirit might linger on this earth makes an intuitive sense to me that the vision imposed upon us by Christianity, of a vague, dull heaven and a horrible, fascinating hell, never will.

Not that I've had much personal experience of ghosts. The only "visitations" I ever received took place over the course of the decade or so following the death of my friend Gaye. Whenever Gaye "appeared," in those years, I would at first question my own sanity, and wonder if I should fly to the nearest asylum, or to Vienna. Then I would question my own rationalism, and wonder if I should wire O. B., who was affiliated with the Society for Psychical Research. Then I would question my own questioning: what was this apparition, after all, if not the belated expression of an old impulse, the one that drives the solitary child to invent an imaginary friend? For I missed Gaye terribly in those years; I missed his voice, and his arch tongue, and his refusal to suffer fools gladly. I wasn't an idiot. I didn't conjure him in the hope that he would console or reassure me. On the contrary, I wanted him to tell me the truth, even when it was brutal. His arrivals not only made me less lonely, they contradicted a doctrine that would have placed him, for a host of reasons, in some deep and terrible realm of a Boschian hell, rather than allow him to float about Cambridge in his smoking jacket and Westminster tie, observing our capers with bemused detachment. In the same way I suspect that my mother's ghost, struck down on the eve of her wedding, represented to her an ideal of marriage all the more alluring for its having been preserved forever in the amber of imminence.

Like me, Gaye was an atheist. As he told it, his war with God dated to very early in his childhood. According to our religious education, God was supposed to be an entity neither animal nor man nor any combination of the two. Nor was God a plant. This entity was supposed to exist, as you or I or the sun or the moon exist, but not as King Lear or Little Dorrit or Anna Karenina exist. And it was supposed to have a mind, not unlike our own minds, but grander, because it had created him and me and everything else in the universe.

Gaye accepted none of this. Neither did I. I've never seen how any sane or rational person could. No doubt in a hundred years only the most primitive of peoples will still worship the Christian God, and then our unbelief will be vindicated.

Oddly enough, given its supposed liberalism, atheism was much frowned upon at Cambridge. Even in the Society there were few who admitted to being atheists. Instead the brethren were forever trying to wrap their religious skepticism in vague, "emotional" statements about "God" and "Paradise." That shit McTaggart, for instance, with his snug little Trinity College of a Heaven, and all the archangel undergraduates buggering one another while seraphim and cherubim fetch cups of tea; or Russell, who envisioned a universe also like Trinity—aloof, rife with inefficiency, arrogant. His idea was that what mattered in religion was not the specificity of the dogma but the feelings that underlay belief: feelings, in his words, "so deep and so instinctive as to remain unknown to those whose lives are built upon them."

As you have no doubt already surmised, I hold no truck with any of these efforts to placate the clerics. Christian devotion of any sort, in my opinion, is anathema to thought. I don't believe Ramanujan was especially devout either, despite all the nonsense he talked about the goddess Namagiri and what have you. He just said what he'd been raised to say, and if he believed in any of it, he believed in it as I believed in Gaye's ghost.

What I have never quite been able to make out is how God can become as real to the unbeliever as to the believer.

Let me give an example. In the spring of 1903, on a sunny afternoon at the very beginning of the cricket season, I went off to Fenner's to watch a match. I was in a good humor. That day the world, as it so rarely does, seemed kindly and beneficent to me. No sooner had I taken my seat, however, than the rain started pouring down. Naturally I had not brought my umbrella. Curses, I thought, and went back to my rooms to change.

The afternoon of the next match was equally beautiful. This time, however, I decided to prepare myself. I brought not only an umbrella—an enormous one, borrowed from Gertrude—but put on a raincoat and galoshes. And wouldn't you know it? The sun shone all the day.

The afternoon of the third match, I risked leaving the umbrella behind. It rained again.

The afternoon of the fourth match, I brought not just the umbrella, not just the raincoat and galoshes, but three sweaters, a dissertation, and a paper that the London Mathematical Society had asked me to referee. Before I left, I said to my bedmaker, "I hope it rains today, because then I'll be able to get some work done."

This time it did not rain, and I was able to spend the afternoon watching cricket.

From then on, I referred to the umbrella, the papers, and the sweaters as my "anti-God battery." The umbrella I saw as being of particular importance. In order not to have to return it to Gertrude, I bought her a new one, with her initials engraved on the handle.

Usually, in this little game, I got the best of God. But sometimes God got the best of me.

One summer, for instance, I was sitting in the sun at Fenner's with my usual arsenal of sweaters and work, enjoying the play, when suddenly the batsman put down his bat and complained to the umpires that he could not see. Some sort of reflection was casting a glare that got in his eyes. The umpires searched for the source of the glare. Glass? There were no windows on that side of the grounds. An automobile? No road.

Then I saw: on the sidelines stood a portly vicar with an enormous cross hung round his neck. The sunlight was bouncing off the cross. I called an umpire's attention to the ungainly medallion, and the vicar was asked, very politely, to take it off.

That vicar: I remember that, though ultimately he complied with the umpire's request, first he had to protest and argue and deny for a while. He wasn't about to give up his cross without a fight. Of course he had an enormous arse. He belonged to that category of men whom I call the "large-bottomed," by which I mean something as spiritual as it is physical: a certain complacency that comes from always having your place in the world affirmed. From never having to struggle or feel yourself to be an outsider.

I can't claim credit for the phrase. It has been drifting around Trinity since the eighteenth century, traceable, I am told, to a geologist called Sedgwick. "No one," he is reputed to have uttered, "ever made a success in this world without a large bottom."

Of course, the world is filled, and always has been, with large-bottomed mathematicians, most of whom claim to believe in God. And how, I have often wondered, do they reconcile their faith with their work? Most don't even try. They just file religion away in one drawer and mathematics in another. Filing things away in different drawers and not thinking about the contradictions is a classic trait of the large-bottomed.

Some, though, aren't content with this solution. These mathematicians are in many ways more vexing because they try to explain mathematics *in terms* of religion, as an aspect of what they call God's "grand design." According to them, any scientific theory can be made compatible with Christianity on the grounds that it is part of a divine plan. Even Darwin's ideas about evolution, which seem to negate the existence of God, can be swaddled in a doctrine that has God stirring the primordial soup, sparking the process of mutation and survival of the fittest with each turn of his magical spoon. Then there are the papers that for some reason large-bottomed men seem always to feel the need to send to me, offering ontological proofs for God's existence. I throw them in the rubbish bin. Because all this effort to make mathematics part of God is part of the effort to make mathematics *useful*, if not to the state, then to the church. And this I cannot abide.

Only once in my life, I am proud to say, have I made a contribution to practical science. Years ago, before we started playing tennis together, Punnett and I used to play cricket. One afternoon after the match, he asked me for help with a question concerning Mendel and his theory of genetics. A geneticist with the unfortunate name of Udny Yule (the war would later make us enemies) had published a paper arguing that if, as Mendel suggested, dominant genes always won out over recessive ones, then over time a condition known as brachydactyly—leading to shortened fingers and toes, and caused by a dominant gene—would increase in the human population until the ratio of those with the condition to those without would be three to one. Although this obviously wasn't the case, Punnett was at a loss as to how he might counter the argument. Yet I saw the answer at once, and wrote it up in a letter that I posted to *Science*.

"I am reluctant to intrude in a discussion concerning matters of which I have no expert knowledge," I wrote, "and I should have expected the very simple point which I wish to make to have been familiar to biologists." It was not, of course, even though, as I phrased it, "a little mathematics of the multiplication-table type" was enough to show that Yule was wrong and the ratio would in fact remain fixed.

Much to my surprise, this little letter made me famous in genetics circles. Soon the geneticists started referring to my little proof as "Hardy's Law," which embarrassed me, both because I never in my life wished to have anything so monolithic as a *law* named in my honor, and because this particular law lent ballast to a theory that has as often been used to argue for God's existence as against it.

Yet I had one reason to be glad. Over the years I had read many newspaper articles decrying what the doctors had just then started calling "homosexuality," complaining of its prevalence and making predictions that if the "disposition," already "on the rise," should continue to "spread," the human race itself would risk extinction. Of course, in my considered opinion, the extinction of the human race is immensely desirable, and would benefit not only the planet but the many other species that inhabit it. Even so, the mathematician in me could not help but balk at the fallacy behind the warning. It was the same fallacy that Hardy's Law had demolished. Just as, if Udny Yule was correct, there should eventually be more brachydactylics than normal-fingered and -toed men and women, so, if the articles were correct, inverts should soon outnumber normal men and women, when the truth, of course, is that ratio will remain fixed.

Yet all that, ultimately, is beside the point—which, I suppose, *is* the point, the one that Ramanujan understood better than any of us.

When a mathematician works—when, as I think of it, he "goes into" work—he enters a world that, for all its abstraction, seems far more real to him than the world in which he eats and talks and sleeps. He needs no body there. The body, with its blandishments, is an impediment. I was foolish, I see now, even to bother trying to explain the tripos to O. B. Analogy can only take you a certain distance, and in mathematics, it's not long before you reach the point where analogy fails.

This was the world in which Ramanujan and I were happiest—a world as remote from religion, war, literature, sex, even philosophy, as it was from that cold room in which, for so many mornings, I drilled for the tripos under Webb. Since then, I have heard of mathematicians imprisoned because they were dissenters or pacifists, and then relishing the rare solitude that a gaol gave them. For them, gaol was a respite from the vagaries of having to feed themselves and dress themselves and earn money and spend it; a respite, even, from life, which, for any true mathematician, is not the thing, but the thing that interferes.

A slate and some chalk. That's all you need. Not pianos or thimbles or nails or saucepans. Not sledgehammers. Certainly not Bibles. A slate and some chalk, and that world—the real world—is yours.

6

I T IS THREE DAYS after New Year's Day, 1914, and Alice Neville—twenty-four years old and newly arrived in Madras—is sitting by herself in the dining room of the Hotel Connemara, doing battle over a slice of cake with a crow. Behind her a turbaned waiter flaps at the crow with a plumed fan, trying to drive it back to the window through which it flew. Every time the waiter shoos it away, though, the crow spirals up to the ceiling. Then, as soon as the waiter has turned around, it descends again to try to eat the cake. It seems to take a mischievous pleasure in the game. So does the waiter, who brandishes his fan like a sword. So does Alice, who's trying not to laugh. Not far away, at a round table, much too large for them, three English ladies wearing hats decorated with elaborate floral displays arch their eyes in disapproval and anxiety as they watch Alice banter with the waiter and the crow. Then a second crow flies through one of the long windows, and aims with gladiatorial precision at their table. Instantly all three get up and scream. They are dressed, Alice sees, in the fashion of twenty-five years ago: high waists cinched by corsets, bustled skirts hemmed half an inch above the toe. Alice, by contrast, wears a flowing, jade-colored dress that brushes the ground. Flat shoes. ("Heels are a disaster when traveling," her aunt Daisy told her.) No corsets or stays. Her hair is still wet from the bath. She has no hat on and, perhaps most scandalous of all, she is sitting by herself in a room all the other occupants of which, with the exception of the trio of ladies, are men. Alice is a more proper girl than she pretends: for example, she has never gone to bed with any man other than her husband, and never intends to. Still, she takes a certain pleasure in raising eyebrows.

Now she puts a cigarette in her mouth and the waiter, before she can even ask him, bends down to light it for her. His proximity provokes in her a mild frisson of pleasure that she makes no effort to disguise. After all, the waiter is handsome and dark, dressed in a white robe with red and gold sashes. His attentions to her must outrage the trio of ladies. No doubt they have already marked Alice as a "new woman," even though today in England the "new woman" is no longer new. In fact the term is rather *démodé*. Yet if, as she suspects, these ladies have lived all or most of their lives in India, it's to be expected that they should be a bit behind the times. Why, for all they know, she might be an adventuress researching a travelogue, someone like the writer who calls herself "Israfel," whose book about India is lying open on Alice's table next to the embattled cake slice. Israfel writes in the guise of a man. (Alice knows she's a woman only from Aunt Daisy, who travels in the same circles as the pseudonymous scribe.) For Israfel, the Anglo-Indians are contemptible "ivory apes" with complexions like "kippered herrings or boiled soles." The typical colonial woman has "never read anything, heard anything, or thought anything; and instead of this blissful state of vacuity making her quite charming, it only makes her dull." By contrast, how reverently Israfel describes Indian women "in gaudy saris, with silver anklets clinking lazily on their dusky limbs, silver studs in their noses, and lustrous soulless kohl-ringed eyes"! Israfel marvels at a nautch dancer's "tinseled skirts glorious with mock jewels." She asks: "Do you think she will ever wear a false fringe and high-heeled shoes?"

Alice, certainly, would never wear a false fringe or high-heeled shoes. Like Aunt Daisy, she is an advocate of dress reform. For if a woman did wear high-heeled shoes, how could she tramp around Madras, as Alice intends to do, and would have done already, had the hotel manager not so strenuously urged her, instead, to ride in a *gharry* driven by a hotel retainer, a man named Govindran, as dark and skinny as his horse? "It is not safe, an English lady alone in Madras," the manager told her, and entrusted her to Govindran—too ugly and devout, presumably, to pose any threat. And so she has explored Madras not, as she hoped, alone, and on foot, but, rather, in a rickety carriage driven by an old man in a dirty turban who—when she tells him that she wants to get out and look around a bit, drag her skirts, for a moment at least, in the dirt of India—squats on the ground next to his vehicle and chews a leaf that stains his few teeth red. Govindran is her closest companion on this voyage, more so than the waiter who protects her from crows, more so, even, than Eric, whom she has hardly seen since their arrival. When she asks Govindran a question, he nods neither yes nor no but waggles his head in a way that seems halfway between the two. In his company, she has gazed up at pyramidal temples encrusted with delicately painted, bas-relief multitudes: deities, horses, elephants. With astonishing ease, even languor, he has maneuvered her around the swift-running, barefoot rickshaw-wallahs (everyone who does anything in India, it seems, is a wallah), and warded off the clutches of beggar children reaching into the carriage to grab what they can, and parted the crowds of humans and cows, the latter usually more colorfully decorated than the former, as if he were Moses parting the Red Sea. Once he stopped, and they watched as a cow, bejeweled and belled and tied to a post, placidly ate its hay. From its behind, grassy cakes of dung fell blithely, from between its legs a urine stream of stunning pungency splashed against the dirt. Everywhere in Madras there are cow pats to step around gingerly, and puddles of cow urine, which, according to Eric, the local people mix with milk and drink.

As for Eric, he's off all day giving his lectures at the University Senate House. Like most of the English buildings in Madras, this one is huge, ostentatious, and, in Alice's view, ugly in the way that only Victorian architecture can be. How much she prefers the narrow streets of Triplicane, the Parthasarathy Temple with its cake decoration deities and the low houses and the doors over which, for good fortune, contorted crosses are painted! Swastikas, they're called. This is the neighborhood, she knows, in which Ramanujan lives, perhaps behind one of the swastika-marked doors. The Senate House, on the other hand, is a Victorian hodgepodge, combining Italianate spires with onion domes and minarets willy-nilly. Its walls are solid British red brick, and though there is the occasional nod to the Indo-Saracenic—in the massive central hall, the stone pillars are carved, like the temple façades, with deities and animals—the final effect is akin to that of her grandfather's sitting room, in which the Indian rugs that he hauled home from his stint in Jaipur underlay a motley of stools and velvet fenders and hulking cupboards stocked with Royal Worcester. Everywhere in that room there were ceramic jars and frilled draperies and lace antimacassars stained a pale yellow by years of hair oil. From the wallpaper, patterned with pansies, a faint but persistent odor of boiled beef emanated. In her diary Alice has written: "My grandparents' sitting room was exemplary of British colonialism, the exotic spoils subdued and made ordinary by what was piled atop them." She aspires to write. She aspires to be a second Israfel.

Now, at last, the waiters seem to have got the crows out of the dining room. (Why doesn't the hotel just hang beaded curtains?) The Anglo-Indian ladies stand uncertainly by their table; it seems that in the course of the fracas, a teacup was upset, and now several of the waiters are laying fresh linens and putting out silverware. From the look of them, two of the ladies are in their late fifties, but the third is Alice's age or even younger. Alas, she wears an expression no less censorious than those of her elders. Through spectacles, she peers at Alice with a frank disdain that Alice answers by boldly ordering something to drink. The waiter she thinks of, now, as hers brings her a glass of yellow juice over chunks of ice.

Despite it being January, despite the fans, despite the open windows, the air is stifling. She takes a gulp; something viscous courses down her throat, at once tart and almost unbearably sweet. Aside from Alice and the ladies, the dining room is nearly empty, which hardly comes as a surprise. Who, after all, would want to partake of afternoon tea in such sultry weather? Of the few men scattered about the place, reading their newspapers, none is drinking tea. The ladies alone are drinking tea. They are buttering crumpets. "Now some women do not dress," Israfel has written. "They pack." Alice's neighbors, in Israfel's words, are "packed in the sort of way that necessitates the footman sitting down on the lid when he locks the trunks." No doubt they will eat fish and roast mutton for dinner. Last night she herself asked the chef to prepare a native dish for her and Eric—"what the locals have" was how she put it—but the chef, whose dark skin had fooled her into assuming him to be an Indian, turned out to be an Italian, and so they were served spaghetti.

Now, from the purse that rests beside her chair, she pulls out a sheet of paper and a pen. She hopes her neighbors will think she's writing a chapter for her travel book, a chapter about *them*, when in fact it's just a letter to a friend; a female friend.

Dear Miss Hardy,
    In all probability my husband has already been in communication with your brother. Nonetheless I trust you will not object to my writing to inform you personally of our safe arrival in Madras. Although the time that you and I spent together, in the weeks before my departure, was brief, I can say with

assurance that from the moment of our first meeting I felt toward
you an affection sisterly in nature.

Is that too much? The truth is, at first glance, she found Gertrude
unnerving, sitting, as she was, with her legs gathered up over her
brother's rattan chair, her dark skirt smoothed over her knees, a white
cat in her lap. She was smoking, blowing smoke rings at the ceiling
with self-conscious lassitude. Her long hair was plaited and subdi-
vided into distinct systems, held in place by a complex and efficient
system of pinning. When Hardy introduced them—"Mrs. Neville, Mr.
Neville, my sister, Miss Hardy"—Gertrude untangled herself and
stood, gaunter than her brother and a bit taller. All bones. Thin
enough to make Alice feel ashamed of her uncorseted hips, the slight
rounding of her belly, the unseemly protuberance of her breasts. Yet
what was most disturbing about Gertrude—it hit Alice only then—
was her left eye. It didn't move with the right one.

I pray you will not take offense at my familiarity, nor, I hope,
object if, during my stay here, I write on occasion to share with
you those aspects of our adventure that might fail to engage my
husband's attention. Mathematicians are more brilliant than
most of us, but heaven help us if Mr. Baedeker were to ask
them to write his guides!

A good line. But will Gertrude think so? Gertrude, she knows, writes
verse. Caustic and clever verse. Verse of a sort that betrays a certain—
well—ambivalent feeling about her life as art mistress at a provincial
girls' school:

> There is a girl I can't abide.
>   Her name? I'll be discreet.
> I feel I'd need some *savoir dire*
>   Should I her parents meet!

> She says "I never could do Maths.
>   When Daddy was at school
>   He could not add!" I'd love to say
>   "Then Daddy was a fool!"

When Gertrude showed Alice these verses, published in her school magazine, Alice smiled wanly. How could she admit that she herself could never do maths? She, the wife of a mathematician? Gertrude, Alice suspects, despised her at first, because she was everything Gertrude was not: feminine, fertile, beloved of a man whom she, too, loved. Or perhaps Gertrude despised her because she assumed that Alice must by necessity despise tweedy, twiggish Gertrude. This would have been ridiculous. The truth is, from the start, Alice only admired Gertrude— her wit, the humor at once cool and cutting. Here was a woman, like Israfel, who did not suffer fools gladly, a woman thin as an exclamation point, and just as emphatic. There was this to be said for invisibility: Gertrude could observe the world from the hidden safety of corners into which Alice, with her large hips, could never possibly fit.

I am sorry to say that I have not, as yet, had the pleasure of meeting Mr. Ramanujan. However, Mr. Neville is to meet him to-day. Indeed, I suspect that Mr. Ramanujan may be the reason why my husband is late returning to the hotel for dinner!

Is that cruel, reminding Gertrude of what she, Alice, has that Gertrude never will? Or, more accurately, what Gertrude has chosen never to have? For if she is a spinster, Alice suspects, it is mostly by choice. Like her brother, Gertrude considers herself far more hideous than she actually is, which is perhaps why, instead of finding a job in London, she has elected to live enisled among pupils whom, if the girl in the poem is any example, she loathes totally:

> "In dictée I got minus two;
> There's not a verb I know;
> I always write the future tense
> Of 'rego,' 'regebo.'"

Her brother is just as strange. A few months before she and Eric boarded the ship for India, he came to tea at their house with Littlewood: two good-looking men, both short of stature, one blond and the other dark. They behaved, she later told Eric, like a married couple, finishing each other's sentences. "Don't tell Littlewood that!" Eric replied.

All through that tea, Hardy ignored her. More than anything, he reminded her of a squirrel, alert and bustling and timid all at once. He talked only with Eric, and only about the Indian, whom he claimed might be another Newton. Littlewood, at least, made an effort. He said he thought the William Morris wallpaper "very aesthetic." He complimented her dress and told her that she would be invaluable to her husband on the journey.

Please tell your brother that I send him my warmest regards and that he may rest assured that my husband and I will do all we can to persuade Mr. Ramanujan to come to Cambridge. That said, I feel that I can confess to you, Miss Hardy, how deeply discomfited I am at the prospect. Like you and your brother, I do not consider myself, in any puritanical sense, to be a Christian. Yet does our decision to live outside the bounds of organised religion give us the right to treat another's piety as superfluous or absurd?

As if in chastisement, a church clock strikes five. Now Eric really is late. Although dusk has yet to fall, the light coming through the windows is getting more diffuse. Through a blur she sees that the men with the newspapers are leaving. The ladies in the plumed hats are fussing with their handbags, preparing to return, no doubt, to husbands awaiting suppers. And suddenly it dawns on Alice that once the ladies leave, she will be the only customer remaining in the vast room. The waiters, without ever betraying their impatience, will continue to light her cigarettes, pretending not to care that she alone is keeping them from getting on with their work, keeping them from replacing the teacups and teaspoons with fish knives and forks and dinner plates: the endless changing of table settings that signifies the progress of morning into afternoon into night, one day into the next . . . Something to write about? Her glass is mostly empty now. What's left of the tart, sugary drink the melted ice has rendered pale yellow. She looks at her watch and discovers that Eric is an hour late.

That afternoon in Cambridge, when the four of them were sitting together in Hardy's rooms—Hardy, Gertrude, Eric, and herself—Hardy said something that disturbed her. This was just before the conversation turned to suffrage. Eric was talking about the Austrian Wittgenstein, how Wittgenstein had said that if it could be proven that something could *never* be proven, he'd be glad to know it. "What do you think of that?" Eric asked Hardy. And Hardy answered, "Any proof pleases me. If I could prove by logic that you would be dead in five minutes, I should be sorry you were going to die, but the sorrow would be very much mitigated by my pleasure in the proof."

After that, there was silence for a moment. Then they all laughed. Gertrude, tangled up in the rattan chair, laughed so hard the cat jumped off her lap.

> "But then my Parents cannot write
> Or speak a foreign tongue."
> Sweet maid, how much the world had gained
> If they had both died young!

Oh, where is Eric? Has he been run down by a *gharry*? Is he lying, unconscious, in some hospital? If so, the Anglo-Indian ladies—they might help. Surely they know doctors, magistrates. But they have gone. She is alone with the waiters. She looks up at the ceiling, and notices another crow, making figure eights among the balustrades. A line comes to her from Israfel—"the spirit of dance incarnate"—and then, with a kind of baleful grace, the crow dives and grazes her table, upsetting the glass, so that the yellowed water spills over the letter she's writing, the book, the tablecloth, and onto her lap.

Instantly the waiter is back with his fan. As he beats at the crow, one of his colleagues mops up the spill, waggling his head and murmuring apologies. For the first time she notices his red teeth. "It's all right, it's nothing," she says, standing uncertainly, while above her, out of reach, the crow swoops and circles.

Is it looking at her? Does it want something from her? On the way home from Hardy's, she asked Eric about Gertrude's unmoving left eye, and Eric said, "It's glass. A childhood accident, I've heard. And to think, she's utterly devoted to him!"

The juice has stained her dress. Probably ruined it. She wants to weep or cry out, because the truth is, she's no adventuress, just a young girl in a strange city who will never tramp the dirt alleys of Triplicane, never taste a native dish, never be brave enough, even, to wander out of Govindran's protective gaze. She misses Aunt Daisy. She misses her husband. She misses a doll she had as a child.

Alice steps away from the table. It's time to return to her room, to change her dress, to do what she can to salvage Israfel. And yet, for the moment, she does not want to go back to her room. She wants to stay right where she is, with the waiters in their glorious robes. Eric bursts in, and she hardly hears him as he fills the echoey chamber with his apologies, his exuberance, details of his meeting with the Indian that he cannot keep from tumbling forward. She stops his hand as he reaches for her waist; points at the ceiling. "Look at the crow," she says. And he looks.

"How did that damned thing get in here?" he asks. "Oh, what happened to your dress?"

"It's nothing," she says. She wants to laugh, as Gertrude laughed. Hand in hand, they walk out of the dining room, Eric talking about the Indian, Alice remembering how, as her brother moved about the room, one of Gertrude's eyes followed him, while the other remained focused on a bust on the mantelpiece, its gaze so steady and merciless you could have sworn it was seeing.

7

My dear Miss Hardy,

A thousand thanks for your kind reply to my earlier letter, which arrived only yesterday. I am delighted to learn that you are recuperating from your head cold, and hope that, as I write this, no symptoms remain to trouble you. Thanks as well to your brother for his kind words of greeting. Please tell him that my husband and I look forward greatly to seeing him upon our return to England.

I am especially glad to learn that I have interested you in the writings of Israfel, whose book *Ivory Apes and Peacocks* has meant so much to me on this journey. I do hope the work gives you as much pleasure as it has me. Alas, I can tell you little about the author's true identity, save that, despite the masculine *nom de plume*, she is, in fact, a Lady, of whom my aunt Daisy has briefly made the acquaintance. Out of respect for this Lady's wish to remain anonymous, Aunt Daisy has refused to share her true name even with me. I do know that she is "musical" and that, among her other works, there is a collection of "Musical Fantasies" including portraits of Paderewski, De Pachmann, and Isaye. Do you go often to concerts? Perhaps, one week-end when we are both in London, we could go together to one. It is a pity that your brother shows so little interest in music. One can only hope that Mr. Littlewood will prove to be a positive influence on him in this regard!

On to other matters: I know that Mr. Neville has written to Mr. Hardy to tell him of his meetings with the Indian genius Ramanujan. Of the four meetings that have taken place so far, I was privileged to be present at two. Mr. Ramanujan is short and of robust stature, with skin less dark than that of most of his countrymen, though of course quite black by our standards. His face is rotund, with eyebrows low over the eyes, a broad, squat nose, and a narrow mouth. The eyes are startling and dark—it would take an Israfel to describe them. His forehead is shaved, while he keeps the rest of his hair gathered back in a sort of tuft known as a *kudimi*. He dresses in the orthodox manner, in a robe and *dhoti*. He wears no shoes, only the flimsiest of sandals.

Fortunately, as soon as my husband and I had sat down with Mr. Ramanujan to partake of Indian tea, any alarm that his outward appearance might have provoked in us fell away. Rarely have I met a man of such grace, charm, diffidence, and delicacy of manner. Mr. Ramanujan's English, while not unmarked by the accent of his native tongue, is fluent, his vocabulary much larger and more precise than that of the average British working man. And though he can come across, at first, as shy, once he reaches a stage of comfort with those in his company, the floodgates open and he reveals himself to be the most congenial of conversationalists.

Our first meeting took place at the canteen of the University Senate House—a building, I might add, Miss Hardy, of incomparable hideousness. My husband launched the conversation by asking Mr. Ramanujan to tell us something about his education. A tale of frustration, disappointment, and injustice now poured from his lips. He comes from a family of high caste but little money, and was raised in the town of Kumbakonam, south of here, in a poor little house on a street with the remarkable name of Sarangapani Sannidhi Street. He is the eldest of three sons. The father is an accounts clerk; from the little Mr. Ramanujan said of him, we understood that the man was unassuming to the point of irrelevance.

For his mother, on the other hand, he had only the highest praise, explaining that, despite her having had only the most rudimentary education (a plight common, I might add, to Indian women), this lady showed from the start an intuitive appreciation of his gifts and did all she could to foster them; that is to say, though she could be of no actual help to him in his studies, she made sure that, while he worked, the house was quiet, his favorite foods were at the ready, and so on. She is also, he said, a gifted astrologer, and, from early on, told him that she had read his stars and that his stars had said he was destined for greatness.

Alas, his schoolmasters showed no such solicitude! Perhaps the truly original are always doomed to be misunderstood. In the case of Mr. Ramanujan, his astonishing talent was largely overlooked. In part this was because, from the earliest days of his schooling, the intensity of his interest in mathematics led him to pay scant attention to the other subjects in which he was obliged to show some facility. The result was that he did not do as well as he might on the examinations necessary for his advancement.

One tale he told I found particularly touching. By way of a mathematics prize, he was presented one year with a volume of Wordsworth's poems. Such a collection, which either of us would have cherished, meant nothing to him. Yet his mother treasured the volume, and today it has pride of place in the tiny habitation he shares with her, his brothers, his grandmother, and his wife on a poor little unpaved alley called Hanumantharayan Koil Street.

Unhappily, this victory was an exception in a career marked, rather, by discouragement and failure, than by support and success. Having done his time at what is known here as the "high school," Mr. Ramanujan won scholarships, first, to Government College in Kumbakonam and then to Pachaiyappa's College in Madras. On each occasion, his interest in his own mathematical researches was so all-consuming that he neglected his more quotidian studies, with the result that he failed his examinations and lost his scholarships. For by this point his explorations of the mathematical universe were all that mattered to him.

He was now adrift. The educational system had rejected him utterly, and he found himself marooned, with no livelihood, income, or prospects, at his mother's house on Sarangapani Sannidhi Street. How, you may ask, did he maintain, through all this, his sense of self-worth? What gave him the confidence to persevere, when every authority had cast him off? This was the next question that my husband put to him.

At this, Mr. Ramanujan rested his hand on his head and thought for a while. Then he looked Mr. Neville in the eye, and explained that he could give no simple answer. There were moments, he said, when his despair became so great that he thought seriously of giving mathematics up altogether. On one or two occasions he contemplated suicide. But then a great rage would well him in him at the institutions that had pronounced him worthless, and he would be seized by a sudden determination to prove them wrong.

Alas, the energy that such tantrums roused in him invariably flagged after a few days. More crucial to his ability to soldier on was the unyielding support of his mother, who bolstered him in his pursuit of matters far beyond her ken with her reassurances and ministrations.

Yet there was another facet to his persistence in those lean and unhappy years. It was this: he remained, quite simply, besotted by numbers. During his days as a scholar, even his mathematical studies were unsatisfactory to him, as he was compelled to drive down well-trodden avenues and engage his fertile imagination in tedious exercises and the exploration of territory of little interest to him. Now that he was cut loose from the academy, however, he could do what he wished. He was no longer beholden to systems in which he believed no more than they believed in him. Instead he was free to spend his days, as he preferred, sitting on the front porch of the house in which he had spent his childhood, working away at formulae and equations on his slate (he could not afford paper), dreaming and inventing. Indeed, he told me that his friends used to make fun of him because his elbow was black; it took too long, he said, to erase the slate with a rag, so he used his elbow instead!

I feel that I should make clear now, Miss Hardy, that our conversation, that afternoon, did not proceed exactly along the lines that I have described. Instead it seemed that Mr. Ramanujan was forever being distracted from his own compelling tale by points of mathematical interest of which some anecdote or other had reminded him. He would then share these points with my husband, writing down figures on scraps of newspaper and packing paper that he keeps in his pocket (yet another sign of his poverty), and the two of them would launch off into a discourse of which I could make neither head nor tail, until Mr. Neville, observing my bewilderment, gently steered the conversation back to subjects within my reach. And though I appreciated my husband's kindly impulse, yet I also regretted that poor Mr. Ramanujan, by virtue of my ignorant presence, was losing a rare opportunity to amplify on matters of which my husband was, without doubt, far more cognizant than anyone he had ever met. Indeed, Mr. Ramanujan's high degree of animation during these rounds of mathematical intercourse convinced me that, should he not come to

England, he would be depriving himself of some essential source of nutrition.

I now asked him about his wife. Here he frowned. As you may know, Miss Hardy, matrimony is in India a far more ritualized business than in our own country. For instance, when Mr. Ramanujan married Janaki (this is the girl's name), she was only nine years old. The marriage was arranged between the families in consultation with astrologers. Before the wedding, the bride and groom met only once; after—again, in keeping with tradition—she returned to her family, and only took up residence in her husband's house when she was fourteen.

Given the circumstances, you might think that Mr. Ramanujan would regard his wife merely as an accessory or impediment. Instead, much to our surprise, he spoke of the girl with affection. True, marriage had brought with it burdens—he could no longer afford to pass his days on the porch doing mathematics; he would have to get work and earn money—yet while he acknowledged these burdens, he never expressed the slightest vexation with the girl who was their cause. Fortunately, over the years, a few gentlemen both English and Indian, some of them amateur mathematicians, had come to recognize Mr. Ramanujan's genius without necessarily grasping its nature. On these gentlemen he had in turn come to depend not just for moral but sometimes financial support. One of them now obtained for him the clerkship at the Port Trust Authority, which enabled him to move his mother and wife to a house in Triplicane, virtually in the shadow of the Parthasarathy Temple.

At this juncture my husband and I were obliged to break off our conversation with Mr. Ramanujan, which had now lasted almost two hours. Before bidding us goodbye, however, he produced a pair of notebooks bound in cardboard and presented them to Mr. Neville. These notebooks, he explained, contained the fruit of his mathematical labors. Would my husband care to borrow them and look through them?

Mr. Neville's eyes widened in wonder. No, he said, handing the notebooks back, he could not in good conscience take into his custody something so precious—yet Mr. Ramanujan insisted, and we returned to the hotel each bearing one of the precious volumes. What would have happened, I wonder now, had our *gharry* been struck by a rickshaw, or a sudden wind come up and knocked the notebooks out of our hands? Later, my husband told me that he considered the loan the most astounding compliment ever paid to him.

That night Mr. Neville did not come to bed. Instead he stayed up until dawn, reading through the notebooks by candlelight. When I awoke the next morning, he told me that he considered them the most significant unpublished documents that it had ever been his privilege to peruse. Far from an onerous task, he now regarded it as his *duty* to persuade Mr. Ramanujan to come to Cambridge.

We met him again the next afternoon. This time he came to our hotel. While the very English atmosphere of the dining room at first seemed to make him uneasy, once again, as soon as he was settled with us and drinking tea, he relaxed visibly.

Mr. Neville now broached the dangerous question: would Mr. Ramanujan reconsider his earlier decision not to come to England? While we understood his fear of breaking a rule of his religion, we also believed that if he remained in India, he would be doing both himself and the world at large a great disservice.

At this, Mr. Ramanujan gazed solemnly at his cup. I feared that Mr. Neville had overstepped his bounds; said too much. Indeed, I was on the verge of apologizing, when Mr. Ramanujan looked up and asked, "Has Mr. Hardy not received my most recent letter?"

My husband replied that he was not certain. He had not heard from Mr. Hardy since our arrival.

Mr. Ramanujan then said that he was worried that Mr. Hardy might lose interest in him once he read this letter, because it was written in his own English; his previous letters, as he put it, "did not contain his language" but were "written by a superior officer." He had then copied them out in his own handwriting. Mr. Neville now asked if this "superior officer" was the same one in whose company he had gone to the interview with Mr. Davies of the Advisory Committee for Student Affairs. Mr. Ramanujan admitted that it was. And then the whole story came out.

The situation both is and is not as your brother surmised. Mr. Littlewood was correct in guessing that, when Mr. Davies asked Mr. Ramanujan, point blank, if he wished to go to Cambridge, the question left him rather flummoxed. He never had the chance, however, to say yes or no, for before he could speak, his superior, Mr. Iyer, answered for him. The answer was an unhesitating no.

He himself is rather confused about the matter. From an intellectual standpoint, he admits, he is quite avid to come to Cambridge. At the same time, he has grave doubts about the venture. Would he, he wonders, be obliged to take an exam such as the tripos? (He has a great fear, it seems, of exams.) My husband told him that he thought not but that he would check with Mr. Hardy.

A more pressing concern is his family. His mother, it seems, objects in the strongest terms possible to her son traveling to England. On the one hand, her qualms are religious; as an orthodox Brahmin, she shares with Mr. Iyer the belief that if Mr. Ramanujan crosses the seas, he will be dooming himself to a kind of spiritual damnation. More practically, however—and in this, Miss Hardy, I cannot help but sympathize with the anxieties of a long-suffering mother—she fears for his well-being in England, worries as to how he will cope with the English winter, has visions of him being forced to consume meat, and so on. Perhaps she also fears his being pursued by English women. (I am speculating here, based on Mr. Ramanujan's reluctance to look me in the eye when he speaks of his mother.)

Then there is the matter of Janaki, his young bride. She has, he told us, expressed to him a desire to accompany him to England; and though he well understands the impracticality, if not impossibility, of bringing her with him, he does not want to disappoint the child. Going to England without her, moreover, would mean leaving her alone with his mother, and given that, in traditional Indian families, the mother-in-law rules over the daughter-in-law with an iron fist, Mr. Ramanujan is naturally worried as to what friction might erupt between the women in his absence, especially as it seems that little Janaki is something of a spitfire!

His last qualm—and that it came last seems to me, Miss Hardy, significant—is religious. Yes, he fears, as his mother does, the consequences, both social and spiritual, of his breaking the rules of his caste and crossing the seas. And yet his anxiety on this point goes well beyond mere religious scruples.

What follows will no doubt sound strange to you and your brother. I will admit that, at first, it sounded strange to Mr. Neville and me, and not only because it reveals the great gulf that separates India from England; also because it indicates the depth of Mr. Ramanujan's religious piety. Nonetheless I ask you to read the next paragraphs with an open mind.

To put the matter quite simply, Mr. Ramanujan attributes his mathematical discoveries not to his own imagination, but to a deity. Since his birth, he believes, he, along with the other members of his family, has lived under the protection of a Goddess, Namagiri, whose spirit occupies the temple at Namakkal, near his place of birth. According to Mr. Ramanujan, it is through the agency of Namagiri that he makes his mathematical discoveries. He does not "come upon" them in the sense that you and I understand the term, nor do they "come upon" him. Instead they are transmitted to him, usually when he is asleep. As Mr. Ramanujan described this process, my husband laughed, and said that he, too, had on occasion "dreamed" mathematics. But Mr. Ramanujan was insistent in distinguishing ordinary dreams from what he called the "visions" supplied to him by Namigiri. The Goddess, as he put it, "writes the numbers on his tongue." His fear is that, if he comes to England, Namagiri might withdraw her divine patronage; and while he understands how much Cambridge has to offer him in the way of recognition, encouragement, and education, he wonders very naturally what use these gains would be to him if, in exchange, he were to lose his access to the very source of his discoveries.

How did we react to such a revelation? My husband, I admit, at first raised his eyebrows, whether in skepticism or simple astonishment I could not tell. As for me, I felt a twinge of disappointment that owes, no doubt, to my own anti-religious disposition. It seemed to me mad that a man of such obvious brilliance should refuse to take credit for his own discoveries. Indeed, after the meeting drew to a close (with the matter of Mr. Ramanujan's coming to Cambridge, I might add, left in abeyance), I could not help but mention to my husband that for me, at least, it was difficult to reconcile this attribution of genius to an outside source with Mr. Ramanujan's obvious pride in his own accomplishments, not to mention his urgent desire to be recognized and even vindicated in the eyes of the Indian authorities. For if what he claimed was true, then it was Namagiri to whom any publications that might arise from Mr. Ramanujan's work ought to be credited, Namagiri whose talents ought to be assessed, Namagiri who should be brought to Cambridge, even if only to Girton or Newnham!

My husband cautioned me not to assume too much. As he reminded me (and he is right in this), we are still strangers here, as yet unfamiliar with the terms of Mr. Ramanujan's religion. It may be that Mr. Ramanujan is, quite simply, anxious to ensure that we should understand the depth of his faith. Still, I cannot help but suspect that his fear of displeasing his mother is tied up intimately with his fear of displeasing the Goddess. I wish I could tell you which, of the two, is the more prominent or, dare I say, the more real fear.

This is where things stand as I write. Tomorrow Mr. Neville will meet, once more, alone, with Mr. Ramanujan. We had hoped to see him sooner, but two days ago we received a message that he had been obliged to make an impromptu journey to his home in the company of his mother. I gather that he is scheduled to return to Madras this evening.

I am sorry not to be able to forward more conclusive news. Please rest assured—and please tell your brother to rest assured—that as soon as we have obtained a definitive answer from Mr. Ramanujan, we will communicate it by cable.

Mr. Neville sends his warmest salutations, and asks me to convey to Mr. Hardy his gratitude at having been assigned the role of "emissary." Likewise we both send our best wishes to your mother and hope that she is feeling better. As for me, I remain, dear Miss Hardy,

Your true friend,
Alice Neville

20 January 1914
Hotel Connemara, Madras

Dear Hardy,

I write in haste, as I must leave shortly for the Senate House. My wife, I know, has been in communication with your sister. She is quite the writer, and so I leave it to her to give the details. The important thing is that I have now read through the notebooks and the content therein is quite extraordinary. Those of his theories that are not original reflect some of the most fruitful and, dare I say, *subversive* ideas already developed on the continent. On the other hand, he makes a lot of errors. If he agrees to come, I'll try to explain to Dewsbury, the registrar here, that, due to his lack of education and so on, he hasn't yet developed the faculty for detecting danger or avoiding fallacies but that, with exposure to proper methods in Cambridge, his will surely become one of the greatest names in the history of mathematics, a source of pride for the university and for Madras, etc., etc. Then maybe we can get them to provide some scholarship money.

A point that might be of interest to you: when I asked him what books had been important to him in forming his ideas, he mentioned, of all things, Carr's *Synopsis of Pure Mathematics*. Are you familiar with that dreary old tome? If that's the only thing he's read, no wonder he doesn't understand how to do a proof!

Finally, a question: one of his (many) worries about coming to Cambridge is that he might be forced to take exams. I told him I'd ask you for assurance that he wouldn't, even though I'm sure that with a little coaching he'd ride roughshod over the tripos. Imagine if, in the old days, he'd been senior wrangler!

Regards to your sister, of whom my wife has become inordinately fond.

Ever yours,
E. H. Neville

8

"THE BLOODY TRIPOS AGAIN," Hardy says, throwing down Neville's letter.

Gertrude looks up at him from her knitting. "Somehow I suspected that would be the first thing you'd land on," she says. "Well, does he have to take it?"

"Of course he doesn't have to take it. It's just a shame that he's wasting his time even worrying about it."

"Then all you need to do is write to Neville and ask him to tell Ramanujan he doesn't have to take it."

"But it shouldn't have even come up in the first place. Neville should have told him, point blank, that he didn't have to take it."

"He might not have known. Or he might not have wanted to give the wrong answer."

"Then he should have cabled me. It's all intentional, I think. You know he was second wrangler the last year of the old system. He's probably needling me."

Gertrude resumes her knitting. It's a cold Saturday afternoon in late January. At present they're sitting across a table from each other in the kitchen of the rather shabby flat on St. George's Square, in Pimlico, that they let together. Hardy stays here when he's got business with the London Mathematical Society, and sometimes loans the place out to friends. Gertrude uses the flat to escape, now and then, the demands of their mother, who is lapsing into senility. Once in a while they meet up for a weekend in London, as they're doing now, only the bad weather has discouraged them from going out to a play or the British Museum. Instead they've spent the day gazing out the window at the sleet falling from the sky, and reading newspapers and letters, including the two from Eric and Alice Neville. Which, if truth be told, is something they enjoy far more than the British Museum.

"You don't like Neville much, do you?" Gertrude asks after a moment.

"I don't *not* like him," Hardy says. "I just don't think he's very . . . distinguished."

She puts the end of one of her needles in her mouth. "He and Alice certainly seem to have hit it off with the Indian," she says,

"Yes, well, let's just hope they don't hit it off with him so well they end up telling him he should stay home to avoid a spiritual crisis."

"Oh, that reminds me, what do you think of the Namagiri business?"

"He's saying what he has to say. To please his mother. To please the priests."

"Are there priests in Hinduism?"

"Or some equivalent thereof."

"Alice's description of him certainly was striking. 'Robust,' she says. I don't know that I've ever seen a fat Indian."

"What he looks like is of no consequence to me."

"Of course not."

"Anyway, you certainly seem to have hit it off with Alice Neville. What's that all about?"

"She's got what my students might call a crush on me."

"Is it lust?"

"Harold, really! Sex doesn't come into it. She's simply . . . enamored of my cleverness."

"And how's this Israel, or whatever it is?"

"Israfel. Not bad. Good descriptions of India"—again, the knitting needle in the mouth—"marred by something a bit too *smart*. For instance, this habit of always comparing everything to Chopin."

"Chopin, eh?"

"Yes, this temple's like Chopin, the Taj Mahal's like Chopin. Rather odd, considering it's India."

"Well, as Mrs. Neville takes such pains to point out," Hardy says, "I wouldn't know anything about Chopin, being a musical ignoramus. Oh, what nasty weather!" He walks the short distance to the sitting room, which is sparsely furnished and very cold. Outside the misted window, the trees on St. George's Square are stark in the winter light. Motor cars and carriages pass by, and men shield women with their umbrellas as they rush for the doors of houses.

After a few minutes he goes back to the kitchen, where he finds that Gertrude hasn't moved. A half-empty cup of tea sits on the table next to the pile of newspapers. Coiled in her chair with her knitting, she snores a little. She looks feline and content.

He sits down across from her. At home, at his parents' house, they more or less lived in the kitchen. All told, they are creatures of kitchens, he and his sister, which is probably why they chose this flat, which has a tiny sitting room and even tinier bedrooms but a kitchen you can actually fit a table into. And so to London they come, one or two weekends a month; to London they come so they can . . . sit in a kitchen. Hardy's life in Cambridge is busy, full of friends and pupils and meals and meetings. For him, these weekends are a respite. For Gertrude, he suspects, they are also a respite, but not from activity; from boredom. It's not that she despises St. Catherine's. From their parents, she has inherited the pedagogical impulse. Still, he knows that she chafes at having to make a life out of showing young girls how to draw and sculpt from clay. Such labors can hardly satisfy a woman of her intellect—or so Hardy sometimes reflects, with a certain detachment, during his morning strolls through the Trinity grounds.

What else might she do? Early on she showed a talent for mathematics, which she never bothered to cultivate. She writes verse, trivial in character. Once he discovered half a novel she had written in a drawer at his parents' house. He read the first few pages, which he thought quite good, but then, when he told her he'd happened upon it and offered what he thought to be some useful criticisms, she blushed, tore the manuscript from his hands, and disappeared into her bedroom. The novel has never been mentioned (or seen) since.

Before he saw her flirt with Littlewood, he wondered if she was a Sapphist. How else to explain her failure to marry? True, exiled as she is in a rural enclave of females, she has little opportunity to meet men. At the same time, she could teach elsewhere. Nor is Bramley entirely lacking in men. There are male teachers at St. Catherine's, and a host of them at Cranleigh, of which St. Catherine's is the female twin. And one or two of those men might even be normal.

In any case, she seems far less taken with Alice than Alice is with her. Earlier, she read aloud to him Alice's letters from Madras in their entirety, interspersing her recitation with occasional snorts of derision to mark those moments when, in her view, the prose was especially idiotic or pretentious. Poor Alice! How horrified she'd be to learn that this letter, obviously composed with such painstaking care, has become a source of condescending laughter for Hardy and this sister of his whom she professes to admire so thoroughly! Fortunately she will never know. And anyway, isn't it tit for tat, given the very condescending tone that Alice takes when describing *him*? Especially that remark about going to concerts! Would she balk if her beloved Ramanujan proved oblivious to music? Of course not! Because being oblivious to music, in Ramanujan's case, would simply be further evidence of maniacal genius . . .

"Stop!" Gaye says, suddenly stepping forward from a broom closet. "Enough of this. You're obviously jealous. Ramanujan's your discovery, and so you can't bear it that the Nevilles are encroaching on your territory."

"That's ridiculous."

"It's not ridiculous. They've got an advantage over you now, because they've met him and even forged an intimacy with him, whereas all you have is a handful of letters. To which I say, if you were so determined to keep him to yourself, why didn't *you* go to Madras?"

"I didn't have the time."

"Don't forget who's talking to you, Harold. You could have made the time. Only you're as afraid as you are eager. That's why you sent Littlewood to the India Office, and Neville to Madras."

"I didn't send him. He was going anyway."

"It comes to the same thing."

Hardy looks away. Gaye's perspicacity, after his death, irritates him almost as much as it did when he was alive. "Oh, go back to your broom closet," he says, but when he turns around, the shade has already vanished.

He looks at Gertrude. She has woken and resumed her knitting.

"Well, I suppose now we just wait," he says.

"For what?"

"Word from the Nevilles."

"Oh, sorry, I didn't realize we were still on that subject."

"What's odd is that the decision's very possibly been made already. Everyone over there may know. And we're just waiting for a letter."

"Didn't he say he'd cable?"

"Would he cable if it was bad news?"

"Monday may bring something."

"Yes," Hardy says. What he does not say is: But how am I supposed to get by until Monday?

January 27th, 1914

Hotel Connemara, Madras

My Dear Miss Hardy,

No doubt the cable that my husband sent has already arrived, therefore you have heard the happy news. After a prolonged sojourn in the region of his childhood home, Mr. Ramanujan has returned to Madras and informed my husband that he will, indeed, come to Cambridge. While I am not entirely clear on the details, I gather that he spent several days at the temple of Namakkal, praying to the Goddess Namagiri for guidance. Yet the strongest impediment to his making a decision in the affirmative was unquestionably his mother, and it was only after that good lady announced that she had had a favorable dream that he was able at last to reconcile his desires with his conscience. In this dream, his mother said, she saw Mr. Ramanujan in the company of white people and heard the voice of Namagiri commanding her to withdraw her objections and give the journey her blessing; in the case of Mr. Ramanujan, Namagiri is reported to have said, the prohibition against crossing the seas could be lifted, as traveling to Europe was necessary to the fulfillment of his destiny.

I cannot tell you with what gratitude and happiness Mr. Neville and I learned of this fortuitous chain of events. Now Mr. Neville says that we must focus our attention on making sure that sufficient funds are available, both in Madras and Cambridge, to pay for Mr. Ramanujan's passage and to make sure that his needs will be met during the period he spends at Trinity.

We depart in a few weeks, and perhaps Mr. Ramanujan will sail with us. Let me reiterate, Miss Hardy, how much my husband and I look forward to greeting you and your brother upon our return. In the meantime, I remain

your affectionate friend,

Alice Neville

PART THREE

Cheerful Facts About the Square of the Hypotenuse

I

I T'S DECIDED THAT they should meet over lunch—Sunday lunch, at Neville's house, where Ramanujan will have arrived the evening before. Hardy loathes introductions, the formality of first handshakes, the rote inquiries about the journey and the throat clearing afterward. If it were possible (and perhaps someday physics will make it possible) he would like to own a device akin to Wells's time machine, but more modest in purpose, designed so that one might leap over awkward moments and into a more tolerable future. Instantly. If you had such a machine, you would never have to wait for the results of an examination to be posted, or judge whether the newly arrived "Ph.D." from Princeton was going to answer your advances with friendliness or hostility. Instead you could just pull a lever or push a button and be already in possession of your exam results, or on the way to bed with the friendly "Ph.D.," or safe at home after being rebuffed by the hostile one. And if you knew that you wouldn't have to go through these things, then you wouldn't have to dread them. As Hardy dreads this first meeting, this first lunch with Ramanujan.

Why does he dread it? Too much expectation, he supposes; too much wrangling with institutional forces, and too many delays, and far, far too many letters. A fat file of them: from Neville, from Alice Neville, from various colonial bureaucrats, from Ramanujan himself. As it happens, finding the money to get Ramanujan to England has proven to be far more difficult than was persuading him to come. In the opinion of Mallet, it was highly unlikely that funds sufficient to support a student at Cambridge could be raised in Madras. Trinity promised only to consider giving Ramanujan a scholarship after he had been there a year. Nor was there any question of the India Office itself contributing so much as a penny. Indeed, Mallet wrote to Hardy, in his opinion Neville had made a grave mistake encouraging Ramanujan to come in the first place; there was "a danger that a student in India might count on Mr. Neville's kindly assurance, and assume that a Cambridge don would find it easy to raise the money required." Which, beyond the £50 a year that he and Littlewood were prepared to pledge, this Cambridge don hadn't.

No sooner, though, had Hardy rushed off a letter warning Neville to "be a little careful" than he learned that Neville, entirely on his own, had managed to persuade the University of Madras to provide Ramanujan with a £250 per annum scholarship, a £100 clothing allowance, the money for his passage to England, and a stipend to support his family in his absence. What the India Office had assured Hardy could never be done, Neville, in the course of three days, had done.

Neville the hero.

And now Ramanujan is in England, and Hardy has still to meet him face-to-face, to see if the reality of him bears any resemblance to the image his mind has conjured—an image, no doubt, to which the descriptions offered by each of the Nevilles has contributed, as has (he cannot deny it) the endlessly fascinating spectacle of the cricketer Chatterjee. Not that it's been easy to forge from these fragmentary and not always complimentary clues a face on which his mind's eye, at least, can gaze. Neville is hardly what one would call a wordsmith. "Stoutish, darkish," he said when he got back from Madras. Well, what else? Tall? No, not tall. A mustache? Perhaps. Neville couldn't recall. Hardy thought of asking Mrs. Neville but feared that if he did, he might give away the game; might reveal to her shades of anxiety that she, unlike her husband, would be perspicacious enough to glean. So he has kept his mouth shut and tried to make do with the little he's been given.

As it happens, he's in London this week, alone in the Pimlico flat. Ramanujan is also in London. His ship docked on Tuesday. Neville went with his brother, who has a motor car, to meet him, after which they ushered him immediately to 21 Cromwell Road, across from the Natural History Museum. The National India Association has its offices there, as well as some rooms that it makes available to Indian students just off the boat in order to ease their transition into British life. Hardy went up for Easter and stayed on—needing a change of air from Cambridge, he told his sister. And if, in the course of the week, he's happened to wander past the Natural History Museum a few times, happened to gaze across Cromwell Road at number 21 and taken note of the Indians coming in and out the front door—well, what of it? It's natural to wonder if he'll recognize Ramanujan, to see if the face matches the image in his mind. A genius. What does a genius look like? What does Hardy himself look like? Hardly the typical messy-haired scientist, who, when on occasion he makes an appearance in a *Punch* cartoon, is usually gazing abstractedly over the tip of his pipe, his jacket misbuttoned and his shoelaces untied. Figures dance above his head, a cloud of Greek letters, punctuation marks, logic symbols, all meant to indicate his remoteness from worldly concerns and occupation of a realm at once too complex and too dull to be worth the effort of trying to enter. The scientist, in such cartoons, is estimable but laughable. Genius and joke. Whereas Hardy is the sort whom those who refer to themselves as "us" would consider "our sort."

And Ramanujan? Standing outside 21 Cromwell Road, Hardy has no idea. Perhaps he comes in or goes out. Perhaps not. Nor will Hardy ask Neville—though he knows that Neville is coming down to London on Saturday to fetch Ramanujan—whether he might accompany him and Ramanujan to Cambridge. He does not want to give, even indirectly, the impression that his attitude toward this momentous arrival is anything but blasé. After all, G. H. Hardy is an important man, with many important things to worry about. Still, on Saturday morning, he takes a last stroll by the Natural History Museum before heading off to Liverpool Street to catch his train.

Back in Cambridge, he returns to the safety of his rooms, to Hermione and his rattan chair and Gaye's bust. Ramanujan, he knows, will be staying with the Nevilles until accommodations can be found for him at Trinity. Everyone agrees—it's much commented upon in Hall—that the Nevilles have been absolutely splendid, have gone beyond the call of duty. Indeed, a few days ago, a classics fellow came up to Hardy and congratulated him on the role he'd played in "bringing Neville's Indian to Cambridge." Hardy smiled thinly and walked away.

The day of the lunch, he meets Littlewood in Great Court. Littlewood is whistling. "A great occasion for us," he says as they head out through the gates on to King's Parade. "After all this effort, we've finally got him here."

"So we have," Hardy replies. "Now we have to decide what to do with him."

"Shouldn't be a problem. Let him continue as he's been going. Oh, and teach him how to write a proof."

"Yes, merely that." Hardy pulls his collar tighter against his neck. The breeze chills his bones even as the sun warms his face. Such a confluence of opposites has a calming effect upon him, so much so that, by the time they reach Chesterton Road, he's nearly forgotten his anxiety. But then, as Neville's house comes into view, his heart starts racing. Prize Day all over again. Were he alone, he might turn around, hurry back to his rooms and send a note to the Nevilles pleading illness. For better or worse, though, Littlewood is with him. Little would Littlewood guess (*Little would Littlewood*) the extent of his terror.

Ethel, the housemaid, answers his knock. Hardy hasn't seen her since the tea the previous autumn. In the interval, she's put on weight, looks like a loaf of unbaked bread. The sitting room into which she leads them is flooded with a natural light that lends to the purple wallpaper a gruesome, almost funereal aspect, exposing the smudges on the window glass and the thin coatings of dust on the mahogany side tables. This effect, of sunlight on a room meant to flatter the dark, enchants Hardy. For a moment he's so distracted that he fails to notice Neville getting up from the Voysey settee, holding out his hand in greeting, guiding Hardy to the spinster armchairs, from one of which a murky figure rises. This is Ramanujan.

The time-skipping machine works: the moment's over before he even blinks.

Familiar names—one of them his own—are repeated. They shake hands (Ramanujan's dry and slippery), and all at once some other voice—some public orator's voice, a headmaster's voice—is booming from Hardy's throat. Words of hearty welcome. A pat on Ramanujan's back, which is warm, meaty. Ramanujan appears to be even more nervous than Hardy is. Sweat beads on his forehead: that's the first detail that Hardy takes in. His skin is the color of coffee blended with milk, and pitted with smallpox scars. He does not have a mustache. Instead there's a shadow that, from a distance, might be mistaken for a mustache, because Ramanujan's nose (squat, pronounced) comes down very low, nearly touching his upper lip. He is neither as short nor as stout as Neville suggested. The appearance of shortness and stoutness, rather, owes to his clothes: a tweed suit a size too small, a collar so tight around his neck he looks as if he's being strangled. The jacket, every button of which he has buttoned, strains to cover his belly. Even the shoes seem to clamp his feet.

Littlewood is introduced—a smoother business. Then they all sit down, and Mrs. Neville comes in, aflutter with apologies for being delayed, and greetings for Gertrude, and questions about Gertrude. She sits next to her husband, who puts his arm over the back of the settee so that his fingers fall lightly on the nape of her neck.

A disquieting silence falls, which no one seems to know how to fill, until once again that headmaster's voice comes crashing forth from Hardy's throat. "Well, Mr. Ramanujan," he says. "And how was your journey?"

"Quite pleasant, thank you," Ramanujan says.

"Although he was seasick for much of it," Mrs. Neville puts in.

"Only the first week."

"And how do you find England so far?" Littlewood asks.

"I must admit, I find it rather cold."

"Not surprising," says Neville. "Today in Madras it's probably a hundred degrees."

"For us, Mr. Ramanujan, this is warm weather," Mrs. Neville says.

"Still," Hardy says, "I'm sure the Nevilles will have made you comfortable." (What idiotic chatter! Every cell in his body resents it. He wants to rip off his clothes, to smash windows.)

"Most comfortable, yes. They have been very good to me."

"He didn't close his door last night! I said to him this morning, Ramanujan, why didn't you close your door? But Alice reminded me, when we were at the hotel in Madras, the Indian guests never closed their doors."

"Eric, don't embarrass Mr. Ramanujan."

"I'm not. I'm just asking a question. Why don't Indians like closed doors?"

"In our dwellings we do not have doors to close."

"Whereas we English do everything behind closed doors!" Littlewood says, laughing and scratching his ankle.

"Yes, I fear we're a prudish people," Alice says. "I've heard that at the department stores in London only ladies are allowed to change the clothing on the female mannequins."

"Is that true?" Hardy asks.

"Of course, times are changing. For instance, I feel I can say with comparative certainty that of those of us present—those of us who are English—not one had parents who slept in the same bedroom."

The silence that greets this supposition also affirms it. Neville coughs in embarrassment. What a saucy character this Alice is, Hardy thinks, or at least aspires to be! Fortunately at that moment Ethel announces lunch. She holds open a door and the five of them file into the dining room, which faces the back of the house. Here the furniture, like the wallpaper, is William Morris, the chairs slat-backed and rush-seated. As for the round table, Hardy can tell from the way it's been set that Mrs. Neville considers this an occasion. She has put out silver, the best wedding china, starched white napkins. At the center there is an arrangement of spring flowers, bluebells and violets and crocuses, in a fluted bowl.

Ethel circles with a bottle of wine, which Ramanujan politely refuses. No doubt another injunction imposed by his mad religion.

And his vegetarianism? For an awful moment, Hardy fears lest Mrs. Neville should have prepared a traditional Sunday lunch—a joint and Yorkshire pudding and two veg and spuds, to welcome the foreigner and introduce him to English ways. In which case, what will he do? Hardy panics at the prospect of this poor Indian having to refuse even the potatoes, which will have been cooked with the meat, until he remembers that, having been to India, Mrs. Neville should know perfectly well that Ramanujan is vegetarian and have made for him, at the very least, a separate set of dishes.

It turns out that she's gone one better. "In anticipation of your arrival, Mr. Ramanujan," she says, "I've been studying vegetarian cookery."

"Much to the chagrin of the cook," Neville adds, laughing.

"Eric, please. The last time we were in London, Mr. Neville and I ate at a vegetarian restaurant—the Ideal on Tottenham Court Road— and we had a very appetizing meal."

"Aside from the meat, the only thing missing was flavor."

"And I purchased a vegetarian cookbook. I hope you're pleased with the results."

Ramanujan waggles his head in a way that might mean yes and might mean no. Such effort on his behalf seems to have left him at a loss for words. Fortunately right then Ethel comes back in, bearing a soup tureen. Lentil soup—not bad, if a little bland—is followed by a salad, after which Mrs. Neville disappears into the kitchen, only to return bearing an immense silver platter covered with a bell. This she lays ceremoniously on the table. "As our main course today," she says, "we have a special dish. A vegetable goose."

With a flourish, she removes the cover. A brown, lumpen mass, surrounded by boiled potatoes and carrots and sprigs of parsley, sits in the middle of the platter. Ramanujan's eyes widen as he takes the thing in. His mouth opens. At this, Mrs. Neville laughs brightly. "Oh, please don't worry, Mr. Ramanujan," she says, "it's not a *real* goose. No fowl of any kind was involved, I assure you. We simply call it a vegetable goose because—well—it's a sort of mock goose. A mock stuffed goose."

"You see, Ramanujan," Neville says, "we English are basically cavemen. Given our druthers, we'd tear raw meat off the bone with our teeth, and so when we eat vegetarian food, we try to create simulacra of the sorts of things we crave. Vegetable goose, vegetable sausage, vegetable steak-and-kidney pie."

Appalled silence greets this menu. "What? Do you think I'm joking? I've had a look at Alice's cookbook, and all these are bona fide recipes."

Ramanujan is blushing. A little smile has crept onto his face. Neville is chaffing him, Hardy sees, and he is enjoying it.

"Call the dish what you will," Mrs. Neville says, slicing into the lump. "All that it is is a vegetable marrow stuffed with bread, sage, and apples and then baked."

Steam escapes from the first incision, carrying with it a strong whiff of cinnamon. A first slice is produced, plated, and put before Ramanujan.

"There's just one thing I don't understand," Littlewood says, as the rest of the plates are handed round. "Why on earth would a vegetarian want to eat imitation meat? I thought the whole point was . . . well . . . *not* to eat meat. To eat vegetables."

"Personally, I'd rather have this than a plate of cold boiled turnips," Neville says, tucking in. "Delicious, darling."

"Thank you, Eric. And what do you think, Mr. Ramanujan?"

"Very tasty, Madam," Ramanujan says—still ill at ease, Hardy can see, with the fork. Primitive implement, designed to pierce flesh. Poor fellow. He must not be used to such flavors. Hardy himself is not used to such flavors. For him, the cloying sweetness of the cinnamon only makes the mush of marrow more repulsive.

The meal concludes with sago pudding, after which the party returns to the sitting room for coffee—which, Hardy is pleased to note, Ramanujan accepts with great enthusiasm. As Mrs. Neville proceeds to explain in her Baedeker voice, coffee is very popular in Madras, even more popular than tea, though it's prepared in a different way: boiled with the milk and then sweetened. They drain their cups, and with exaggerated apologies—perhaps this has been pre-arranged with Neville—she explains that she has some "household matters to attend to" and leaves the room. Now, Hardy, supposes, they are supposed to talk mathematics. Good God, how awful! Even worse than the small talk! He wants to escape, and wonders if Ramanujan must feel the same way. But then Neville asks Ramanujan a question about the zeta function, on which Ramanujan proceeds to expatiate, at first haltingly, then with growing confidence. It seems that he has been shown Hardy's proof—just now published— that there are an infinite number of zeros along the critical line.

Only now does Hardy have the presence of mind to really *see* him. The heavy-lidded eyes, dark and searching, glance out from beneath a massive, furrowed brow. The hair, though short, is thick and luxuriant. Perhaps because Mrs. Neville is no longer present, he has unbuttoned his jacket, with the result that he looks altogether more comfortable. He says that he's becoming interested in what he calls "highly composite numbers." Littlewood asks what he means. "I suppose I mean," Ramanujan says, "a number that is as far from a prime as a number can be. A sort of anti-prime."

"Fascinating," Littlewood says. "Could you give us an example?"

"24."

Hardy raises his eyebrows.

"None of the numbers up to 24 has more than 6 divisors. 22 has 4, 21 has 4, 20 has 6. But 24 has 8. 24 can be divided by 1, 2, 3, 4, 6, 8, 12, or 24. So I define a 'highly composite number' as a number that has more divisors than any number that comes before it."

What a strange mind! What a strange, ranging mind!

"And how many of these numbers have you calculated?"

"I have listed every highly composite number up to 6,746,328,388,800."

"And have you drawn any conclusions about these numbers?" Neville asks.

"Well, yes. You see, you can work out a formula for a highly composite N—" He makes a grasping motion with his fingers, as if reaching for an invisible pencil, at which Neville stands and says, "Hold on a minute." Then he goes out of the room and returns, a few seconds later, bearing a blackboard on legs and some chalk. Awkwardly Ramanujan stands beside the blackboard. "Well," he says, "if we say N is a highly composite number, then the following formula can be written for N."

And he's off. At the blackboard, any self-consciousness he might feel about speaking English leaves him, just as Hardy's discomfort evaporates. They're lost now, and when, an hour later, Alice Neville peers down from the top of the stairs, she sees four men she hardly recognizes, speaking a language she cannot hope to understand.

2

ALICE STROLLS DOWN the corridor and steps into the spare room, the door of which Ramanujan has left ajar. His trunk—dark leather, barely scuffed—sits neatly packed on the floor. The surface of the bureau is empty, the washbasin clean. The bed appears not to have been slept in. How is this possible? She feels under the blankets, and realizes that the sheets haven't been touched. So has he slept on the floor? Or perhaps on top of the candlewick bedspread, the beige surface of which he smoothed upon waking? No unfamiliar odor has penetrated the room, as if, in his modesty, Ramanujan has held back even the exhalations of his body. She smells only the clean scent of the scrubbed wood floor and the cold spring air.

Earlier in the week, when she was preparing this room for Ramanujan, she found herself wondering what he would make of the stiff, high bed, the varnished bureau, the walls unadorned except for a few Benozzo Gozzoli reproductions, picked up on their honeymoon trip to Italy. Back in Madras, she knows, Ramanujan had no bed. Like most Indians, he and the other members of his family slept on mattress rolls that could be folded up and put away during the day. Any spare piece of floor would serve as a bedroom. And now here he is in England, where the trees are just coming into bud and, in order to sleep, he must climb up onto a bed. What must he make of it all? Does the strangeness terrify him? Will he curl into himself? Hide from it? Or will he find, in this strange, high bed, that a new Ramanujan—a version of himself that can only be born abroad, as some new version of Alice was born in India—is, like the trees, just coming into bud?

She pushes the door to. Downstairs, the men's voices rise with excitement and impatience. No one is likely to interrupt her as she opens the trunk, gazes at the neatly folded clothes and the notebooks lying atop them. In a toiletry kit—also new, matching the trunk—she finds a hair brush, hair tonic, tooth powder, and a toothbrush. Feeling under the clothes, she fishes out a book called *The Indian Gentleman's Guide to English Etiquette*, a photograph of a young girl whom she assumes must be the wife, and a small, awkward brass object that, when she pulls it free of its wadding of shirt, turns out to be a statue of Ganesha, the Hindu elephant god, god of success and education, of new enterprises and auspicious starts, of literature. Ramanujan's Ganesha has a potbelly and wears a crown. In the first of his four hands he holds a noose, in the second a goad, in the third a broken tusk to write with, and in the last a rosary. His trunk curls around a sweet and to his right sits the rat that he rides as men ride horses.

Why doesn't Ramanujan take him out? Put him on the bureau next to the basin? Why doesn't he unpack his uncomfortable clothes, and lay out his hairbrush and his tooth powder, and pull apart the bed so that he can lie between the sheets? She wishes she could do these things for him. She knows that she dares not do these things for him. He likes her—that much is clear—but he is too shy to show outward affection. And how can she force him to?

Very carefully, she returns the book and the statue of Ganesha to the trunk, which she closes and clasps shut. Then she sits on the bed, disrupting the perfect suavity of the spread. She thinks of the men downstairs, and for some reason, for an instant, she feels as if she might die of loneliness.

Why does she care so much? Why does it matter to her, his being here in her house? Israfel wouldn't care. *She* would look forward to getting rid of him, getting him delivered to Trinity, after which she would clap her hands together and say, "Well, thank goodness *that's* over." Only Alice is not Israfel, and so what she feels is grief.

Very gently she stands. She smoothes the wrinkles she has left in the bedspread—enough to create an effect of seemliness, not enough so that Ramanujan will not know that someone has been sitting on his bed. Then she wanders back out into the corridor. The sun is setting. The men keep talking. She should get them tea. She knows that. She should go downstairs, put some biscuits on a plate, and get the water boiling. But she doesn't move.

3

RAMANUJAN STAYS WITH the Nevilles for six weeks. There are regular dinners, to which a variety of Trinity luminaries are invited so that they can lay eyes, at last, upon the "Hindoo calculator," as one of the newspapers has recently dubbed him. Russell comes, as do Love, Barnes, Butler. One night Hardy is asked to bring Gertrude. By this point the horrid food at the Nevilles' has become so much the stuff of gossip around Trinity that Hardy knows to dine Littlewood and his sister first, in his rooms, so that when they are compelled to confront the latest aberration culled from Mrs. Neville's cookbook—vegetable trout, vegetable shepherd's pie—they will be able to plead small appetites with impunity.

This night, though, a surprise awaits them. Rather than prepare some caricature of the flesh, Mrs. Neville announces that—thanks to the recent arrival of certain spices ordered from London—she has prepared a vegetable curry. "In Mr. Ramanujan's homeland, of course, we would eat with our fingers," she tells Gertrude. "But as I've explained to him, most English people are as uncomfortable with this habit as he was, at first, with his fork. Now you've become quite the expert with our cutlery, haven't you, Mr. Ramanujan?"

Ramanujan waggles his head. It took Hardy a while to get used to this curious gesture of his, a sort of bobbling from the neck that, he has now come to understand, signifies a provisional yes. Make no mistake: Hardy feels nothing but gratitude toward the Nevilles. They have cared for Ramanujan and made him feel at home, shown him how to navigate the byways of Cambridge and the corridors of Trinity, fed him and bedded him and seem prepared to continue doing so for the duration of his stay. That said, it rather annoys Hardy the degree to which they treat him, at least when others were present, as *theirs*, an intelligent pet ape in the process of being trained to act like a man. And look! Tonight, as a treat for the ape, we shall dine on bananas! Well, perhaps that's too harsh. What's certain is that, in preparing a curry, Alice Neville is showing off for Gertrude. For some reason it seems of paramount importance to Alice that she make a positive impression on Gertrude.

Hardy turns to glance at his sister. Her face registers no reaction whatsoever. There is no one in the world to whom he feels closer than Gertrude, and yet, in certain fundamental ways, he cannot make sense of her. What does she think, for instance, of the Nevilles' décor, which she takes in, as she takes in everything, coolly, without comment? Littlewood flirts with her every time they meet. What can he see in her? She is bony and flat-chested and wears a brown sack of a dress, neither new nor fashionable. So perhaps that's it—perhaps what attracts him is her absolute lack of self-consciousness. The same quality drew Hardy to Littlewood once.

They sit down to eat. Rice is served from a ceramic bowl, the curry—which is soupy and yellowish, bobbing with bits of unidentifiable vegetables—from a silver tureen. "Of course, Miss Hardy," Mrs. Neville says, "in Madras a curry of this sort would be far more highly spiced. I've made certain modifications to suit the English stomach."

Indeed she has. If anything, the curry is blander than those versions of it that Hardy's mother, on occasion, prepared. That said, it provides a welcome respite from vegetable goose. Indeed, he observes, Ramanujan himself is tucking into it with relish, no doubt grateful even for this vague counterfeit of the food he is used to. And meanwhile Mrs. Neville natters on about Madras, and the Indian way of eating—wrapping up the food in a sort of pancake—while Neville watches her, amused and serene. Ramanujan says nothing; he only occasionally waggles his head. For it must be as clear to him as it is to Hardy that the performance is really for Gertrude. Women are such unfathomable creatures, so conscious of one another as potential competitors, allies, or prey! If you didn't know either of them, you might assume that Gertrude would be envious of Alice: Gertrude, the very embodiment of the English spinster schoolteacher. And yet instead it is Alice who longs to win Gertrude's approbation. Why? Perhaps she imagines that Gertrude is some paragon of cool wit and urbanity, the avatar of a world in which Alice, as it stands, would feel hopelessly ill at ease. Nor does it matter that Gertrude is not that kind of woman at all, that in fact she would be as intimidated by the Stephen sisters, or Ottoline Morrell, as Alice would. For Gertrude, to her credit, is good at games. She knows that, once you're handed the ball, you run with it. And so, in Alice's presence, she plays the role that she has been assigned. She is aloof and faintly condescending, ever refusing to bestow the kiss of approval for which Alice longs. She withholds, and, in withholding, makes Alice curse herself for needing the love of a man even to know herself.

Both women watch Ramanujan closely. It's as if, for them, every facet of the Indian, even his genius, has an aroma as exotic and pungent as the food Alice is describing. And does their gaze disconcert him, at least a little? He cannot be used to such attentions. He is used to solitude.

Every morning, having been first breakfasted and dressed by Mrs. Neville to suit the weather conditions, he crosses the Cam, walks across Midsummer Common, then takes King Street, Sussex Street, and Green Street to Trinity. Half an hour's walk, in shoes that still blister his feet. For the rest of the morning, he and Hardy work together, usually just the two of them, though sometimes Littlewood comes over. They work on Riemann. By now Hardy has established irrefutably that there is an infinity of zeros along the critical line. But, as he told Miss Trotter, that does not mean that there is not, also, an infinity of zeros *not* along the critical line. So really, Hardy has proven nothing; just made a step in the right direction.

The first job is to explain to Ramanujan why his own improvement on the prime number theorem is wrong. This turns out to be something of a balancing act. On the one hand, Hardy needs to make him understand why his thinking was flawed, and, in particular, to drive home the fact that accuracy to 1,000 integers, in mathematics, means nothing. On the other, he doesn't want to discourage Ramanujan. He wants him to understand why his failure—and it is a failure—is in some ways more wonderful than any of his triumphs. For the problem to which he dreamed his way in Kumbakonam is one that in Europe it took the finest mathematicians a century just to articulate. And none of them—not Hadamard, not Landau, not Hardy—has solved it. Ramanujan may.

Unfortunately, he is impatient. He is itching to publish, he tells Hardy, so that he can show the men in Madras who encouraged him that the time and money they spent was not wasted. And there is more to it than that, Hardy is sure. No human being, no matter how spiritually evolved, is free of vanity. Even Ramanujan must dream of flaunting his success before those who failed to value him, and, by doing so, making them feel as wretched as they made him feel. And not just the petty provincial bureaucrats who took away his scholarships in Kumbakonam. The longing extends to Cambridge itself.

For instance, from early on—indeed, from the day he received Ramanujan's first letter—Hardy guessed that he was not the first authority to whom Ramanujan had written. Now he asks, and receives verification that, well before he wrote to Hardy, Ramanujan wrote to two of his Cambridge colleagues, Baker and Hobson. Neither took the trouble to reply.

The next morning Ramanujan wants to find out everything he can about Baker and Hobson. When and where do they lecture? If he asks the porters at their colleges, can he find out where they live? Hardy tells him, though reluctantly. It's not that he fears that Ramanujan would go so far as to confront these men, neither of whom he has met. He is far too shy. And yet Hardy would not put it past him to slip newspaper announcements of his arrival in England under their doors.

Teaching him doesn't prove to be easy. The first two or three mornings Hardy spends trying to explain what a proof is, but Ramanujan's attention keeps wandering. In many ways he is still the child making magic squares to amuse his school chums. He won't focus, as Hardy would like him to, on Riemann; instead his mind moves in twenty directions at once, and though Hardy tries to keep him on track, he dares not interrupt flights of associative fancy that might lead to unexpected discoveries.

One morning, for instance, they are talking about π. Hardy knows that during the lonely years he spent on his mother's *pial*, among the many formulae Ramanujan came up with were several intended to approximate the value of π. Some of these struck Hardy as quite remarkable, if for no other reason than because they were so peculiar; for instance:

$$\pi = \frac{63}{25} \times \frac{17 + 15\sqrt{5}}{7 + 15\sqrt{5}}$$

Or:

$$\frac{1}{2\pi\sqrt{2}} = \frac{1103}{99^2}$$

Now Ramanujan is on to something more sophisticated. On his own, he has discovered that, by means of what are called modular equations, it is possible to come up with new and incredibly rapid routes to π: series that converge with amazing speed, allowing the calculator, in a very short time, to write out the value of π to a very great distance. And where did he come up with these equations? To amuse himself, Hardy imagines him sleeping in the Nevilles' guest room, imagines Namagiri—dark-skinned, in his mind's eye, with a Cleopatra fringe and painted cheeks and thirty arms—patiently inscribing the formulae on his tongue. What a genius that goddess must be to be able to do what Moore could not, to journey at her leisure into uncharted forests of the mind and return bearing jewels and treasure! There is a path Hardy is beginning to discern, faint amid the foliage, leading from Ramanujan's flawed effort to improve on the Prime Number theorem to the Riemann hypothesis and perhaps beyond. The question is, will his ambition help him or hinder him in his navigation of that path? Or to put it another way: now that Ramanujan has crossed the ocean, will Namagiri follow?

So they pass their mornings, and then, in the afternoons, Ramanujan goes to lectures, or returns to the Nevilles' house, where he does who knows what with Mrs. Neville until the sun sets, at which point there are those terrifying dinners, one or two a week at least. What Mrs. Neville feeds Ramanujan when no guests are present Hardy dares not guess.

One night he proposes that he and Littlewood take Ramanujan to dinner at Hall. They pick him up at the Nevilles', walk away with him as Mrs. Neville waves goodbye from the doorway, as forlorn as any mother sending her child off to school for the first time. Neville meets them at Trinity, where a flurry of attention greets Ramanujan's arrival. For the first time he wears his robe. Various men welcome him, and though it's not the usual thing—he isn't a fellow—he sits, on this occasion, between Littlewood and Hardy at high table. Because the cook has been alerted to his vegetarianism, an unappetizing arrangement of boiled potatoes, carrots, and turnips is placed before him, which he regards with suspicion. Who can blame him? Then again, it's not for the food that he's come tonight.

Russell is across the table. He is avid to know Ramanujan's opinions—about Indian independence, about the suffrage movement, about Home Rule in Ireland. To this interrogation Ramanujan appears unequal. His replies are flustered and hasty, especially when suffrage comes up, as he doesn't even know the word. And how, after all, can he be expected to render an opinion on suffrage when he comes from a country where most of the women cannot even read or write? It's not that Russell's baiting him, or teasing him, it's just that he's off base. To Russell, Ramanujan is the very opposite of the exotic specimen that he is to Gertrude and Alice: he's an emissary from another part of the world whose views Russell wants to solicit in the hope, no doubt, of enlisting him in his own fledgling efforts to create a new England. Yet it's a useless effort, as Russell himself soon seems to recognize, for he changes the subject. He asks about the work Ramanujan is doing.

Now Ramanujan relaxes. He speaks of some of the modular routes to π that he has come up with, including one that provides a value of π to eight decimal places in the very first term. Russell is rapt. If there is one subject that can drag him away from politics, it's mathematics, and the conversation saves the evening.

Afterward, Hardy and Littlewood walk Ramanujan and Neville back to Chesterton Road. Along the way Ramanujan says little. He limps from the tight shoes. And if he's exhausted, no wonder! Even if it's the thing he wanted most in the world, or claimed to want most in the world, it must still be bewildering, to have moved so swiftly from the solitude of his mother's *pial* to the frenzy of the Trinity high table. And all as a result of a letter that Hardy might have thrown away as casually as did the other men to whom it was sent, in which case Ramanujan would still be in Madras, still working at the Port Trust Office.

Perhaps it's too much for him—as if a sailor, after years spent shipwrecked on a desert island, is finally rescued and told that, as a reward for his privations, he may now take all his meals at the Savoy. And what happens? Such an abundance of rich food makes him ill, he whose stomach has become accustomed to leaves and thistles and fish caught with his hands. In the same way Ramanujan survived, for years, on only the thinnest diet of affirmation. So: have they made a mistake in imagining that his stomach could match his appetite?

Mrs. Neville is waiting up for them when they arrive at her house. "Hello, darling," Neville says, and kisses her on the cheek. "I'm afraid we've put poor Ramanujan through it tonight. Questions, questions, questions!"

"It was quite stimulating," Ramanujan says.

"How are your feet?" Alice asks.

"Fine, thank you."

"Well, you're home now." Suddenly Alice looks at Hardy with alarm, as if she's let escape some sentiment of which she would prefer that he remain unaware. Foolish. He's seen it all along.

Afterward, on the way back to Trinity, he talks the matter over with Littlewood. "I'm having trouble working out what she feels about him," he says. "On the one hand, her attitude's very maternal. Yet she also seems a little in love with him."

"With women," Littlewood says, "it often comes to the same thing."

"What, mother love and—"

"Exactly. Very common."

"Yet Neville has no idea."

"Of course he does. He's just not particularly interested. You know Neville."

"So you don't believe they're—"

"Oh, they might be. Who knows? And how ironic it would be if they were! Because isn't that what every Indian mother fears most when her son goes abroad? Seduction by an evil foreign lady? Yet who would have guessed it would be Alice?"

Hardy frowns. He can't tell if Littlewood's joking and he doesn't want to admit that he can't tell.

"Well," he says after a moment, "if you want to know my opinion, they're not. I mean, look at them. Alice with her inexplicable devotion to Neville, Ramanujan, who seems such a child. And not very interested in women, from what I can see."

"You can never be sure. Whatever the case may be, I hope at least he's having a good time. Because tonight he seemed miserable."

"Crowds frighten him."

"He should move out of the Nevilles' house. Move to Trinity. I've checked, and as soon as term ends, there should be rooms in Whewell's Court."

How shrewd of Littlewood! To have Ramanujan close at hand, after all, would not only make their collaboration simpler to orchestrate, but eliminate, once and for all, the complication of Mrs. Neville, her vegetarian cookbook, her dinners.

"Shall we broach the subject tomorrow?" he asks.

"Let's," Littlewood says. "How he answers may tell us everything we need to know."

4

A RAINY AFTERNOON on Chesterton Road. The fire crackling. Alice and Ramanujan sit across a table from each other, gazing at a half-finished jigsaw puzzle, an old one from her childhood. Five hundred pieces. Since they've been working on the puzzle, an image has begun to emerge against the dark wood grain: two gentlemen in Victorian dress, sitting at a table not unlike the one at which Alice and Ramanujan are sitting. An Oriental carpet patterned in rich red and yellow hues covering the floor. A third man, dressed in the garb of an innkeeper, standing to the table's left. Is this a tavern? One of the men may be holding a glass. Years before, when she was perhaps fourteen, a business acquaintance gave the puzzle to her father, who took no interest in it, with the result that it eventually migrated to the nursery in which Alice and her sister, Jane, still did their homework. Every year or so they would make a valiant attempt to put it together, only to be distracted by the charming shapes into which many of the pieces were cut: a head in profile, a dog, a heart, a half-moon. They might get so far as to finish the frame and a corner of the carpet before Jane would lose patience and blow at the table, gusting the pieces to the floor. For Jane had tantrums. She was always the impetuous one, whereas Alice was always the one to get down on her knees, scrabble to collect the detritus of her sister's fury. Perhaps for this reason, when their father died and their mother closed up the house, she laid claim to the puzzle and brought it with her to Chesterton Road. When Ramanujan arrived, she dug it out. He had never before seen a jigsaw puzzle. She barely had time to explain to him what it was before he was at work on it.

And now here he sits, staring down at the three Victorian gentlemen, holding in his right hand a piece in the shape of a tiny pumpkin, patterned in the hues of the carpet. For a moment he studies the carpet—piecemeal still, as if rats have chewed holes in it—and then, with a sweeping gesture that makes her think of aeroplanes, he fits the piece into place. The pumpkin disappears as another chunk of carpet realizes itself. This rather disappointed Alice in her youth. After all, putting together the puzzle meant losing the delightful shapes.

"Have you worked out a method?" she asks Ramanujan, when what she would like to ask him is: "Does Namagiri help you with puzzles, too?"

"I wouldn't call it a method," he says. "But I do have . . . well, an approach. That is to say, having completed the frame, I gather the like colors together and work from there."

Alice suppresses a smile. How funny, she thinks, to be sitting across a table from one of the greatest geniuses in the history of humankind, watching him lose himself in a jigsaw puzzle! Nor is her husband, the Trinity fellow, any better. Indeed, she knows perfectly well that as soon as he gets home this afternoon, as soon as he's dried off and had some tea, Eric will sit down and work on the puzzle with Ramanujan until supper. Like children they'll work. Not thinking. And Alice won't mind. Even so, she'll feel obliged to get up from the table. To leave them alone. And why? She can't say for certain. All told, everything is nicer when it's just her and Ramanujan. Then she can talk to him in a way that she never can when Eric's there.

He's holding now what appears to be a lobster, or something lobsterlike, in his hands. As always, he's wearing a jacket and tie. He's not wearing his shoes. Recognizing, early on, the suffering they caused him, Alice bought him a pair of soft slippers, which, she told him, it was customary in England to put on when one was at home. To make him feel more at ease, she bought slippers for herself and Eric as well, and now all three of them wear them. Indeed, the only person in the household who doesn't wear slippers is Ethel.

Still, when Ramanujan leaves the house, he has to put on the dreaded shoes. She knows what a torture it is to him, walking to Trinity with his toes so constricted, and wishes it was warm enough for him to wear sandals. But then again, would he, even if he could? On outings in Cambridge, she has noticed other Indians dressed in garb more befitting their origins. She asked Ramanujan about this once, and he told her that when he made the decision to come to

England, Littlehailes, one of his champions in Madras, rode him in the sidecar of his motorcycle to Spencer's, the city's grand old department store, through the doors of which Ramanujan had never before set foot. There he was fitted for shirts, suits, trousers. He was taken to an English barber, who snipped off his *kudimi*, something he would not allow until after his wife and mother had left for Kumbakonam. "How did it make you feel?" Alice asked, remembering the book she'd seen in his trunk: *The Indian Gentleman's Guide to English Etiquette*. And after a moment, he answered: "I felt merely ridiculous in the clothes. But when the barber cut off my *kudimi*, I wept. It was as if I was losing my soul."

The lobster Ramanujan has been holding lands on the table, and as it does, a sensation of empathy passes through Alice, bringing her, quite literally, to her feet. Ramanujan looks up. "Oh dear," Alice says, for the mere act of standing has slightly disarranged some of the puzzle pieces.

"No matter," Ramanujan says, fitting them back into place.

She walks to the piano. It's an old Broadwood upright with lanterns on either side, inherited from her grandfather. Of late she's taken to playing in Ramanujan's presence—simple pieces, for she's not much of a pianist. "Greensleeves," a Handel minuet, a few Schubert impromptus. And then yesterday, looking through the music that she inherited with the piano, she happened upon the score for *The Pirates of Penzance*. It was a simplified score, intended to assist in home performances. She played "Poor Wandering One" but didn't sing.

Now she opens the score to the Major General's song. She tests out the melody. And then some unsuspected vein of audacity announces itself in her, and, really without preparation, she sings:

I am the very model of a modern Major-General,
I've information vegetable, animal, and mineral,
I know the kings of England, and I quote the fights historical,
From Marathon to Waterloo, in order categorical.

Ramanujan looks over from the table.

"Mr. Ramanujan, come and join me at the piano," Alice says. "I rather suspect you'll enjoy this song."

Hesitantly he gets up. Alice makes room for him on the bench and he sits, close enough so that she can feel the heat of his body, not so close so that their clothes actually touch. "This song is from a famous comic opera called *The Pirates of Penzance*. The singer is a gentleman officer trying to impress some pirates. But really, the point is that he's rather full of himself. Listen."

I'm very well acquainted, too, with matters mathematical,
I understand equations, both the simple and quadratical,
About binomial theorem I'm teeming with a lot o' news
With many cheerful facts about the square of the hypotenuse.

"Of course," Alice continues, "when it's done properly, it's sung much faster than I've sung it. And by a man."

Ramanujan is looking at the score. "Binomial theorem," he says, in a tone that might mean amusement, might mean disdain.

"That's why I thought you might enjoy it," Alice says. "Now come along, let's sing together."

"Sing? I can't sing."

"How do you know? Haven't you sung in the temple?"

"Yes, but . . . I've never sung an English song."

"Well, I can't sing either, and who'll hear us? Just Ethel. So we'll do it together. At the count of three. One, two, three . . ."

She sings, and, quite to her delight, Ramanujan joins in:

I'm very good at integral and differential calculus;
I know the scientific names of beings animalculous;
In short, in matters vegetable, animal, and mineral,
I am the very model of a modern Major-General.

"There, you did very well."

"Did I?"

"You've got a lovely tenor voice. And better yet, a very good ear. You might have perfect pitch."

Ramanujan looks at his lap. He is breathing hard. Sweat beads on his forehead, as it always does when he's happy.

"Now come on," Alice commands. "Let's keep going. We'll finish the song, and then we'll sing the whole thing together."

Ramanujan takes a deep breath.

"One, two, three—"

I know our mythic history, King Arthur's and Sir Caradoc's,
I answer hard acrostics, I've a pretty taste for paradox,
I quote in elegiacs all the crimes of Heliogabalus,
In conics I can floor peculiarities parabolous.

"Peculiarities parabolous!" Alice repeats. And they both start laughing. They laugh like children. Outside, the rain pours down. On the table, the puzzle sits placid, immobile, seemingly content in its half-finished state. Comfortable in their slippers, Alice's toes wiggle, as, she supposes, do Ramanujan's.

And then, quite unexpectedly, the door opens. They both stand, embarrassed, as if they're being caught in the midst of some impropriety. "Hello, darling," Neville says, walking through, his footsteps preceding other footsteps. Hardy's and Littlewood's.

"Hello," Alice says, and drifts over to accept her husband's kiss.

"I've brought Hardy and Littlewood for tea. Hope you don't mind."

"Of course not."

"What have you two been doing? The puzzle, I see. They're hard at work on a jigsaw, Hardy. And what's this? The piano open! Have you been teaching Ramanujan to play?"

"No, to sing." Alice rings a bell for Ethel as Neville walks over to the piano to inspect the score.

"The Major General's Song," he says. "I say, Ramanujan, have you been doing Gilbert and Sullivan?"

Ramanujan says nothing. He sits stiffly on the settee.

"Mrs. Neville, you never cease to amaze me," Littlewood says. "What a service you're doing us, introducing Ramanujan to everything English! Whereas we only ever talk mathematics to him."

Alice sits across from Ramanujan, in one of the spinster chairs. "So what brings you home so early?" she asks, as Ethel brings in the tea things.

"Marvelous news. Littlewood's found rooms for Ramanujan in the college. On Whewell's Court. He can move next week."

What does her face say? Nothing, she hopes. Not that her husband would notice even if her face did show something. Behind his kindness, she knows, lie obliviousness and self-absorption.

Hardy would, though. That's what frightens her. That he should see something in her face, and tell Gertrude.

And Ramanujan? Does *he* notice anything? Ethel hands him his tea and he stares into the cup. Takes the milk and stirs it in.

Alice smiles. Later, she will draw pride from that. But for that moment it's as if a furious girl has just filled her cheeks with air and blown the little shapes that make up the world all over the floor.

She takes her tea. "What wonderful news," she says. "Not having to do all that walking. It will be so much better, Mr. Ramanujan, for your feet."

5

June 8th, 1914
Cambridge

My Dear Miss Hardy,

I hope you will not consider it impertinent of me if I write to you in confidence about a matter with which, on the surface at least, you and I are not directly concerned. On Mr. Hardy's suggestion, Mr. Ramanujan will shortly be leaving my house, where he has lived contentedly for six weeks, to move into rooms at Trinity. I cannot emphasize how strongly I feel that this would be a disastrous course to take. Here Mr. Ramanujan is well cared for. I make sure that he gets all the milk and fruit that he desires, and remain scrupulously attentive to his needs, dietary and otherwise. In college, how is he supposed to fare? He cannot stomach the food and says that he will cook for himself on a gas ring.

While I understand Mr. Hardy's desire to have Mr. Ramanujan closer to hand so that they may devote more hours of the day to mathematics, I fear also that your brother is failing to take into account the necessity of insuring that Mr. Ramanujan has a life outside mathematics. He has made a very great journey and is adjusting to a world radically different to his own. He misses his wife and family. Surely it is worth half an hour's walk each morning if as a result he is both healthier and more contented.

I know that you wield considerable influence with your brother and would ask you to intercede with him on Mr. Ramanujan's behalf. I also beg you not to mention my name in this connexion or that I have written to you.

I remain, as always, your dear friend
Alice Neville

"Well, what do you think of that?" Gertrude says, putting down the letter.

"I suppose," Hardy says, "that it merely confirms what we've suspected all along."

"And what's that?"

"That she's in love with him."

He draws on his pipe. It's a Saturday morning in June, and they're in the kitchen of the flat on St. George's Square. Littlewood is with them, up for the day to make a rendezvous with Anne, though he hasn't said so. Although he's sitting at the table, pretending to read the *Times*, he's been listening with great care to Gertrude's recitation, wondering how it is that she can ignore so casually Mrs. Neville's entreaty that she keep the letter to himself.

"If you want my opinion," Hardy says, "this clinches it. He must move into the college as soon as possible."

"Why such urgency?" Littlewood asks.

"It's obvious. As long as he's under the Nevilles' roof he's also under Mrs. Neville's thumb. He needs his freedom."

"But maybe he's happy there. You saw the pretty domestic scene, Hardy. The fire and the puzzle and the piano. Looked pretty cozy to me."

"Suffocating's the word I'd use."

"But that's you. And she's right about the food."

"I don't see how. Ramanujan doesn't seem the least anxious about cooking for himself. In fact, I rather got the impression he's looking forward to it. A respite from those horrific concoctions Mrs. Neville's always dragging out of the George Bernard Shaw cookbook or whatever it's called."

"Of course I won't disagree on that point."

"I should hope not. You're the one who found him the rooms."

"Still, I can't help but wonder if in the end he might not be better off staying under Neville's roof, being cared for—"

"—by a woman with a morbid erotic obsession."

At this Gertrude laughs. Her laugh surprises Littlewood; it's higher and flutier than he would have expected.

"What's so funny?"

"You two," she says, laughing more.

"Why?" Hardy asks. "Why on earth are we funny?"

"Has either of you considered asking him where *he* wants to live?"

6

RAMANUJAN'S TRUNK is packed. It sits by the front door at 113 Chesterton Road, alongside its owner, who stands stiffly at attention, as if he is attending a military or religious ceremony. Before him stand the Nevilles and Ethel. All are dressed to suit the occasion. No one is wearing slippers.

In a few moments Neville's older brother will arrive in his Jowett car, the same car in which they fetched Ramanujan when his ship docked. The brother will stay the weekend. "And to think, that was only—what, Alice, six weeks ago?"

"Seven," Alice says.

"Seven weeks. I must say, Ramanujan, it feels as if you've always been here."

Ramanujan stares at his shoes. His forehead is covered with drops of sweat.

"We'll miss you around here, won't we, ladies?" Neville puts his arm around Alice, who shudders. But to everyone's surprise it is Ethel, the housemaid, who bursts into tears.

"Now, Ethel, please," Alice says, shutting her eyes.

"I'm sorry, ma'am," Ethel says. "It's just that it won't be quite the same around here without sir to cut up fruit for."

"I can tell you one thing," Neville says, laughing. "I'm expecting a joint of mutton for dinner tonight."

All of them laugh at that. Ethel takes a handkerchief from her pocket and blows her nose.

Then a honking sounds. "There's Eddie," Neville says, opening the door to wave. "Right on time as always!" he shouts, before turning to Ramanujan. "No, to be perfectly direct about it, we'll miss you around here. All of us will."

"But I won't be so far away," Ramanujan says. "Only at the college."

"Yes, and you can come to dinner whenever you like. Right, Ethel? I promise you, you haven't cooked your last vegetable goose."

"Oh, sir!" Ethel says, covering her face.

Eddie Neville comes inside. He's red-faced and jovial—an older version of Eric. He pats Ramanujan hard on the back, then the brothers hoist the trunk and carry it out to the car. Ramanujan turns to Alice.

"I thank you very deeply for your kindness," he says. "And not only that, my mother thanks you."

"Does she?"

"Yes, she wrote so in a letter and asked me to tell you."

"And Janaki?"

"Janaki I have not received a letter from. But I am certain that she too would thank you."

They shake hands, then. All very innocent and amiable. And, as Alice reminds herself, it's not as if he doesn't want to go. He could have refused.

After the men have left, the house seems very quiet. Ethel disappears into the kitchen, no doubt to begin preparing the requested joint. Nor can Alice deny that her own mouth waters a little, at the prospect of meat again after such a long hiatus.

She walks across the sitting room, toward the piano; notices, for an instant, the puzzle on the table . . . and takes in her breath. Is it possible?

Yes. He has finished it. He must have stayed up most of the night. There they are: the quaint-looking guests, the innkeeper. A glass and the top hat rest on the table. Floorboards lead up to the tufted edge of the carpet. And yet—she leans over the table, being careful not to let out her breath. Yes, there is something wrong. A piece is missing. In the lower left-hand corner, where the rug ends and the floorboards begin, the wood grain of the table shows through. Indeed, the real wood and the wood in the picture are so similar in tone that if you didn't look carefully, you wouldn't notice it. But Alice does notice, and as she does, she remembers her sister's tremendous gusts of rage, her own scrabbling on the floor afterward. Of course it makes sense that a piece should have gone missing. Indeed, it's a miracle that more weren't lost.

With her finger she traces the shape of the gap. She thinks of the old nursery, the settee and the faded floral curtains. Somehow, the last time she swept the pieces back into their box, one, brown with black stripes, must have remained behind. Its absence is what she cups now in her hands, and so she opens them, letting it free into the room: the shape of a butterfly.

7

New Lecture Hall, Harvard University

SOMETIME IN THE mid 1920s (Hardy said, in the lecture he did not give) Mrs. Neville came to see me. I was at Oxford by then, and had been for several years. Neville was at Reading. In fact we had left Trinity the same year, 1919—I because, after the business with Russell, I could no longer bear the place, Neville because his fellowship had not been renewed. Correctly, I think, he suspected that this was in retaliation for his having been such a vocal pacifist during the war. Almost as vocal as Russell.

We had not stayed in touch, though I had heard, through Little-wood, that the Nevilles had had a child, a boy, and that the boy had died before he was a year old. Littlewood and I were then publishing several papers a year together, written through an exchange of letters. We saw each other at most once every few months.

I should say that she did not just waltz into my rooms at New College unannounced. She sent a note first, explaining that she and Neville were to be in Oxford for a day as he was giving a lecture at one of the other colleges. Neville himself would be very busy but she had time at her disposal and was hoping that she might call. I replied that of course she would be welcome.

I instructed my scout to arrange tea and sandwiches with the kitchen—for those of you unfamiliar with such arcana, what we call a "gyp" at Cambridge we call a "scout" at Oxford—and in due course, the polite five minutes after the appointed meeting time, Mrs. Neville arrived, a bit stouter than she had been in her youth, but still with that rather humid look, as if she had just emerged from the bath. The various pins and stays with which it was studded still could not contain her hair, which was still red. Her perfume—of

Parma violets—was the same as before, the same one my mother had worn.

She sat down across from me, and, after a few minutes of the most tedious and polite exchange (I did not mention the dead child), she got down to business, explaining that a few weeks previously, an Indian mathematician had come to see her. His name was Ranganathan, and he had recently come to study the workings of the Reading library. Like Ramanujan, this Ranganathan was from Madras, and so, upon learning that Neville was in Reading, he had asked if he could come to talk to them about Ramanujan, who, it seems, in the years since his death, had become something of a myth to the Madrasi mathematicians. Indeed, Ranganathan had it in mind to write Ramanujan's biography.

Being the woman she is, Mrs. Neville prepared for the visit by brewing Indian coffee and making some sort of Indian sweet, a recipe for which she had found in one of her cookbooks. She made a point of this to me, which, I realize now, I should have recognized as a sign of the outburst to come; back in Cambridge she'd always tried to undermine my friendship with Ramanujan by pointing out how much better she "understood" him. And in the case of Ranganathan, the ploy must have paid off, for he was very confidential with her. He arrived in due course at their house, she said, and he was wearing a turban. This simply astonished her, she said, because, back in Cambridge, Ramanujan had often complained to her that he found it a torture to wear a hat. Wouldn't he have been more comfortable wearing a turban? she asked.

Before I could answer, she was back to her tale. Having absorbed the turban, it seemed that she asked Ranganathan if his wearing it had ever caused him any trouble in England, and he had replied that only on two occasions had anyone even remarked upon his headwear. Once was in Hyde Park, at Speakers' Corner, when a speaker advocating Irish independence pointed to him from his platform and said something to the effect that this "friend from India" should surely understand the persecution by England of a slave nation. The other was when Ranganathan was riding a train to Croydon, a train moving slowly due to some repairs on the track, and the gang coolies stared at him through the window and called him "Mr. A.," which was what the newspapers were then calling an Indian prince involved in a lawsuit. Neither incident, Ranganathan said, upset him in the least—which led Mrs. Neville to ask him why, then, poor Ramanujan had not been allowed to wear his turban. Ranganathan replied that perhaps at the time, in Madras, it was assumed that a man walking down the streets of an English city wearing a turban would be laughed at or even stoned. Few of Ramanujan's Indian champions, after all, had ever been to England, while his English champions had been away for many years.

All this Mrs. Neville explained in a voice that, as she spoke, became increasingly agitated, even accusatory—as if, somehow, I was complicit in the edict that Ramanujan could not wear a turban, when in fact his wearing a turban would have meant nothing to me. Before I could tell her this, however, she moved from the turban to the *kudimi*, the religiously prescribed tuft of hair that Ramanujan had had snipped off before his departure. Did Ranganathan still have his *kudimi*? she asked him, and he told her that he did, and took off his turban to show her the little tuft, at which point, she said, tears filled her eyes, as indeed tears now filled her eyes. "Why in the world," she asked, "was he forced to cut it off? He would have been so much happier had he been able to keep it." But again, I had no chance to answer, for she was now on to clothes. Although Ranganathan wore Western-style clothes, he told her that when he was at home, he wore his *dhoti*, and that his landlady did not mind at all. Nor, Mrs. Neville said, would she have minded had Ramanujan worn his *dhoti* when he was staying at her house. And why had he not been allowed to wear his *dhoti* at Trinity? "This may seem a small matter to you, Mr. Hardy," she said, "but it would have made for Ramanujan the difference between happiness and misery."

Please bear in mind that, so far, to this putative "conversation," I had contributed not so much as a word. Mrs. Neville had not given me the chance. Now, though, she was wiping her eyes, and I took advantage of this brief caesura in her harangue to say, "I agree with you completely. No doubt Ramanujan would have been much happier had he allowed himself these concessions."

She looked at me in surprise. "Allowed himself!" she said. "Are you supposing he had any choice in the matter?"

I said, "There have been Indians at Cambridge for many years. He had Indian friends. Some wore turbans. He could have followed their example. At Trinity, anyway, he wore slippers most of the time, not shoes."

"I gave him those slippers," she said, almost jealously.

"That was kind of you," I said.

She strangled her handkerchief. "It was a terrible mistake, his moving into the college. I'm sure that, had he stayed under my roof, he would never have become ill. He might be alive today."

So this was what it came down to. I looked at her with the compassionate disbelief that one reserves for the insane. And in a sense, I think, she *was* insane at that moment. Women are so inclined to confuse things. Perhaps, through Ramanujan, she was mourning the death of her own child.

In any case, having now made her point, she pulled back. She became, suddenly, very bright, very friendly, as if the strained intercourse of the past half hour hadn't even taken place. What a pleasure it was to see me again. Was I happier in Oxford than in Cambridge? Eric had asked her to pass on his regards and to say how sorry he was that he would not have a chance to call.

And then she left. Her odor of Parma violets remained behind. It is a great and painful irony that even accusations of the most unjust and ludicrous sort still leave a sting—of what? Guilt? No, not exactly. Doubt. For now she had put into my head the idea that by moving Ramanujan into the college, I had brought about or at least hastened his death. Such an idea, of course, was madness. What, after all, could where he lived have had to do with his illness? And yet, perhaps, had he been kept away from such a mass of men as was passing through Trinity through the war years, had he not taken to cooking his own food . . . Do you see? Once the splinter of doubt is under the skin, there is no teasing it out. She had done her job admirably.

But I have moved ahead of myself; I have moved not only into but beyond the years of Ramanujan's illness, when what I wanted to tell you about were those first happy weeks before the war started, weeks distilled, for me, into the image of him waddling across New Court wearing a pair of slippers. And now I see that it was the slippers that made me remember Mrs. Neville's visit today. Because, as she so bitterly reminded me, she had given them to him.

Waddle, of course, is not a kind verb. Nor is it an entirely accurate way of describing Ramanujan's walk. If he seemed to teeter a bit, I am convinced, it was mostly due to the constrictions of his clothes, which, as I have said, were too small for him. On this matter Mrs. Neville and I remain in complete agreement: Ramanujan was born to wear a *dhoti* or some other loose garment. In flowing clothes he would have looked as regal as that "Mr. A." with whom the coolies confused Ranganathan. In English dress, on the other hand, he did come off a bit absurd.

In any case, as I'm sure you've heard a thousand times before, that was an extraordinarily beautiful summer, that last summer before the war; never before had so many trees so fragrantly shed their blossoms, and so on. As it happened, it was the height of May week when he moved into his rooms, delivered to Whewell's Court by Neville's brother in that terrible motor of his. That same day, the tripos results were posted, the names now in a plain vertical row. Littlewood and I took Ramanujan to see them, and he studied them scrupulously. All a far cry from the old days when a crowd would fill the Senate House to hear the reading of the Honors List . . . I had put a stop to that, I told him, an achievement in which I took what I considered to be a justified pride. And Ramanujan, I think, understood that pride, he whom exams had so betrayed and cornered.

The weather being exceptionally fine, Littlewood and I walked him down to the Cam to watch the punts gliding by, the men in their flannels and college blazers, the girls with their bright frocks and colorful Japanese umbrellas. None of this, he later told me, struck him as particularly spectacular—he who was habituated to the bright colors of the women's saris in Kumbakonam, and who had drifted down the holy river Cavary in boats not so different from our punts. All along the banks of the river picnics were laid out. We watched the bumps races for a while—he seemed to find them quite dull—then went over to Fenner's for a cricket match, Cambridge versus the Free Foresters. I am sorry to report that he took as little interest in the match as he had in the bumps race. And then in the evening we attended a rather frivolous entertainment put on by the Footlights Dramatic Club, a revue entitled *Was it the Lobster?*, at the silly songs and sketches of which, to my amazement, Ramanujan laughed heartily. He had a very memorable laugh, loud enough to startle, at which point he would cover his mouth with his hand.

If he were alive today, I'm sure he could tell you whether, in fact, it *was* the lobster. That was the sort of thing he remembered. I can tell you only that I shall always recall those days with happiness, and in particular the sight of Ramanujan, his face turned toward the sun, making his way across New Court toward my rooms. It was a sight that filled me with satisfaction and a certain pride, for I knew that he was there entirely thanks to me, that without me he would never have been walking those cobblestone paths.

He would arrive, most mornings, around nine-thirty. For a few moments he and Hermione would stare at each other. Then we would drink coffee and chat a bit before getting down to work. How was he settling into his rooms? Quite nicely, thank you. And was he comfortable cooking for himself? Quite, thank you. He bought vegetables each week at the market (admittedly, he found them strange and tasteless at first, but he got used to them), in addition to which he was able to order rice and rice powder and spices from a shop in London. A friend in Madras had also sent him a special kind of cooking pot, I forget what it was called, made of brass lined with silver, in which he made one of his favorite dishes, a thin, spicy lentil soup called *rasam*. In his home province, the people had a taste for food that was sour as well as spicy. At first he tried to give his food the proper note of sourness by squeezing in the juice of lemons, but our lemons, he said, were not nearly so sour as those in India. Fortunately another acquaintance from Madras, a youth also on his way to study mathematics at Cambridge, was due to arrive any day, bearing with him a large supply of tamarind, the preferred souring agent of the region, with which Ramanujan would be able to make *rasam* almost, if not quite, as tasty as his mother's.

On one of those occasions, while we were drinking our coffee, he noticed the bust of Gaye. "Who is that man?" he asked. And I explained that he was a dear friend, possibly the best friend that I had ever had, and that he had died, at which Ramanujan looked soberly at his lap. He, too, he said, had had friends who had died. Fortunately he had the good graces not to ask *how* Gaye had died.

And then, the coffee finished, we set to work. In those early days I was still trying to hammer home to him the importance of writing proofs—a futile effort, I see now. Such values must be imparted early to a mathematician; in Ramanujan's case, I realize, it was already too late. Still, I tried.

I have very particular ideas about proof. I believe that proofs should be beautiful and, to the extent that this is possible, concise. A beautiful proof should be as slender as one of Shelley's odes, and, like an ode, it should imply vastnesses. I tried to impress this upon Ramanujan. "A good proof," I told him, "must combine *unexpectedness* with *inevitability* and *economy*." There is no better example than Euclid's proof that there are infinite prime numbers—a proof I am going to walk you through now, just as I walked him through it so many years ago, not because you don't know it (I should hardly wish to insult you by implying such ignorance) but because I want to call attention to aspects of the proof of which your professors, in teaching it, may not have taken note.

This is, of course, a *reductio ad absurdum* proof, and so we begin by assuming the opposite of what we want to prove: we assume that there is only a *finite* number of primes, and we call the *last* prime, the *largest* prime, P. We must also remember that, by definition, any non-prime number can be broken down into primes. To choose a random example, 190 breaks down as $19 \times 5 \times 2$.

Assuming, then, that P is the largest prime number, we can write out the primes in sequence, from smallest to largest, and the sequence will look like this:

$$2, 3, 5, 7, 11, 13, 17, 19, 23 \ldots P$$

Then we can propose a number, Q, that is 1 greater than all the primes multiplied together. That is to say,

$$Q = (2 \times 3 \times 5 \times 7 \times 11 \times 13 \ldots \times P) + 1$$

Either Q is prime or it is not. If Q is prime, this contradicts the assumptions that P is the largest prime number. But if Q is not prime, it must be divisible by some prime, and that cannot be any of the primes up to and including P. So the prime divisor of Q must be a prime bigger than P, which again contradicts our original assumption. Therefore there is no greatest prime. There is an infinity of primes.

I cannot tell you what pleasure I continue to take, even today, in the beauty of this proof; in the brief yet extraordinary journey it represents, from a seemingly reasonable proposition (that there is a greatest prime) to the inevitable yet utterly unexpected conclusion that the proposition is false. Nor would I be telling you the truth if I said that Ramanujan was oblivious to the beauty of the proof. He understood that beauty; he appreciated that beauty. And yet his appreciation was rather akin to mine of the novels of Mr. Henry James. That is to say, I *admire* them yet I cannot *love* them. In the same way I never had the sense that Ramanujan had much *love* for the proof. What he loved were numbers themselves. Their infinite flexibility and yet their rigid order. The degree to which natural laws, many of which we barely understand, check our ability to manipulate them. Littlewood thought him an anachronism. According to Littlewood, he belonged to the age of formulae, which ended a hundred years ago. If he had been German, if he had been born in 1800, he would have changed the history of the world. But he was born too late, and on the wrong side of the ocean, and even if he never admitted this, I feel sure that he knew it.

These were, I believe, days of great happiness for Ramanujan, no matter what Mrs. Neville might say to the contrary. Nor was she in any sense out of the picture. One weekend, for instance, I recall her hauling Ramanujan off to London, to meet Gertrude for a visit to the British Museum. He might have made friends. Sometimes I would see him in the company of other Indians. Above all, he worked, and before the summer was out, he published his paper on modular equations and routes to π.

Occasionally I would visit him in his rooms, which were on the ground floor of Whewell's Court. They were extraordinarily tidy and contained almost nothing in the way of possessions, aside from the requisite bed and dresser and, for some reason, a pianola that did not work. He lived ascetically, like one of those Hindu mystics about whom one reads from time to time. From the little kitchen an odor of curry and that clarified butter so beloved by the Indians—ghee, it is called—always emanated. If a shadow of trouble passed over our conversations during those days, it was due to his wife's failure to write him any letters. Forget that the poor thing was barely literate: he longed for *some* communication from her, in addition to which, in India, there were apparently scribes and such to whom you could go when you needed a letter written for you. From his mother, letters arrived regularly, pages densely filled with a script as mysterious to me as the language of theorems must be to any non-mathematician. His wife, though, wrote nothing, even though he wrote to her, unfailingly, once a week.

One wonders what would have happened had the war not broken out. Many wonder this, for all sorts of reasons. There is of course no answer.

PART FOUR

The Qualities of the Isle

I

GERMANY INVADES BELGIUM, and at first Hardy feels as he does about a beautiful proof: the onset of war seems at once *inevitable* and *unexpected.*

Almost everyone he speaks to now claims to have seen it coming, yet as he looks back over the past month, he can remember only Russell saying that he saw it coming. Instead domestic crises—strikes, unrest in Ulster—dominated the conversation at high table. The assassinations in Sarajevo, of course, provoked a bit of comment. Yet Servia was so far away! A small, primitive country. Nothing that happened there could touch Cambridge.

Russell, by contrast, was in a panic. Most of July he spent shuttling between London and Cambridge, running about announcing that he knew no one who was in favor of war, that everyone he had spoken to considered the prospect of war folly. As if public opinion ever influenced the decisions of government. As if saying that something could never happen would stop it from happening.

The day after the news broke, he chased Hardy down in the middle of Great Court. "So it's come," he said, not with any sort of "I told you so" glee, but in a tone at once stunned and drawn. "Everything we believe in is over." And now declarations of war are being presented like visiting cards.

It's all very bewildering to Hardy. War with Germany, after all, means war with Göttingen, beloved Göttingen, land of Gauss and Riemann. Yet Germany has now invaded Belgium on its way to France. To protect Belgium, England must forge an alliance with Russia—savage, autocratic Russia—and all in order to defeat Germany, land of Göttingen, land of Gauss and Riemann . . . How à propos that Russell alone predicted the worst! Hardy's imagination spins in an infinite regress, the barber who shaves only those men in his town who do not shave themselves. And the town (where else?) is Göttingen.

As soon as war is declared, the tone among his acquaintances changes from one of dismissal to one of denial. Instead of reassuring one another that Britain will remain neutral, they start reassuring one another that the war, should it actually commence, will be swift. Over by Christmas. Lord Grey, for instance, has just admitted to secret talks with France. Might these lead to a quick armistice? Heartening words resonate through New Court and Nevile's Court, but behind them Hardy can hear the thin, ceaseless babble of despair.

"It is the end," Russell says. He is just back from yet another trip to London. The day before war broke out, his lover, Ottoline Morrell, summoned him, as her husband was to give a speech to Parliament, urging the British government not to enter into the fray. Unable to gain admission to the gallery, Russell paced up and down Trafalgar Square and was appalled to hear the men and women sitting under the lions voicing enthusiasm, even delight at the prospect of war. "Today is not yesterday," Russell says, speaking of the reactions of the "average" person. Yet even here at Cambridge, where supposedly no one is average, subterranean rumblings of patriotism sound. Even among the brethren. Rupert Brooke, for instance, has said he's ready to volunteer—"no doubt the influence of that odious little Eddie Marsh," Russell says—while Butler has offered up all the facilities of Trinity College to the war effort. "It is the end," Russell repeats, then goes back to London because he cannot bear to be too far from the center of things. "Horrible as it is," he says, "I have to get the news as soon as it arrives."

The irony, of course, is that often the news arrives at Trinity sooner than it does at the office of the *Times*. The brethren have enviable connections—Keynes to the treasury, Marsh, through Churchill, to 10 Downing Street. Norton writes to Hardy that he saw Marsh at a party in London, "parading about in evening dress, immaculate, enjoying his importance." Brooke was with him. "He is living in Marsh's flat. He has spurned Bloomsbury and boys in favor of manliness and uniforms. Yet isn't it funny that he should have chosen Edwina, of all people, as his mentoress?"

And in the meantime, it does not stop being summer. That is the heartbreak. Cambridge has more or less emptied out for the long Vacation. Littlewood stays in Treen, returning, presumably, only when Dr. Chase takes up residence. Hardy divides his weeks between Trinity and his mother's house in Cranleigh. When he's at Trinity, whole days pass during which he sees no one but Ramanujan, with whom he takes walks along the river, and sometimes sits on the banks. Heliotropic by nature, he raises his face to the sun whenever it passes between the clouds. Truth be told, he appreciates the quiet. It seems inconceivable that the world could end in such a season.

He tries, as much as he can, to *see* Ramanujan. Standing in shadowed profile before the river, his arms folded behind his back and his stomach protruding slightly, he might be the silhouette of a Victorian gentleman, cut from black paper and pasted against a white ground. Restraint and discipline, a certain aloofness, or perhaps even elusiveness: these are his most distinguishing traits. Except when they're talking mathematics, he rarely speaks except when spoken to, and when he is questioned, almost always answers by dipping into what Hardy envisages as a reserve of stock replies, no doubt purchased on the same shopping trip in Madras during which he was supplied with trousers, socks, and underwear. Replies such as: "Yes, it is very lovely." "Thank you, my mother and wife are well." "The political situation is indeed very complex." Here he is, after all, in English clothes and on English land, and still Hardy can't begin to penetrate his carapace of cultivated inscrutability. Only occasionally does Ramanujan let something slip, a whiff of panic or passion slips through (Hobson! Baker!), and then Hardy feels the man's soul as a mystery, a fast-moving prickle beneath his skin.

Mostly, those afternoons, they talk mathematics. Definite integrals, elliptic functions, Diophantine approximation. And, of course, primes, their diabolical tendency to confound, of which Hardy wants to make sure Ramanujan never loses sight. For example, Littlewood has of late made another important discovery. It has to do with a refinement that Riemann made of Gauss's formula for counting primes. Up until recently, most mathematicians took it for granted that Riemann's version would always give a more accurate estimate than Gauss's. But now Littlewood has shown that, though Riemann's version may be more accurate for the first million primes, after that Gauss's version is sometimes more accurate. But only sometimes. This discovery is of vast importance to about twenty people. Unfortunately, half of those people are in Germany.

As they walk, he asks Ramanujan if he knows the story of Riemann's terrible housekeeper, and when Ramanujan waggles his head, he tells it. "Of course," he concludes, "the story's probably false."

"How old was he when he died?"

"Thirty-nine. He died on Lake Maggiore, of tuberculosis. So why would the housekeeper feel compelled to burn his papers? It all seems suspiciously convenient, a way of saying, 'Yes, there's a proof out there, you've just got to find it.'"

Ramanujan is silent for a moment. Then he asks Hardy about Göttingen, and Hardy tells him what little he knows of the place; he describes the *rathaus* on the front of which is emblazoned the motto "Away from here there is no life," and the cobbled streets down which, in his imagination, Gauss and Riemann—freed, now, from the constraints of time—stroll together as they discuss the hypothesis. Every few paces, when Riemann comes to a crucial juncture in his lost proof, the pair stops, diverting the passersby as a rock diverts a stream. Likewise, when they are talking mathematics, Hardy and Ramanujan sometimes stop; only this time of year, there are few passersby to impede.

He asks Ramanujan about his childhood. Did he ever play chess? Again, Ramanujan waggles his head. He only learned chess once he arrived in Madras, he says. However, when he was very small, he and his mother played a game with eighteen pieces, fifteen representing sheep and three representing wolves. "When the wolves surrounded a sheep, they would eat it. But when the sheep surrounded a wolf, they would immobilize it."

"I would imagine," Hardy says, "that it would be rather difficult for the sheep to win."

"Yes. Very quickly, however, I was able to calculate the probabilities of the game, and from then on, whether playing wolf or sheep, I always won over my mother."

"Did she mind?"

"No, not at all."

"How old were you?"

"Six. Five, perhaps."

Hardy is not surprised. At five he was beating his own mother at chess.

"Both my parents were, as they say, mathematically minded," he says. "My mother especially. Not that she ever had the chance to cultivate her talents. She was a schoolteacher."

Ramanujan says nothing.

"And your parents?"

"They are poor people. They did not have education. My father is a *gumasta*, a simple accounts clerk."

They stop to look at the river. No punts glide by. Hardy hears birdsong, the faint whoosh of branches in the breeze. Ramanujan turns to face him, as he rarely does, and his eyes, so black and deep, astonish Hardy. Such eyes, he thinks, would drive even the most rigorous mind to bad poetry: *Liquid pools of molten ore, / These portals to a world beyond* . . . At night, sometimes, in his head, he works on the poem, which he never writes down.

"Hardy," he says, "is it true that in Belgium the Germans are setting fire to whole villages?"

"That's what the newspapers tell us."

"And that they are killing the children and throwing away the old people?"

"So I am told."

Ramanujan frowns. "I am worried about two young men from Madras who are coming here to study. Ananda Rao and Sankara Rao. They are carrying much food for me, including tamarind."

"There's no need to worry," Hardy says. "No one's going to attack a British passenger ship."

"But they are not traveling on a British ship. They are traveling on an Austrian ship. Their intention was to get to Austria and come here by train. What will happen to them now?"

"Oh, an Austrian ship." A robin flies by. "Well, once they arrive in Trieste, they'll just . . . I don't see why anyone should give them trouble. After all, they're students."

Again, Ramanujan frowns. "Last night I dreamed that they were trapped in a burning village," he says. "I saw them burn."

"Oh, I shouldn't think that would happen. They're not going anywhere near Belgium."

Silence now. They continue their walk. Ramanujan has his eyes fixed on the ground in front of him. And for a moment Hardy, turning to glance at him, asks himself a terrible question, a question he berates himself for even entertaining. Is what really worries Ramanujan the fate of the young men or of his tamarind?

2

THE FRIDAY AFTER war is declared, Hardy takes part in an expedition to Leintwardine Manor, on the Welsh border, to watch an open air performance of *The Tempest*. Alice Neville organized the trip at the beginning of July, before anyone guessed that war was imminent. She has people near Leintwardine, and the performance is to benefit some charity to which they have connections. On Thursday, Hardy sent her a note asking if, under the circumstances, she might not prefer to cancel the outing, and she replied that she could see no reason why they should. "There is no fighting in Hertfordshire, or so I'm told," she wrote. This both irritated and disappointed Hardy, who had been hoping, at the very least, that the war would give him a reasonable excuse not to do things he did not want to do.

And so that Friday morning he finds himself gathered at the Nevilles' house, along with Ramanujan, Littlewood, Neville's brother Eddie, and Eddie Neville's friend Mr. Allenby. Of all the invitees, only Gertrude has begged off, pleading a fictitious cold. Ramanujan and the Nevilles will ride with Eddie in his Jowett, Hardy and Littlewood with Mr. Allenby in his Vauxhall.

Once they set off, Cambridge thins out quickly, giving way to open countryside. The weather is fine. Still, Hardy's dismay at the roar and stink of the Vauxhall inhibits his ability to take any pleasure in the view. He sits in the back, alone. Littlewood is up front with Allenby, who has red cheeks and heavy jowls. Like the elder Neville, he lives north of London, in High Barnet. Both are members of a motoring club; "mad for motoring," he tells Littlewood, who nods and smiles in that irritating, inevitable way of his—Littlewood, with his confounding ability to make himself at home anywhere, no matter how dire the circumstances. Hardy, on the other hand, finds that the older he gets, the more ill at ease he feels venturing beyond the walls of Trinity. He's never liked cars, and Allenby is not what you would call a conservative driver. He takes the turns with a ferocity that brings Hardy's heart to his throat, all the while laughing and chattering with Littlewood above the engine's clamor, while Hardy hallucinates rifle tips pointing up from the roadside hedgerows. Hours turn into weeks, then years, the rifle tips seem with every mile to poke him more urgently in the bowels, until at long last they pull up outside Leintwardine Manor. Hardy is let out of the backseat. He has been sitting for so long, his legs feel as if they're going to collapse under him. He needs a loo. He stumbles over to Ramanujan, who looks complacent enough, if a bit dusty.

"Enjoy the ride?" he asks.

Ramanujan merely smiles. "The scenery was splendid," he says—yet another of the department store replies.

A visit to the toilet, followed by a pint in a nearby pub, restores Hardy's composure a bit. By now the sun is setting, and the group heads off—on foot this time, thank God—to the manor. A great lawn sweeps away from the house, toward a tennis court on which a makeshift stage has been erected, complete with footlights. Some members of the audience, mostly old women, sit in folding chairs, while others picnic in groups—and indeed, not to his surprise, Hardy now discovers that Alice, too, has brought a picnic, a gallimaufry of her vegetarian horrors, which she proceeds to lay out on a cloth of faded red ticking. Vigorously she divvies up the goods, passing a plate of something stuffed with something else to Mr. Allenby, who gazes at it with a stunned expression. Another plate she hands to Hardy. As he examines its contents, he takes in, as if from a great distance, fragments of talk about Shakespeare, Alice's charity, Vauxhalls versus Jowetts. What a strain it must be, all this effort to direct the conversation away from the subject it yearns for, like trying to hold a magnet away from a pole! And why are they bothering? Why are they even here?

He is just starting to butter a piece of bread—the only eatable there he can stomach—when he hears his name being called. He looks up. Harry Norton is striding toward him, accompanied by Sheppard, Taylor, Keynes, and, lingering a few paces behind, Count Békássy.

Hardy stands. Crumbs drop from his trousers to the grass. Later he will reflect grimly that there is something inevitable about coincidences of this kind. Far from negating randomness, they confirm it. Hence 331, 3331, 33331, 333331, and 3333331 are prime, but 33333331 is not.

"Hello, Hardy," Norton says. "And what on earth brings you to these parts?"

"I could ask you the same question."

"We've come to see Bliss, of course. Oh, sorry if we're interrupting—"

"Bliss?"

"You know Bliss." Norton leans closer. "The new recruit. He's Caliban and his brother's Ferdinand. We're here to look on with Békássy as his boy has his moment in the limelight. Isn't that right, Feri?"

Békássy, whose back Keynes is now touching, nods.

"But I had no idea Bliss was in the play," Hardy says. "We came because Mrs. Neville . . . Forgive me. May I present Mr. Norton? Mrs. Neville . . ."

Oh, the horror of introductions! As Hardy rattles out the names, how-do-you-do's cross like swords; the requisite "Won't you join us?" is followed by the requisite "We couldn't possibly . . ." "But there's plenty to eat." "Well, if you're sure . . ." "Of course. Do sit down."

And then, before Hardy knows what's happening, space is being cleared; a second picnic cloth, this one blue, is being laid out. *The quadrants touching.* Sheppard, recklessly abandoning any pretense of discretion, points at Ramanujan and whispers to Taylor, who gapes. His hair looks even whiter in the dusk light than it does in his rooms at King's. And what does Ramanujan make of these curious men? Does he take Sheppard's pointing as a signal of his celebrity ("the Hindoo calculator") or of his obvious foreignness? The duskiness of his skin? The squatness of his nose?

Plates are moved out of the way. With his terrible inquisitive gusto, Sheppard sidles up to Ramanujan, asking him the usual questions— how is he settling in, is he happy at Trinity—but also ones of a decidedly more Apostolic nature, such as, "Speaking as a Hindu, do you believe Heaven can accommodate worshippers of your Gods as well as of our God?"

"There are many Christians in India," Ramanujan says. "And

Muslims. Generally speaking, the adherents respect one another's beliefs, though of course some conflict is inevitable." (Answer purchased at Spencer's, price 1 rupee.)

"Naturally, naturally. Still, the Hindus must have feelings on the matter, when for instance they see Christians entering a church, or Jews a synagogue."

"It is my personal view that all religions are more or less equally true."

"Really?" Keynes says. "How fascinating. A pity McTaggart isn't here." He and Sheppard are now peering at Ramanujan assessingly, as if he's an embryo. Is he an embryo? Is all this a set-up? In which case, why hasn't Hardy been informed? And who is the father?

Dusk is falling. Footlights flash, the crowd quiets, the play begins. From the darkness behind the stage, young Bliss emerges, his good looks set off, oddly enough, by the stoop he affects, the rags and smears of grease paint on his face. Not a bad Caliban, all told. Hardy closes his eyes as Bliss utters some lines that Gaye loved especially:

> When thou camest first,
> Thou strok'dst me and mad'st much of me; wouldst give me
> Water with berries in't, and teach me how
> To name the bigger light, and how the less,
> That burn by day and night: and then I lov'd thee
> And show'd thee all the qualities o' th' isle,
> The fresh springs, brine-pits, barren place, and fertile:
> Cursed be I that did so!

Hardy turns to look at Békássy. Tears glisten beneath those heavy Hussar lids. So this is what it's like, then, true love or comradeship or what have you, between men! What Hardy thought he knew with Gaye; what sometimes he still dreams of knowing. And will he ever know it again? Perhaps because the world's about to end, that old yearning for romance, for passion, seems to have reawakened in him; he looks, haltingly, about him, wondering if there's anyone here tonight, anyone at all . . .

Then the first act ends. Norton gets up to smoke, and Hardy follows him. They stand huddled together, out of earshot of the picnickers.

"Honestly, Harry," Hardy says, "I had no idea about Bliss. Our being here is pure coincidence."

"Very like you, hiding your lights under a bushel," Norton says. "But really, you should have at least introduced him to *me*. Sometimes I think you forget I'm a mathematician."

"Only because you forget yourself."

"Yes, yes, I know. It's just that trying to do the degree nearly drove me to bedlam."

"Sheppard certainly seems keen to get to know him."

"Sheppard is doomed to be a conversationalist." Norton blows out smoke.

They are quiet for a moment, and then Norton says, "Beastly thing, this war, isn't it?"

Hardy almost laughs. After so much strained evasion of the topic, to hear it mentioned straight on—and so casually!—comes as a relief.

"I'm surprised Keynes could get away, what with his work at the Treasury."

"It was for Békássy's sake."

"How so?"

"Haven't you heard? He's going back to Hungary to join the army. To fight against Russia. Supposedly we'll be at war with Hungary next week, so if he doesn't get out before that, he'll be interned. Of course, Keynes tried desperately to talk him out of it, but Feri wouldn't hear of it. So now Keynes has agreed to pay his passage, since the banks are closed, and Feri can't get his own money. But he's wretched about the whole thing. We all are."

"And Bliss?"

"He says he's signing up, too. Following Rupert Brooke's lead. Rather romantic, isn't it, the lovers fighting on opposite sides? We brought Feri down tonight because, well, really, it's his last chance to see Bliss before he goes off."

Hardy looks toward the house, where presumably the actors have set up their dressing room. Békássy is emerging from a side door.

"How very noble," Norton says.

"What? That they're going off to die?"

"No, that they're going off to defend their respective fatherlands."

"I despise this war. I can't believe every intelligent human being doesn't despise this war."

"Well, from what Keynes tells me, Moore hasn't made his mind up yet one way or the other. And McTaggart's already declared himself a rabid anti-German."

"This from the man who wrote 'Violets or Orange-Blossom?'"

"Still, you've got to admit the Huns are proving to be rather brutal. A cold military machine. I've read they're bayoneting children."

"That's just propaganda."

"It wouldn't surprise me. You know, Nietzsche and the whole *übermensch* business. Not every German's a Goethe, Hardy."

"They're defending their interests. They're afraid of Russia, just as we're afraid of them. The dreaded German Navy. Everyone's afraid, everyone's acting in anticipation of someone else acting in anticipation of someone else acting in anticipation."

"Like Russell's infinite regress."

"Exactly."

The footlights flash, indicating the end of the interval.

"We should be getting back," Norton says. "Oh—are you stopping the night?"

Hardy nods. "The Nevilles are staying with her cousin. The rest of us are putting up in some inn. Knighton, I think." He blows out smoke. "And you?"

"Some friend of the squitter-squatter's. At least that's where Sheppard and Keynes and the squitter and I are headed. Maybe I'll finally get a look at *the three*. Tristan and Isolde, who knows?" Norton lowers his eyelids. "Isn't it a pity we can't . . . well . . ."

But the second act is about to begin. They stub out their cigarettes, then return to the lawn to watch the rest of the play. Which goes on. And on. All told, the slowest performance of *The Tempest* through which Hardy has ever been obliged to sit. By the time it's over, his legs have fallen asleep under him. But then he looks at his watch and sees that only two hours have passed. In fact the performance went rather swiftly.

And then, perhaps even more anguishing to him than the introductions, the farewells begin. Ramanujan could probably produce an equation to calculate T, the amount of time it takes before everyone finally leaves, based on P, the number of people present, and I, the interruption variable, which of course multiplies the length of time required for each goodbye by an uncertain quantity. And oh, the words!—*So charmed . . . We must meet again soon . . . Fascinating to have learned of your motor club*—endless words before, finally, Norton kisses Alice's cheek, and Littlewood shakes Keynes's hand, and Békássy rushes off toward the house to find Bliss, with whom he will no doubt soon be escaping into the shadows of the summer night, the forest and its dark canopy.

At last it's over. Hardy climbs into Allenby's beastly car, which carries him and Littlewood to Knighton, to the George & Dragon Inn, where they learn that an error has been made; instead of reserving five rooms, as Alice requested, the innkeeper has put aside only two. Indeed, the inn doesn't even have five rooms! One room has one double bed; Eddie Neville and Allenby cheerfully agree to share it. As for the other: "There are two large beds, sir," the innkeeper tells Hardy. "Certainly big enough for the three gentlemen."

"Doesn't bother me," Littlewood says.

Of course it doesn't! And Ramanujan? His expression is impenetrable. Maybe he doesn't care. Back at home in India, don't they sleep willy-nilly, all over the floor?

And so the innkeeper, carrying a candle, leads them up to the room, which is in the attic, spartan and frowsty, the two big beds arranged opposite each other, one against the north and the other against the south wall. There is no electric light. Instead the candle that the innkeeper sets on the mantel imparts to the room its warm, flickering glow.

Littlewood stretches his arms. "Well, that was a thoroughly draining entertainment," he says, stripping off his waistcoat. "I don't know about you chaps, but I'm knackered."

At which, with the insouciance for which he is famous, he yanks off his clothes, flings back the covers of one of the beds, and lies down. No thought, apparently, of washing. "Goodnight," he says, and within seconds he is snoring.

Hardy and Ramanujan are left, for all intents and purposes, alone. They look at each other.

"I believe the bathroom is downstairs," Hardy says.

"Thank you," Ramanujan replies. He opens his little valise and removes from it a toiletry kit and a pair of pyjamas. Bearing these with him, he opens the bedroom door and tiptoes out.

Hardy blows out breath. Now he has time to visit the water closet and change—quickly, surreptitiously—into his own pyjamas. Having done so, he surveys the two beds, one tidy, the other thrown into disarray by Littlewood's splayed and naked form. Littlewood has pushed the covers down to just below his navel. For a moment, Hardy watches the expansion and compression of his diaphragm, notes the sparse hairs on his chest . . . Oh, which bed to climb into? If he gets into the bed with Littlewood, he won't sleep a wink. But if he gets into the empty bed, he'll merely be passing the burden of choice on to Ramanujan. And what will Ramanujan do?

Then he hears a door open somewhere—the bathroom door below, perhaps—followed by footsteps on the stairs.

Almost without thought, he makes his choice. He climbs into the empty bed.

Five minutes pass. He counts them. The door to the room opens and shuts again. He hears the floorboards creaking under bare feet. Then there is a moment of stillness, before Ramanujan blows—hard—and Hardy both hears and smells the guttering of the candle. Darkness smothers the room. He feels the heft of another body pressing down on the mattress, which tilts away from him. Sheets and blankets tighten around his rib cage. He smells wool, the outdoors—and then he realizes what has happened. Ramanujan has not actually got into the bed; he's only got onto it. He is sleeping atop the bedspread and sheets and blanket, with his coat draped over his torso.

Well, how strange! Hardy hardly knows how to interpret *that*. And yet, he must confess, he likes the way that, thanks to Ramanujan's weight, the sheets pull away from him, and push down on him, and envelop him. It's like being cocooned.

He falls asleep, and wakes what seems an instant later to see dawn light coming through the window.

"Harold," a voice says—Ramanujan's? But no. It's only Gaye.

He sits on the edge of the bed. "Well, look at you," he says. "Quite a night, wasn't it?"

"How do you mean?"

"Drama off the stage as well as on. I mean, it's the sort of thing Shakespeare should have written, and might have written, though not for performance, of course. You know, soldier lovers divided by war. Like something out of Greek poetry."

"You're the classicist."

"I've always loved *The Tempest*." Gaye takes what appears to be a file out of his pocket. "And Bliss made a perfectly serviceable Caliban, don't you think? Not brilliant but . . . serviceable."

"Are you filing your nails?"

"Do a dead man's nails grow? I'm sure you remember what I always used to say, you have to see Shakespeare performed to really grasp him. And what poetry! Listen." He puts his hand to his diaphragm. " 'And then I lov'd thee, and show'd thee all the qualities o' th' isle . . .' Much like you've shown your Indian friend the qualities of the isle, Harold. 'The fresh springs, brine-pits, barren places, and fertile . . .' And then at the end, the brutal envoi: 'Cursed be I that did so!' It undoes everything that comes before. Because what Caliban recognizes is that he has loved, which is noble, but because he's loved, he's lost the thing that matters most to him. 'Cursed be I that did so!' "

Hardy almost sits up. He almost starts to argue. But he knows Gaye won't be there to hear him.

Just like him to leave him like that, the words hanging, and no opportunity, ever, to reply.

3

END OF AUGUST. Not far from the Nevilles' house, the Third Battalion of the Rifle Brigade (Irish) has encamped on Midsummer Common. At seven Alice wakes to the sound of their training exercises, the officer in charge shouting out his orders in a brogue. Eric is already gone, at his study in the college. She breakfasts with Ethel, who shows her a postcard that her son has sent her from Woolwich Arsenal. He is in the Territorials. All morning long, Ethel bangs pots in the kitchen, while Alice sits by the dining room window, looking out at the soldiers, waiting—for what? For the world to end? For Ramanujan to visit?

He arrives just after eleven. Unannounced. When she hears the knock at the door, she composes herself on the piano bench and waits for Ethel to bring him in. She doesn't want him to see how glad she is to see him, or how glad she is that Eric is away. The jigsaw puzzle sits where he left it. Much to Ethel's annoyance (and Eric's amusement) she will not hear of it being dismantled. She serves him coffee—she has taught Ethel to boil the milk in the Madrasi way—and then they sit together at the piano. She teaches him songs. She is teaching him "Greensleeves."

> Your vows you've broken, like my heart,
> Oh, why do you so enrapture me?

There is a sudden report of rifle fire—the soldiers practicing in the Common. "Why must they always do that when I'm playing?" Alice asks crossly. "All right, let's begin again."

> Your vows you've broken, like my heart,
> Oh, why do you so enrapture me?
> Now I remain in a world apart
> But my heart remains in captivity.

Whom does he see when he sings these words? Janaki? Each time he visits, she asks if he has heard from his wife, and each time, he says no. At first he claimed not to be troubled by this. "I'm sure," he'd said, "that I shall have a letter next week." Then, when no letter came, he'd said, "No doubt the war is interfering with the delivery of the post." But letters keep arriving from his mother.

More rifle fire. And no letter. "It's probably nothing," Alice says. "Perhaps she's gone to visit her family."

"She would have told me."

"Well, does your mother mention her in her letters?"

"No."

"Could you ask your mother?"

"It would not be . . . No, I could not."

He rests his elbow on the wooden lip of the piano—delicately, so that it doesn't touch the keys. Then he rests his head on his hand. And how she longs to stroke his black hair! But she would no sooner touch him than admit to the surge of hope, even joy, that she feels each time he tells her that he has still not heard from Janaki. For if Janaki has, in fact, left him, or moved away, or died, then he will need her more than ever. And if he needs her, he will come more often; perhaps even move back into the house.

After he has gone, she unpins her hair. She brushes it. She looks at herself in the mirror. "You are a terrible woman," she says, and feels it as true. She has been thinking terrible thoughts. For example, she has been thinking: what a pity that Eric has such weak eyesight! For if Eric had normal eyesight, he might enlist and go to France. Then strangers would treat her with great kindness, knowing that she had a husband fighting in France. She would be alone in the house. She could be alone with Ramanujan.

It is not exactly that she is in love with him. Or at least, she is not in love with him the way she was (or is) in love with Eric. For Eric's appeal is his familiarity. From the start, he attracted her precisely *because* he was so simple to know. He was the proverbial open book, the sentences written out in the large, legible print of a child's primer. In this regard he could not have differed more from her sister Jane, a creature of strata and stratagems, whose words were often fishing lures or traps. Eric, by contrast, was incapable of subterfuge. Bespectacled and virginal and perennially cheerful, he lived for his work—the prospect of returning to

it in the morning was enough to keep him awake much of the night—
and for lovemaking, at which he is clumsy. Still, he tries. Now he is
slower than he was. He waits for her. For all her exasperation, she
cannot help but be touched by his grunts of pleasure and the gratitude
afterward. Oddly, it is those aspects of her husband's character that she
finds most irritating—his absentmindedness and his thickheadedness—
that evoke in her the greatest tenderness.

And then there is Ramanujan. With Ramanujan, nothing, or next to
nothing, is straightforward. Far from a child's primer, he is a text
written in a language she does not know how to read. Even when he is
in her presence, even when he sits physically by her side, she cannot
guess his thoughts. Eric's thoughts she can guess easily, and she's
almost always right. Ramanujan, on the other hand, she sees as a
closed door behind which lie untold treasures. Things she cannot guess
at. Mysterious Eastern lovemaking techniques, and occult lore, and a
certain ancient wisdom. No specifics are available to her, only the
vague sense of an atmosphere very different from that of her living
room: a tent draped in spice-colored fabrics from which bits of mirror
wink, scented by jasmine petals drying in a silver bowl.

Her life, she sometimes feels, has been reduced to alternating
anticipation and anxiety. Mornings she frets as to whether he will
come. If he does not come, she lapses into despair. If he does, she
begins to worry, almost from the instant of his stepping through the
door, about what she will do once he leaves. And once he does leave,
the dread closes in like dusk in winter.

The next morning she wakes, as always, to the voice of the battalion
commander, and finds that she can bear it no longer. Not the waiting,
not the rifle reports. Without telling anyone, not even Ethel, she
gathers her umbrella and hat, walks to the station, and boards the
first train to London. The platform is full of young men on their way
to join regiments. Only some are in uniform. *Every day Cambridge's
reservoir of youth empties a little more*, she thinks, as she sits down in
a compartment the other occupants of which are three of these young
men, one in dusky khaki, the other two in Norfolk jackets. The ones in
Norfolk jackets discuss the latest news from Belgium in animated
voices, as if war was a football match, while the one in khaki gazes
listlessly out the window.

Not wanting to call attention to herself, Alice opens her handbag and takes out a copy of the *Times*. "Nearly all the persons I interrogated," she reads, "had stories to tell of German atrocities. Whole villages, they said, had been put to fire and sword. One man whom I did not see told an official of the Catholic Society that he had seen with his own eyes German soldiery chop off the arms of a baby which clung to its mother's skirts."

With a wheeze, the train moves out of the station. Alice puts her paper down; watches the tracks give way to another train going the opposite direction, and then the backs of mean houses. In one of them a child is staring at an iris. The listless young man takes a book from his satchel: *The War of the Worlds*. One of Eric's favorites. And what *will* happen if Germany invades England? Will this young man protect her? Will she be raped by the Huns? Will they bayonet poor Ramanujan? She shouldn't be asking such questions, she knows. She is a pacifist, after all. And these boys—they could be Eric's students, the ones he sometimes brings home for tea and differential geometry.

She resumes her reading:

All the men with whom I talked were agreed that, apart from their heavy guns and overwhelming numbers, there was nothing about the German soldiers which need be feared. They describe the behaviour of the enemy as too brutal for any civilized nation, and most of them had seen Belgian villagers drawn in front of the Germans to act as a screen for them. One man declared that a favourite trick of the Germans is to terrify Belgian villagers by driving them along immediately in front of their heavy guns, where, owing to the elevation of the guns, they are really quite safe. Their experience has been that the Germans have no respect for the Red Cross, and that in fact they wait until the wounded have been picked up, and then fire.

At Liverpool Street, she throws the paper in the dustbin. She catches a cab and rides to St. George's Square, to an address she looked up furtively in Eric's diary just before leaving. Not that she has any reason to assume that Gertrude will be there; still, she hopes so. She needs to talk to someone, to a woman.

Having paid the driver, she approaches the building. It is narrow, upright, one of a sequence of houses pushed somehow too close together, like books crammed onto a library shelf. The window trim needs new paint. One of the bells (bronze, needing to be polished) is marked "Hardy." She rings it, and is relieved when, a minute or so later, the door opens and Gertrude is standing before her, dressed in a rather dreary frock, blinking with surprise.

"Mrs. Neville," she says.

"Hello," Alice says. "I hope you don't mind my just showing up like this, I—I had to get out of Cambridge."

"But my brother's not here."

"I know. It's not your brother I want to see."

Gertrude does not appear especially happy to hear this. "Oh, well, come in," she says after a moment, making space in the constricted corridor. "I'm afraid I haven't much to offer you," she adds as they climb a narrow staircase, the treads of which creak under Alice's shoes.

"I wasn't expecting anything."

"Nor is the flat particularly tidy."

"Really, it doesn't matter."

They go in together. Gertrude shuts the door, then leads Alice through a sitting room that is musty and nearly empty of furniture into a kitchen with a pebbled brown linoleum floor and a table over which newspapers are spread. "Do sit down. Would you like some tea?"

"Thank you, yes." Alice takes off her hat. She cannot say why, but for some reason she feels immense in this room. It's not that it's so small, or that she's so large—it's just that whenever she moves, she knocks into something. First her elbow upsets the dish rack. Then her head hits the door frame. Then, as she's pulling the chair Gertrude has indicated out from under the table, she shoves it accidentally into the wall.

"Oh dear," she says. "I hope it won't leave a mark."

"It doesn't matter. Do you take milk?"

She shouldn't have come.

"Yes, please." Gertrude's copy of the *Times* is, as it happens, open to the article about the Belgian atrocities. "Did you read this yet?" Alice asks.

"Yes, just now."

"I wonder if the stories are to be believed—if German soldiers really are chopping the hands off of babies."

"I can well believe it, coming from the nation that gave us *Struwwelpeter*."

"Who?"

"Slovenly Peter. It's a book of German children's stories. And in one of them there's a little boy who sucks his thumbs, and his mother warns him that if he keeps sucking them, the great tall tailor will come and cut them off with his great sharp scissors, and he keeps sucking them, and lo and behold, the great tall tailor does come and he does cut off his thumbs."

"How gruesome."

"The illustrations are quite fabulous, with vivid red blood spurting from the points of amputation."

"And this is given to children?"

"Well, why do you think it is that German soldiers never suck their thumbs?"

Gertrude places the cup of tea before Alice, sits down opposite her, crosses her arms. She looks impatient, suddenly, as if to say, all right, enough fun and games, why have you come to bother me? And why has Alice come to bother her?

"I suspect you're wondering what I'm doing here," she says. "The truth is, I'm not sure myself. Cambridge simply . . . feels rather sad right now."

"So my brother tells me."

"The train today was full of young men. Students. Every day Cambridge's reservoir of youth empties a little more."

No response. And Alice was proud of that line.

"A battalion is encamped across the street from our house. From Ireland. Each morning they go through their exercises, starting at dawn."

"And your husband?"

"He is getting on. At the college, the wounded are being bedded outdoors, in Nevile's Court. Officers dine in Hall."

"So my brother tells me."

"And will Mr. Hardy volunteer?"

"He says he hasn't decided, though it's hard to imagine him in uniform. What about Mr. Neville?"

"He has weak eyes." Alice sips her tea, then adds: "It's a pity, too, because he's very brave. He's a very strong swimmer. Last winter he jumped into the Cam and saved a child from drowning."

Why did she say that? No doubt Gertrude is well aware that, even if Eric's eyesight were perfect, he'd never volunteer. He makes no bones about his pacifism. And yet it seems suddenly urgent that Gertrude know he's not a coward. "The other night, Eric overheard someone saying, 'The way things are going, soon Trinity's going to be emptied out save for Hardy and a bunch of Indians.'"

"That seems rather an exaggeration."

"Perhaps . . . Still, wouldn't it be astonishing if in a few months time he and Mr. Ramanujan were all that was left of Trinity?"

"Your husband will be there too. And the Master."

"I know. I was exaggerating."

"And how is Mr. Ramanujan faring?"

"As well as can be expected, I suppose. Not that I see him very often these days."

"You mean, since he's no longer under your roof?"

"Of course he does come to visit a few times a week. I'm teaching him to sing."

"To sing?"

"He has a lovely voice. Yesterday I taught him 'Greensleeves.'"

"I should like to hear that."

"Of course, he's far too shy to sing in front of strangers—only me."

"It's good to know that he has found such a friend in you, Mrs. Neville."

Alice looks up. So far, she has managed to evade Gertrude's gaze. Now, however, she meets those alarming eyes. The right one is peering at her assessingly, while the left one . . . how to say it? It floats.

And suddenly, without even thinking to ask, she asks, "How did it happen?"

"What?"

"How did you lose your eye?"

Gertrude seems to rear up in her chair. Like a cat. Good. Ever since she's arrived, Alice has wanted to get the upper hand. To make Gertrude flinch. Good.

"I hope you don't mind my asking."

"Do you imagine you're the first to ask?"

"Well—"

"You're not. People ask all the time. Women especially."

To Alice's surprise, she uncrosses her arms.

"If you must know, it was when I was nine. Harold hit me in the face with a cricket bat. An accident. I was knocked out cold. And then, when I woke, I was in the hospital, and it was gone. The eye was gone. That's all."

"But that's terrible."

"I suppose so. I was so young I hardly remember what it was like—before. Of course, afterwards, the important thing was to protect Harold."

"Why?"

"Because it was an accident, wasn't it, and he was so terribly fond of cricket, he shouldn't be made to feel any sense of responsibility or guilt. And so I was told never to speak of it."

"By your father?"

"My mother."

"Did you mind?"

"Only at first. But then I realized that she was being quite sensible, really. You see, she was determined that no one be steered off course. Even then, we knew Harold was a genius. The last thing we wanted was that this should hinder his progress. And it helped me, too. Having to act, from the start, as if nothing had happened—it made it possible for me to make that my . . . modus operandi."

"Let me see it."

"What?"

"The eye. Take it out. Let me see it."

Gertrude laughs.

"Why is this funny?" Alice asks.

"Because everyone who's ever wanted to see it thinks she's the first to ask to see it."

"Is it always women?"

"Always. Anyway, happy to oblige. Only please look away while I take it out."

Alice looks away. She hears, or imagines she hears, a sort of unscrewing, a plop and a pop, and then Gertrude says, "All right. You may turn now."

Alice turns around. Gertrude has her back to her. She holds her right hand behind her back, the fingers curled around . . . something.

The thing is passed from Gertrude's palm into Alice's. Alice examines it. The eye is white and globular and heavier than she would have thought—the size of a large marble, with the iris and the lens slightly raised. And what a piece of craftsmanship it is, the brown a perfect match for Gertrude's real eye, the white etched with tiny red lines, to suggest veins!

"May I have it back now?"

"How does it work? How do you insert it?"

"You just pull back the lid and pop it in. The socket closes right around it."

"Is it uncomfortable?"

"It was a bit strange, at first. This alien immense *thing*. But one gets used to it. Now I hardly think about it. May I have it back now, please?"

"Does it dry out? Do you have to keep it lubricated?"

"The tear glands weren't affected. May I have it back now?"

Once again, Gertrude reaches her arm behind her back. Alice deposits the eye in her palm.

"Don't look."

Alice closes her own eyes. Then Gertrude says, "It's all right now," and when Alice looks again, Gertrude's face is across the table. An expression of warmth, even affection, seems to have suffused it.

"Well," she says. "Are you satisfied?"

"Quite, thank you."

"Good, I'm glad we got past that." She looks toward the kitchen window. "It's becoming a lovely day, isn't it? What would you say to going to the zoo?"

"The zoo?"

"Yes, why not?"

"I'd say it's a wonderful idea," Alice says. And she stands, in the process knocking her chair, once more, into the already bruised wall.

4

THERE IS A ROOM, a flat, a place they sometimes go when they're both in London. Usually at Littlewood's behest. Like C. Mallet of the India Office, the owner is a friend of his brother's. They stay there an hour or two and then, when they leave, Anne can't seem to get her underclothes adjusted. Because the flat is near Regent's Park, they walk to the zoo, where they sit on a bench in front of a cage inside which a Bengal tiger paces. It is the very end of September, and Littlewood has just told her that in a month he will be leaving, possibly going to France. He is joining the Royal Garrison Artillery as a Second Lieutenant. "Apparently I might be useful for gunnery calculations," he says. "Ballistics. Hardy will keel over when he hears."

"I wish you hadn't done it."

"I thought of not doing it. But then I thought, look, it's not like we're going to have much choice in the matter for long. Conscription's coming, I promise you. Churchill's already putting in for it."

"How do you know?"

"Hardy. Churchill's secretary is one of his Apostles."

Anne lights a cigarette. Across the pathway, the tiger lies down and licks its huge paw. Like Hardy's cat, only it gives off a muskier smell. What Littlewood thinks impatience must smell like. And now a child approaches with her nurse to gaze at the tiger. She clings to the nurse's hand. Keeping a safe distance.

"When will we see each other?"

"With any luck I'll be in London in a few months. Or nearby. Woolwich, probably."

"But will you be able to get down to Treen?"

"Not as often as I do now, I'm afraid."

She takes his hand. She is holding back tears. Suddenly the tiger bounds up, giving an ill-tempered roar, which frightens the child, who starts to cry. The nurse leads her away, toward the elephants.

"What will become of you?" Anne asks, weeping.

"Darling, there's no need for this. I'll be fine."

"But what if they send you into battle? I've read the reports."

"But that's the whole point, they won't send me into battle. They don't send men like me into battle. We're too valuable behind the scenes."

"I'm sorry." She takes a handkerchief from her handbag; wipes her eyes. "I feel so foolish. Maybe it's the children. They ask, you know. This is just—it's so awful. I can't believe I have to explain this to my children."

"I'm so sorry that you have to."

"And in the meantime, Hardy just goes about his business . . . I see *he* hasn't felt duty bound to volunteer."

"He may volunteer still. I know he's thinking about it."

"Then why can't you do as he does? Wait?"

"Because if I put it off, I may not get such a safe position."

"But with all his connections, couldn't Hardy make sure you did?"

"His influence doesn't extend that far, I'm afraid. I'm not part of that circle. He can protect himself, probably."

"And he says he can't work without you!"

"Don't blame him."

"Why not? I have to blame somebody."

"Blame Kitchener, then. Blame Churchill. You've never even met Hardy."

"Only because you never—"

"Ssh. That's his sister."

Anne looks up. Two women are strolling down the path, toward the tiger's cage.

Without thinking she pulls her hand out of Littlewood's. He stands. "Miss Hardy, Mrs. Neville. What a lovely surprise."

Gertrude gives Anne an assessing glance. "Hello, Mr. Littlewood," she says. "And what brings you to the zoo?"

"Simply—a lovely afternoon. And you?"

"It's a little ritual of ours," Alice says. "Whenever I happen to be in London."

"Oh, may I introduce Mrs. Chase?"

Anne gets up too now. She has to shake Gertrude's hand with her left hand, because the handkerchief is balled up in the right.

"And may I offer you ladies some tea?" Littlewood asks, ever the gallant, ever able to adjust to what confronts him.

"Oh no," Alice says. "We wouldn't want to interrupt."

"You're not interrupting."

"Well, if you're sure . . ."

"No, we must be going," Gertrude says firmly, and takes Alice by the arm. "A pleasure to see you, Mr. Littlewood. And a pleasure to meet you, Mrs . . ."

"Chase."

"Chase. Good day."

They move on. A few feet along the path they stop before the elephants, at which they peer with academic earnestness. They don't seem to be talking.

He and Anne sit down again, and all at once Anne begins to laugh. She laughs so hard she has to wipe her eyes again.

"What on earth's the matter now?"

"It's nothing, it just seems so funny . . . Well, I mean, who cares anymore? If they guess everything."

"I hate to tell you, darling, but we're hardly a state secret."

"I know. That's why I'm laughing."

"Why didn't you want to stop for tea?"

"Because they were obviously having a row. Or something."

"But who is she?"

"Can't you see?"

"Oh! . . . But he introduced her as *Mrs*. Chase."

"Well, how do you expect Russell would introduce Ottoline Morrell?"

They are approaching the bat house. Gertrude's expression is one of wicked amusement, but for Alice, it's as if a new idea has entered the world. Russell and Mrs. Morrell. Littlewood and Mrs. Chase.

Well, why not?

She resolves, then, that she will meet Mrs. Chase again. She will seek her out. That woman with the brown hair and the sun-darkened skin and that look of—well—radiance, Alice would call it—even in tears, a kind of radiance—this is a woman she can talk to. This is the kind of woman she might, if she's lucky, end up learning how to be.

5

New Lecture Hall, Harvard University

IN THAT LECTURE he did not give, Hardy said:

There is, I believe, an unfortunate tendency today—one, I suspect, that will only intensify as the years pass—to portray Ramanujan as one of those mystic vessels into which the inscrutable East has poured its essence. This isn't surprising. Here we have, after all, a young man who never wore shoes until he boarded a ship for England; who would not eat the food in Hall for fear of contamination; who claimed publicly that the formulae he discovered were written on his tongue by a female deity. Nor did he discourage this myth of himself—on the contrary, he did much to enhance it—which is why, for those who did not know him, his legacy will always carry the scent of incense and temples. And yet, for those of us who did know him, how do we explain that the myth has nothing to do with the man we knew?

The Ramanujan I knew was, above all else, a rationalist. Despite his occasional eccentricities of behavior, in my company he was never less than sane, reasonable, and shrewd. By temperament he was an agnostic, by which I mean that he saw no particular good and no particular harm in Hinduism or any other religion. As he told us that afternoon when we went to watch *The Tempest* in Leintwardine, all religions were for him more or less equally true. In Hinduism, as I understand it, observance matters far more than belief. Belief, as a concept, belongs to Christianity. It is part of Christianity's pernicious effort to enslave its disciples by holding before them the bejeweled dream of a new Jerusalem, a reward to be paid out in recompense for a life of piety. Nor is it sufficient to go through the motions. The Christian must accept in his heart that God is real if he expects to reach heaven.

The Hindu's fate in the afterlife, on the other hand, hinges entirely on how he behaves. If he heeds the rules, he will be reincarnated as a member of higher caste. If he breaks the rules, he will return as a beetle or an untouchable or a weed or some such thing. It does not matter what he believes. And so when the Hindu adheres to certain prohibitions and strictures for the sake of propriety and decorum, rather than because he accepts the doctrines of his religion as literally true, he is not acting as a hypocrite in the way, say, that I would be if I were to attend chapel, or participate in a mass, or thank the Lord for my supper.

I can guess how Mrs. Neville would react to this statement. She would say, "Well, Hardy, if that's the case, then why didn't he just eat meat? Especially once the war started, when it became so difficult to obtain supplies from India, why did he elect to ruin his health rather than violate his religion's dietary proscriptions? It *must* have been because he believed."

No, Mrs. Neville, it was not because he believed. He remained vegetarian, first of all, because vegetarianism was second nature to him. He had never in his life eaten meat and found the idea of doing so repellent. Also he worried that, if word got back to his mother that he was adopting Western ways, she would make things very difficult for him when he returned to Madras. For Komalatammal, as she was called, was hardly the devout and devoted figure whom her son's Indian admirers have portrayed. This must be put on the table once and for all. On the contrary, she was what my old bedmaker, Mrs. Bixby, would have called a "right piece of work." She was clever, possessive, and exploitative. It would not surprise me to learn that she employed other Indian students in Cambridge as spies in order to insure that her son did not stray from the path of righteousness. She might also have hounded him, or threatened to hound him, through occult means.

An admirer of Ramanujan's recently sent me her picture. In it, a very short woman sits in a very tall chair, so tall that her bare feet barely touch the ground. She has a low, mean face, not stupid in the way, say, that a sheep's face is stupid: no, in this face there is the gleam of a primitive intelligence. She stares boldly into the camera as if to challenge its potency, or mesmerize the viewer, by drawing him into the black dot painted between her eyes. No, it is not a picture that I can look at for long.

Let me give a brief account of her life. She came from a poor but cultured Brahmin family. Her father was some sort of petty court official and, as is the usual thing in India, her parents arranged her marriage for her. From what I have gathered, for the first few years after she was married she could not get pregnant, and so her father and grandparents decided to intercede by praying to the goddess Namagiri. Reportedly the grandmother already had an established relationship with Namagiri, occasionally going into trances during which the goddess would speak through her, and on one of these occasions she had announced that if Komalatammal bore a son, she would speak through him, too. So they got on their knees and prayed to the goddess to grant Komalatammal fertility and, lo and behold, nine months later she gave birth to a boy.

From then on, whenever she spoke of her son's conception, Komalatammal invoked the name of the goddess. She never mentioned her husband, Kuppuswamy, even though he must have had something to do with the business. Nor did Kuppuswamy protest. From what I have been told, he was a meek, ineffectual person, who recognized early on the advantages of keeping out of his wife's ferocious path. For Komalatammal was nothing if not ambitious. Early on, it is said, she read her son's horoscope and deduced from it that he would either become famous all over the world and die young or remain obscure and live to a ripe old age. Reputedly she was quite proficient at matters both astrological and numerological. She must have decided that if there was a chance that he was going to die young, she should take advantage of his talents while she could. Accordingly, from the moment when he first showed signs of mathematical precocity, from when he was three or four, she enlisted his assistance in the various numerological manipulations in which she indulged toward the end of interpreting her own future and insuring that harm should come to her enemies. With the father simpering in the background, mother and son labored together, their bond in many ways more intimate than that of husband and wife.

Not surprisingly, Komalatammal also professed to be a skilled interpreter of dreams, and to have passed on this skill to her son, who later claimed proficiency at it. I have no doubt that the latter part of this statement, that Ramanujan *claimed* proficiency at the skill, is entirely true. For it would have been just like him to pretend to possess psychical capacities if by doing so he could secure his social footing or assist a friend. Nearly all so-called prophecy, after all, is mere inductive reasoning dressed up in gypsy scarves.

Two examples, taken from letters sent to me by Ramanujan's Indian acquaintances, will suffice.

In the first, Mr. M. Anantharaman writes to say that once, in the Kumbakonam of their childhood, his older brother described a dream he had had to Ramanujan. Ramanujan then interpreted the dream to mean that there would soon be a death in the street behind their house—and, lo and behold, a few days thereafter, an old lady who lived in that street died.

Let us look at the case closely. Ramanujan had lived in Kumbakonam nearly all his life. He would have known most of the townspeople, and, through his mother, been up to date on their financial misfortunes, the conditions of their marriages, and the various ailments from which they suffered. Imagine, then, that Ramanujan's mother informs him one day that old lady X, who lives in the street behind the brothers Anantharaman, is at death's door. The next day he is asked to interpret a dream. It would require no psychic talent to foresee—and announce—this old lady's imminent demise.

The second example comes from Mr. K. Narasimha Iyengar, who also hails from Kumbakonam and, for a time, shared lodgings with Ramanujan in Madras. In his letter, this gentleman describes preparing for an examination at Madras Christian College, the mathematics portion of which he feared he would fail. As he recalls, on the day of the examination, Ramanujan "instinctively felt" that they should meet, and, when they did, provided him with "prophetic tips" as a result of which he was able to pass the mathematics exam with the required minimum score of 35 percent. Without Ramanujan's intervention, Mr. Iyengar says, he would have failed.

This is, of course, a more subtle case. What Mr. Iyengar is implying is that the "tips" for the exam were provided to Ramanujan by an outside force. Perhaps they were written on his tongue. In fact, though, as a mathematician and a longtime victim of the Indian educational system, Ramanujan would have known exactly what types of problems Mr. Iyengar was likely to encounter on such an exam. By explaining these problems patiently, and then crediting his insight to spiritual intervention, he was able to reduce the youth's anxiety and instill in him the confidence he needed to score better. For he was above all else—and this is often forgotten—a kindly man.

I offer these examples because I want to emphasize that Ramanujan, though he may have acted the role of the devout Hindu, and even claimed supernatural capacities, was in fact not remotely susceptible to the vagaries of the so-called religious sentiment. He was, instead, at heart and soul a rationalist. This may sound like an oxymoron. In my view it describes him perfectly. If, on occasion, he practiced economies of truth, he did so because he had weighed the pros and the cons and concluded that in certain cases it was necessary, if not to lie, then to allow certain false impressions to linger. For instance, you will recall that, when it came to traveling to Europe, a very convenient "dream" made it possible for him to sidestep the Brahminic injunction against crossing the ocean. His mother had this dream. She, too, I suspect, is far from the reverent creature she has been portrayed as being. On the contrary, she understood the advantage to herself of his going to England, and, just as she had exploited his talents in his childhood by compelling him to assist her in her numerological enterprises, she tried to leech from him not just a certain measure of fame, as the saintly mother of the "Hindoo calculator," but, after his death, a certain quantity of cash.

Yes, Mrs. Neville, I hear you. You protest. I am judging the poor woman too harshly. She sacrificed much for her son, labored hard to pay for his schooling and to care for him, never wavered in her faith in his genius even when all doors were shut in his face. All of this is true. And still she was a grasping, self-interested woman.

Nowhere is this more evident than in her dealings with his child-bride, Janaki.

Of Janaki herself, I have an uncertain impression. Ramanujan seemed to feel very fondly toward her. He called her "my house." When, after a long time in Cambridge, he still had not received a single letter from her, he told Chatterjee, the cricketer, "My house has not written to me." "Houses don't wrote," Chatterjee replied cheerfully—perhaps an ungentle witticism, for in fact the failure of the expected letters to arrive was a source of great pain to Ramanujan, though whether this was because he missed the girl, or feared that his mother had killed her, I cannot say. According to Mr. Anantharaman, Ramanujan knew "no conjugal happiness" with Janaki, as she was, in his words, "most unfortunate." Yet Mr. Anantharaman also reminds me that shortly before his marriage, Ramanujan was operated on for a hydrocele—a swelling of the scrotum due to the build-up of serous fluids—after which he was unable to engage in sexual activity for more than a year. Other sources imply that Komalatammal refused to let the couple sleep together, using the hydrocele as an excuse. Probably she wanted Ramanujan all to herself. I cannot tell you whether Ramanujan regarded this enforced abstinence, whatever its cause, as a curse or a blessing.

In any case, he must have been pretty well able to guess what was going on at home. Even under the best of circumstances, the Indian mother-in-law is a tyrant, given leave by convention to berate and even beat her poor daughter-in-law, to force her to do any number of unpleasant chores, and to dispense punishment freely. In turn, the daughter-in-law is expected to treat her mother-in-law with reverence, to simper before her and accept whatever abuse she inflicts without protest. Vengeance, she knows, will come later, when she has her own son and *he* marries and she has the chance to perpetrate upon *her* daughter-in-law the same cruelties to which she was subjected. Thus the cycle continues, generation to generation, in pretty much every Indian household. And when you consider the circumstances—Komalatammal's volatility; the absence of the mediating son and husband; the daughter-in-law's youth and defiant nature— well, you can imagine what a powder keg that house in Kumbakonam must have been.

I am sure Ramanujan divined it all: the vituperative asides, the coarse saris, the slop pails. Poor Kuppuswamy, now nearly blind, spent most of his time trying to keep out of the way of the flying pots. And, the whole time,—this is the great irony—the poor girl *was* writing letters to her husband—long, lamenting letters, begging him to arrange for her to come to England, if for no other reason than so she could escape her mother-in-law's despotism; only Komalatammal would intercept the letters and destroy them before they were sent. Just as she intercepted Ramanujan's letters to his wife before Janaki could get hold of them. Once Janaki tried to sneak a note into a package of foodstuffs being sent to Ramanujan, but Komalatammal fished it out before the package went. You can imagine the heat Janaki must have got then.

It was an intolerable situation—and Ramanujan, even from a great distance, felt its repercussions. Later, his mother let it drop that her resentment toward Janaki owed to certain peculiarities in the girl's horoscope that her family had deliberately camouflaged before the wedding. Apparently the horoscope, when properly read, revealed that marriage to Janaki would hasten Ramanujan's death. Her parents, knowing this would imperil the chances of their none-too-desirable daughter finding a husband, resorted to fraud in order to be rid of her. Though, as it happened, they weren't rid of her for long.

I wish that, at the time, I had understood as clearly what he was suffering as I do now. By means of the same powerful intuition that, in earlier days, he had passed off as a gift for prophesy, he must have "seen" the horrifying scenes in Kumbakonam. Yet he could do nothing. Due to the U-boat attacks, he could not go home. And in the meantime, in the absence of letters, he tried to read the silence. This is a dangerous undertaking in the best of circumstances. I know, having often tried it myself. When those you long to hear from do not or cannot speak, you speak "for" them, just as, in the days of our youth, Gaye used to speak "for" the cat, saying things like, "I'm not feeling very well," or, "Hardy, you're cruel, you won't rub my tummy." In the same manner, Ramanujan must have spoken "for" Janaki, and in turn replied to this Janaki who, for all we know, bore not the slightest resemblance to the girl he had left behind in India.

And this was only one of his many troubles. The war frightened him, as it did all of us. The foods he craved, in particular the fresh vegetables that were a staple of his diet, were becoming increasingly hard to obtain. And then English customs, he told me, seemed very strange to him. There's no nice way to say this: he thought us dirty. Once, for instance, we overheard a woman at a tea shop complaining that if the members of the working classes smelled, it was because they bathed just once a week. "If only they would bathe, as we do, once a day!" this woman said. Ramanujan looked at me in alarm. "Do you mean to say you only bathe once a day?" he asked.

Our ablutionary habits were not the only ones that puzzled him. Why, he asked me, did children not stay with their parents after they married? Did they not love their parents? Would they not be lonely? I answered that the English valued independence, and this concept, too, he found strange. Used to sleeping anywhere at all, in a small house shared with many people, he even found it strange to have his own room.

Autumn drew to a close, and the weather started getting cold, colder than anything he had ever known. This is perhaps the aspect of his English experience that I am least able to imagine—I, who from early childhood became habituated to the vagaries of winter: numb fingers, chapped lips, the struggle to compel the blanket to exert a few extra degrees of warmth. Clothes, which he had always looked upon purely as a kind of decoration, a way of embellishing the body while protecting his modesty, he now had to use, for the first time, as layers of defense against the encroachments of winter. Not only did he have to contend with the terrible, pinching shoes, but with gloves, scarves, galoshes, greatcoats, hats. Rain he knew from the monsoons—but warm rain, leaving steam and moisture in its wake. Here, on the contrary, even the brief walk to New Court could be a struggle with wind gusts that threw sheets of sleet and hail into his eyes, and broke the spine of the umbrella I'd given him. Bathing was an ordeal. No wonder the English were, from his point of view, so filthy! For who could endure more than one bath a day when the temperature in the bathroom was below freezing?

When he got to my rooms in the morning, I would watch him unwrap himself and then give him coffee, which he drank gratefully and in quantity. I toasted crumpets for him over the fire. Still, he never seemed to be able to get warm enough. I myself thrived in cold weather; the morning found me bright and vigorous, my cheeks red from a brisk walk. Ramanujan, on the other hand, would be pallid. He wasn't sleeping well, he told me. Perhaps I should have taken this as a warning sign; and yet there was so much to distract the attention in those days of war!

Inattention: the schoolboy's perpetual excuse. I was looking at something else. The other boy hit me first, I wasn't listening, sir. What right have I to resort to it now when I would never accept it from a student?

No, what I am offering is *not* an excuse. It is a confession.

PART FIVE

A Terrible Dreaming

I

B Y SEPTEMBER, Trinity is a different world. Whewell's
Court is a barracks. When he goes to meet Hardy each
morning, Ramanujan must navigate bunks and tents and a
mess. Nevile's Court is an open-air hospital. Wounded soldiers, their
faces and limbs bandaged and bloodied, lie in neat rows on metal
frame beds under the arcades of the Wren Library. Across the way,
lights have been strung from the ceiling of the south cloister, which has
been made into an operating theater.

To the extent that he can, Hardy stays in his rooms. Soldiers
parade everywhere. In Great Court, Butler preaches to the troops,
warning them to resist French temptresses. Colonels and captains in
khaki dine at high table, toasting with champagne if the next
morning one of their fellows is to be shipped off. This spectacle
is so distasteful to Hardy that he starts eating alone in his rooms.
Eggs and toast. The food of his childhood. When he does go out, he
finds himself strangely drawn to the library arcade, to the soldiers
who were running fresh not a month earlier. Now dozens of them
arrive every day, feverish from infected wounds, suffering from
lockjaw, typhoid, spotted fever. As he passes, they ask him for
cigarettes, which he provides, much to the chagrin of the sisters. The
sisters don't like to see their patients smoking.

Few others are around, which leaves Hardy feeling a certain sadness
that he recalls from his childhood, a sadness associated with the
September days before school began, each one shorter than the last,
during which it seemed that everyone in the world except him had
something to do, somewhere to be. Now, when he walks the river, he
never runs into anybody. Littlewood is gone, a second lieutenant in the
Royal Garrison Artillery. Keynes is at the Treasury. Russell is off
speechifying against the war. Rupert Brooke, thanks to Eddie Marsh's

intervention, has got himself a commission in Churchill's Royal Naval Division. Békássy is in Hungary, Wittgenstein in Austria. It doesn't matter that they're fighting on the other side. What matters is that each is defending his fatherland, and, in doing so, taking part in some exalted, immemorial rite of manhood. Or so Norton explains it. Norton makes it his business to explain things. He makes it his business to understand.

One weekend he arrives back at Trinity from London. He carries, or so it seems to Hardy, the redolence of Bloomsbury, its cloistered, bookish gloom. He asks Hardy what he's planning to do should conscription come, and Hardy replies, "I suppose I'll go to war."

"You mean you won't be a conscientious objector?"

"I disapprove of conscientious objectors as a class," Hardy says, by which he means that he disapproves of Norton as a class; of Bloomsbury as a class; of the image he has conjured up, of Strachey and Norton and Virginia Stephen (now Woolf) sitting in their London libraries, gazing out at the rain and muttering, "Oh, the horror!" Strachey, Norton tells him, won't talk about the war. He spends his evenings reading books that take him as far from the war as he can get. Right now, for instance, he's reading *Memoirs of the Lady Hester Stanhope*. And why does the idea of Strachey sitting up in bed, no doubt in a nightcap, with *Memoirs of the Lady Hester Stanhope* open on his lap, fill Hardy with such distaste? He's no better, really. His cloister is New Court. And instead of Lady Hester Stanhope, he's rereading *The Portrait of a Lady*.

As for Norton—well, if there's evidence of the degree to which he's muffled himself, it's that he fails entirely to pick up on Hardy's insult, and says simply that *he* will certainly declare himself a conscientious objector should the necessity arise—not, Hardy senses, out of conscience but simply to protect himself. And how is Hardy supposed to respond to that? It seems to him that every day he and his old friend have less to say to each other, even though they still sleep together now and then.

What preoccupies him most is this question of what he should call himself. Is he a pacifist? Certainly his disapproval of this shameful war is as absolute as Russell's. And yet he can't claim that he disapproves of *all* war. He would fight a just war. So the question is: has this war, despite its beginnings, now *become* a just war? The wounded soldiers, when he sits with them, cannot stop speaking of the atrocities in Louvain, the sacking and burning of houses, shops, farms, and, worst of all, the library, the famous library, as celebrated for its collection of rare and precious books as the one in the shadows of which they now lie. It's curious: few of these men are educated. Most, Hardy imagines, don't read at all. Yet the sacking of the library seems to have shaken them to the marrow. "To burn a library to the ground," Hardy tells Moore, with whom he now strolls the arcades of Nevile's Court as once they strolled the meadows of Grantchester . . . But he can't finish the sentence. Who could finish such a sentence? Among the books burned there must have been German books, books by Goethe and Novalis and Fichte. And who burned them? The countrymen of Goethe and Novalis and Fichte.

The trick is to try to maintain some sense of balance, and in this regard, writing letters helps.

To Russell, who is giving a lecture tour in Wales, he writes: "How is it possible that England hungers to crush and humiliate Germany? What is wanted is peace on fair terms."

To Littlewood, with whom he tries to keep collaborating after a fashion, he writes: "It is proving harder than I suspected to teach him. His mind is like Isabel Archer's, it keeps jumping out the window. I can never keep him on any one topic for long."

To Gertrude, whom he can see far less often now than before, he writes: "Please tell Mother not to worry. In all likelihood, if called up, I should be rejected on medical grounds—*entre nous*, I hope not, but don't tell her that."

Ramanujan, too, is writing letters. He writes to both his parents. "There is no war in this country," he tells his mother. "War is going on only in the neighboring country. That is to say, war is waged in a country that is as far as Rangoon is away from Madras. Lakhs of persons have come here from our country to join the forces. Seven hundred Rajas have come here from our country to wage war. The present war affects crores of people. The small country Belgium is almost destroyed. Each town has buildings fifty to a hundred times more valuable than those in Madras city."

His letter to his father is much shorter. "I have all the pickles," he writes. "You need not send anything more. Except what you are sending now, do not send any other thing. I am getting on well. Do not allow the gutter to run as usual. Pave the place with bricks. I am getting on well."

2

THAT AUTUMN, Ramanujan begins to publish. The *Quarterly Journal of Mathematics* brings out his "Modular equations and approximations to π." To celebrate, Hardy takes him to a pub, where he refuses to drink anything. He tells Hardy that he's at work on a big paper on highly composite numbers. His equation is ingenious, and distinctly Ramanujanian (an adjective that Hardy has no doubt will soon be in circulation). It looks like this:

$$n = 2^{a_2} \times 3^{a_3} \times 5^{a_5} \times 7^{a_7} \times \ldots p^{a_p}$$

where n is the highly composite number and $a_2, a_3, a_5 \ldots a_p$ are the powers to which the successive primes need to be raised so that the number can be written out as a multiple of primes. Thus, if we are dealing with the highly composite number 60, we can write it out as

$$60 = 2^2 \times 3^1 \times 5^1$$

Here $a_2 = 2$, $a_3 = 1$, and $a_5 = 1$. If we are dealing with the largest highly composite number that Ramanujan has found, 6746328388800 (he writes it out on a torn piece of newspaper; he has not lost his Indian habit of hoarding scraps of paper), we would write

$$6746328388800 = 2^6 \times 3^4 \times 5^2 \times 7^2 \times 11 \times 13 \times 17 \times 19 \times 23.$$

What Ramanujan has managed to prove is that, for any highly composite number, a_2 is always going to be bigger than or equal to a_3, a_3 is always going to be bigger than or equal to a_5, and so on.

15

And for every highly composite number—an infinity of highly composite numbers—the last factor is always going to be 1, with two exceptions: 4 and 36. In many ways it's the exceptions that intrigue Hardy the most, in that they reveal, once again, how notoriously resistant numbers are to the ordering impulse that, by their very nature, they invoke. Whenever you seem to be getting close to seeing the whole in all its lovely symmetry—the palace emerging from the autumn mist, with all its stately storeys, as Russell once put it—mathematics throws you a ball you can't hit. This is why, despite all the evidence to the contrary, Hardy won't accept the truth of the Riemann hypothesis without a proof. The numbers 4 and 36 come early on. But with the zeta function, the exceptions could come at lengths so remote from the human capacity to count that Hardy can barely conceive them. As Ramanujan has learned the hard way—as every mathematician has learned the hard way—the world of numbers brooks neither compromise nor shortcut. You cannot cheat there. You will always be caught out.

In any case, no one he has ever met seems to know the numbers as intimately as Ramanujan does. "It's as if each of the integers is one of his personal friends," Littlewood said early on, a witticism that misses, in Hardy's view, the eroticism of working with numbers, the heat that rises off them, their vibrancy and unpredictability and, sometimes, danger. As an infant his mother gave him a set of numbered blocks, and then lamented that all he would do with them was hit them against one another, the 7 with the 1, the 3 with the 9. What she failed to recognize was his need, even then, to penetrate to the rumble of life within. Attractions and repulsions, euphonies and banshee screeches. Soon he had broken all of them except for the 7. All his life 7 has been his favorite number. Despite his atheism, he respects its mystic allure, just as he respects the less salubrious association carried by two other numbers that he refuses to speak, much less write down. It's not that he believes in the specific superstitions; it's that he's convinced that the numbers themselves give off vapors of malevolence. Other numbers that most people would consider perfectly benign he also despises: 38. And 404. And 852. Still others he loves. He loves nearly all the primes. He loves, for reasons that elude him, 32,671. And, now that Ramanujan has introduced him to them, he loves the highly composite numbers, and

...umbers, he loves 4 and 36 the most, ...ely Ramanujan's rule—4, and 36, and 9, the bridge between them; 9, which is 3^2. He crosses the bridge and steps into fields in which he knows Ramanujan has already tarried. So far as he can see, nothing edible grows here. They are sterile, or picked clean.

3

THE *TIMES* HAS made it official: half the men at Cambridge are gone to war. "Among the 50 percent of those left in residence," Hardy reads, "many are foreigners and Orientals, and many of the others are beneath the age limit or have been rejected by the doctors on account of physical defects."

So where does that leave him?

The *Times* also tells him the university has halted organized athletics for the present: "there are no men, there is no mind for the river and the playing-fields." Well, he's tempted to write, there's at least one man who has a mind for cricket—indeed, for one man at least, the prospect of a spring without cricket is almost unbearable to contemplate. But this letter, even though he copies it out, he never sends.

Everywhere he goes, he sees Indians. They never take off their gowns and mortarboards, perhaps to insure that no one question their presence here. Under the best of circumstances they would be nervous. Now the war seems only to have amplified their self-consciousness. One afternoon, for instance, as he's walking through the Corn Exchange, he watches a gust of wind yank the mortarboard off the head of an Indian youth in King's College robes. With amusement and pity, he observes the comic turn of the youth chasing the mortarboard and bending to retrieve it, only to see it dashed off once again— playfully, cruelly—by the wind. Finally the mortarboard lands at Hardy's feet. He rescues it, dusts it off, and hands it to the Indian, who is out of breath from running. The Indian thanks him, then hurries in the opposite direction.

A few minutes later, Hardy sees him again, gathered at the corner of Trinity Street and Bridge Street with three of his countrymen. One is Chatterjee, the handsome cricketer with whom (it seems an eon ago) he conflated Ramanujan. The second is tall and stooped and wears spectacles and a turban. The third is Ramanujan himself. He waggles his head at Hardy. And what is Hardy supposed to do in response? Wave? Walk over and say hello? He chooses, on this occasion, just to wave.

The next morning, he asks Ramanujan who he was with. "Chatterjee," Ramanujan says. "He is from Calcutta. And Mahalanobis— he is also from Calcutta, studying natural sciences at King's—and Ananda Rao."

"Oh yes," Hardy says. "Isn't he the one who was coming to England on an Austrian ship? As I recall, you were worried he might not make it."

"He had quite an adventure. By the time he and Sankara Rao reached Port Said, the war had begun. Near Crete an English ship started firing on them and ordered them to stop. Luckily their ship carried no guns. If the ship had carried guns, and the sailors had shot back, they would have been sunk."

"What happened after that?"

"Everyone was taken prisoner and brought to Alexandria, where the ship was seized. The Indians and the Englishmen were put on another ship and sent to England. So he and Sankara Rao arrived safely."

"And the tamarind?"

"It was undamaged."

"What do you make with it again?"

"*Rasam*. It is a thin soup of lentils. Very spicy and very sour. The English in India call it 'pepper water.' If you like, I shall make some for you, Hardy. It tastes like *rasam* now. It did not when I used your lemons."

"I should like to try it."

"Perhaps I shall have a dinner. I shall invite some friends. Chatterjee and Mahalanobis, perhaps."

"I would enjoy that," Hardy says. But Ramanujan either changes his mind or forgets that he made the offer in the first place, for the invitation—to Hardy's mild regret—doesn't come.

4

New Lecture Hall, Harvard University

ON THE LAST DAY of August, 1936, as the light outside waned, Hardy continued his imaginary lecture, all the while writing equations on the board and disquisiting, with his voice, on hypergeometric series:

I wonder (he did not say) if I can convey to you tonight—young Americans that you are, raised by your fathers to feel yourself victorious, and rightly so, flush with the knowledge that you both won and profited from the war—I wonder if I can convey to you how dark and lost and strange those years were for England. For me it was at once a busy time, my finger stirring a thousand pots, and trying to stop, as it were, a thousand dykes; and yet it was also a dull and dreary time, during which the rain never seemed to cease, and there was always ample opportunity to fret and anticipate, no matter how full the days might be. For we longed to feel that our lives, and the world we lived in, were real, despite the governmentally sanctioned unrealities that the newspapers routinely fed us. Sometime in the autumn of 1915, for instance, we were told that Servia would from now on be known as "Serbia," in order that its honorable people should not think that we looked upon them as "servile." Advertisements for "war kits at short notice" shared the same newspaper page with ones for motor cars. Most recreational sports having been more or less forcibly put on hold, the popular press took to likening the war to a cricket match. A certain Captain Holborn of the artillery division made it his habit to kick a football into enemy territory before launching an attack. This was regarded as behavior worthy of laudation. Even the puzzles in the *Strand* began to have war-related titles: "Exercising the Spies," "Avoiding the Mines." Which did not stop me from doing them.

Today, of course, we know the truth. We have the memoirs and the letters, testimony to what a horror France was, the rats and the lice and the severed limbs flying. Things that those of us who were not there have no right, no license, to describe. And we also know what an outrageous waste it was ("wastage" was the bureaucratic term for death in the battlefield), and how stupid the war was in conception and practice, and how stupidly we played it.

At the time, though, even as the rationalist in me tried to keep in mind the delusive purpose of the propaganda, the sentimentalist took pleasure and sometimes comfort in the notion that the war was a sort of jolly game. "All great fun," as Rupert Brooke once put it. Nor did it help when Brooke waxed poetic, in his letters, about bathing with the "naked, superb" men in his regiment. Of course, Brooke could feel himself naked and superb in his own right, which I never could. Still, the very idea of bathing naked with a corps of handsome youths—I cannot pretend that it did not excite me. As a boy I had devoured tales of battle and glory and victory. I was a little in love with young Prince Harold. When he took the arrow in the eye at Hastings, I longed to have been there with him, to have ministered to his wounds and cradled him in my arms. I used to have a very strong erotic fantasy—I think it was the fantasy in which I indulged the first time I touched myself with carnal intent—that I was lying injured on a battlefield, my clothes somehow half torn away, and two officers, one a doctor, lifting me onto a stretcher and carrying me into a tent, where they proceeded to strip away the clothes that remained, until I was naked . . . The fantasy never progressed beyond this moment. What would happen next I could not imagine. And now, in the first years of the war, this fantasy returned, more powerful than ever, perhaps because I had had, in the intervening years, experiences that allowed me to extend the vision beyond the moment when my clothes were stripped off, to the one where the doctor leaned over to kiss me, and beyond that as well . . .

Somehow I dreamed, even gloried in, the possibility of my own death. When I read the lists of the Cambridge dead that the *Cambridge Magazine* published, I tried to insert my name among those of the men from Trinity, all of whom, of course, I had known, at least by sight, and some of whom I had taught. Hardy between Grantham and Heyworth. How lovely that sounded! Grantham, Hardy, Heyworth.

And the names of the regiments! Only England could make poetry from the naming of its regiments: 7th Seaforth Highlanders, 1st Royal Welsh Fusiliers, 9th Sherwood Foresters, presumably with Robin Hood in command and Friar Tuck and all the other members of that merry band.

You see, the action, not to mention the grisliness, was in France. Back at Trinity, the nights were quiet enough for dreams. I tried to convince myself that I appreciated the silence, when in truth I missed the drunken singing that used to wake me, and the philosophical arguments under my windows, the morose declarations uttered—as only the young can utter them—with rhapsodic joy. For this had always been the flavor of the first weeks once the term started. One could revel with the young in their newfound freedom, the freedom to stay up late, and argue, and say, "When youth ends, life ends. I shall kill myself when I turn thirty." (The voicer of this particular sentiment, I happen to know, didn't make it past nineteen.) I even missed those rituals I'd once claimed to despise: the bloods invading the rooms of the aesthetes, breaking their crockery and throwing the pieces down into New Court. For now there were no bloods—the hale and hearty were off fighting—and few aesthetes, for many of these were fighting, too, and of those who remained, none seemed to have the heart to sing or argue.

Early that winter I was sitting, one morning, reading in my rooms, with Hermione on my lap, awaiting Ramanujan. I looked up and saw that the first snow was falling. And somehow its innocence, its seeming obliviousness to the condition of the world, moved me and saddened me. For possibly the snow was falling also on the riven farmland of France and Belgium, falling into the trenches in which the soldiers waited for what might be their last sunset. And it was falling on Nevile's Court, to be gazed upon by the injured lying on their camp beds. And it was falling in Cranleigh, where my mother, half out of her mind, watched it through her bedroom window, and my sister through the window of a classroom in which uniformed girls were painting a vase of flowers. Lifting Hermione off my lap, I got up and walked to the window. It was still warm enough outside that the snow didn't stick; it melted instantly when it touched the ground. And there, standing in the court below me, was Ramanujan. The flakes melted on his face and ran down his cheeks. He stood there like that for a full five minutes. And then I realized that this must have been the first time in his life that he had seen snow.

He came upstairs and we went to work. I cannot say exactly what we were working on. It's so hard to remember with Ramanujan, for he was always busy with two or three things at once, or he had had another dream, and had another oddity to share. Were we, for instance, already on to the theory of round numbers? This was the sort of thing in which he could lose himself for days at a time, counting through all the numbers from 1 to 1,000,000 and then ordering them by roundness. "1,000,000, Hardy, is very round," he said to me one day. "It has 12 prime factors, whereas if you take all the numbers between 999,991 and 1,000,010, the average is only 4." I liked to imagine him sitting in his rooms, making lists like this. Yet he was doing much more than that. He was laying the groundwork for the asymptotic formula for roundness that we would later perfect.

By the middle of October, the last of the wounded had been moved out of Nevile's Court. New hospital facilities were being built on the cricket grounds of Clare and King's colleges—one of the best pitches in town, I noted ruefully at the time.

Still, I visited the hospital. The first time, I took Ramanujan with me. The wards stretched for three-quarters of a mile, ten blocks of them, with sixty beds each. What was strangest about them was that they only had three walls each. In each one, where the fourth wall should have been, there was open sky, clouds, lawn.

I asked one of the sisters why the walls were missing. "It's for the fresh air," she said, rubbing her arms for warmth. "Fresh air blows away germs. Also headache and lassitude."

"And what happens when it rains?"

"There are blinds. Though if I'm to tell the truth, they don't work very well. Not that it matters. These men are used to sleeping outdoors, and under far worse conditions."

Not far off, a soldier started wailing. His words were unrecognizable. Perhaps he was Belgian. The sister went off to tend to him, and I looked at the men, most of whom were wrapped in cocoons of blanket and bandage. How would they stay warm in the winter? I wondered. Or perhaps that was the point. Perhaps the thinking was that, should they be made too comfortable, they might be less willing to return to the front. I could imagine such an idea gaining credence in military circles.

Afterward Ramanujan expressed his bewilderment at the missing wall. "Tuberculosis patients are treated the same way," I told him—having no idea, of course, what was to come. "Fresh air! Fresh air! The English are great believers in the healing powers of fresh air."

"But what happens when it rains?"

"Then they will get wet."

That afternoon, on target, it rained. Great sheets of rain came down. Somehow I could not sit in my room, watching the deluge, so I took my umbrella, the one I had stolen from Gertrude, and went back to the ward. The sister was now fighting the blinds, which rattled and flapped in the wind. At her feet, rainwater pooled. She had put on galoshes. When the wind gusted, shards of rain splattered the men lying nearest the blinds, some of whom cursed or laughed, while others lay still, seemingly oblivious to the lashings.

The quietest of them—I noticed him only then—was a lad with dark blond hair and green eyes. Hair only slightly darker than that on his head tufted out from his nightshirt. I stepped gingerly to his bedside. "May I?" I asked, opening the umbrella over his head.

"I don't think I should thank you," he said.

"Why not?" I asked.

"Because opening an umbrella indoors is bad luck," he said.

"Not this umbrella," I said. "This is a lucky umbrella. And besides, we aren't exactly indoors. We're sort of . . . on the threshold, aren't we? Between outdoors and indoors."

"Are you a don?"

"Yes. How did you know?"

"You talk like a don."

"Do I?"

"All sorts of daft things."

I was pleased that he considered me young enough to tease. I asked if I could sit with him a bit.

"There's no law against it," he said. And I sat down in the chair next to his bed, being careful, all the while, not to let the umbrella sway.

"What's your name?" I asked.

"Thayer," he said. "Infantry. Birmingham. Took a hunk of shrapnel in the leg near Wipers."

"Wipers?"

"You know, in Belgium."

"Ah, Ypres."

"Yes, *Ee-pray*."

"Are you in pain?"

"Not the leg. I don't feel anything in the leg. They say it's fifty-fifty if I lose it." Suddenly he looked up at me. "Is not feeling pain a bad sign? Does it mean I should consider the leg gone? Because Lord knows you can't get a straight answer out of anyone around here."

"I wish I could tell you," I said. "But I'm only a mathematician."

"I was never any good at long division."

"Neither was I." I said this without even thinking what effect the words might have on him. He laughed.

"So are you in pain anywhere else? Besides your leg, I mean."

"It's just that my head aches. A sort of pounding. Ever since the explosion." He pointed to a bowl next to the bed, in which a wet cloth lay. "The sister drenches this with hot water and puts it on my forehead and that seems to help. Could you ask her if she'll do it now? It's got cold."

"Of course I will," I said. And I got up to look for the sister. But she was still doing battle, valiantly and hopelessly, with the blinds, a struggle from which she would be called away intermittently by a patient's yelp.

I glanced around the ward. There were one or two other sisters about, tending to patients. Then I noticed a stove in the corner. On one of the hobs was a pot of water from which steam rose.

"Just a minute," I said. And I leaned the umbrella, as best I could, on the chair, so that it might continue to keep him even a little dry. "I'll be right back," I said. And then I took the cloth from the bowl and carried it over to the stove, where I dipped it in the hot water and wrung it out.

"Here we are," I said, returning. "May I?"

He lifted his chin with a kind of knightly forbearance. Very cautiously I brushed back his hair. Then I took the cloth and draped it over his brow. He shuddered and gave out an audible sigh of relief.

All that afternoon I sat with him. He talked to me, not, I sensed, because he took any great interest in me, but because he had things to say and I was someone to listen. I must be honest about this. He talked about the front line, and the rats that were as big as dogs, and the curious fact that one almost never saw the enemy—"never saw Jerry" was how he put it—but always felt his sinister proximity. Somehow you knew he was there, in his own trench, not two hundred yards away, and when, on occasion, some sign of life would emerge from the other side of No Man's Land—when one heard a bit of singing, or smelled food frying—it came as a shock.

"What kind of singing?"

"Jerry songs. Only once—it was the oddest thing—I heard a radio playing, and it was a British program. A comedy. And they were laughing at it."

All the while the rain came down. Men moaned and wailed and asked—begged—for cigarettes. Every twenty minutes or so I would take his cloth and warm it in the hot water. The bother was, during those intervals when I was away at the stove, the umbrella, propped up against my chair, kept falling over. Rain would mat his hair and soak his blankets. I'd do my best to dry him. Then I'd sit again and try to keep the umbrella steady, even though doing so made my arm ache. You see, I was determined that no drop of water should land on him, other than the water from the cloth on his head.

Finally the storm let up. The exhausted sister was now able to remove her galoshes and retire for a cup of tea. Thayer stretched; his eyes fluttered. At that moment I would have done anything to protect him. I would have stayed, holding up the umbrella, all night. But I feared that my prolonged presence might be thought unseemly, either by the sister or by Thayer himself. So I picked up the umbrella and said, "Well, I'd best be going." And much to my surprise, he asked me if I would return again tomorrow. And if I might, before I left, wet the cloth, one more time, and lay it on his brow.

I said that of course I would—both wet the cloth and come back tomorrow. And I did come back. Every day for two weeks I came back. We talked and talked. He asked me to tell him what kind of mathematics I did, and I tried to explain Riemann to him, and, much to my amazement, he grasped the essentials. Or we talked cricket. (He shared my admiration for Shrimp Levison-Gower.) Or he told me about his mother and his sisters, and his friend Dick Tarlow, to whom one of his sisters had been engaged, and how, at Wipers, Dick Tarlow had been blown to bits, and how much he missed him, and how much his sister missed him.

Thayer did not, in the end, lose his leg. Instead I arrived, one afternoon, at the hospital, bearing a gift for him—the first gift I had dared bring, a copy of Wells's *The Time Machine*—only to be told by the sister that he had been discharged that very afternoon, and sent to his people in Birmingham, for a few weeks' rest before going back to the front. A month or so later he sent me one of those horrible form letters that the government issued to the soldiers in those days, with the line checked off that read "I am being sent down to the base. Letters follow at first opportunity." Only his signature at the bottom—J. R. Thayer—indicated any connection between the form and the lad who had filled it out.

That winter was famously cold—so cold that I could not bear to visit the hospital anymore, for fear of witnessing too much suffering and feeling hopeless at my own inability to ease it. This included my own suffering. Thayer, at least, I had helped make comfortable, though I never touched any part of him besides his forehead, on which I laid, time and again, that warm, wet cloth. It was for his sake, those days, that I prayed for rain. Every morning I would rise and beg God to bring rain. Sometimes He would oblige, which annoyed me. I worried that He was onto the game. Most days, though, the clouds never broke, and once or twice the sun even shone through the vast space where the south wall of the ward should have been, raising the spirits of the soldiers and giving some cause to smile. On such days I was grateful for the umbrella, which I was able to rest, closed, against the wall next to Thayer's bed. Closed, it had brought luck. Open— who knows what it had brought?

I must confess that I fear myself, now, ever finding out.

5

I N MARCH 1 9 1 5 , Russell sends him a note saying that he has
invited D. H. Lawrence to visit Trinity. Would Hardy join them,
after dinner, for sherry in Russell's rooms?

Most of the officers have left by now, so he goes that evening to
Hall. A man he supposes to be Lawrence sits across from Russell and
next to Moore. Hardy is too far down the high table to overhear their
conversation. Still, he can tell it's strained. There are long silences,
during which the eupeptic Moore eats with relish, while Lawrence
merely stares at his plate, a morose expression on his oblong face.
Although Hardy hasn't read any of his books, he's heard much about
the writer: about his childhood in a coal-mining town near Notting-
ham, and the years he spent as an elementary schoolteacher, and his
recent marriage to a zaftig German divorcée, the daughter of a Baron,
six years his senior. And what must he make of these Trinity men,
sawing at their meat while Byron and Newton and Thackeray look
on? Do they seem ridiculous in their gowns? Is he overawed? Is he
repulsed?

As requested, Hardy arrives at Russell's rooms around nine. A few
others are there: Milne—former editor of the *Granta*, now at *Punch*—
as well as Winstanley, who makes it his business to know more about
the history of Trinity than anyone else, and is currently pontificating
to Lawrence about the building of the Wren Library in 1695. Moore is
there too, and Sheppard (without Madam Cecil, thank goodness),
waiting his turn to address the author.

What impresses Hardy most about Lawrence is his gauntness.
Gauntness like that you have to work at. With his big head and
hunched shoulders, he might be an underfed gargoyle. His hair is thick
and brown, and looks as if it has been cut the old-fashioned way, by
placing a bowl over the head, which is strangely shaped, thick and

protuberant at the brow, then tapering into a chin the sharpness of which his beard, cut to a point, only accentuates. He doesn't speak much. He seems to be listening very intently—at the moment to Russell, who has just received, by post, an article that Edmund Gosse wrote for the *Edinburgh Review* at the beginning of the war. "Listen to this," Russell says. " 'War is the great scavenger of thought. It is the sovereign disinfectant, and its red stream of blood is the Condy's Fluid that cleans out the stagnant pools and clotted channels of the intellect.' " He throws the review down. "Have any of you ever actually seen a bottle of Condy's Fluid? I had to ask my bedmaker. She showed me one. Purplish stuff. She says she uses it to 'get out the odors.' And this from a man who hasn't left London in ten years! What does he know? What do any of us know?"

"War is not fine," Lawrence says. "This abstract hate of a fairy-tale German ogre—there are finer things to live and die for."

Then he is quiet again. Does the mention of the ogre owe to the influence of the German wife? From what Hardy has heard, she left her first husband, also an Englishman, to marry Lawrence.

"Gosse is a shit," says Russell. "And Eddie Marsh—even worse. Selling this bill of goods just so he can dress up and go with Churchill to parties. These men are insects, obscene, venturing out from their crevices into the darkness, crawling over corpses, polluting them with their slime."

"Oh, come now, Bertie," Milne says. "Surely they're not *that* bad."

"They are that bad."

"Well, haven't we got into a gloom!" Sheppard says. "And when the whole purpose of this evening is to welcome Mr. Lawrence to Cambridge." With that, he strides up to Lawrence and starts talking to him about his books. And really, he is a marvel, with his gift for shepherding (*Sheppard shepherds*) a conversation along. Whether he's actually read the books is immaterial: what matters is that he gives the impression, brilliantly, of having read them. And clearly he's read *something*, for now he starts quoting to Lawrence from Lawrence's own work. "*Sons and Lovers*, of course, is a masterpiece," he says, "though personally I shall always feel a special fondness for *The White Peacock*. And that early chapter, 'A Poem of Friendship,' the two boys frolicking in the water and drying each other off afterwards!" He clears his throat. " 'He saw I had forgotten to continue my rubbing, and laughing he took hold of me and began to rub me briskly, as if I were a child, or rather, a woman he loved and did not fear. I left myself quite limply in his hands, and to get a better grip of me, he put his arms round me and pressed me against him, and the sweetness of the touch of our naked bodies one against the other was superb.'" Sheppard breathes deeply. "What language! You see, I've memorized it."

Silence greets this unexpected declamation. Lawrence says, "Thank you," then turns away.

Now Russell introduces him to Hardy, whose hand Lawrence grips warmly, fervently, for too long. Perhaps he simply finds it a relief to have been saved from Sheppard's insinuating little performance. Much more pleasant, no doubt, to listen as Hardy, at Russell's request, rambles on about the Riemann hypothesis. Indeed, even after Russell's gone off to chat with Winstanley, Lawrence sticks close to him; leans into him; clings to him almost as a life raft. And how ironic *that* is, considering Hardy's own—how to put it?—predilections. Yet he takes a certain pride in the misreading; if Lawrence takes him to be normal, if he does not ally him with Sheppard, so much the better.

And meanwhile, in the background, Sheppard doesn't stop declaiming. It's the oddest thing. He has no audience. He knows Lawrence is valiantly not listening. And still he declaims, with an almost vicious irony: "'It satisfied in some measure the vague, indecipherable yearning of my soul; and it was the same with him.'"

"There must be a revolution of the state," Lawrence says to Hardy. "Everything must be nationalized—all industries, all the means of communication. And of course the land. In one fell blow. Then a man shall have his wages whether he's sick or well or old. If anything prevents his working, he shall have his wages all the same. He shouldn't live in fear of the wolf."

Sheppard: "'When he had rubbed me all warm, he let me go, and we looked at each other with eyes of still laughter, and our love was perfect for a moment, more perfect than any love I have known since, either for man or woman.'"

Lawrence: "And every woman shall have her wage, too, until she dies, whether she works or not, so long as she works while she's fit to."

Sheppard: "'The cool, moist fragrance of the morning, the intentional stillness of everything, of the tall bluish trees, of the wet, frank flowers'—Isn't that marvelous? 'Wet, frank flowers'—'of the trustful moths folded and unfolded in the fallen swaths, was a perfect medium of sympathy.'"

Lawrence: "But for now we live trapped within a shell. And the shell is a prison to life. If we don't break the shell, our lives turn in upon themselves. But if we can smash the shell, then anything is possible. Then and only then we shall begin living. We can examine marriage and love and all. But until then we are fast within the hard, unliving, impervious shell."

Hardy, in imitation of Ramanujan, waggles his head. Lawrence frowns. "You must have patience with me. I know sometimes my language isn't clear."

Hardy doesn't expect to see Lawrence again. The next afternoon, though, as he's crossing Great Court, he hears a voice calling his name, and turns to see Lawrence running toward him, on storkish legs.

"What a boon," he says, taking Hardy's arm. "I've had a very terrible morning. Please, may I walk with you?"

"Of course."

"It was one of the crises of my life."

They head toward the river, Hardy feeling at once flattered and embarrassed by the rapacity with which Lawrence clutches him. "I don't know whether Keynes is a friend of yours," he says. "And if he is your friend, and you come to loathe me, that is regrettable, but I must speak or I shall die."

"What you say shall remain between the two of us. That goes without saying."

"Russell wanted me to meet him—Keynes," he says. "So this morning we went to his rooms, but he wasn't there. It was very sunny, and Russell was writing him a note when Keynes came out of the bedroom, blinking from sleep. And he was in . . . his pyjamas. And as he stood there some knowledge passed into me. I can't describe it. There was the most dreadful sense of repulsiveness. Something like carrion. A vulture gives the same feeling."

"Oh my."

"And the pyjamas . . ." He shudders. "Striped. These horrible little frowsty people, men lovers of men, they give me a sense of corruption, almost of putrescence. They make me dream of black beetles. Of a beetle that bites like a scorpion. In the dream I kill it, a very large beetle, I scotch it and it runs off, but it comes again, and I must kill it again."

"How awful . . . and in striped pyjamas . . ."

"I have thought a lot about sodomy. Love is this: you go to a woman to know yourself, and knowing yourself, to explore the unknown, which is the woman. You venture upon the coasts of the unknown, and open what you discover to all humanity. But what nearly all English people do is, a man goes to a woman, he takes a woman, and he's merely repeating a known reaction, not seeking a new reaction. And this is simply self-abuse. The ordinary Englishman of the educated classes goes to a woman to masturbate himself. And sodomy is just a nearer form of masturbation, because there are two bodies instead of one, but still it has the same object. A man of strong soul has too much honor for the other body, so he remains neutral. Celibate. Forster, for instance."

They have circled back to Trinity. All this way they have encountered no one, but now two soldiers pass by, student soldiers, in uniforms under their gowns. "How ugly they are," Lawrence says. "I think of that line from Dostoevsky: 'to insects—sensual lust.' One insect mounting another—Oh God, the soldiers! So ugly. Like lice or bugs. Steer me clear of them!" Hardy steers him to Nevile's Court, and he lets go, at last, of Hardy's arm. "I feel better," he says. "The bond of blood brotherhood is a crucial one." Then he steps nearer. "Oh, how can you bear it here? I loathe Cambridge, its smell of rottenness, of marsh-stagnancy. Come visit me and Frieda. We live in Greatham. In Sussex. The air is fresh, the food plain. Come and see us."

"I will," Hardy says, rubbing his arm, which has gone numb. And then Lawrence shakes his hand—his handshake is so weak, so ineffectual, so moist, Hardy recoils—and walks through the door that leads to Russell's staircase.

Black beetles in striped pyjamas . . .

6

A GAIN, HE ENCOUNTERS Ramanujan with his Indian
friends. This time they are sitting by the river. The shadows of
an elm afford him the chance to study them more carefully.
The stooped one with the turban is reading something aloud to the
others. The youngest one—the one whose mortarboard blew away—
has intense, darting, faunlike eyes. When he notices Hardy, he turns
away.

The next morning, Ramanujan says, "Ananda Rao is quite in awe
of you."

"Why?"

"Because he is studying mathematics, and you are the great mathematician. The great Hardy. But he is shy to introduce himself."

"He need not be."

"I tell him that, but he won't listen. He is a youngster."

"Tell him he can come to see me anytime."

Hardy opens his notebook, indicating that the time has come to go
to work. "Ananda Rao is preparing an essay for the Smith's Prize,"
Ramanujan says.

"Oh, good for him."

"Might I submit an essay for the Smith's Prize?"

"But the Smith's Prize is for undergraduates. You're well beyond
that."

"I do not have a B.A."

"Yes, the requirement was waived in your case."

"I should like to have a B.A."

"Well, I suspect we could arrange that."

"How?"

"You could do it 'by research,' as they say. Maybe your paper on
highly composite numbers. You'll need to ask Barnes."

The next morning Ramanujan says, "I have asked Barnes, and he agrees. I can do the B.A. by research with the paper on highly composite numbers."

"Fine."

"Then I can submit my research for the Smith's Prize?"

"But you're eons beyond the Smith's Prize! Why should you even bother with the Smith's Prize?"

"You won the Smith's Prize."

"Prizes are meaningless. Just things to gather dust on the mantel." Then he catches himself. For how can he convey the meaninglessness of prizes to one who has suffered so from not having won enough?

"Hardy," Ramanujan says, "may I ask you a kindness?"

"What?"

"I wonder if you would allow me . . . if I did not come to see you for the next three days."

"Oh? And why's that?"

"Chatterjee has invited me to go to London with him."

"To London?"

"With him and Mahalanobis and Ananda Rao. He has found a boardinghouse with a very pleasant landlady who serves, he says, excellent vegetarian food."

"And what will you do in London?"

"We will see *Charley's Aunt*."

"*Charley's Aunt*!" Hardy suppresses a laugh. "No, of course. I mean, yes. You should start getting to know more of England than the corridors of Trinity."

"Thank you. I promise that I shall continue my work in London. I shall have the mornings free."

"There's no need for that. Take a break from work. It'll clear your head."

"No, I shall work every morning, from eight to noon."

Four days later he's back at Hardy's fireside.

"So how was London?"

"Very pleasant, thank you."

"And you enjoyed *Charley's Aunt*?"

"I laughed very much."

"What else did you do?"

"I went to the zoo."

"The zoo in Regent's Park?"

"Yes. And I saw Mr. Littlewood and his friend. They took me to tea." He waggles his head. "She is very amiable, Mr. Littlewood's friend."

"So I've heard."

"And then after tea they took me to see Winnie."

"Who is Winnie?"

"Winnie is a black bear cub from Canada. She was brought by a soldier. Her name is short for Winnipeg, not Winifred. But then the soldier's brigade was sent to France, and now Winnie lives at the zoo."

"And what is Winnie like?"

"She is very tame. A gentleman from the zoo fed her. I stayed and watched her for an hour, with Mr. Littlewood and his friend."

"So you shall go to London again?"

"I think so, yes. The boardinghouse was very comfortable. It is in Maida Vale."

"Very convenient for the zoo."

"And the landlady—Mrs. Peterson—she has taught herself Indian cooking. She even made *sambar* one night. Well, a sort of *sambar*."

"That would no doubt please your mother."

"She would be pleased. May I ask your guidance on a small matter?"

"Of course."

"On the train back, Mahalanobis showed us a problem from the *Strand* magazine. They are published every month—mathematical puzzles—and this one he could not solve."

"What was it?"

Ramanujan fishes a magazine cutting from his pocket and hands it to Hardy. "Puzzles at a Village Inn"; the setting, familiar to Hardy, is the Red Lion Inn in the Village of Little Wurzelfold. Only now the men speak of the war.

"I was talking the other day," said William Rogers to the other villagers gathered round the inn fire, "to a gentleman about that place called Louvain, what the Germans have burnt down. He said he knowed it well—used to visit a Belgian friend there. He said the house of his friend was in a long street, numbered on his side one, two, three, and so on, and that all the numbers on one side of him added up exactly the same as all the numbers on the other side of him. Funny thing that! He said he knew there was more than fifty houses on that side of the street, but not so many as five hundred. I made mention of the matter to our parson, and he took a pencil and worked out the number of the house where the Belgian lived. I don't know how he done it."

"Well," Hardy says, "and what is the solution? It shouldn't be difficult—for you."

"The solution is that the house is number 204 out of 288. But that is not what is interesting."

"What is interesting?"

"It is a continued fraction. The first term is the solution to the problem as stated. But each successive term is the solution for the same type of relation between two numbers as the number of houses increases toward infinity."

"Very good."

"I think I should like to publish a paper on continued fractions. Perhaps this continued fraction. You see, with my theorem I could now solve the puzzle no matter how many houses there were. Even on an infinite street."

An infinite street, Hardy thinks, of Belgian houses. And Ramanujan pacing the rubble, holding his continued fraction before him like a sextant. And all the houses burning.

"I suspect that it would make an excellent paper," he says.

"Might it be a paper," Ramanujan asks, "with which I could win the Smith's Prize?"

7

WATCHING RAMANUJAN with Chatterjee has the odd-est effect on Hardy: he remembers trying, back before he met Ramanujan, to form an image of what Ramanujan might look like, and seeing Chatterjee. And now Ramanujan is *with* Chatterjee, and it's like watching two incarnations of the same person. Much as he tries, he can't recapture the image of the Senior Combination Room that he formed after reading *A Fellow of Trinity*; the real Senior Combination Room has obliterated it. Chatterjee, though, remains, and as long as he does, so will the image of Ramanujan that Ramanujan, by virtue of his arrival, should have erased.

Is he jealous? It's not exactly that he misses the summer days when he and Ramanujan strolled alone along the riverbanks. Nor does he begrudge him his new friends. And yet he can't help feeling . . . what? Left out? He tries to be logical with himself. He asks himself: what do you want? For the Indians to invite you to join them on one of their London jaunts? To share a room with Ramanujan at Mrs. Peterson's boardinghouse? To go with him to the zoo, and visit Winnie the black bear cub from Canada, and take tea with Littlewood and Mrs. Chase?

Surely not. After all, he has his own flat. His own life.

Whenever they see each other in public, Ramanujan gestures to Hardy, Hardy nods, and they move on. One afternoon on Great Court, though, Ramanujan actually waves. Hardy has no choice but to cross the lawn, where Ramanujan introduces him to his friends. Chatterjee has a firm handshake, Mahalanobis bows, Ananda Rao will not meet his eye. They talk about the Gallipoli campaign for a few minutes, and then Chatterjee says, "Well, I must be off. Goodbye, Dear Jam."

"Goodbye," Ramanujan says.

Dear Jam?

"What is this, a nickname?"

"It is what they call me."

Dear Jam. So far as Hardy can surmise, Ramanujan doesn't even like jam. At least he's refused it every time Hardy's offered it. True, in the words there's a faint echo of his name. Even a partial anagram. ARJAM is in RAMANUJAN. So is that where the name comes from? And does having heard it give Hardy the right to use it?

"Dear Jam." He tries it out when he gets back to his rooms. "Dear Jam." He can barely get his mouth around the words.

"Why fret?" Gaye asks. "Indians are always giving each other silly nicknames. Pookie and Bonky and Oinky and Binky. It's a boarding-school affectation."

Hardy turns. Gaye is kneeling by the fireplace, stroking Hermione.

"How did you become such an expert?"

"I listen."

"And what do you hear?"

"That you're jealous. Admit the truth."

"I'm not jealous!"

"Then you're envious. You *want* his friends. Especially that crick-eter . . . And I can't blame you for that."

"You're utterly wrong. It was the same when you were alive, Russell, you always assumed I was in love with everyone. You were ridiculous about it."

"So what's the truth?"

"Just that I'm curious as to the origins of this pet name. And the very fact that he *has* a pet name—it seems out of character for him."

"Or perhaps *he* isn't the man you assume—or should I say require him—to be?"

"I don't require him to be anything in particular."

"Yes you do, Harold. You need him to be shy and reclusive and obsessed with his work, because then you don't have to bother taking him around. He doesn't interfere with your life. But if he keeps *you* in the dark, you don't like it, which, if you ask me, is rather hypocritical, given that you've done next to nothing to introduce the poor man into your own, shall we say, social sphere."

"That's not true. Littlewood and I took him to dinner at Hall and he despised it. He hates the food. We tried. What can you do when you offer someone something and he doesn't want it?"

"Well, I can't say I'm surprised." Gaye strokes Hermione's neck, so that she purrs. "After all, you did the same thing to me."

"What did I do?"

"You know perfectly well what. The thing you can't speak of. The Saturday night thing."

"Oh, that."

"Yes, that."

"It was an entirely different situation."

"Was it? You shut me out. Just as you're shutting him out."

"But he doesn't want to be brought in."

"Fine." Gaye stands, releasing Hermione. "Well, clearly you know everything about the case, so I'll be off then, shall I?"

"Don't go."

"Why? What's the point of my staying when you obviously have no interest in hearing what I have to say? It was the same when I was alive, Harold. You heard me out but you never listened."

He moves away. Hermione tests her claws on the carpet. Then Hardy says, "Wait."

"What?"

"You told me earlier there was something you wanted me to admit. Well, what is it?"

"That you want to keep him all to yourself. That you're afraid of losing him."

"All right, I want to keep him all to myself. I'm afraid of losing him. There. Are you satisfied?"

"And you'd like to have it off with the cricketer."

"And I'd like to talk cricket with the cricketer. Then we could see what develops."

Hermione tests her claws on the carpet. Gaye smiles. "I'm glad you said that. It's a relief to hear you speaking the truth for once."

"Does it sound like the truth to you?" Hardy asks. "It doesn't to me. But then again, since the war started, nothing does."

8

T HE POT, the same sort that his mother used all through his youth, is made of beaten brass with a layer of silvering on the inside. The recipe is his mother's, too. First he soaks the tamarind pulp in boiling water. Then he mashes the pulp with his fingers, to squeeze all the liquid out of it. Into the pot he puts lentils and turmeric and water and lets them cook until the lentils have broken apart, until he has a sort of yellow gruel. He stirs the lentils to break up any lumps, then adds more hot water, and lets the broth rest so that the solids sink to the bottom. Then he strains the broth, leaving aside the solids, which he will use for *sambar*. To this broth he adds coriander and cumin powder, chili powder, sugar, salt, and the tamarind juice. He lets the broth cook for a further fifteen minutes, and then the *rasam* is ready—to be finished off later with a garnish of mustard seeds fried in *ghee*.

At home, his mother would make the *rasam* fresh every day. He does not have the time to do this. Nor could he eat all that *rasam* in one day. So he makes the *rasam* at the beginning of the week, and then, all week, he has it to hand and can reheat it every time he wants some. In this way he need not be distracted for long from his work.

His friends notice the smell whenever they visit him. Sometimes he offers them a cup. They talk or work together and, in the meantime, the tamarind in the *rasam* corrodes the silvering, exposing the brass and leaching out the lead. If he does not taste the lead, it is probably because the spiciness of the chili powder and the sourness of the tamarind would be enough to cover flavors far more acrid.

So the months pass. He eats his *rasam* over rice, or drinks it from a cup. The pot sits placidly on the stove.

9

RUSSELL COMES TO Hardy's room to tell him that Rupert Brooke has died—something Hardy already knows from the *Times*. He comes in without knocking, interrupting a conversation Hardy is having with Sheppard. " 'Joyous, fearless, versatile, deeply instructed,' " Russell reads aloud, " 'with classic symmetry of mind and body . . .' And they say Winston Churchill wrote this!"

"I sense a distinctly *Edwardian* pen behind those words," Sheppard says.

"They reek of what our friend Mr. Lawrence might call *Marsh*-stagnancy," adds Hardy.

"Very funny. Fine time to joke, with a young man dead. And Marsh's paw prints all over his body."

Hardy looks at his lap. The truth is, he has never subscribed to what he's lately heard called "the cult of Rupert Brooke." To him, Brooke was merely a handsome, rather pallid young man who radiated an aura of self-regard and anomie; inclined, out of the blue, to make the most scabrous remarks: against Jews, against homosexuals—this, though at meetings of the Society he often spoke of sleeping, in his youth, with boys; of having lost his virginity to another boy. Brooke liked James Strachey and hated Lytton; seemed always to be having sexless affairs with women; wrote what Hardy thought to be banal and sentimental verse. And now he is dead. Is Marsh to blame?

Sheppard says he doesn't think so. "Admit it, Bertie," he says, "you're being too hard on Eddie."

"He might as well have murdered him. He seduced him. Brought him into his posh circles, introduced him to Asquith, put it in his mind to be the great hero. Wasn't Brooke living in Eddie's flat?"

"Still, it was Brooke himself who enlisted."

"Eddie got him the commission."

"Only because he insisted upon it. He would have gone regardless."

"Yes, but so quickly?"

"Eddie might have been trying to save him," Hardy says. "He might have been trying to get him the safest commission he could find."

"Not that it did any good. Brooke was hell-bent on dying," Sheppard says.

"And now he has died—of sunstroke, the *Times* tells us," says Hardy.

"Apparently not, in fact," Russell says. "That was only what they thought at first. It was blood poisoning, from a mosquito bite."

"A mosquito bite!"

"Sunstroke makes better propaganda, though."

"Brought down by glorious Phoebus' rays," Sheppard intones. "Buried, like Byron, where Hellenic light bathes his grave, far from home."

"And to think that he never even saw battle."

"Didn't he? I thought he was in Antwerp."

"He was, but his battalion never fought."

"Felled by a mosquito en route to Gallipoli. A pity, when he hoped so badly to be shot, or blown up by a mine."

"He managed to get those war poems published quickly enough."

"Have you read them?"

"I have." He recites:

> To turn, as swimmers into cleanness leaping,
> Glad from a world grown old and cold and weary.
> Leave the sick hearts that honour could not move,
> And half-men, and their dirty songs and dreary,
> And all the little emptiness of love!

"I suppose we're the half-men," Hardy says. "Singing our dirty songs."

"Into Condy's Fluid leaping, more like it," Russell says, crumpling the obituary in his fist.

E THEL, IN SORROW, as an act of silent, sorrowful protest, continues to make the coffee the Madrasi way, boiled with milk and sugar. Even when Neville complains—"Can't we just have ordinary coffee?" he asks—she still makes it that way.

"There's nothing you can do about it," Alice tells him. "You know Ethel. Once she sets her mind to a thing—"

Ethel is stout, red-faced, about fifty, from the look of her, though she might be younger. She comes from Bletchley, and returns there every Wednesday to visit her daughter, who works in a corset factory. No husband has been mentioned.

"Any news of the son?" Neville asks Alice.

"She doesn't say and I don't ask. I gather he's in France."

"Poor lad. Well, go on."

Because of her husband's poor eyesight, Alice makes it her habit, each morning, to read aloud to him from the newspapers. " 'At Bow Street Police Court on Saturday,' " she reads, " 'Messrs. Methuen and Co., publishers, Essex Street, Strand, were summoned before Sir John Dickinson to show cause why 1,011 copies of Mr. D. H. Lawrence's novel *The Rainbow* should not be destroyed.' We should hold on to our copy, Eric. It might be worth something. 'The defendants expressed regret that the book should have been published, and the magistrate ordered that the copies should be destroyed and that the defendants should pay ten pounds, ten shillings costs.' "

"So they just gave in?"

"I'm not surprised, given the mood these days. 'Mr. H. Muskett, for the Commissioner of Police, said that the defendants, who were publishers of old standing and recognized repute, offered no opposition to the summons. The book in question was a mass of obscenity of thought, idea, and action throughout, wrapped up in language which he supposed would be regarded in some quarters as an artistic and intellectual effort.' "

"Such as at 113 Chesterton Road."

"It must be the Sapphist scene. The two women."

"Alice, you're not supposed to know about such things."

"Ssh. Ethel."

"You're the one who said it!" Neville butters some toast. "Anyway, the obscenity business is just a cover. It's really because the book is so overtly antiwar."

"Has it really become that dangerous to be antiwar?"

"I fear so." He winces at the sweetness of the coffee. "And his being married to a Hun-ness doesn't help. Any more news on the Derby business?"

"Yes, there's a piece about that."

"Oh? What's up?"

Alice scans the article, then says, "It's nothing. Just more back and forth." She says this to spare her husband worry, for in fact the article touches on a point of great concern to them both. According to the terms of the Derby Scheme, men under forty-one may "attest" voluntarily their readiness to enlist without actually enlisting. What the article discusses is the order in which the "Derby men," as they've been dubbed, will be called up. To quell the anxieties of married men—and to make sure that they attest—Asquith has offered his assurances that no married man will be called up until every last single man, including those who haven't yet attested, has been hunted down and sent to the front. The result has been a sudden upsurge in the number of recorded marriages.

Neville has not attested. Neither has Moore. Others that they know have. You can recognize a Derby man by the armband he wears, gray with a red crown. In Neville's case, of course, whether he attests or not is of no practical import; his eyesight is so bad that he would be turned away at the medical exam. Still, his refusal to go through the formalities is enough to provoke disapproval. For the whole purpose of the Derby scheme (or so the cynics say) is to put such an onus on those who don't attest that they'll be shamed into attesting. It's a discreet form of conscription. Coercion is the rule of the day. Yesterday, for instance, Neville heard that James Strachey had quit his job at the *Spectator* rather than attest, as his editor insisted. And his editor was his cousin! And though things haven't got that bad at Trinity, still, Neville knows full well that every day he doesn't go to the recruitment office, he puts himself at greater risk. Butler has made it clear how strongly he disapproves of pacifist activities within the college. He keeps a careful tally of which fellows are members of the Union for Democratic Control and the No Conscription Fellowship. Neville, like Russell, belongs to both. And unlike Russell, he doesn't have a reputation to protect him.

"We're reaching a point where if you're not wearing an armband, you look rather conspicuous," he says.

"What about Hardy? Has he attested?"

"I don't know. Why do you ask?"

"No reason. I'll just be curious to see if he has the courage of his convictions . . . the courage not to."

The truth, of course, is that Alice hopes that Hardy *will* attest, and that, as a single man, he'll be called up. Sooner rather than later.

"Well, from what I've heard," Neville says, "no matter what happens, he won't fight. He's got some medical condition."

"What kind?"

"How should I know, darling? I'm not his doctor. Ethel, more toast please."

"But if you know that he's got *some* sort of condition—"

"That's just the rumor. It's what I picked up in the Combination Room."

"Who told you?"

"I don't remember. Chapman, I think."

"Ask him. Find out what's wrong with him. He could be planning to buy a medical exemption certificate. I've heard you can buy them on the black market for fifteen pounds—"

"Steady on!" Neville leans across the table; takes his wife's hand. "Alice, what's this about? Why are you so het up about Hardy?"

She pulls her hand away. "I'm not het up. I just wish he'd make up his mind and take a position."

Neville removes his spectacles and cleans them. "This is about Ramanujan, isn't it?"

"In part. In part it's about him. I won't deny that. I've always had the sense that Hardy looks upon him as—I don't know—a sort of mathematics machine, to be milked for everything he's worth before he breaks down. But he doesn't care at all about the poor man's happiness, about what he might need, or how he's managing with the cold weather. He works him like a dray horse."

"Well, from what I saw of them the other day, Ramanujan seemed perfectly all right."

"What? What did you see?"

"They were walking together, and Ramanujan was smiling. Laughing. And besides, it's not as if he's doing maths twenty-four hours a day. He went to London last week."

"Did he? Who with? Did Hardy take him?"

"No, he went with some other Indians."

"Oh, I see. Well, that's all right, then."

"And he's changed rooms. He's moved over to Bishop's Hostel."

"Why?"

"To be closer to Hardy, I suppose." Neville stands. "You've got to stop worrying about him, Alice. He's fine."

"I wish I could believe that."

He bends over her. "My dear little mother," he whispers into her hair. "What you need is a child. A little miniature Eric Harold—"

"That's not entirely in our hands."

"More than you think, it is. You know what I mean." Neville pauses for effect. She looks away. Then he pats her head, as if *she's* the child. "Well, I must be off."

"Goodbye."

He kisses her on the cheek; hesitates a moment; kisses her on the mouth. His hand is on her neck.

Ethel comes in, and they part.

"Clear away these things, will you?" Alice says. Then she gets up from the table and walks into the sitting room. The puzzle, after all this time, is still there. She looks at it. Trembling. And why? Damn all these men—Hardy, Eric, Ramanujan. Hardy doesn't leave. Ramanujan does. Eric may be forced to. Damn them all.

She looks at the puzzle; at the Beau Brummell-y gentleman, and the innkeeper handing them their drinks. Three more men. And how long have they been sitting there? A year? A year and a half? Guarded, protected by her? And why?

All at once she flings out her hand so that the puzzle falls to the ground. It's done before she thinks to stop herself. So this is what it feels like—what Jane must have felt, those afternoons in the old nursery. Exultant with rage.

Alice's heart is racing. Fragments—a single piece or two pieces, clinging together—fly across the carpet, while big swaths of picture, ten or twenty pieces stuck together, hang and then fall over the table's edge, like rubble in a landslide. And as they fall, something falls inside her. The consequences. Always the consequences.

By the time Ethel comes in, she is on her knees, picking up the pieces.

"Mr. Ramanujan's puzzle," Ethel says.

"An accident," Alice says. "I knocked against the table."

"Let me do that, ma'am." Now Ethel, too, is on her knees.

"Thank you. Oh, look, this one is shaped like a teapot."

"I must say, I'm glad to see it gone. Now I can polish the mahogany."

"Really?" Alice stops, looks up at Ethel. "Are you really glad?"

"Dust catchers, that's all they are," Ethel says. Very efficiently she breaks up the big chunks and sweeps the remains into a pile. By the time she and Alice are done, no sign will remain that any violence took place here. And if Eric asks, Ethel will say nothing to contradict Alice when she tells him, "We decided it was finally time to take it apart."

11

E VEN FOR HER—even for a woman who rode through
Madras on a *gharry*, and reads Israfel—it is a bold move.
She knows this. It's one thing to travel to London on the train,
to arrive unannounced on the doorstep of a lady friend. It's another to
walk through the courts of Trinity College in broad daylight—a
woman, wife of a fellow—and to step, in full view of the dons and
the gowned undergraduates, through the door to staircase D, Bishop's
Hostel.

She can't say what's come over her, only that, under the circumstances, the codes of propriety that governed her youth no longer seem
to bind her. It's all very simple. He doesn't visit her. So she will visit
him. She is curiously unfrightened. As in a dream, she climbs the stairs
and knocks on the door she knows to be his.

When he answers, the look of bewilderment on his face shakes her
out of the dream. Good heavens, what is she doing? But it's too late
now.

"Mrs. Neville," he says.

"Hello," she says. "I hope I'm not disturbing you."

"No. Please come in."

He backs up; lets her through the door, which he quickly closes. It is
then that she realizes that he's dressed in Indian clothes, a loose shirt
and a *dhoti* dyed a pale shade of lavender. On his forehead is his caste
mark, on his feet are the slippers she gave him. His legs are more
muscular than she would have guessed, and hairier.

"I hope I'm not interrupting."

"No, not at all. May I offer you some tea?"

"Yes, that would be lovely. Indian tea?"

He waggles his head, then disappears into the gyp room in which,
she sees, he has set up his makeshift kitchen. The room is clean and

spartan. There is his trunk, in the corner. Other than that, there is little furniture: a desk, a chair, and an old armchair from Alice's own attic. Through a half-open door, she sees the bed, tightly made. No pictures on the walls. Indeed, the only decorative object she can discern is the statue of Ganesha that she first happened upon when she rummaged through his trunk. Now it sits on the mantel over the hearth.

"Your rooms are very nice," she says.

"Thank you."

"I understand you moved recently."

"Yes. In Whewell's Court I was on the ground floor. Here I am on the second floor."

"And you prefer that?"

"There is less noise."

She inspects the book on the armchair, which is in Tamil. "What are you reading, Mr. Ramanujan?"

He darts out of the gyp room. "It is nothing."

"Some mathematical text?"

"No, it is the *Panchangam*. What we call a *Panchangam*. A sort of almanac."

"How fascinating." She picks up the book, leafs through it. "And what do you use it for?"

"It is only an old tradition," he says. "The *Panchangam* goes through the year, charting the positions of the stars and the moon. And so back home, they consult it to determine the most auspicious time and day for . . . important events."

"Such as?"

"Weddings. Funerals."

"But we're not having any weddings or funerals here, are we?"

"No, not just that. Also travel. Which are the most auspicious days to travel, and which days not to travel, and so on."

"You mean, there are certain days when you would and when you wouldn't want to go to London?"

He waggles his head.

"Or change your rooms?"

He is silent.

"Oh, I must sound horrible," Alice says. "As if I'm interrogating you. I don't mean to. You see, I'm not like the others, Mr. Ramanujan. I really want to know."

She looks him in the eye. He meets her gaze; his eyelids flutter but he doesn't turn away.

Then the kettle sings. "Excuse me," he says, and returns to the gyp room, from which he emerges, a few minutes later, bearing two cups on a tray.

"Please sit."

"Where will you sit?"

"Here."

So she sits in the armchair, and he sits, not far from her, on the floor. Cross-legged. At her knees, more or less. He hands her the tea.

"And do you always wear your *dhoti* in your rooms?"

"Not when I am expecting visitors."

"Then it's fortuitous that I didn't tell you I was coming."

He smiles and tries to hide his smile.

"Would you ever wear your *dhoti* to a lecture, Mr. Ramanujan? Or when you went to see Mr. Hardy?"

"Oh, no. Of course not."

"Why not?"

"It would not be correct."

"You are welcome to wear it when you visit me."

"I'm sorry I haven't been to visit you lately. I've been very busy with my work."

"Of course. And that's why you're here. To work." She puts down her cup. "You know, Mr. Ramanujan, I meant it when I said I wasn't like the others. Like Hardy and even—my husband. The others, they don't believe in your religion. And they think you don't believe in it, either. That you simply practice your . . . rituals . . . out of habit, or to please your people. But I do believe that you believe. And I'm interested. Genuinely interested. What a pity I can't understand your language! Then you could teach me to read the stars."

"I am not an expert."

"I hope I'm not offending you by asking. And it's not just out of idle curiosity. You see, Mr. Ramanujan, I want so much something to believe . . . Especially these days, with the war. It seems that all the old guarantees, that if you lived right and ate your vegetables . . . but that doesn't guarantee anything anymore, does it? Because all those young men, most of those young men . . . But if you could read the stars, if you could read the future—"

"It's not something you can teach."

She leans in toward him. "Tell me about the first time you had the dream."

"What dream?"

"When Namagiri wrote on your tongue."

"But the first time it was not Namagiri in the dream. It was Narasimha."

"Who is Narasimha?"

"He is the lion-faced avatar of Vishnu." Ramanujan puts his cup down next to him, on the floor. "I'm sorry. I must explain. In the Hindu religion a God can manifest himself in many forms. And Narasimha is one of those forms that Vishnu takes. The fourth form. The angry form. Well, there was a demon king called Hiranyakashipu who despised Vishnu. He performed many acts of penance to obtain a boon of immortality from Brahma, but Brahma only granted him the chance to choose the condition of his death. So Hiranyakashipu replied that his condition was to be killed neither by animal nor man, not during the night nor during the day, not inside or outside his house, not on earth or in space, neither by an animate nor an inanimate weapon. He thought he had tricked Vishnu, and was now immortal, and he declared himself king of the three worlds. But what he did not know was that his son, Prahlada, was devoted to Vishnu. So when he learned it, Hiranyakashipu tried to kill the little boy. He tried to have him boiled and set on fire and thrown away. But Prahlada was protected by his devotion to Vishnu. And then one afternoon at dusk in his palace, Hiranyakashipu smashed a pillar in a rage, and from the pillar Narasimha jumped out. Because he was half-man and half-lion, he was neither animal nor human. Because it was twilight, it was neither night nor day. They battled, and then, on the threshold of the palace, which was neither inside nor outside, Narasimha laid the demon on his knees, which was neither on earth nor in space, and using his nails, which were neither animate nor inanimate weapons, he tore Hiranyakashipu to shreds."

"What an extraordinary story."

"My grandmother told me this story many times when I was a child. She told me that the sign of Narasimha's grace is drops of blood seen in dreams. That was the first time. The drops of blood fell, and then it was as if . . . as if scrolls were unfolding before me, containing the most beautiful and complex mathematics. Endless scrolls. Endless formulae. And then, when I woke, I hurried to write down what I had seen."

"How old were you?"

"I was ten."

"And since then?"

"It is always like that. What I see in the dreams is boundless. The scrolls never cease."

"It must be beautiful," she says. "The scrolls unfolding."

"Oh, no, it is terrible."

"Terrible? Why?"

"Because what I can bring into the world is only the smallest fragment of what I read on the scrolls. There is always so much more that I cannot bring! And each time, leaving it behind, it is like being torn to shreds. Yes, it is a terrible dreaming."

He looks down as he says this. He is not weeping. He has his hands crossed placidly over his lap.

"You suffer, don't you?" Alice asks.

He doesn't answer.

Then she stands up. And Ramanujan, perhaps because he assumes that she is intending to leave, stands up too, and looks at her. "You're not much taller than I am," she says. "An inch at most." And, just as earlier she reached out and pushed the puzzle to the floor, so now she reaches out across the little distance to touch his cheek.

He flinches. He does not move.

She steps closer. Still he does not move.

She puts her hand on the back of his neck, as earlier that morning Eric put his hand on the back of her neck. She feels moisture and heat and small, sharp prickles of stubble. She pulls him closer and he does not resist when she puts his lips against hers. Neither, though, does he kiss her back. He is absolutely still. Their lips are touching. But it's not a kiss.

What is she supposed to do now? She senses that she could lead him into the bedroom, push him down on the bed, pull up his *dhoti* and her skirts and mount him, and he would not protest. But he would not encourage her, either. He would neither encourage nor discourage her.

His breath is warm and tastes of the tea. His lips are dry. Still they do not open.

Finally she steps away. He seems about to speak, and she puts her finger to her mouth—a universal gesture, she hopes. And he doesn't speak. He doesn't even move.

She walks away from him slowly, as if there's nothing left to hurry for. Then she opens the door and lets herself out.

12

New Lecture Hall, Harvard University

THE ARMBAND IS made of steel-colored wool (Hardy said in the lecture he did not give), emblazoned with a shining crown in imperial scarlet. I wore it just once or twice. To wear it in Cambridge was to draw the approval only of men I detested.

Now it sits in the second drawer from the top, left side, of a walnut chest I've had since I first arrived at Trinity, back in the last century. In the same drawer, there's a pair of Gaye's five-gloves, and a cricket ball, and some tennis balls with which we used to play indoor cricket, using a walking stick as a bat. Also our collection of train tickets. Gaye and I shared a passion for railwaydom. We used to make a game of planning routes between outrageous places—Wolverhampton and Leipzig, say—and seeing which of us could come up with the one that required the most changes. We loved the Underground, and when the Bakerloo line opened in 1906, we went into London just to ride it.

There are no letters in the drawer. We never wrote letters to each other. Nor are there cats' collars, or empty jars that once contained worm medicine. The things that you save—you save them, I suppose, so that when you're old, you can fondle and caress them and feel the breeze of nostalgia brushing your face.

What no one tells you is that by the time you're old, remembering is the last thing you want to do. That is, assuming you can remember where you put all that stuff.

I attested on the very last day that attestation was possible, the day before the Derby Scheme closed. This was in the middle of December, 1915. I did it in London, so that none of my Cambridge friends would see me. By mid-December, conscription seemed a certainty, and though no one in the government said so in so many words, most of us were convinced (wrongly, as it turned out) that if we attested, we would receive preferential treatment when the time came. Besides, Littlewood had of late written to tell me that, allowances having been made for his mathematical talents, he was being excused from artillery training and put to work improving the accuracy of anti-aircraft range tables. He would not leave England. I suppose I hoped that, if worse came to worst, I, too, would be put in a position of that sort—which raised the dilemma of whether I should agree, for the sake of my own safety, to apply my abilities to the prosecution of a war in which I did not believe. This was assuming, of course, that I was asked to do so. For all I knew, I might be sent to France as punishment for having attested so late.

I remember that the afternoon I went, I waited five hours in a queue, in wet, sleety weather. By the time I got to the recruiting office, it was well past midnight, and the women volunteers had run out of forms. So I had to come back the next morning and wait another five hours. Although medical exams were supposed to be given on the spot, the rush was by then so frantic that these had to be dispensed with. Instead we were told that we would be examined when we were called up, or summoned before the tribunals that would decide whether to grant us exemptions.

Of course, others refused. Pointedly. Neville, James Strachey, Lytton Strachey. I could have refused, too. Somehow, though, I couldn't see myself spending the next years, as some of the Blooms-berries would, doing "agricultural labor" and bickering with one another on Ottoline Morrell's farm. Nor could I stomach, as Lytton seemed calmly prepared to, the prospect of going to prison. Given the choice between prison and the trenches, I preferred the trenches.

Why? I suppose it came down to that romance of battle that I was spoon-fed from so early in my childhood. There was no equivalent romance of Wormwood Scrubs. Few of you here tonight, I would guess, can imagine what it was like to grow up in a world that had not yet known the Great War. Yet this was the world of my youth, in which war belonged to the distant past, or a distant realm: Africa or India. What notions we had of war came from books we read as children, in which boys scarcely older than we were wore armor, and rode steeds, and fought with swords. And the ministers of the government, because they had read the same books that we had, took advantage of this shared heritage to vilify the Germans. The Germans, they told us, routinely gathered up the bodies of dead Englishmen and used their fat for tallow. They had crucified two Canadian soldiers. They kept French women in their trenches as white slaves. They were descendants of ogres, just as we were descendants of knights.

Odd . . . today I have so few specific memories of those months! No doubt I was busy—I know this from looking at my diaries—and yet, when I recall them, I see myself, always and only, standing before my window at Trinity, staring out at the rain. This isn't, of course, possible. My diary for 1916, for instance, tells me that from January on, I spent a part of each week in London. Diaries are useful only as signposts to memory. And now, lo and behold, I find myself once running into Ramanujan, purely by chance, at Kensington Gardens, where the government, as part of its strenuous campaign to persuade the people at home that the war was going marvelously well and that the front was a sort of rustic, robust holiday camp, had dug "exhibition trenches" for the public to inspect and even climb down into. These trenches were a joke. They were tidy and dry, cut in a zigzag, with fortified walls and clean duckboard flooring. They had bunk beds and chairs and little kitchens in them. That day some soldiers were inspecting the exhibition trenches, home on leave from a world at once frighteningly remote and yet, as the crow flies, so close that people in Devon could hear the artillery fire in their kitchens. And these soldiers were laughing. They didn't even bother to say anything. They just looked down into the trenches and laughed.

It was inside the pseudo-trench that I found Ramanujan, peering at the walls in that strange, spectral way of his. He was by himself. I patted him on the back, surprising him, and he jumped. "Hardy," he said, and smiled. He seemed glad to see me.

After we climbed out, he asked me about the real trenches. "Is it true," he asked, "that the soldiers must stay in them all day?"

"And much of the night as well."

"And that the trenches are continuous, from the Belgian coast to Switzerland? I heard that if he wanted to, a man could walk, underground, the length of France."

"That may be possible in theory. I doubt it is possible in reality."

We strolled together, out of the park, Ramanujan with his hands shoved in his pockets for warmth. He was staying in Maida Vale again, at the boarding house run by his beloved Mrs. Peterson. With relish he described the route by which he had traveled to Kensington. He had begun his journey at the brand new tube station at Maida Vale, then changed at Paddington from the Bakerloo line to the District. He told me that he had been studying the Underground, and now knew which was the deepest station, and what was the longest distance between stations, and the shortest. He told me about a poster he had seen that day, a poster I had seen myself. Below a picture of children frolicking in a dusk meadow were the words:

WHY BOTHER ABOUT THE GERMANS INVADING THE COUNTRY?
INVADE IT YOURSELF BY UNDERGROUND AND MOTOR-BUS

He asked me if this was supposed to be funny, and I said that I supposed it was—a sort of "gallows humor," a term I then had to define for him.

After that, when we both happened to be in London, we sometimes went about together. Wherever we were going, he would insist that we go by tube, even when it would have been quicker to take a taxi or a bus. I never argued this point with him. How could I, when as a child I had dreamed that letters traveled by themselves from postbox to postbox, via underground tunnels? Verne's *Journey to the Center of the Earth* had been my favorite novel. Now I went to Foyle's and bought him a copy, which he devoured in one night—and no wonder! Suddenly ours was a world half-subterranean. Trenches crisscrossed Europe like tube lines, while beneath the German trenches, though we did not know this at the time, miners were patiently tunneling, digging shafts to fill with dynamite. A million pounds of dynamite.

One afternoon we went by tube to the zoo. The zoo was Rama-nujan's other passion. He seemed to know all the animals personally, and went so far as to apologize for the giraffes. "Their odor is offensive," he said, "though the zookeepers tell me that we smell as bad to them as they do to us." Then he introduced me to Winnie, the bear cub from Canada of whom he had grown so fond, and about whom he now seemed to know everything there was to know: that back in Quebec, her mother had been shot, and she captured by her mother's killer, and subsequently sold to a member of the Canadian

Mountain Rifles, a veterinarian named Colebourn. When Colebourn joined up, Winnie crossed the Atlantic with him and then stayed with him at his brigade headquarters on Salisbury Plain, where she followed the men around and ate out of their hands. Colebourn wanted to take Winnie to France with him, but his commanding officer would not allow a bear at the front, and so she was sent to live at the London zoo until her master returned from battle.

Perhaps subsequent events—in particular Milne's transformation of Winnie into Winnie-the-Pooh—have colored my memories of the many visits that Ramanujan and I paid to her cage. Milne, whom I will always think of as Russell's literary friend, editor of the *Granta*, young and quick and clever, is now, of course, famous for a series of books about a bear and a toy piglet and a donkey, books which I have read and from which, I am perfectly willing to admit, I have derived far more pleasure than I have from most of the so-called serious literature published in the last decades. (Give me Milne over Virginia Woolf any day!) In any case, when I recall those visits, I see Winnie black, as she was, not golden like her namesake; and yet I also see her scooping honey with her paw from a jar that a zookeeper holds out to her. Is it possible that such a scene ever took place?

I can't know. So much remains a blur. Dream and reality merge, and I can't keep anything in order. When was the *Lusitania* sunk? And in what sequence did the battles come? Ypres, Second Ypres, the Somme, Mons, Loos, Passchendaele. And the names of the dead—Brooke, Békássy, Bliss. Such an alliterative trio. *Brooke, Békássy, Bliss*. There you have it, the music of loss.

Every week I read the lists of the dead, and tried to keep clear in my head which of the men I knew at the front had been blown up, which were missing, which were maimed. More names each week, most of them only remotely familiar, attached to faces hurrying past in Great Court . . . Have you ever contemplated the curious fact that the population of the dead only ever gets larger, while on earth our number remains more or less constant? I used to think that, with all the young men dying, purgatory in those years must have been terribly crowded. It must have resembled a tube station into which, due to some cosmic signaling error, no trains ever arrive, so that the platform just gets more and more mobbed. All on one platform: the weeping, the furious, the suffering, waiting for the trains that will take them to judgment and, perhaps, rest. Here on earth, on the other hand, there were fewer youths than there should have been. Everywhere there should have been a youth, there was a cross, and a mother weeping, and offering up more sons, gladly, to the glory of England.

And all through it—how busy I must have kept myself! Perusing the diaries, I discover that, at different points, I was secretary of: (a) the Cambridge branch of the Union for Democratic Control and (b) the London Mathematical Society (L.M.S.). That the first of these, while hardly as radical as the No Conscription Fellowship, should have been considered subversive will come as no surprise: during the war any group that advocated peace as a goal was considered subversive. The second might seem the least likely organization in the world to arouse the suspicion, much less the attention, of the government. Yet the London Mathematical Society had always worked for the free exchange of ideas across borders, and continued to do so once the war began. "Mathematics," Hilbert would later famously declare, "knows no races. For mathematics, the whole cultural world is a single country." This was an even more radical idea in 1917, viewed as likely to undermine the hatred of the Other on which the war's popularity depended. Had we been able to, we in the London Mathematical Society would have gladly published in German periodicals. Short of that, we made a point of publishing in as many non-English journals as we could. Now I see that between 1914 and 1919, I published in the vicinity of fifty papers, some with Ramanujan, some with Littlewood, and nearly all of them abroad: in *Comptes Rendu*, and the *Journal of the Indian Mathematical Society*, and the *Tohoku Mathematical Journal*, and the marvelously named *Rendiconti del Circolo Matematico di Palermo*. More dangerously, from the point of view of the jingoists, I published frequently in *Acta Mathematica*, the Swedish editor of which had the audacity to include articles by Germans and Englishmen in the same issues. I even coauthored a short book with the Hungarian Marcel Riesz, written through correspondence. Our epigraph, in Latin, concluded: "Auctores Hostes Idemque Amici." *The authors, enemies and, at the same time, friends*. This alone was probably enough to get my name put on some government list of internal agitators.

And what of that other society, the secret one, from which I had taken wing, and yet to the activities of which I remained, sometimes reluctantly, attuned? It limped along, in its fashion. Every year we had a dinner in London: in 1915, at the dinner, Rupert Brooke's memory was toasted. Yet the animosity that had arisen, for example, between Dickinson and Moore, on the one hand, and McTaggart on the other could not be healed. Dickinson and Moore considered McTaggart a traitor to peace. McTaggart considered Dickinson and Moore traitors to England. They remained at opposite ends of the table and would not speak.

All that united us was mourning. Of the three lost boys, Békássy was the second to die, a few months after Brooke, a year or so before Bliss. It was Norton who came to break the news to me and to tell me how bad I must feel. No matter that I had barely even met that poor lovelorn Hussar! Norton had a way, especially in those days, of assuming that his own grief, joy, distress, longing—choose whichever emotion you like—had of necessity to be everyone else's. He often began his sentences, "Don't you?" or "Aren't you . . . ?" Irritating enough when the sentence is: "Don't you think this lemon cake delicious?" (I despise lemon cake.) But when the sentence is "Aren't you just grief-stricken about poor Békássy?" I could have struck him. For what could I say? No, I'm not, and I'd thank you not to supply my reactions to me ready-made? The truth was, I considered Békássy's death a stupidity. Like so many others, he had the idea in his head that the war would ennoble him, that he should go because, as he told Norton, it was part of "the good life" to go. But while he was waiting to be sent to the front, he wrote that he did not want to think about *why* he had gone: "I want to *be in it* and forget what I think." And of course, as he was an aristocrat, he joined the cavalry. According to Norton, he put three red roses on his horse's head because they were part of his family's coat of arms, and then he rode off to the Russian front, no doubt on some "trusted mount," scion of generations of Békássy equine nobility, and there he died.

And now the crisis (with Norton there was always a crisis) was whether to tell Bliss. No one knew exactly where Bliss was—in France, or still in England, training—or if breaking the news that his great love was dead was even a good idea, given that he was himself enlisted. I tried to help. I tried to find Bliss's brother—now, of course, renowned as a composer, though, given my equally famous tin ear, I'm not supposed to care about that. But Arthur Bliss was already in France. I didn't dare involve the parents. So I gave up. I have no idea if Bliss ever learned that Békássy was dead. He died himself not long after in the Somme, killed by a piece of shrapnel that lodged in his brain.

Today I cannot get too worked up when I think of these deaths. Too many others were lost whose lives would have mattered more. Nothing of consequence, I suspect, would have come of these three anyway.

One death in those years did affect me, profoundly, and that was Hermione's. Sheppard, if he were here today, would interrupt now to say that my suspicions about this matter are "paranoid." (Like so many others, he has become an aficionado of psychoanalysis, and likes to pepper his conversation with its jargon.) In turn I would tell him that he is far too inclined to assume the best of people. For the facts are what they are. Hermione died suddenly of a digestive ailment that went undiagnosed. And I am convinced that it was poison. Yes, I am sure that someone gave her meat or fish laced with poison. It would have been easy to do. I never locked my door. And she died at the beginning of 1916, just as I was becoming actively involved, along with Moore and Neville, in a war with the Trinity council.

This is what happened. As I mentioned, I was secretary of the Cambridge branch of the Union for Democratic Control, a comparatively benign organization the official goal of which was to agitate for a just settlement once the war was over and to insist that in future the government enter into no more secret "arrangements" with allies without parliament first having a chance to vote. As a goal, of course, this was hopelessly naïve, in that it was predicated on the assumption that the war would end quickly. Once it became obvious that the war was not going to end quickly, we in the U.D.C.—privately at least— began to think in terms of a draw and a compromised peace. This was, to say the least, an unpopular line to take, and as rumor spread that our secret and real ambition was to broker a ceasefire with the Germans, so the conviction that the U.D.C. was not at all what it pretended to be, that, on the contrary, it was a radical group bent on undermining the aims of England, took hold.

Not surprisingly, the Cambridge branch was very active. Indeed, by the end of 1915, we had already held a number of private meetings, and hosted a public one at the Guildhall. The trouble began when we put a comparatively innocuous notice in the *Cambridge Magazine*, announcing that we would be holding our annual general meeting in Littlewood's rooms and that Charles Buxton would speak on "Nationality and the Settlement." Although Littlewood was in Woolwich at the time, he, too, was a member of the U.D.C. (More of our members were in uniform than you might guess.) Littlewood had agreed to let us use his empty rooms for the meeting, while Buxton was an expert on the Balkans whose wife, Dorothy, each week, culled articles from the foreign press and published them in a column in the *Cambridge Magazine* that offered an alternative to the relentless jingoism and Boche-bashing of the *Times*. All, in other words, perfectly aboveboard, if a bit anti-government. But the meeting never took place. A week after the announcement was posted, a letter appeared in the same publications. Its author was the secretary of the Trinity Council, and in it he communicated the Council's decision to prohibit the U.D.C. from holding any meetings within the precincts of Trinity. No private communication preceded the publication of this letter, from which fact we deduced that the message was meant not just for us in the U.D.C. at Trinity, but for Cambridge at large. The day we had arrived as freshmen, Butler had told us that the university would "feed men of culture as God feeds the sparrows." Now even peaceful dissent, it seemed, was no longer to be tolerated.

Moore had his own solution. A week later he published a sort of "modest proposal" in the *Cambridge Magazine*, in which he applauded the Council's "spirited" action and suggested, along the same lines, that the Council should "suspend all services in the College Chapel until the conclusion of the war" on the grounds that "at services of the Christian churches young men are liable to have brought to their notice maxims quite as dangerous to their patriotism as any which they will hear at a meeting of the Union of Democratic Control." It was, I thought, a brilliant move, in that it threw into relief the Council's hypocrisy: how, after all, could an institution that claimed to be built on Christian doctrine suppress an organization that was striving for peace? A contradiction! *Reductio ad absurdum*. What I did not understand, then, was that as part of their training, agents of authority learn to adjudge when it is advisable simply to say nothing. Nothing was said now, and in short order the reading public—those members of it, that is, perspicacious enough to have gleaned Moore's Swiftian intention—let their attention wander from this tempest in a Trinity teapot to more pressing matters of political victory and trench defeat.

Still, we felt obliged to do something, and in January, Neville and I called a special college meeting to protest the Council's ejection of the U.D.C. In retrospect, the proceedings are comical to relate, as may be typical of such gatherings. First we put forward a resolution "that in the opinion of this meeting a Fellow of the College should be entitled to receive in his rooms as guests members of a society invited to promote its objects, these being neither illegal nor immoral." Before this resolution could be voted upon, however, an amendment was proposed "that the word 'privately' be inserted between the words 'society' and 'invited.'" This was carried by a vote of 41 to 2. (I was one of the dissenters.) Then a second amendment was proposed "to add at the end of the resolution the words 'provided the interests of the College are not prejudiced thereby.'" This amendment was carried by a vote of 28 to 14. So now the resolution read "that in the opinion of this meeting a Fellow of the College should be entitled to receive in his rooms as guests members of a society *privately* invited to promote its objects, these being neither illegal nor immoral *provided the interests of the College are not prejudiced thereby*."

All this Neville and I observed, as it were, open-mouthed. It was astonishing: with a kind of bureaucratic judiciousness, and by means of a discussion as rancorless as the letter that the Council had sent to the magazine, the fellows at the meeting had managed to transform the original resolution into a statement noteworthy only for its absolute impotence. And all this through the addition of eleven words. Democracy, though it may be the only choice we have, can by its very patience sometimes make one long for benevolent dictatorship.

I remember that at this meeting, I was sitting between Butler and Jackson, the classicist, who must have been in his late seventies by then, and was both shortsighted and rather deaf. As I recall, I was in the midst of making a statement—a response to the addition of the final clause to the proposal, the clause that was its undoing—when Jackson interrupted me, perhaps because he could neither see nor hear me speaking. "I am an old man," he said, "and I hope that the war may continue many years after my death." This is—I swear it—what he said.

The next afternoon I found Hermione dead. Whether she suffered agonies to equal those of the soldiers who died alone, abandoned in No Man's Land, I shall never know, for I was away in London most of the day in question, and only returned late, to find her lying quite still before a pool of vomit. She looked peaceful, and had stretched out her body in much the same way that she did in sleep. And while she was not atop her favorite ottoman, she was near it. There was vomit on the ottoman too, a tidy pile. Hermione always was a very tidy cat.

I carried her corpse to the Backs, and buried her near where Gaye and I had buried Euclid. And then I decided that, as soon as I could find a means to, I would leave Trinity.

Euclid's death had been less sudden. He suffered from worms. We had taken him to the veterinarian, who explained that whenever he tried to eat, the worms would come up from his stomach into his esophagus and nearly choke him. The veterinarian gave us a powder, which we mixed with milk. Unfortunately, whenever we tried to get the milk and powder mixture down his throat, he would be sick.

My recollection of the afternoon before he died is far more vivid than most of my memories of the war. Leonard Woolf had come to see us, along with a chap called Fletcher who now told the most disgusting story. At a circus in France he had seen a woman, bare-breasted and immense, crawl around a pit in a pair of bright red drawers, catching rats with her teeth and killing them. I can't recall exactly what led Fletcher to tell this story, only that the telling was vivid, and that he punctuated it with the same repetitive expressions—"It was really too repulsive"; "It really was too filthy"—to which he customarily took recourse in conversation. When he was done, Euclid, much to our amazement, got up and started walking backward, which led Gaye to inquire whether walking backward was a bad symptom in a cat. No one seemed to know. And then Woolf and Fletcher left, and Gaye and I were alone with Euclid, who continued to walk backward about the room, hitting walls and knocking over furniture. We dared not stop him, as one dares not wake a sleepwalker, and when, once or twice, Gaye made an effort to turn him aright, he would resume walking backward within seconds.

Finally he hit the door to my room and collapsed. We carried him to his basket and tried, once again, to give him some of his medicine. Again he vomited it up.

Shortly thereafter Gaye and I bade each other goodnight. Although we had been sharing the suite for a year, we had not yet spent a night in the same bed. But that night he came into my room, woke me, and said, "Harold, may I get in with you?" And I said that, of course, he could. And then he embraced me from behind—we were both wearing our pyjamas but even so, as he embraced me, I could feel that he had an erection and was pressing it into my backside. And I pressed back.

We lay there like that for an hour or so, alternately pressing and sleeping, until Gaye complained that his left arm was falling asleep, at which point we switched positions, and I did the pressing, and he the pressing back. Then my right arm fell asleep. All night we kept shifting position as our respective arms feel asleep.

Sometime during that night, Euclid died. We buried him the next morning near the river. But the next night, and for many nights thereafter, Gaye slept in my bed. And though, when we were with others, we continued to call each other "Gaye" and "Hardy," in private we started to call each other "Russell" and "Harold."

Soon enough the pyjamas came off.

PART SIX

Partition

I

ONCE AGAIN, Ramanujan is making *rasam* in his gyp room. It's the middle of January, 1916. He's wearing two jumpers and a woolen muffler made especially for him, Hardy told him, by a writer who, having developed acute insomnia as a result of war worries, has taken up knitting as a means of passing the long nights. Now the writer generates upwards of twenty mufflers a week, most of which he sends to the troops in France. This one, however, he made specially for Ramanujan when he learned of his difficulties coping with the English winter. The muffler is green and orange—"no, not green and orange," Hardy corrected himself, when he presented it to Ramanujan, "mint and saffron. Strachey insisted that I say mint and saffron." In fact, the green is more the shade of banana leaves than mint leaves, while the orange lacks saffron's hint of gold. It brings to mind ripe mangoes or turmeric. As it happens, Ramanujan is just now spooning some turmeric into a bowl. The lentils for the *rasam* sit in a second bowl. Picking through them for bits of grit, as his mother taught him to do, he spills a few on the table top. As he sweeps them together, he counts them. Seven lentils. How many ways can you divide up seven lentils? Well—he tests it out—you could divide them into 7 groups of 1 each, or one of 6 and one of 1, or one of 5 and two of 1 each, or one of 5 and one of 2, or one of 4 and one of 3, or one of 4 and one of 2 and one of 1, or three of 2 each and one of 1, or . . .

15 in all. Yes, you can divide 7 lentils up 15 ways.

So how many ways can you divide up 8 lentils?

Carefully he takes a single lentil from the bowl and puts it on the table with the others.

Eight groups of 1 each, one group of 7 and one of 1, one group of 6 and one of 2, one group of 6 and two of 1 each . . .

22 ways.

And 9?

30 ways.

He keeps going. He does not eat. It is well past midnight by the time he has worked out the number of ways you can divide up 20 lentils, and by then lentils are everywhere: spread out over the table in neat configurations, on the floor, under the hob. Some, he will soon discover, have migrated into his bed. They stick to the fibers of the muffler made by the famous writer. For the next year his bedmaker, when she does the sweeping, will find them in her dustpan. In 1994 an engineering student from Jakarta, while trying to retrieve a lost contact lens, will excavate one from the gap between two floorboards.

The *rasam* remains uncooked.

627 ways.

2

IN THE MORNING, he goes to Hardy's rooms. When he takes his coat off, lentils fall from the lining.

"What's wrong?" Hardy says. "You look exhausted."

"Last night I was cooking. I am hosting a dinner. Tuesday week. I wonder if you would do me the honor of attending."

"Of course," Hardy says. "What's the occasion?"

"Chatterjee is getting married."

"Is he now? How lovely for him. So—round numbers."

"Yes, round numbers."

Hardy steps up to the blackboard. At present he's trying to get Ramanujan to focus on a proof that almost all numbers n are composed of approximately $\log \log n$ prime factors. This proof Hardy feels especially determined to complete, not only because the result will be their first joint publication, but because, if they finish it, he'll feel that he's succeeded, at last, in converting Ramanujan to his own religion: the religion of proof.

The trouble, as usual, is that Ramanujan won't concentrate. He fidgets with his pen. He keeps blowing his nose.

"Are you sure you're all right?" Hardy asks.

Ramanujan waggles his head.

"I'm only asking because you seem a bit distracted. Is it the dinner?"

"Oh, no. The lentils."

"The lentils?"

"For the *rasam*." And Ramanujan proceeds to explain that, as he laid out the ingredients for his *rasam*, he started counting lentils, and that got him thinking about partitions.

This is not the first time they have talked about partitions. Indeed, partition theory has been on their minds, albeit in a rather scattershot way, ever since Hardy received Ramanujan's first letter, and encountered a statement about a theta series the very inaccuracy of which opened up a startling new angle on the question. Calculating p (n)—the partition number of a number—is easy when n is 5 or 7; the problem is, as you climb up the number line, p(n) increases at an astounding rate. For instance, the partition number of 7 is 15, while the partition number of 15 is 176. So what's the partition number of 176?

476,715,857,290.

What, then, would be the partition number of 476,715,857,290?

"And where have the lentils led you?"

"I have an idea for a formula for calculating the partition number of a number. Even a very large number." He stands. "May I?"

"Of course." Hardy wipes the blackboard clean, and Ramanujan steps up to it. He starts to draw diagrams: little dots representing lentils. Then he writes out the theta series from his original letter. Then Hardy mentions a generating function that Euler came up with, leading to the power series

$$1 + \sum p(n)x^n = \prod_{n=1}^{\infty}\left(\frac{1}{1-x^n}\right)$$

And they're lost. On the blackboard the first crude terms of the formula emerge. What they're trying to build one might think of as a sort of machine into which you insert a ball emblazoned with an integer—n—only to see it emerge, a few seconds later, emblazoned with a second integer—p(n). Yet what permutations the ball must be put through in the course of its journey! And what unexpected elements must go into the building of the machine! Imaginary numbers, π, trigonometric functions. Once again, a simple question is proving to require a very complicated answer.

By noon, Hardy is exhausted, elated. He wants to break for lunch, then immediately get back to work, only Ramanujan demurs. "I have some other business to attend to," he says.

"Oh, very well," Hardy says, his voice thick with impatience. "But try to get here early tomorrow. This is most exciting. We're really on to something here."

The next morning Ramanujan arrives late, disheveled, and smelling peculiarly sour.

"I was preparing the *rasam*," he says by way of excuse.

"But I thought you made it the night before."

"I meant to, but the lentils—"

"I don't see why this particular *rasam* is turning out to be such a production," Hardy says, wiping the blackboard clean.

"But this is no ordinary *rasam*. It is a very refined *rasam*. With tomatoes. And I must make it in quantity."

"Let's leave off cookery for the moment and move on to more important matters, shall we?" And Hardy starts to write. He wants to talk about Cauchy's theorem, and some ideas he's had concerning the unit circle on the complex plane that, though at first glance they don't seem to bear on partitions at all, may in fact illuminate the route they're looking for. He talks, and though Ramanujan seems to take everything in, he says almost nothing. The dinner, it seems, has obsessed him. When, later, Hardy asks him what he's planning to prepare, he won't answer. Clearly, though, esoteric supplies are needed, for the next morning he disappears—leaving only the briefest of notes—only to return that afternoon (the porter reports this to Hardy) bearing three bulging paper bags. Has he been to London, then? And who else, besides Chatterjee and his fiancée, is he planning to invite?

"Miss Chattopadhyaya will be there," Ramanujan says. "She is studying ethics at Newnham and is the sister of a distinguished poetess. Also Mahalanobis."

"What about Ananda Rao?"

"I thought of asking him, but he is too immature."

"And the Nevilles?"

Ramanujan hesitates. "I do not think that this would be the sort of occasion that Mrs. Neville would enjoy."

"Really? I suspect she'd enjoy it thoroughly."

"No, she would not. I am sure."

Hardy decides to leave that one alone.

3

FOR THE NEXT several days, Ramanujan frets about the dinner. He cannot focus on anything else. This frustrates Hardy no end. After all, the phase of imaginative ferment in which he now finds himself—who knows how long it will last? Such episodes are notoriously capricious. One day you wake up ready to do the best work of your life, the next, for no clear reason, you discover that both your inspiration and your energy have withered away. He wishes Ramanujan could understand this. Yet he also knows that, were it Littlewood he was dealing with, he'd give him a wider berth. Indeed, the success of his collaboration with Littlewood owes, to a great degree, to their willingness to give each other latitude. So why, with Ramanujan, does this feeling always creep in that somehow Ramanujan owes him, as recompense for his having brought him to Cambridge in the first place, the full and constant benefit of his genius? To make such a demand, he knows, is completely unreasonable. After all, as everyone is always reminding him, Ramanujan has needs of his own. And some of them have nothing to do with mathematics.

At last Tuesday arrives. Not surprisingly, Hardy doesn't see Ramanujan at all that morning. He works alone, then does the puzzles in the new issue of the *Strand*. After lunch, which he takes in Hall, he meets up with Neville and Russell to discuss the burgeoning crisis of the U.D.C. Neville says nothing about the dinner. Is it possible he hasn't heard about it?

Dusk descends. Hardy bathes, shaves, polishes his shoes, and puts on his tie and jacket. He is just about to leave when he remembers that he's neglected to fill Hermione's water dish—and then he remembers that Hermione is dead. The dish is now on the mantel, next to Gaye's bust, which seems, tonight, to glare at him with more fury than usual. "Well, what can I do?" he asks. "I'm not ready for another cat—

though Mrs. Bixby's sister . . ." But he's tired of conversing with the dead. So he descends the staircase, steps into the cold air of New Court, makes the one-minute walk to Bishop's Hostel, and climbs the nearly identical staircase that leads to Ramanujan's rooms. On the other side of the door, voices murmur in an unrecognizable language. He knocks, and Ramanujan—his face scrubbed shiny, his jacket straining at the buttons, stretched tightly across his torso—lets him in.

Instantly all conversation ceases. Hardy looks around in amazement. The armchair and desk have been pushed to the side to make room for a long dining table covered with a white cloth, no doubt borrowed for the occasion from the college. Chairs from Hall and place settings and place cards have been laid out. The table is so big, and the room so small, that there's hardly anywhere to stand. Ramanujan's guests are backed into corners or up against the wall. And they are absolutely silent.

Ramanujan leads Hardy to one of them, a dark-skinned woman in her late twenties, elegantly dressed in a green and blue sari shot through with gold thread.

"May I present Miss Chattopadhyaya?" he says.

Miss Chattopadhyaya reaches out her hand. "How do you do?" she says.

"Very well, thank you," Hardy says. "And you?"

"Very well, thank you."

Such niceties! Rather than reaching out his hand, the turbaned Mahalanobis bows; still, the exchange is virtually identical to the one that Hardy has just had with Miss Chattopadhyaya. By contrast Chatterjee, who must come from a more sophisticated background, greets him with the casualness of a public school man: a slap on the back, an old-chummy salute, after which he introduces his fiancée, Miss Rudra (what names these Indians have!), who has a young, fresh mouth to which she chronically lifts her hand, as if to hold back a fit of giggling. She is a student, Chatterjee announces proudly, at the local teachers' college. They will be married at the end of the month. It is difficult, their families are so far away . . . At the mention of the families Miss Rudra puts her hand to her mouth, while Chatterjee, his lean musculature barely discernible beneath the layers of jacket and dress shirt, places his hand on her back.

Ramanujan, in the meantime, has gone into the gyp room, from which a complexity of aromas emanates: sourness, smoke, the prickle of cumin and the musty sweetness of coriander powder. Hardy follows him in. The little table is crowded with food: not only the *rasam* in its silvered pot, but steamed white cakes (of rice?), and triangles of stuffed dough, and yogurt with cucumber and tomatoes, and fried potatoes, and a red stew.

"And you managed to prepare all this on a single gas ring?"

Ramanujan nods his head.

"No wonder you've been working so hard." Hardy rubs his hands together. "Well, it all smells delicious. You've done a remarkable job, my friend." He pats Ramanujan on the back, and Ramanujan jumps. "Easy! No need to be nervous. You're among friends."

"I have burned the *pongal*."

"It doesn't matter. No one will mind."

"But I labored over the *pongal*. Only one shop in London had the green gram. Mrs. Peterson found it for me."

"It doesn't matter."

"And the rice is overcooked."

"I tell you, it doesn't matter. The important thing is the company."

"Well, it cannot be helped. We must go on." Then he leaves the gyp room, with Hardy in tow. "The meal is prepared," he says, almost grievously. "Shall we sit?"

Once again, all conversation ceases. The guests take their places. Ramanujan carries in the pot of *rasam*; ladles the soup—what was it he said the English called it? Pepper water?—into bowls.

Hardy tastes. The liquid in his spoon is thin, reddish brown, and seems to distill a dozen flavors, none of which he can name. There is tartness, and sweetness, and fire, and a certain muddiness; what he imagines dirt would taste like. "My compliments," Miss Chattopadhyaya says. Miss Rudra waggles her head. Chatterjee eats fast and recklessly, Mahalanobis with a gentility verging on indifference. Ramanujan doesn't eat at all.

Suddenly he bounds up. "Oh, but I have forgotten the pappadum!" he says. And he rushes into the gyp room, only to return a few seconds later bearing a basket of crisp wafers. "Now they are cold."

"Never mind," Hardy says, breaking his into pieces. He has finished his bowl of soup. They have all finished their bowls of soup, except for Miss Rudra, who eats extremely slowly. It's not that she eats little—

she empties her bowl—but rather that she manages to keep each spoonful in her mouth for longer than any human being Hardy has ever known. What a trial of a wife she will make!

Second servings of the *rasan* are ladled out. The talk turns to cricket, a subject at which Mahalanobis proves to be surprisingly conversant. That Chatterjee knows his cricket, of course, comes as no surprise. He speaks of the game's history in India, the great players he admired as a boy, Calcutta's Maidan. All the while the women listen, Miss Rudra, for once, with her mouth uncovered. The bowls are empty now. "And who would care for a third helping?" Ramanujan asks.

"I wouldn't say no," Hardy says.

"That is most gracious of you, Mr. Ramanujan," says Miss Chattopadhyaya, "but I must decline."

"Miss Rudra?"

She covers her mouth with her hands; shakes her head no.

"I see. Very well."

Ramanujan returns to the gyp room. Hardy starts naming his favorite cricket players, including Levison-Gower, of whom Chatterjee proves to be less admiring than he ought to be. A friendly argument starts up. The ladies smile. Then Hardy hears, or thinks he hears, a door clicking shut.

For a few seconds, no one says anything. The conversation dissipates. Cautiously Hardy looks over his shoulder, into the gyp room.

"Has he gone out?" Mahalanobis asks.

"Perhaps he needed something from the college kitchen," Chatterjee says.

They wait. Finally Hardy gets up and opens the door to the corridor.

"No sign of him," he says.

An uneasy silence falls. There are certain possibilities that none of the men wants to bring up in front of the ladies, and so Hardy is rather surprised to hear Miss Chattopadhyaya say, "Shouldn't someone go downstairs to the toilets? He might need help."

"I'll go," Chatterjee says.

"I'll go with him," Mahalanobis says. And they march out the door, only to return, a few minutes later, alone.

"He is not in the toilet," Chatterjee says.

"What could have happened?" asks Miss Chattopadhyaya.

Another expedition is organized. Leaving the ladies behind, the three men walk briskly to the college kitchens. No, Mr. Ramanujan has not passed by, the chef reports. So they go to the porter's lodge.

"He left fifteen minutes ago," the porter says.

"Where was he going?"

"He didn't speak to me. But I must say, it struck me as odd, seeing as he didn't have his overcoat on."

"Which direction was he heading?"

"Towards King's Parade."

Hardy strides out the college gates; looks up and down the street, in both directions. No sign of Ramanujan.

"He's gone," Chatterjee says, with more surprise than distress in his voice.

"What else is there to do?" ask Mahalanobis.

"Nothing," Hardy says. And they head back to Ramanujan's rooms, where the ladies await them.

Now the dilemma is what to do with all the food. Should they wrap it up? No one is sure.

In the end they leave it. No doubt Ramanujan will return later. Were they to pack up the food, or throw it away, he might be offended.

It goes without saying that they will not continue eating.

At the foot of the stairs the members of the perplexed party bid each other farewell, and head their separate ways.

Hardy—still hungry—wishes he had had the third bowl of *rasam*.

4

THE NEXT MORNING Ramanujan fails to show up at Hardy's rooms. "Curious," Hardy says to no one. But he goes about his business anyway. He reads the papers; works, as best he can, on the partitions formula; finding that he cannot concentrate, picks up the *Cambridge Magazine*, and then throws it aside. How vexing! The moment of ferment is fading—he can feel it. Important work may be lost, and it will all be Ramanujan's fault. But there's no point in dwelling on that, so he retrieves the *Cambridge Magazine* from where he's dropped it. Since a few months ago, Mrs. Buxton, wife of Charles Buxton, who was to have spoken at the ill-fated meeting of the U.D.C., has been editing a section entitled "Notes from the Foreign Press," which consists of excerpts of articles from dozens of foreign papers, including enemy papers, which she has managed to obtain permission to import from Scandinavia, translated into English. *Neue Freie Presse* (chief Vienna daily), *National Tidende* (Copenhagen, conservative), *Vorwärts* (German, Social Democratic) . . . How varied are the responses to the war, how right every side believes itself to be! His eyes wander to the adverts. *Under the Red Robe* is playing at the Victoria Cinema, accompanied by *His Soul Reclaimed* ("a very Dramatic Episode of the Staircase Life") and footage of "20,000 German prisoners captured in Champagne." Chivers' Olde English Marmalade, Officers' Uniforms at Joshua Taylor & Co., "Health Über Alles" at Le Strange Arms and Gold Links Hotel, Hunstanton. *Hun*stanton? . . . Outside his window, the sun has come out. Why not a walk? So he puts on his coat, heads downstairs, happens to stroll by Bishop's Hostel.

On Ramanujan's landing, he encounters a bedmaker. "No sign of him, sir," she says. "And all that food going to waste."

"Why don't you eat it?"

She blushes. "Oh, sir, it's rather strange food what he eats. I'd be afraid."

"Well, let me know when he comes back, would you? Or tell Mrs. Bixby."

"Of course, sir."

That night, at Hall, Russell asks what's happened. "I suspect he's gone to London," Hardy says. "Nothing to be concerned about." But afterward, when he gets back to New Court, he finds young Ananda Rao waiting at the foot of his stairs in his gown and mortarboard.

"He is not in London," Ananda Rao says. "I telegraphed Mrs. Peterson. He is not at her boardinghouse."

"I wouldn't worry. I'm sure he'll be fine."

Ananda Rao doesn't move. Is he hoping that Hardy will invite him upstairs? *Should* Hardy invite him upstairs?

"Well, goodnight," he says finally.

"Goodnight, sir," Ananda Rao says. And he turns away. Is there a look of regret on his face as he walks toward the archway?

Hardy closes the door. A missed opportunity perhaps. If so, one better not taken up. After all, he is a student. And, as Ramanujan himself said, "immature."

5

FOUR DAYS PASS, and not a sign of him. Finally Hardy tells Mrs. Bixby to give Ramanujan's bedmaker permission to throw away the food from the dinner party, which is starting to stink. He sends a note to Chatterjee, asking if he's heard any news. "I have not," Chatterjee replies. "But I am told by some who know Ramanujan better than I that such disappearances are not out of character for him. He has done the same thing before."

Then another note arrives, from Mrs. Neville.

Dear Mr. Hardy,

I am deeply distressed to learn from my husband of Mr. Ramanujan's "dinner party" last week and his subsequent disappearance. What distresses me far more, however, than the question of what provoked his disappearance (a matter on which I can only speculate), is the impression I have that nothing is being done. Has it not occurred to you that he may be lying ill or injured on a roadside somewhere? Did he have money with him when he left? Should the police not be notified?

Please inform me as soon as possible what steps have been taken. If I do not hear from you by the end of the day I shall take steps to notify the police myself.

Alice Neville

Interfering bitch. What business is it of hers, anyway? But he writes the required reply.

Mrs. Neville,

While I understand, of course, your concern over Mr. Ramanujan's well-being, I would beg you not to jump to conclusions.

He is a grown man and capable of taking care of himself. Nor, I gather, is it unusual for him to "disappear" from time to time. The genius often has odd habits. Until there is reasonable cause to do so, I cannot see what benefit would be gained from contacting the police, short of humiliating Mr. Ramanujan and leading him to believe that he is not, in our country, free to go where he pleases and do what he pleases.

G. H. Hardy

No reply is forthcoming, at least not from Alice. Gertrude writes, though.

Dear Harold,
   Alice is in a state of extreme anxiety over Ramanujan which your note did little to allay. Can you do nothing to ease her worry? Short of that, will you promise me no longer to add to it? She is very sensitive and genuinely cares about Ramanujan.

Your loving sister,
Gertrude

Well, what's this about? And from Gertrude, of all people! Has Alice somehow won her over? Gertrude, he knows, has little patience for hysteria. So how is it that suddenly she has become Alice Neville's advocate?

The ways of women will never cease to perplex him.

6

TUESDAY, A WEEK since the dinner party, there is a knock on his door. He opens it and sees Chatterjee.

"I have received a telegram from Ramanujan," Chatterjee says.

"Thank God. Where is he?"

"Oxford."

"What's he doing there?"

"He doesn't say. He only asks me to send him five pounds."

"Good lord!"

"The address is a boardinghouse. I suspect he has to pay the bill and his train ticket back to Cambridge."

"Have you sent it?"

Chatterjee looks at the floor. "I could do so in a week," he says, "but at the moment, old chap, I don't have five pounds to spare . . . the wedding arrangements . . . I could manage two . . ."

"Not to worry," Hardy says. "I'll send it. What's the address?"

Chatterjee hands him a slip of paper. They walk together to the telegraph office. "Do let me know when you hear from him, will you?" Hardy says afterward, as they're heading out into the street.

"Of course. Good of you to help him out."

"And I'm sorry about the dinner . . . I hope Miss Rudra wasn't offended."

"She's a simple girl. Such things don't affect her."

They shake hands and part. Hardy returns to his rooms. All that afternoon and evening he fights the impulse to stroll by Bishop's Hostel, or—stronger still—to check the train schedule, to wait at the station for the trains from Oxford.

Instead he asks Mrs. Bixby to ask Ramanujan's bedmaker to let her know once he's come back.

"He returned late last night, sir," Mrs. Bixby tells him the next morning.

"Good. Thank you," Hardy says. Then he runs about, setting things up in the room to give the impression that in the interval, he hasn't even missed Ramanujan. Newspapers spread on the table, figures on the blackboard, paper on the desk.

As expected, around nine, there is a knock on the door. Hardy opens it.

"Good morning," Ramanujan says.

"Good morning," Hardy says.

Ramanujan steps inside. He is holding what appears to be a page torn from the *Daily Mail*, soiled and crumpled. "I believe I have made some refinements to the partitions formula," he says.

"Excellent. I'm eager to see them."

Ramanujan unballs the page from the *Daily Mail*, the margins of which, Hardy sees now, he has covered with tiny figures and symbols, written in his familiar, tidy hand. "It is far from complete. Still, with low values I obtain a result that is fairly close to p(n). About five percent off."

"Yes, I obtained much the same result, working on my own, while you were gone."

"Did you? Well, then . . ."

Ramanujan folds up the ball of paper; sits. Hardy sits across from him.

"The trouble is, we need a table of high values in order to have accurate solutions with which to compare the results of the formula."

"Indeed." Hardy is quiet for a few seconds. Then he says, "Ramanujan, I don't want to pry, nor are you in any sense obliged to answer, but . . . Well, we were all rather worried when you left. Tell me, why did you go to Oxford?"

Ramanujan looks into his lap. He rubs his hands together.

"It was the ladies," he says after a moment.

"The ladies?"

"Miss Rudra and Miss Chattopadhyaya. They would not accept the food I offered."

"But they did accept it."

"I offered them third bowls of *rasam* and they would not accept. I was hurt and insulted, and I went out in despair. I didn't want to come back. Not while they were there. But I had a little money in my pocket, so I went to the station and caught the first train to Oxford."

"But the ladies had already eaten two bowls. I don't know how it is in India, but you must remember, in England, at least, ladies like us to think, well, that they have smaller stomachs. They feel it would be impolite, unfeminine, to eat too much."

"I worked for more than a week preparing that meal. They insulted me. I could not sit by while—"

"Still, you could have let me know. The fact is, it was quite an inconvenience, your being away."

"I wasn't idle. As I said, I made some improvements on the formula. And now if we could just obtain some high values for the function, we would be in a position to test it out."

"Oh, don't worry about that. We'll ask Major MacMahon."

"Who is Major MacMahon?" Ramanujan asks.

"You shall soon see," says Hardy. "He's very curious to meet you."

7

W HO *IS* MAJOR MACMAHON? He is the sort of man who might best be summed up by his titles. Among other things, he is, or has been, Deputy Warden of the Standards of the Board of Trade, Member of the *Comité International des Poids et Mesures*, General Secretary of the British Association, Fellow of the Royal Society, Former president of both the London Mathematical Society and the Royal Astronomy Society, Member of the Permanent Eclipse Committee, and Member of the Council of the Royal Society of Art.

Major MacMahon is the son of Brigadier-General P. W. MacMahon. For some years he was with the Royal Artillery in Madras, where he participated in a famous punitive attack against the Jawaki Afridis in Kashmir. Upon his return to England he was named professor of mathematics at the Artillery College in Woolwich, where Littlewood now toils. Then he retired from the military, and now he lives with Mrs. Major MacMahon on Carlisle Place in Westminster. He has enormous whiskers, and would be the first to tell you that he enjoys nothing better than a glass of good port and a game of billiards.

In March of 1916, Hardy takes Ramanujan to see him. When they arrive at his house, the maid leads them not into the sitting room but the billiards room, the floor of which is laid with Indian carpets pillaged, in all probability, during that famous raid in Kashmir. All the furniture—the sofa, the Queen Anne chair with its ball-and-claw feet, even the billiards table itself—drips gold and red bullion fringe. From over the hearth, a deer's head gazes down with that expression of mingled contempt and boredom at which taxidermists seem to specialize. Ramanujan looks at it, then turns away, clearly disconcerted.

"Haven't you ever seen a hunting trophy?" Hardy asks.

He shakes his head no.

"In England they kill for sport. I say 'they' because I myself would never take part in such a barbaric form of self-amusement."

"And do they eat the deer?"

"Only occasionally."

Now Major MacMahon comes into the room, accompanied by Mrs. Major MacMahon, who immediately announces that she doesn't understand a thing about mathematics and must go to the kitchen to oversee some bottling. Then she leaves. The major motions for Hardy and Ramanujan to sit on the sofa. He opens a box of cigars, takes one out and lights it; offers the box to Hardy and Ramanujan, both of whom decline. "Well, I'll smoke alone then," he says, with a twinge of mild affront. "So, Mr. Ramanujan"—blowing smoke in his direction—"I understand you're a crack calculator. As Hardy may have told you, I'm rather decent at mental arithmetic myself. How about a little contest?"

"Contest?"

"Yes, contest." The major stands again, and pulls a blackboard on wheels from the corner. "Here's what I want you to do, Hardy. I want you to write down a number, any number you like, and then we'll see which of us can break it down first."

He throws Ramanujan a piece of chalk, which Ramanujan fails to catch.

"You stand here, next to me. When you've got the answer, put it on the blackboard."

But Ramanujan is on the floor, trying to find the piece of chalk, which has rolled under the sofa. Only once he's retrieved it does he walk to the blackboard.

"All right," the major says, rubbing his big hands together. "First number?"

"Let's say . . . 2,978,946."

A few seconds pass. Then both men are scratching with the chalk. The major finishes first—the answer is $2 \times 3^2 \times 167 \times 991$—though Ramanujan isn't far behind.

"Too close to call?" asks Hardy.

"I believe the major bested me," Ramanujan says.

"Then let's go on." And Hardy calls out another number. And another. More often than not, the major wins.

Finally Hardy throws out the number 4,324,320.

Instantly Ramanujan writes the answer: $2^5 \times 3^3 \times 5 \times 7 \times 11 \times 13$.

"But that's not fair, Hardy," the major says. "That's one of his highly composite numbers. He has the advantage."

"I don't see why that should matter," Hardy says. "Though it's true that he's figured them out to—how many?"

"6,746,328,388,800," Ramanujan says.

"Yes, but you missed one," the major says.

"He missed one?"

"I've been looking forward to telling you." And now the major fishes in his jacket pocket, drawing out a crumpled sheet of paper. "29,331,862,500," he reads. He hands Ramanujan the paper, at which Ramanujan stares with a stricken look on his face.

"How did you find it?" Hardy asks.

"It's my specialty," the major says. "It's why you've come here."

Combinatorics is an old science. As the major explains, it has its origins in Ramanujan's country, in an Indian treatise of the sixth century B.C. entitled the *Sushruta Samhita*. "It's actually a cookery book," the major says. "What it does is take the six different flavors, which are bitter, sweet, salty, hot . . . Oh damn, what's the fifth? Now let me see. Bitter, sour, sweet, salty, hot . . ."

"Tart?"

"Yes, tart. Thank you." As he speaks, he's setting up a game of billiards.

"Anyway, so the treatise takes the six flavors and combines them, first one at a time, then two at a time, then three at a time, and you end up with sixty-four possible combinations in total if you add in the possibility of English cookery—no flavor at all. Ha! And that, in essence, is enumerative combinatory analysis. Only of course our methods today are somewhat more sophisticated." The major hits a ball into a pocket. He aims again, misses, and hands the cue to Ramanujan.

"Have you ever played billiards before?"

"No."

"It's simple, just hold the stick like so"—he stands behind Ramanujan, lines him up—"and aim for the white ball."

Ramanujan concentrates. With surprising expertise, he cues,

shoots, and gets a ball into the pocket. "Bravo," the major says, applauding. "Now go again." Again, Ramanujan aims. This time, however, he stumbles, nearly ripping the green baize with his cue stick. The white ball goes bouncing over the edge of the table, then rolls along the floor, only to bump against one of the armchair's clawed feet.

"Never mind," the major says, retrieving the ball. "It's your first time out."

Ramanujan says that he'd prefer to watch and learn, so Hardy takes the stick from him. As he and the major play, they talk about partitions. What Hardy and Ramanujan are after is a theorem: that machine into which you would insert the billiard ball emblazoned with one number only to see it emerge, a few seconds later, emblazoned with another. Of course, because the theorem will be derived from an asymptotic formula, the number won't, in all probability, be exact; it will have to be rounded off. This bothers Ramanujan more than it does Hardy. "The great weakness of young mathematicians confronted with a numerical problem," Hardy says, "is that they can't see where accuracy is essential and where it's beside the point."

"You might think of combinatorics as a machine, too," the major says. "A different sort of machine, though. Have you heard of Babbage's analytical engine? He never built it. Well, combinatorics is like that machine that Babbage never built. And Byron's daughter— she was a mathematician, you know, worked with Babbage—she said of it"—the major clears his throat as he cues up—" 'We may say most aptly, that the Analytic Engine weaves algebraic patterns just as the jacquard loom weaves flowers and leaves.' Nicely put, which is no surprise, coming from Byron's daughter." He hits and gets a ball into a pocket. "Well, that's what I do. I weave patterns. I have an analytic engine of my own—right here." He taps his own skull.

"And am I correct in understanding that of late you've been weaving partition numbers?" Hardy asks.

"You are indeed correct. I'm working my way up the number line, roughly, skipping a few here and there."

"How far have you got?"

"Yesterday I got $p(n)$ for 88."

"How long did that take?"

"A few days."

"And what was the answer?

"You expect me to have it memorized?" The major chuckles. Then he puts his right hand on his chest, thrusts out his left arm, and declaims, "44,108,109."

"44,108,109," Ramanujan repeats. As he stands there, he seems to fondle the number.

"A man after my own heart," the major says, patting him on the back.

8

I N T H E M I D S T of all the great tragedies, small ones stand out with a curious pathos. For example, Littlewood learns that the landladies of Cambridge are now threatened with destitution, as so few students remain to let their rooms. "In the meantime, however," he reads aloud from the *Cambridge Magazine*, "it may console many in their hour of distress to learn that all that has happened has been in perfect order, and in strict conformity with the laws, both of logic and philology: *the tenants have left—to become lieutenants*."

Anne doesn't laugh. It's late morning in the flat near Regent's Park. Across the room from where Littlewood's sitting, across a shaft of sunlight that penetrates the window like a saber, she's pinning up her hair.

"If you want to know what I think, they should just turn all those boardinghouses into brothels," he says.

"That's a bit callous of you," she says, taking a pin from her mouth. "Those women depend on the students for their livelihood."

"Only a joke," he says. "What's become of your sense of humor?"

"Nothing seems very funny to me at the moment."

"If you can't laugh, you'll go insane, is what I say," he says. And he lights a cigarette. Although Anne's nearly dressed, he's still in his shorts and vest. He's postponing as long as he can the moment when he'll have to put on his uniform, because putting on his uniform will mean that his leave is really over and that he must return to Woolwich. And not only that, Anne must return to Treen. If "must" is the right word. In fact she seems impatient to get away. Why, you'd think (he thinks) she'd be happy to have three days with me. Instead it's been all worry. Worry about the children. (One had a toothache.)

Worry about the dogs. Worry that her husband would find out she's not, in fact, visiting her sister in Yorkshire. Nor has she wanted sex much, which isn't in and of itself a catastrophe—they are well past the phase where sex is a necessity to them—and yet one would hope she'd realize that after all these weeks cooped up with a bunch of men, he might appreciate the chance to run his hands over a woman's body. Which Anne hasn't much allowed. So has she stopped loving him?

The thought pierces him as the beam of sunlight pierces the window, cleaves him, passes through the other side. Impossible. Impossible.

She finishes doing her hair. He stubs out one cigarette; lights another. "Care for some breakfast?" he asks.

"No thanks, I'll be late for the train."

"Tea then?"

"Ugh, the thought makes me sick."

He laughs. "One would think you were pregnant."

"I am, actually."

The cigarette hangs from his lips. "What did you say?"

"I wasn't planning to mention it, but now that you've brought it up—"

"Pregnant!"

"Don't sound so surprised. It happens to women."

"But how—"

She does up the buttons of her blouse. "Jack, I know boys of your generation grew up in virtual ignorance of the laws of nature, but really, one would assume that by now—"

"Don't be ridiculous—Of course I—" He stands, looks around as if he's forgotten something. And then he realizes that what he's forgotten is joy. "Darling!" he says. And he embraces her. "But this is marvelous, marvelous!"

"Steady on." She pushes him away. "It complicates things."

"Why?"

"Arthur."

"But you're not saying that you and Arthur—"

"Of course not. Don't be daft. Arthur and I haven't—well, for years. And that's just the trouble. He'll know it's you. So things could get a bit sticky."

"But shouldn't we get married?"

She turns to face him. "What are you saying, Jack?"

"Well, why not? You and Arthur—as you say, you haven't—"

"But you never said anything about marriage before."

"I know. But now—"

"Because I'm pregnant?"

"No, of course not. It's that your being pregnant—it makes me realize how much I love you, how much it matters. This."

"You could say that with a little more conviction."

"I'm absolutely convinced."

"You don't sound it."

She's right. He doesn't sound it. Quick, he must find a reason for her not to think him despicable.

"That's only because it's such a surprise. I've hardly had a chance to get used to it."

She puts on her jacket. "Let's make one thing perfectly clear," she says. "I have no intention of divorcing Arthur *or* of marrying you. And if you think the matter over carefully, you'll see that I'm right. You and I aren't meant for marriage—at least to each other. We're meant to live outside the rules." Suddenly she puts her hand on his cheek. "It's not that I don't love you. Perhaps it's that I love you too much." Or perhaps—he doesn't say this—it's that you love Treen too much; that you love too much this life of yours into which I come and go, come and go. But never there permanently. You don't want me there permanently. And if I'm to be honest, I don't want to be there permanently either.

"What will Arthur say? Will he be angry?"

"Probably. And if he is—well, there's nothing to do about it, is there?" She picks up her hat. "The child will be raised as his. He or she will think of him, Arthur, as his father, and you as Uncle Jack. Just like the others."

Littlewood puts his hand to his forehead. Much to his own astonishment, he is weeping. "I don't know what to say," he says. "I don't know how to get used to this."

"You've got used to worse things. We all have." She kisses his forehead. "And now I must go or I shall miss my train."

"But it's my child too!" He says this as if he has just realized it.

"Our child," she corrects.

"Will nothing change?"

"Oh, everything will change." She is at the door now. "Though not necessarily for the worse."

"Anne—"

"No," she says firmly, suddenly prim. And then she's gone.

9

WITHOUT ANNE, the flat seems squalid; improbable. A place for assignations, not only his own. Other men, he knows, come here. With other women. And, for all he knows, with other men.

Quickly as he can, he washes, puts on his uniform, and packs his bag. On the way downstairs, he passes a woman carrying a parcel of groceries. She looks him up and down as if to say, I know which flat you're coming out of. She has a scarlet birthmark on her left cheek, a sort of permanent flush that he finds strangely attractive. But when he offers to help her with the groceries, she says no, thank you, and hurries past him up the stairs.

He steps outside. It's cold and raining a little. A gust of wind hits him in the face like a fist, like the knockout blow he knows he has coming to him, that he deserves and even desires. Soon the left side of his face is numb. He walks—street follows street, namelessly—and then he stops walking and looks at his watch. Four hours and twenty minutes until he's due back at Woolwich, one hour and twenty minutes until he's due to meet Hardy at a tea shop near the British Museum, seven minutes until Anne boards her train. And how is he supposed to face Hardy—dry, sexless Hardy—and talk mathematics, or Trinity politics, or cricket, now that Anne has torn a gash in the very fabric of his life? His life: a surface that stretches without tearing, a surface "the spatial properties of which are preserved under bicontinuous deformation." Topology. That's how he's thought of it until this morning. But then Anne tore a gash right down the middle. He wants a beer. He can't face Hardy without a beer.

He goes into the first pub he sees. It's noon exactly. These days, thanks to the Defense of the Realm Act, pubs are only open from noon until two-thirty and then from six-thirty until eleven. He downs a pint, then orders another. He thinks: what am I to her? To him, she is a mystery. She always has been. They met more or less by accident, five years ago, when he was in Treen on holiday. There was a garden party, and she was there with Chase, who had heard of Littlewood from Russell, and started up a conversation. Obviously Chase wanted to make an impression, but it was his wife, obliviously capering with a dog, who made the impression. While Chase talked, she danced the dog up onto its hind legs, and kept it standing on its hind legs—he counted—for a full forty-five seconds, simply by dangling in front of its face an imaginary bit of something, conjured up between her fingers. She had brown, freckled skin. Shoes looked wrong on her somehow. She seemed so much a part of the shore outside the window, the rough surf and the sand and the rocks, that he assumed she had been born and raised in Treen, when in fact she had grown up in the Midlands. She had only come to Treen after marrying Arthur, to whose family the house belonged. "No one believes it," she told him when they finally got to talk, "but until I was seventeen I'd never seen the sea. And then I came here, and the moment I stepped down from the carriage, I knew I'd found the place I belonged. I consider myself extremely fortunate. I have a theory that for each of us there's a place in the world where we belong—only very few of us ever find it, because God is capricious. No, not capricious. Malicious. He scatters us over the earth at random, he doesn't plant us in our places. And so you might grow up in Battersea and never know that your true place, the one place you belonged, was a village in Russia, or an island off the coast of America. I think it's why so many people are so unhappy."

"And are you happy," he asked, "now that you've found your place?"

"I would be happier," she said, "if finding it didn't require me to give something else up. But perhaps we're all doomed to such bargains."

The morning after he met her, much to his regret, he had to return to Cambridge. He was eager to get back to Treen, though, and when, a few weeks later, he wrote to tell her that he was planning another visit, she invited him to stay as her guest. And then he arrived, and conveniently—it seemed suspiciously convenient at the time—Arthur was not there; at the last minute a medical emergency had obliged him to stop the weekend in London.

"You're my place," he said to her that night. It was true. Much as he liked Treen, it was not Treen to which he belonged. It was to Anne. She seemed an extension of the coast, as if a beach, fleeing the advances of a sea god, had taken human form and stepped up onto the earth on shaky legs of sand. In this myth that Littlewood invented, you could recognize the beach naiad by the sand that she always left in her wake, no matter how far inland she journeyed, the sand that you could follow backward, like a trail of breadcrumbs, to the cliffs and the beaches of Cornwall. Somehow he knew, even that first night, that he would spend whatever he had left of his life, or much of it, trying to trace that trail back to its source.

After that, they settled into an adulterous routine. Commitment, for both of them, meant routine. Most Fridays he would take the train down to Treen. She would meet him at the station, feed him a late supper in the sitting room. The next day, at eight precisely, coffee in bed, then, in the morning, work on the sun porch, sitting on a broken chair, his feet on a log and his papers held down by stones gathered from the beach. At noon he would take a swim of twenty minutes, timed exactly. Then lunch. Then a rest. Then, in the afternoon, another swim, or, if it was too cold out, a walk. After tea, patience. After patience, dinner with beer. After dinner, more cards, more games, sometimes with the children. More beer.

More beer! That's what he needs! He orders a third pint. Those weekends before the war, he always slept in a spare room on the third floor, away from the children. She would join him there after putting them to bed, returning to her own room just before dawn. Arthur (somehow this was understood) would come down the third weekend of each month, and that one weekend, Littlewood (this was also understood) would have some pressing obligation that kept him away. For it was clear that she had made a contract with Arthur, that somewhere in the depths of the bedroom they shared (as far as he knew they shared it), words had been traded, perhaps recriminations, negotiations entered into and terms agreed upon. Just exactly what those terms were he didn't ask: it was part of her arrangement with him that he would not ask. Nor was protest to be tolerated. For he sensed that if Anne accepted as inevitable a certain equalizing, a balancing of pleasure with sacrifice, it was because she believed that such a balancing was part of the natural order. Anne wanted Treen and she wanted Littlewood. She got both, but how much she had to give up in return she would not say.

And now she is pregnant.

He finishes his third pint; looks at his watch. In twenty minutes he's due to meet Hardy. A bother. So he pays his bill and steps back out into the cold. Once again, the wind punches him in the face. Now it is his right cheek that goes numb. He crosses a street. A motor car passes by, so close he can feel the metal graze his skin. The driver shouts at him: "Bloody idiot, watch where you're going!"

You could say that with a little more conviction.

Could he have? He supposes he could have. *Marry me*, he might have said, on bended knee. If he'd pleaded with her, would she have relented? She'd thrown out just that one hint, opened, for just an instant, a door he might have pushed open wider. But he didn't, and now, he knows, the door is shut again. He has lost his chance, and the beach naiad has gone back to her beach.

Another motor car flies past. Across the street from him a woman is walking a dog that resembles that one Anne kept on its feet for so long, dancing. As she has kept him dancing.

And where is *his* place? The place to which he himself—Anne or no Anne—belongs?

He stops; shuts his eyes. He sees a fireplace, a window through the old glass of which he can make out architraves and the shadows of trees. Trinity is ancient. It went on for decades before he came stumbling through its gates. No doubt it will go on for decades after his coffin is carried through those same gates. (If, that is, anything goes on; if he doesn't die in the war; if the Germans don't win the war.) Is Trinity, then, where he belongs? If so, it's an illusion. After all, those rooms he calls his own, they are his only in the sense that a piece of Imperial Roman marble he once pilfered from the Forum is his. Such things outlive us. We claim them, house them, house ourselves in them. But only for a time. And still he thinks of those rooms as *his* rooms.

Curiously, in his youth, he hardly ever worried about God. But then he met Anne, and Hardy, and now he is convinced that God, on His throne, whiles away His off-hours mapping out those routes by which His subjects will be led most quickly to unhappiness. Human souls tossed willy-nilly over the face of the earth, connivances with nature to insure rain at cricket matches. And in Littlewood's case? Passion for a woman he can never possess, combined with attachment to a place he can never own. A sort of doomed, perpetual bachelorhood.

Once again, he looks at his watch. Quarter to one. Soon he will have to meet Hardy. Does he dread it? No. To his surprise, he finds that he's rather looking forward to it. For he will never marry Anne. He will never have a child who bears his own name. But Hardy—Hardy isn't going anywhere. Hardy is permanent. Spouse or collaborator, it comes to the same thing. And there is work to be done. Always, always work to be done.

H E G E T S T O the tea shop first; claims a table; watches through the window as Hardy, in a bowler hat and raincoat, saunters toward the door. Saunters, yes—that's exactly the word for Hardy. He is laconic and sleek, like an otter. He steps inside, closes his umbrella, signals with his chin. "Littlewood," he says, ungloving a hand, which Littlewood shakes. So dry, that hand. Which rather contradicts the otter notion. A thin wedge of a man, all edges. What would it be like to embrace him? He shudders to think.

"Sorry I'm late. I'm just off the train."

"No bother."

"You're doing fine, I trust."

Such a statement brooks no possibility of an answer. "I'm doing fine."

"Good."

"I've got something to show you." Littlewood reaches into his bag. "It's my first ballistics paper. Just printed. See that little speck at the bottom of the last page?"

"Yes, what is it?"

"A tiny sigma. The last line was supposed to read, 'Thus σ should be made as small as possible.'" Littlewood leans back. "Well, the printer did his job. He must have scoured the print shops of London to find one so tiny."

Hardy laughs so loud the waitress turns and gives him a look.

"I'm glad you think it's funny," Littlewood says. "I've missed having someone around who'd understand why that was funny."

"I may be joining you soon. Who knows? Conscription seems a certainty."

"And this from the secretary of the U.D.C.! How goes all that, by the way?"

"The college is in an uproar. Butler's trying to root out everyone who has anything to do with us. Rumor has it he's working to throw out Neville. And in the meantime none of us can complain because three of his sons are at the front. Butler's. And the poor man's in an absolute state. He can't seem to fix his attention on anything, he hardly hears what you're saying." The waitress approaches. "Oh, yes, hello. Earl Grey, please."

"And you, sir?"

"The same. Anything to eat, Hardy?"

"No, I wouldn't care for anything."

The way Hardy says he "wouldn't care for anything" vexes Littlewood. Now if *he* asks for anything to eat—and how alluring the pastries look!—Hardy will doubtless look him up and down reproachfully. And while it's true that, since they last met, Littlewood has put on a few pounds—well, what's to be done about it? He's enlisted now. You can't stay slim on range tables and military potatoes.

"Just tea. Nothing to eat."

"Very good, sir."

The waitress walks away.

"I've been thinking a lot about our friend Ramanujan lately," he says. "You know, I was never sure if I believed all his talk of dreaming up mathematics. But then the other night I had a dream in which I saw, clear as day, the solution to a problem, and of course the next morning I'd forgotten it. So I began keeping a pad and pencil by the bed, and the next time it happened I woke up, wrote it down, and went back to sleep. And then in the morning I looked at the pad, and you know what I'd written?"

"What?"

" 'Higamus, bigamus, men are polygamous. Hogamus, bogamus, wives are monogamous.' "

This time Hardy does not laugh.

"So what brings you to town this time?"

"Mathematical Society business. We're trying to help a German physicist who got stuck in Reading. Now he's been interned."

"Good of you."

"Well, there are Englishmen stuck in Germany. And the Germans are trying to help them too."

"Strange to think that we're here and they're there. On opposite sides."

"It's merely a change of sign. Trivial. Plus into minus, minus into plus."

"Is that all you think it is?"

"This war is a joke."

"Still, if the Germans win—"

"It might be a fine thing for England."

Littlewood smiles. "One thing I do miss is hearing you make outrageous statements. You know that outrageous statements aren't permitted at Woolwich."

"Nor should they be. They belong to Cambridge."

"The truth is, I don't miss that side of Cambridge. The bright talk, the witticisms flying. All the goods in the front window."

"So is Woolwich any better?"

"At least there's a certain naked honesty about it. There's a job to do, and you do it."

"Careful, Littlewood, you're starting to sound like an engineer."

"I don't see why I shouldn't end my days as one. I expect I'll lose the gift once I hit forty. And then what's the alternative? Mathematicians gone to seed make excellent vice-chancellors."

"I could see you as a vice-chancellor."

"I'd rather be shot."

"Given the work you're doing now, you'll certainly be able to position the gun."

"Yes, that I will. Although I'm not exactly a crack marksman. That's why they leave me to work things out on paper."

The waitress brings the tea. Two women with very straight backs sit at the next table. A three-tiered tray has just been delivered to them, stacked with sandwiches, scones, crumpets, and those pastries, studded with sultanas, that Littlewood covets.

And why aren't they eating? With studied nonchalance, the women sip their tea, exchange a few words, ignore the delicacies. They do not put sugar in their tea. In all likelihood, no sugar has been used in the pastries; no eggs, either, for this is wartime, and Hardy has chosen a fairly expensive tea shop, the clientele of which cares about appearances. Heaven forbid that these women should be confused with workers for whom nourishment must be taken in quantity, and fast, if the job is to be done! Or that they should be seen as not respecting the sumptuary laws imposed by war—at least in public. Who knows what they have hidden away at home?

On the other hand, at working-class tea shops—there is one in Woolwich that Littlewood frequents—all the customers put sugar in their tea.

If any of this concerns Hardy, he doesn't show it. He pours out. He does not ask for sugar. Come to think of it, has Littlewood ever once seen Hardy take sugar in his tea? It's as if, his whole life, he's been obeying sumptuary laws of his own invention.

"Ramanujan sends his regards, by the way," Hardy says.

"And how fares Ramanujan?"

"All right, I think. I wish I could get him to concentrate."

"Don't make him concentrate too much, though. Is he happy?"

"To be honest, he seems a bit depressed. Perhaps it's all the reading he's doing. My hunch is that he's finally recognizing how much he doesn't know."

"Then maybe he shouldn't read so much."

"But even if he didn't, he's too intelligent not to see what he couldn't see in India. Now he realizes that he's handicapped. The very thing that was always his calling card—his lack of schooling—he understands now how it's hurt him."

"What was it Klein said? Mathematics has been advanced more by those distinguished for intuition than by those distinguished for rigorous methods of proof."

"Easy for Klein to say, with his education."

"I think we should just leave Ramanujan in an empty room with a slate and let him come up with whatever he likes."

"If only. The trouble is, he's ambitious. And this in spite of the goddess Namby-Pamby and the dreams and what have you. You know he still keeps pestering me about the Smith's Prize? An undergraduate prize! And he's getting his B.A. By God, he's determined to take that B.A. back to India with him."

"B.A.s matter in India."

"So better a B.A. than proving the Riemann hypothesis? Better a B.A. than immortality?"

"But what is immortality?"

"Whoever proves the Riemann hypothesis will be immortal."

"The difference between a great discovery and an ordinary one is a difference of kind, not a difference of degree."

"Ah, but is the difference between a difference of kind and a difference of degree a difference of kind or a difference of degree?"

"The answer is elementary." Littlewood gazes, for a few seconds, into his tea. Then he says, "Hardy, a few years ago—I never mentioned this at the time, but Norton told me you were writing a novel. A murder novel."

"That's ridiculous."

"Well, he said that you were. And in it the victim proves the Riemann hypothesis and the murderer steals the proof and claims it as his own." Littlewood empties his cup. "It's a very good idea."

"And when am I supposed to have time to write novels?"

"I just wouldn't want you to think, well, that I'd be bothered if you, let's say, based a character on me. Maybe the murderer. You could work in the ballistics angle. And the tiny sigma."

"Never listen to Norton. Half of what he says is deranged fantasy. We need more milk." Hardy looks over his shoulder. "I wish I could get that waitress's attention! They're always looking the other way when you want to signal them! I think they do it on purpose."

"Are you in a rush?"

"No, I just haven't been to the flat yet."

"Anne is pregnant."

Hardy pauses; swallows.

"No need to pretend you don't know about us. She told me this morning."

"Well, I'm not sure what to say . . . Are congratulations in order?"

"Decidedly not. She won't marry me. She insists on staying with her husband." He puts his head in his hands. "Oh, Hardy, what am I to do? It's not that I want to marry her, I can't see us living like the Nevilles on Chesterton Road . . . But I love her. And the child. Is it wrong of me to want the child to know me as its father?"

"No, it's not wrong . . . Only if she doesn't want to marry you, what can you do?"

"Nothing. I can't do anything." He runs his fingers through his hair. "Well, that's it. I just needed to tell someone. I hope you don't mind."

"Of course not."

Once again, Hardy tries to signal the waitress. He reached out his arm, and Littlewood takes it in his hand; pushes it, gently, down onto the table.

"Not yet. Just a few minutes. Just wait with me a few minutes. I'm hungry."

Now Littlewood waves to the waitress. She comes instantly.

"Those pastries look awfully good," he says. "The ones with the sultanas. I'll have one, please. You too, Hardy?"

"No, I wouldn't—" He coughs. "Oh well, why not?"

"Very good, officer," the waitress says to Littlewood, backing away, her eyes on his face.

And Littlewood winks.

F ROM THE TEA SHOP, Hardy turns left and walks to the Underground station. In his pocket is a letter from Thayer. Not much of a letter; then again, Thayer's letters never contain much beyond the basic information (when he has a leave coming up, which day he plans to be in London) and the basic question: at what hour might he call at Hardy's flat "for tea"? Whether Thayer employs this euphemism for the benefit of the censors or to satisfy some standard of his own, Hardy does not know; he only knows that he finds this whole business of answering Thayer's letters—the reply sent to a military address, and consisting solely of a suggested hour for the "tea" appointment, as if he were some benevolent great-aunt—as exciting as it is annoying.

In any case, the system seems to work. Twice, now, they have convened at the flat in Pimlico for early afternoon assignations. The first time Hardy was anxious; he actually took the trouble to purchase biscuits, to boil water and put out the tea things, all of which turned out to be quite unnecessary. No tea was poured. Instead Thayer, almost the instant the door was shut, hurled himself into Hardy, enveloped him in the woolly, wet stink of his greatcoat, pressed his mouth into Hardy's mouth, so that their teeth knocked. Then they were on the floor, clothes were being pulled off so roughly Hardy could hear buttons breaking. That Thayer, as it turned out, wanted to be buggered came as no surprise. Keynes had alerted him to the curious fact that nearly all the soldiers home on leave wanted, when they met up with queers, to take the passive role. "Mind you, I'm not complaining," Keynes said, "only it does strike one as a bit strange, doesn't it? I'd have thought *they'd* want to do the buggering, so that they could tell themselves they weren't 'really' queer, that they were simply taking advantage of an opportunity, cheaper than whores and all that—but no." Instead, it seemed that they wanted, as one of Keynes's paramours phrased it, "to see what it felt like." It was as if, after so many weeks in the trenches, after taking lives and nearly dying, they required a more extreme variety of erotic stimulation than ordinary intercourse could provide. Nor was Hardy unwilling to oblige when Thayer got on his knees and thrust his rear end in the air—this despite the fact that, though he had admitted this to none of his friends (not even Keynes), he had never actually engaged in buggery before, his sexual repertoire having been limited to some of the various unnamed "acts of gross indecency" that the law punished with a less severe sentence. Wanking and sucking, though in Hardy's case, much more of the former than the latter, due to his mother's inculcation in him of the belief that germs enter mostly through the mouth. Gaye had laughed at him for that.

And what would Gaye have thought had he seen him that first afternoon with Thayer, on his own knees and thrusting away while Thayer writhed and grunted under him? Indeed, he must have been doing a fairly decent job of the thing, from the way Thayer moaned and swore—so decent a job that for a moment he wondered whether he might not, after all, try having it on with a woman. But no. What he really enjoyed wasn't the fucking itself so much as the obvious paroxysms of pleasure that Thayer was experiencing. Thayer disengaged himself, turned on his back, put his legs on Hardy's shoulders. Now the scar from the shrapnel wound was just to the left of Hardy's mouth—red and jagged—and as he plunged into Thayer he could not help running his tongue along the length of it. Thayer howled, shot off. Hardy shot off too. "Damn," Thayer said, pulling himself back along the length of the floor with his elbows. "My damn leg."

"Did I hurt you?"

"No, it's just the position I'm in." Then he stood. He seemed far more naked in the wake of the act than he had in the course of it. "May I wash now?" he asked. And Hardy said that yes, of course he could wash.

And afterward—*then* he wanted the tea. That was the oddest thing. You might have thought he'd have tried to get out of there as fast as he could, that shame or horror at his own gluttonous passivity would have overwhelmed him. Nothing of the kind. Instead he put his uniform back on, and they sat down to tea and biscuits, and Thayer talked. He talked once again about his sisters, and his parents, and about a girl named Daisy with whom he had for some years had, well, they had known each other for some years and, though nothing had been put into words or writing, it was sort of understood—but now, with the war, was it fair of him to marry her if the likelihood was that he would leave her a widow? But if they waited until the war was over—and who could guess how long that would be?—it would be rather late to start a family, wouldn't it? And he wanted children. He wanted a boy, whom he would name Dick, for his friend Dick Tarlow.

Hardy listened. They might as well have been in the hospital again, with the rain coming through the blinds and the cricket field outside. Then Thayer stopped talking, and looked at his watch, and said, "Well, I'd best be going. I've got to catch the train for Birmingham." And he got up, and Hardy got up, and they walked to the door, where Thayer put on his greatcoat and turned to him. What Hardy hadn't realized at the hospital was how tall he was. "Look," Hardy said, "won't you take some—" He was reaching for his wallet. Thayer stopped his hand; shook his head no. "Please," Hardy said.

"No," Thayer said. And held out his hand. They shook hands manfully. Suddenly Thayer pulled him close again, kissed him hard enough this time to draw blood. "Ta-ra" was his last word, along with a military salute, before he turned on his heels and went hobbling down the stairs.

This happened twice more. Then, yesterday, another letter arrived. Telegrams were exchanged. Today their appointment is set for two o'clock, and Hardy is eager to get to the flat, to prepare the bed and himself before Thayer arrives.

From Ramanujan he has picked up the habit of going everywhere by tube. Now he descends at Russell Square, rides the Piccadilly Line to South Kensington, then switches to the District, which he takes to Victoria. At the station he buys a packet of biscuits (Bath Oliver, the kind, he has learned, that Thayer likes best) as well as some flowers to put in the vase on the kitchen table. It's a sunny afternoon, albeit a cold one, and while the prospect of seeing Thayer fills him with what he would be willing to call joy, nonetheless an awareness of trouble in the world, in his life, in Littlewood's life, darkens his humor. Increasingly, it seems that one only has these brief moments, and then trouble comes again. And what intensifies his joy at seeing

Thayer, every time he sees Thayer, is of course the blessed fact that Thayer isn't yet dead.

Some crocuses are blooming in St. George's Square. Removing his gloves, he bends down and picks a few, which he adds to the bouquet he's purchased, then trips up the stairs to the flat. He is whistling—what? Something silly, something he must have heard on the wireless somewhere:

> For Belgium put the kibosh on the Kaiser;
> Europe took the stick and made him sore;
> On his throne it hurts to sit,
> And when John Bull starts to hit,
> He will never sit upon it anymore.

He checks his watch. One-thirty. Only a half an hour, then, to wait until Thayer rings his bell.

He opens the door. A woman screams. From the doorway to the kitchen, Alice Neville stares at him, her hand on her chest.

12

"**G**ood god," Hardy says.

"You terrified me," Alice says.

"What are you doing here?"

"Didn't Gertrude tell you?"

"Tell me what?"

"That I've been staying here."

"She most certainly did not."

"Since last week," Alice says. "She said she wrote to you and told you—"

"Gertrude knows I don't always read her letters." (It's true; a side effect of working with Littlewood.)

Alice begins to weep very quietly. "I warned her that this might happen," she says. "I told her you wouldn't like it once you found out."

"Oh, for God's sake—"

"But she said it was as much her flat as yours, and so long as I was sleeping in her bedroom—and that you only come on weekends, while on the weekends I go back to Cambridge—"

"I don't only come on the weekends. What kind of absurd notion is that?" (But it's true that the last time he saw her, he told Gertrude he was only coming up on the weekends.)

"Then you must ask Gertrude."

"Oh, for heaven's sake. Please stop crying."

She does not stop crying. She takes a handkerchief from her pocket and brings it to her nose. And in the meantime, absurdly, Hardy is still standing in the vestibule, with the door open, and the neighbors, for all he knows, listening in.

"Look, there's no need for this. Please just—just don't wail." He shuts the door behind him; hangs his coat on the peg; steps past her into the kitchen and lays the flowers, in their wet wrapping of newspaper, on the table. "I can't bear wailing."

"And how do you think I feel? Here I am, minding my own business, when the door flies open and you—I could have been in my dressing gown."

"A good thing you weren't."

He sits down. She remains standing.

"Why are you here, anyway?" he asks.

"I'm working with Mrs. Buxton," she says.

"Mrs. Buxton?"

"The 'Notes from the Foreign Press,' in the *Cambridge Magazine*. I'm one of her translators."

"What language?"

"Swedish and German."

"Swedish! Where on earth did you learn Swedish?"

"In Sweden, as it happens. I spent some time there as a girl. My mother's half-Swedish. I speak French too, but Mrs. Buxton needs more help with the German than the French, because she publishes more from the German press and she's got a surfeit of French translators. Gertrude's working with her, too. Gertrude's doing French."

"I had no idea."

"If you'd bothered to read her letters, you'd have known everything."

Hardy looks at the table. Now that he understands why Alice is in London, he feels a little ashamed at his reaction to finding her in the flat. After all, he can't help but appreciate Mrs. Buxton. Her column in the magazine is practically the only place you can find out what's actually going on in the world. "An intrepid lady," Russell said the other night in Hall, "and doing a great service, providing an alternative to that bilge in the *Times*." So if Alice is working for Mrs. Buxton—well, he has to applaud her.

"Won't you sit down?" he asks.

"No, thank you."

"Or I could make some tea."

"Or *I* could make some tea."

"Whichever of us makes it, some tea might be in order."

"I'll make it." Alice moves toward the stove, where she fills the kettle, femininity trumping ownership.

"And where do you do all this translating?" he asks after a moment.

"Much of it I do here," she says. She is dry-eyed now. "Though generally I'm in Golders Green in the mornings. That's where the Buxtons live—Golders Green. It's their HQ. I go and collect the articles that Mrs. Buxton has assigned me, and then either I work there—if there's space, it can get awfully crowded—or I take my work and come back here. I've a desk set up in Gertrude's room. With dictionaries."

"You mean you're here all week? How long has this been going on?"

"Just a week now. We all need work to do, Mr. Hardy. Especially at this dark hour."

"Yes, but how does Neville feel about your being gone?"

"He understands. I have to do my part."

"But doesn't he mind your not being there?"

She wipes her hands on a dishcloth. "Really, Mr. Hardy, there's no need to drop such unsubtle hints," she says. "It is obvious that my presence here displeases you. Very well, then I—"

"No, it's not that."

"—then of course I shall, at my earliest convenience, seek other accommodations. However, given the hour, and the fact that the magazine goes to press tomorrow and I've an article due in the morning, I trust you'll give me leave to pass one more night under your roof."

"It's fine, please—"

"In your sister's bedroom, of course, for which, I should add, I pay her rent."

"Mrs. Neville, please. It's fine. It's fine if you stay here. I didn't mean—it was just a bit of a shock for me as well, seeing you there, I—I didn't expect it."

She remains by the stove, back erect, while the kettle sings.

"Needless to say I wouldn't think of doing anything that might interfere with your liberty or incommode you."

"You're not putting me out. Gertrude's right, usually I am only here on the weekends. Today's an exception. And of course I'm a great admirer of Mrs. Buxton—everyone admires Mrs. Buxton—and I want to do everything I can to support her, and you, in a very noble effort."

"For which, needless to say, we receive no financial recompense."

"Needless to say."

"Well, I'm relieved that you see it that way." She switches off the kettle; pours the hot water into the pot. "And of course it goes without saying, Mr. Hardy, that I shall stay out of your way. Once I've had my tea I'll lock myself up in Alice's bedroom. I'll be as quiet as a mouse. You won't even know I'm here."

Suddenly the bell rings. Hardy jumps. "Oh my God," he says.

"What's the matter?" Alice asks.

"A friend—an appointment. I forgot."

"Well, let her in. Or would you prefer that I—"

"No, I'll go. Never mind." He hurries, and beats her to the door. "Just a delivery, I'll get it downstairs." And shutting the door behind her, he races down to the entryway; opens the front door, where he finds Thayer, radiant, smiling in the rain. Rain in his hair.

"Thayer," he says.

"Hello, Hardy," Thayer says, and is about to step through when Hardy blocks his way.

"What's the matter?"

"I'm afraid—" Hardy steps outside, shutting the door behind them. "I'm afraid there's been something of a mix-up," he says, lowering his voice. "You see"—he leans in, to whisper—"I share this flat with my sister, and, well, without telling me, she lent—a friend of hers is staying the night in her room. And so I'm not alone. A lady is in there."

A shadow darkens Thayer's face. "Oh, I see," he says. "A lady."

Hardy nods and shakes his head at once; without being aware of it, he realizes later, he is mimicking Ramanujan. "I'm being perfectly truthful," he says, "she's a friend of my sister's. From Cambridge. She's working in London, and Gertrude, without telling me—"

"Well, that's smashing, isn't it? And when you think that I came by train from Birmingham just to—"

"I'm sorry. I'm so sorry. If I'd had any idea she'd be here—"

"Of course." Thayer smiles again, but this time his smile is mocking. "Well, I guess that's that, then. Ta."

He turns. Hardy puts his hand on his arm. "Wait," he says. "Look, if you wait a minute—let me think—we could go somewhere else. We could meet later at—a hotel."

"A hotel? What do you think, I'm some tart?"

"It's not like that."

"You could have said, 'I'm sorry, Thayer, *my sister's friend* is here, on account of *my sister's friend* I'm afraid I can't offer you more than a cup of tea, come upstairs and sit down and take the chill off and let me introduce you to *my sister's friend* before you get back on the train—"

"I'm sorry."

"'Sister's friend, this is Thayer, of the First West Yorks Regiment. Thayer, this is sister's friend.' 'How d'you do?' 'How d'you do?' Instead of which it's, 'I'm ashamed for anyone to see you, you wait down here in the street and later we'll meet at a hotel.'"

"Please don't be so angry—"

"Well, fuck off."

"Wait, please—I'm sorry, I should have. I didn't think. Of course you can come up." He coughs. "Let me start again. Thayer, won't you please come up and—"

"Too late."

"Won't you come up for a cup of tea?"

"You rich toffs, you never understand, do you? You can't just start again once you've fucked it up. Try it in the trenches with your arse full of goddamned Jerry shrapnel."

Once again, Hardy puts his hand on Thayer's arm. Thayer pushes him away. "Don't touch me!"

"I'm sorry, I wish—"

Thayer turns; walks across the street, toward the square.

"Thayer—" Hardy calls. He is close to weeping now, as earlier Alice wept. "Thayer, please—"

"Forget it," Thayer says, from a distance, over his shoulder.

"Thayer, wait for me."

And at that moment, just as he's about to take after him in pursuit, a constable passes by. Picking up the scent of discord, he walks over to Hardy. "Everything all right, sir?" he asks. "This chap bothering you?"

"No, everything's fine, thank you," Hardy says.

"You bothering him?" the constable calls to Thayer.

"Bothering *him*?"

"No, it's fine." Hardy fixes his face into some simulacrum of ordinariness. "Thank you, officer. Goodnight."

And turning around, he goes back into the building.

13

THERE IS, for Alice, something heartbreaking about her husband's ignorance. He doesn't understand. What's worse, he doesn't know that he doesn't understand. Whereas she understands everything perfectly—too perfectly.

That weekend, for instance, she's sitting in the room she's come to think of as Ramanujan's room—the guest room, made over now as an office, a place for her to work on her translations—when he tiptoes through the door and puts his hands on her shoulders. She jumps. "Please don't startle me like that," she says.

"Sorry," he says. "I just had an urge to touch my lovely little wife."

"Yes, all right, but the next time you get an urge, knock first, will you?"

"Of course, darling. So what are you translating now?"

"An article."

"About what?"

"England and peace."

"What do they say?"

"That we're delaying peace."

"Let me see." He reads over her shoulder: "'England blamed Germany for a desire for war during July 1914, but since the end of August 1914, she has repeated that Germany would like peace, but that the time is not yet here.' Wouldn't it be better to say, 'the time has not yet come?'"

"Mrs. Buxton likes to keep the translations as literal as possible."

"Ah, Mrs. Buxom. Luring my wife away to work at her brothel five days a week."

"Yes, Eric, I know you think it's very funny."

"And who knows what odd sorts of men you're expected to cater to?"

"Thank you, Eric. Now if you don't mind—"

"But you're always working! Can't you take a few hours off?"

"What about all the hours you spent working, when you were finishing your degree? Hours and hours I spent alone, and did I even once raise my voice?"

"Now darling—"

"It's perfectly true. You can't expect me to spend the rest of my life sitting here, idle, at your beck and call."

"All right, darling."

"And it's not as if I'm off every week shopping or going to concerts, this is important work. It's war work, of a sort."

"All right, you've made your point. It's only that—well, you're gone so much these days, I—and then when you're back, you're always locked up in here. If I didn't know better, I'd think you were trying to avoid me."

She closes her eyes. So it's come at last. Understanding. She's almost relieved.

"But of course I do know better than that—"

Damn.

"I'm sorry, I'm being terribly selfish." He nuzzles her hair. "And you're right, you were patient with me, all those years. And now I shall be patient with you."

He backs away on exaggerated tiptoe; shuts the door behind him; opens it again and peers in.

"Can I get you anything? A cup of tea?"

"No, nothing."

"Something to eat?"

"No, I'm fine, Eric."

"Sorry, then." His voice a whisper. And once again he shuts the door.

Alice breathes deeply. Then she looks at the page in front of her—the translation—and notices a blot just at the end of the sentence she was working on. No doubt her pen slipped when Eric surprised her.

Well, at least he's gone.

And how is it possible, after all this time, that he doesn't grasp the truth, doesn't recognize—yes—that she's left him, leaving him?

And why? Does she not love him anymore?

When she first started working for Mrs. Buxton, the reason she gave herself was that she couldn't survive another day cooped up in the house with Ethel, while frighteningly nearby a war raged. Despite his best efforts to appear jaunty, Eric could not hide his worry. She knew that he was in trouble with Butler because of his opposition to the war. She understood that there was a chance he might lose his fellowship. She admired his stoic devotion to his ideals—how could she not?— and yet, for all the respect she felt, she could not bear for him to touch her. Even after her fantasy of Ramanujan falling in love with her ended in humiliation, she could not bear for him to touch her. And he was being unbelievably dim.

He asked her what was wrong. In words, she complained only of boredom, her wish to be doing something, not just sitting around the house. He mentioned all sorts of possibilities. In Cambridge, the Women's Emergency Corps had initiated an effort to employ women in making toys. Other women were working as train guards, or tilling the land. She tried not to laugh at his naïveté. What she wanted to be doing, of course, was writing—savage, oblique essays that decimated English complacency about the war without ever once mentioning the war; that sort of thing. Even if she had the talent, however, she lacked the connections. She did not travel, as Aunt Daisy and Israfel did, in literary circles. And so she stayed at home, growing more and more irritable, until one morning she received a note from Gertrude telling her in the most casual tone that in her spare time she had started translating for Mrs. Buxton. And of course, as Alice had become, like her husband, a devotee of the "Notes to the Foreign Press," immediately the possibility entered her head that perhaps she, too, could lend a hand with the translating. After all, how many English people could there be who understood Swedish?

That was how it began. Immediately she wrote to Gertrude, who replied the next day that Alice should come to London as soon as possible. Gertrude had told Mrs. Buxton about her, had mentioned her facility with both Swedish and German, and Mrs. Buxton had begged her to ask Alice for her help. And what a fillip that was, to feel, at last, needed for something, by someone! And so on Saturday she took the train to London, and the Underground to Golders Green, where the Buxtons lived. Gertrude opened the door to admit her. All sorts of noises issued from within: typewriters, voices arguing in languages only some of which she recognized. A little boy tore past—the Buxtons' son. Then Gertrude led her into the sitting room, which was in chaos, newspaper cuttings covering every surface and large portions of the floor, while on the various chairs and sofas and in some cases, cross-legged, on the carpet, men and women sat, reading aloud to each other in a host of languages, and turning, restlessly, the thin pages of dictionaries and thesauruses, and testing out possibilities on one another. One man working on an Italian article asked a woman who was typing: "What would you put for *maggari*?"

"Perhaps?"

"No, that would be *forsé*. *Maggari* is more—'If only,' or 'I wish.' "

"What's the sentence?"

But before Alice could hear the sentence read—and her Italian was good enough for her to be capable of offering an opinion—Gertrude had taken her into the dining room, where two women sat at opposite ends of a table covered, like the sitting room floor, with newspapers. One of the women rose. Her face was beautiful and severe, rather like a Wedgwood vase; she was dressed elegantly but comfortably, in a long skirt and a blouse the crenellated patterns of which brought to mind stained-glass windows in churches. "You must be Mrs. Neville," she said, reaching out her hand. "Welcome, please sit down. May I introduce my sister? Eglantyne Jebb."

The sister rose. She was at once more mannish and less forthright than Mrs. Buxton, the effect of her sturdy handshake undercut a little by her reluctance to look Alice in the eye. When she spoke, she kept her hands in the air, gesticulating, Alice suspected, less in order to add emphasis to her words than to keep her face covered.

Mrs. Buxton, by contrast, was a beacon of calm in the midst of the pandemonium into which her house had been transformed, a pandemonium she acknowledged cheerfully, if with an undertone of regret, telling Alice, "I do apologize for this disorder. The papers have just come in. You read German, is that correct?"

"And Swedish."

"Excellent. With Swedish I am at sea. I can make neither head nor tail of it. German, however, I read well enough to be able, at the very least, to offer an opinion on the translations rendered by those whose knowledge of the language is deeper than my own." She opened a copy of *Vorwärts*. "Perhaps you could help us by offering your opinion, Mrs. Neville. A rather impertinent reader has sent in a letter complaining that we mistranslated the word *Ausnahmegesetze*. This isn't the sort of word you'd find in a dictionary. How would you translate it?"

Alice sat rigid. Was she being tested—ever so subtly?

"Well, let me see. *Ausnahme* would be—exception, I suppose, and *gesetze*, legislation? So: exceptional legislation?"

Mrs. Buxton smiled. "Exactly. See? I told you, Eglantyne, he was wrong." She passes Alice a letter. "After several paragraphs of grudging praise, this correspondent, one Mr. Marx, slips in rather superciliously that in his view we have mistranslated the word, which ought to be rendered 'emergency legislation.' But 'emergency legislation' would not be *Ausnahmegesetze*, it would be something more like *Notstandsgesetze*." She closed the newspaper. "You see, Mrs. Neville, one has to be very careful. And no matter how hard we work, someone will complain. Still, it must be done."

"I cannot say," Alice said, "how much I admire the integrity of your enterprise."

"Thank you," Mrs. Buxton said, then exclaimed suddenly, "Oh, good heavens, I've offered you nothing to eat or drink. Would you like anything? Luckily I have two women here who, as they cannot type and speak no languages other than English, have volunteered to run the kitchen. Something, I might add, that my husband and children appreciate. You see, I'm immensely lucky. There are so many people eager to help. Well, what can we offer you?"

"I wouldn't care for anything," Alice said, "but thank you for asking. In fact, I'm rather eager to get to work."

"That's marvelous. Well, why don't you start with this piece from *Vorwärts*? It'll be very useful in my argument with Mr. Marx, as it contains both the contentious *Ausnahmegesetze* and *Sondergesetz*, which is closer to what he's speaking of."

"It's very exciting," Alice said, taking the newspaper, "to have this opportunity."

"I fear you won't think so after a few days. You may want to run away screaming! But never mind. We shall be grateful for however many minutes or hours you grant us."

"I shall not run screaming," Alice said, and wanted to add: this is the place to which I have run. But she said nothing.

So this is what her life has become: five days in London, staying in

Gertrude's flat, then the weekend at home. She arrives late on Friday, leaves late on Sunday. Two nights are all she can bear with Eric. As if to celebrate her presence, Ethel has taken to preparing elaborate meals on the weekends, joints of meat and roasted pheasants and a curried duck that makes her remember, with a distant fondness, the days when they cooked for Ramanujan. None of this can she stomach. In London her life is marked by a cultivated frugality. She drinks weak tea, eats sandwiches consisting of the thinnest imaginable slivers of cheese placed between the thinnest imaginable slices of bread. The occasional orange. She has lost weight, which upsets Eric. "I like a woman with some meat on her bones," he says, slapping her no longer ample rump.

She ignores him. How can she explain herself to a man who hardly understands his own sorrow? Perhaps she might say to him, "Eric, what you're feeling is grief, because your wife, whom you love, no longer loves you," and he would understand. But if she were to say to him, "I cannot bear, at this moment, to be comfortably fed or comfortably bedded, I must walk in the cold without boots or an umbrella, I must sleep in an underheated flat on a bed that pains my back"—would he be capable of understanding this need for penance, for penitence? A need, perhaps, to experience an iota—if only that—of the suffering that the soldiers are experiencing. Or a need to rid herself of that terrible taste in her mouth, that taste of tea that was on Ramanujan's breath, when she pressed her lips against his and he . . . he just stood there.

Impossible to contemplate, that she did such a thing. That she shamed herself like that. It's something she could never tell Eric.

And if she can't tell Eric, if she can't articulate to him, much less to herself, what she felt that afternoon, as she walked home from Trinity, how can she explain to him why it is that she needs the austerity of Gertrude's narrow bed, in that drab flat?

Hardy has not returned. Not since the one visit. Nor has she asked Gertrude if she has spoken with her brother about Alice's staying there.

Odd that all during the course of that one night, the night that she and Hardy both slept in the flat, they never once spoke of Ramanujan. She never mentioned, and neither did he, the dinner to which she was so pointedly not invited. Or Ramanujan's disappearance, and reappearance, afterward. Or the rather testy correspondence that his disappearance provoked.

Eric never mentions Hardy, either. Or Ramanujan. Why is this? Is it perhaps because, without recognizing it, he senses the uneasiness that their names call up in her? Obviously he must see them both. Hardy every day. When they don't talk mathematics, they must talk politics, Russell's refusal to keep his mouth shut, the almost willful effort he's making to provoke Butler. Eric is happy to tell Alice all about what's going on at Trinity. But for some reason, when he does, he never mentions Hardy's name.

Dusk is falling. She is glad. One more night, one more day, and she'll be able to return to London. She longs to return to London. And not just because she is happier there, these days, than here. Also because someone has entered her life whose presence alone is enough to revive Alice's sense of possibility. Prospects of pleasure, if remote, rise before her whenever she sees this person. This person whom she saw, for the first time, last week, at Mrs. Buxton's. A new recruit. "Ah, Alice," Dorothy said—they were now on a first-name basis—"I wonder if you might show this lady around. She's come to pick up some work to take home with her. She lives in Cornwall and speaks perfect Italian."

Alice turned. Standing before her, radiant and very pregnant, was Mrs. Chase. Littlewood's friend, whom she and Gertrude had met, albeit briefly, at the zoo.

"We know each other," Alice said.

Mrs. Chase's face buckled with confusion. "I'm sorry, do we?" she asked. "My memory's terrible these days. It's curious, this is the third time I've been pregnant, and each time something very odd happens. Last time I was constantly thirsty."

"It's all right," Alice said. "I'm Alice Neville. We met at the zoo— oh, it feels like years ago. I was with Gertrude Hardy."

Memory, then, a reawakening that was visible in Mrs. Chase's eyes. But a good memory?

"Of course," she said, smiling. "How lovely to see you."

And she reached out her hand, and took Alice's arm, and mysteriously, thrillingly, kissed her on the cheek.

I 4

New Lecture Hall, Harvard University

BY THE END of 1916, we had the partitions formula. Here is what it looked like:

$$p(n) = \sum_{1}^{v} A_q \phi_q + O\left(n^{-\frac{1}{4}}\right)$$

where

$$A_q(n) = \sum_{(p)} \omega_{p,q} e^{-\frac{2np\pi i}{q}}$$

$$\phi_q(n) = \frac{\sqrt{q}}{2\pi\sqrt{2}} \frac{d}{dn}\left(\frac{e^{c\lambda_n/q}}{\lambda_n}\right)$$

the sum being over p's that are positive integers less than and prime to q, v is of the order of $\sqrt{n}$, and $\omega_{p,q}$ is a certain 24q-th root of unity and

$$C = \frac{2\pi}{\sqrt{6}} = \pi\sqrt{\tfrac{2}{3}}, \lambda_n = \sqrt{n - \tfrac{1}{24}}$$

Today whenever I write out the formula, I think: what an extraordinary creature! It is like one of those circus bears trained to balance a motor car on its nose, or some such thing. There is dazzle in its every baroque convolution; yet the dazzle belies the laborious process by which we got to it: a process, sometimes, of trial and error, as if we were standing in a room the walls of which were lined with thousands upon thousands of light switches, and we had to try each one with the goal of eventually arriving at a very particular degree of brightness. One switch would bring us close—and then we would try another and the light would be blinding, or the room would go dark. Still, over weeks, we got closer, and then, almost without noticing, one day we had the light almost right.

Now I must address, once again, the mystic faction that accepts, without a hint of incredulity, Ramanujan's claim that his mathematics came to him in dreams, or that formulae were inscribed upon his tongue by a deity. I am sure that he believed this to be the case, just as I am sure that, on occasion, he did haul up from the depths of his imagination treasure chests from which glittering jewels gleamed forth, while the rest of us were chiseling away in the diamond mines with our pickaxes. And yet, the ability to voyage on a regular basis (as poor Moore could not) into regions of the mind from which most of us are barred does not necessarily require the intervention of a goddess. On the contrary, all of us experience, on occasion, such "miracles."

Let me give an example. All of you who know him would agree that no mathematician is less "mystic" than Littlewood. Yet even Littlewood described to me once an occasion on which, while working on the $M_1 < (1 - c)M_2$ problem for real trigonometrical polynomials, his "pencil wrote down" a random formula that turned out to be the key to the proof. According to Littlewood, this episode was "almost unattended by consciousness"—a claim which, had psychoanalysis been in vogue during the war, would have been of considerable interest to its adherents. In those years it would have been of interest only to adherents of the Ouija board. And that is just my point. Were I to announce, today, that a goddess was writing formulae on *my* tongue, you would show me the way to the asylum. But Ramanujan was Indian, and so he was labeled a "visionary." Yet what this label neglects is the price he paid for his vision, and how hard he had to work to attain it.

While it is true, for instance, that the formula sprang from one of the conjectures that he had brought with him from India, it must be borne in mind that the journey from that initial conjecture to the final product was laborious and long. It was a process of refinement, and while it is fair to say that, had I not brought to the table certain technical know-how that I possessed and that he did not, we couldn't have got there, let me emphasize that my contribution was not *merely* technical. I contributed my own share of vision.

I remember it was Christmas when we finished. I was at Cranleigh, at the house in which I had grown up, the house my mother shared with my sister, and to which I returned on holidays. My mother, at this point, had been dying for several years. Every few months, it seemed, she would come close to death, she would see the angels beckoning her, and then, at the eleventh hour, something would pull her back from the brink, and before we knew it she would be out of bed, making tea and proposing a game of Vint. To this game—does anyone now remember it?—she was devoted. It was Russian in origin, a variant on Contract Bridge. (I'm told "Vint" means "screw" in Russian.) That Christmas we played it for hours every day, with our neighbor and Mother's friend, Mrs. Chern, making up the fourth. Mrs. Chern cheated, I think. I wonder if Mother noticed.

I may have already mentioned that she possessed a certain degree of mathematical talent—a talent, I am sorry to say, that in her later years she applied exclusively to the playing of Vint, which at least has the advantage of being a harmless pastime, in contrast to the occult evils in which Ramanujan's mother indulged. And Mother, to her credit, was a very good Vint player. Almost as good as I was. That year I had the idea to write a book on how to win at Vint, and make enough money from it that I could give up teaching. My goal, I told Russell, was to score a million points, so that later, when people asked me what I'd done in the Great War, I could say that I'd become head of the Vint League and given the world at large the benefit of my expertise. But I never wrote the book, just as I never wrote the murder mystery about the Riemann hypothesis, and now, when people ask me what I did during the Great War, I tell them, "I took care of Ramanujan." Perhaps, in my dotage, I shall write both.

But I am straying. To get back to partitions: that Christmas, Ramanujan sent me a postcard from Trinity, providing the last piece in the puzzle and asking me to write up the final proofs. By then MacMahon, who was really the dearest of creatures, had provided him with the typewritten copy of values he had come up with for $p(n)$ up to $n = 200$, and Ramanujan had made his comparisons. The formula was not precise. Instead it gave an answer that was correct only when rounded to the nearest integer. Yet the difference was extraordinarily small. In the case of n = 100, for instance, our formula gave a value for p(n) of 190569291.996, whereas the actual value was 190569292. A difference, to be precise, of .004.

Ramanujan was thrilled with the results. He called them "remarkable," which was unusually expressive, coming from him. It was exciting enough news that I mentioned it to Mother, to whom I rarely spoke about my work, but as the question had no bearing on Vint, she responded only with an air of contrived vagueness, saying something along the lines of "How nice" before drifting back to the card table.

You see, she was really sharp as a tack. Vagueness was a convenience for her, to which she resorted when a subject bored her. Her illness let her get away with all sorts of things she could never have got away with had she been well. And in the meantime my poor sister danced attendance on her, indulging her every fancy and never managing to distinguish between the real complaints and those that were purely fictitious. Poor Gertrude. In this regard she was far more credulous than I was.

Was the Russell business in full swing then? I think so. But no: most of the action—his arrest, the court case, his dismissal from Trinity—must have happened in the late summer and early autumn, because I remember light coming over my shoulder as I read one of his letters while drinking tea; at Christmas it would have been dark already at teatime, a darkness which the wartime prohibition on streetlights only deepened. The habit of memory (my memory, at least) is to organize by category, not date. It's as if some immemorial secretary has plucked events out of their natural sequence and then filed them away under such headings as "Ramanujan," "The War," "The Russell Affair," so that now, in order to see clearly the chronology, I have first to dig out from each file the pertinent details of a moment and then place them alongside the details of another moment, dug out of another file. Nor, once I've completed this elaborate reconstruction, am I quite convinced of its veracity.

By the way, this is an episode of which, if you Harvard men have heard of it at all, you have probably heard only because it touches lightly on the history of your own illustrious university. For in 1916 not only was Russell dismissed by Trinity, he was refused a passport by the Foreign Office, and this meant that he could not take up a position he had been offered at Harvard. All of which suited his intentions perfectly.

I shall try to be as brief as possible. Russell was not, as is commonly believed, dismissed by Trinity *after* he was sent to prison. In fact, by the time he was sent to prison, two years had passed since his dismissal. This second arrest resulted from an article he wrote for the *Tribunal* that was adjudged likely to muck up relations between England and the United States; my own personal belief is that he wrote the article *in order* to be sent to prison, and thereby prove once and for all his willingness to endure sufferings, if not equal to, then at least approaching those of the men at the front. For it was difficult, in his position, to escape being labeled a shirker, and prison would show the manliness of his opposition.

But this is jumping ahead. In 1916 I don't believe prison was as yet on Russell's mind. What he had done was acknowledge, in a letter to the *Times*, authorship of a leaflet issued by the No Conscription Fellowship. The leaflet contained language the government considered inflammatory and possibly illegal, and so when Russell announced that he had written it, the Crown had no choice but to prosecute. The exact charge was that in the leaflet Russell had made statements "likely to prejudice the recruiting and discipline of His Majesty's forces." This was just what he wanted, for now he could use the trial as a soapbox for his pacifism. By getting himself prosecuted and, if possible, convicted, he hoped both to draw attention to the injustices being suffered by the conscientious objectors and to obtain a larger audience for his tirades.

The trouble was, his tirades could go over the heads of their intended audience. At the trial, he was in every way the logician, dismantling the prosecution's case as if it were a piece of specious mathematical reasoning. For instance, in addressing the principal charge against him—that the leaflet prejudiced recruiting—he noted that, at the time that the leaflet was issued, single men were already subject to conscription, while married men were not. Therefore the only deleterious influence that the leaflet might have would be on married men who were considering voluntary enlistment and were therefore, *ex hypothesi* (Russell actually used this phrase), not conscientious objectors. The leaflet, Russell summed up, merely informed such men that, if they chose to "pose" as conscientious objectors, they would be liable to two years' hard labor. "I do not consider that knowledge of this fact," he said, "is likely to induce such a man to pretend that he is a conscientious objector when he is not": an argument that, while it might dazzle a Trinity undergraduate, was only likely to antagonize a Lord Mayor.

And antagonize the Lord Mayor it did. Indeed, I would say that the strategy backfired completely, with the result that Russell was found guilty and fined £100, which he refused to pay. And the irony is, he could easily have got off. The Crown's case against him was incredibly weak. Now I suspect that in fact his game was far more subtle than any of us guessed; that, having recognized the weakness of the case, he had deliberately chosen to employ an approach that would annoy the Lord Mayor and insure his conviction. Now, because he refused to pay the fine, all the goods in his rooms at Trinity would go on the auction block. The newspapers would report the auction, and he would look every inch the martyr.

On the other hand, I very much doubt that he expected the Trinity Council actually to dismiss him. I certainly didn't expect it. After all, it is one thing to refuse a pacifist group permission to meet on the college grounds; it is another to rescind the fellowship of a man as eminent, respected, and famous as Bertrand Russell. And though the college bylaws gave the Council the *right* to dismiss any fellow convicted of a crime, it did not *oblige* them to do so. There was a choice to be made, and in making it, the Council revealed itself to be despotic and cowardly, undermining—perhaps permanently—the very foundations of intellectual freedom on which the college was built, and drawing ire from both inside and outside Cambridge.

Yet it was worse than that. Of the eleven members of the Council who voted against Russell, five were Apostles—McTaggart and Jackson among them. That ghastly shit McTaggart, I still believe, should have been cursed and roby-ized for what he did, for roby had merely decided that the society was not worth his time, while McTaggart turned against a brother who had once regarded him as a mentor. That year, every time I saw McTaggart creeping along a wall, or riding by on his decrepit tricycle, I would walk the other way, for fear that, should we encounter each other, I might lose my temper and kick him. Finally I understood why, in his school days, other boys had found kicking him such an irresistible temptation.

Of course, if Russell was shaken, he seemed to get over it quickly enough. Indeed, within a few days, he was telling me that the dismissal was the best thing that could have happened to him because, as he put it, it "decided the issue." Now he would be free of Trinity once and for all, and could travel around the country offering "intellectual food" to working men, miners and the like. Whether he really believed this or had merely struck a bargain with his pride I cannot say. But he did go off, to Wales and other places, and give lectures. Nor did he appear, when on occasion I saw him in London, to miss Trinity in the slightest. I cannot blame him. I loathed Trinity myself.

Yes, I loathed Trinity. I say this today without regret or embarrassment, even though, in the interval, I have left for Oxford and returned again. In dismissing Russell, we all agreed, the Council had at last gone too far. And yet we were divided as to how we should respond, some (myself included) feeling that militant action was called for, others believing that we should lie low until the war was over. And in the end, we compromised. Instead of a strongly worded statement published in the *Cambridge Magazine*, we settled for a weakly worded petition circulated only within the college:

> The undersigned Fellows of the College, while not proposing to take any action in the matter during the war, desire to place on the record that they are not satisfied with the action of the College Council in depriving Mr. Russell of his Lectureship.

What astounds me, in retrospect, is that even with this diluted language we collected only twenty-two signatures. It was mostly the enlisted fellows, the ones whose signatures would have carried the most weight, who refused to sign. Nor did Russell make the job any easier for us when he wrote to the Trinity porter and asked that his name be struck from the college books. That such a gesture should be considered provocative may strike you as puzzling, but in the Trinity of those years, any action that could be interpreted as expressing contempt for tradition was taken very seriously indeed. Because of it, we very nearly gave up on the whole effort, reasoning that if Russell had no desire to be helped, we ought not to risk our futures to help him. For he was having a fine old time right then, drinking beer with his new Welsh miner mates and sleeping with three women at once, though how they could withstand his breath I cannot imagine.

What did Ramanujan make of it all? Was he even aware that it was happening? I wish I knew. I wish I had asked him. But I didn't.

No doubt the most absurd moment in the affair, and the one in which Russell took the greatest satisfaction, was the auctioning off of his goods. This was necessitated, you will recall, by his refusal to pay the fine. Yet from the beginning he maintained an underhanded control of the proceedings. Remember, he had two domiciles. In addition to his rooms at Trinity, he kept a flat in London. Somehow he had managed to persuade the court to leave the London flat alone, and impound only what was at Trinity. I suspect that, from his vantage point, auctioning off the stuff at Trinity would be doubly beneficial: not only would the spectacle of the auction secure his public reputation, it would relieve him of the necessity of returning to Trinity to clear out his rooms, which he would be vacating anyway. Now his Welsh lecture tour need not be interrupted. And of course—at least this is what he said at first—he didn't really care about any of the stuff at Trinity. The truth was, it didn't have much value. Under ordinary circumstances it would never have fetched the £110 (a £100 fine plus £10 in costs) that Russell was required to pay if he was to avoid prison. For it was hideous stuff, chosen deliberately, or so Norton and I believed, to suggest the sort of studied indifference to environment that Russell considered befitting an intellectual.

Now, when I look over the advertisement for the sale (the immemorial secretary has kindly preserved it), I am really quite astonished at its brutality. The auctioneers, Messrs. Catling and Son, were experts at the use of a certain kind of language the sole intention of which is to whet the appetites of antique dealers and predatory collectors. For you must understand, most of the stuff was tasteless and worthless, which was why it made Norton and me laugh to see a particularly ugly little table described as a "Coromandel Wood Tea Caddy, mounted with 10 plated medallions," or Russell's battered desk transformed into a "Walnut Kneehole Writing Table," or the stained rugs described as "Superior Turkey Carpets." Indeed, of all Russell's furniture, only one piece—a six-legged Chippendale sofa—was any good, and this, in the end, I bought myself.

Any mirth that this advertisement might have aroused, however, ceased with the first paragraph. For immediately after listing "upwards of 100 ozs. of plate, Plated Articles, Gentleman's Gold Watch and

Chain," Messrs. Catling and Son skipped a line and announced—the text here is centered and in capital letters—the pièce de résistance: "COLUMBIA UNIVERSITY BUTLER GOLD MEDAL, awarded to Bertrand Russell, 1915." And then the books: *Royal Society Proceedings and Transactions, London Mathematical Society Proceedings*; the complete works of Blake, Bentham, Hobbes; *Baldwin's Dictionary of Philosophy and Psychology*; *Cambridge Modern History*. To sell a man's medal! And his books! Even Russell must have felt enough of a spasm at the prospect of these losses to reconsider his desire to see *everything* sold off, for a few days before the auction took place he was writing that, though he did not mind giving up the philosophy and mathematics books, he should not like to lose the literature books. And then—a further refinement—while it was true that he did not mind giving up the philosophy and mathematics books, he did think that he should like to keep the complete sets of the great philosophers, as these had belonged to his father. And then there was the tea table for which he seemed to feel a disproportionate attachment. But the medal could go. It would make good copy, this emblem of his fame overseas melted down and put on the market as raw gold. He could not resist that.

The morning of the auction, I asked Ramanujan if he would like to go with me, and he said that he would. It was the sort of warm day in which I would have taken far greater pleasure in peacetime. For now I did not want sun and leaves and river. I wanted gloom that would at least approximate the gloom of the Somme. And I suppose others must have felt the same way, for when we got to the Corn Exchange, we saw that the auction had drawn only a small crowd. Norton, of course, was there, pad and pencil in hand, for he was keeping the accounts for the collection, and needed to write down the prices that the lots fetched. There were no representatives of the press, not even from the *Cambridge Magazine*. Even the auctioneer seemed to feel the paltriness of the affair, for his patter lacked conviction, and he lowered the gavel with neither enthusiasm nor force. Had Russell been present, I suspect he would have been hugely disappointed.

The first lot, the auctioneer said, was already sold. This consisted of the silver, the watch and chain, the medal, and that tea table to which Russell felt such an attachment, and had been paid for with the funds collected by Morrell and Norton through their subscription. By now most of the books had been withdrawn too, which left only the furniture, the linens, the carpets, and a few odds and ends fished out from the backs of drawers. These fetched, in total, a little over £25. I got the Chippendale settee for just over £2, the one gesture of subtle retaliation I allowed myself. Norton bought some Denmark table-cloths, while Ramanujan, much to my surprise, bid on a little picture of Leibniz that I remembered having seen on Russell's mantelpiece, propped up between two silver candlesticks. No one bid against him, and he got the picture for almost nothing.

Afterward, the three of us took a walk along the river. "Of course I'll give him back the tablecloths," Norton said.

"Why?" I said. "Some tea-stained tablecloths. He probably doesn't even remember he owned them."

"But it's a matter of principle," Norton said. "You'll be giving him back the settee, I trust?"

"No, I think it will look much better in my rooms than it did in his," I said. "I might even have it recovered. I was thinking a *toile de Jouy*. Blue on white. Wouldn't that make a nice change, Ramanujan, when we're working on the partitions formula?"

Ramanujan said nothing. Clearly he did not know what a *toile de Jouy* was.

"No doubt Mr. Ramanujan finds our British preoccupation with furnishings and decoration somewhat curious," Norton said.

"That reminds me, why did you buy the Leibniz picture?"

"Leibniz was a great mathematician. But of course I shall return it to Mr. Russell if you feel that I should."

"No, keep it. If he'd wanted it, he'd have let Norton know."

We sat down on a bench. Some swans were stepping up out of the river onto the grass. "Vicious creatures," Norton said, and began to tell a story about how a swan had attacked him and his mother when he was a child. Before he could finish, though, Ramanujan broke into a loud cough, stood, and said, "Excuse me, I'm afraid I must return to my rooms." Then he left.

"That was odd," I said, watching him stumble away. "I wonder if he isn't feeling well."

"I should say so!" Norton said.

"What do you mean?" I asked.

"Haven't you noticed?" he said. "These last weeks he's looked like death warmed up."

I gazed at the swans. Their preening beauty, the careful attention they were paying to their own white down, belied fearlessness and brutality. They floated by, their apparent obliviousness to our presence, I knew, an illusion, the perpetual illusion perpetrated on creatures with eyes on the fronts of their heads by those with eyes on the sides. Our mistake, as always, was presuming that the other's perspective was our own; construing hostile surveillance as inattention. Yes, they were watching us.

We got up and walked back to the college. Perhaps one should be forgiven for failing to notice physical changes in the companion with whom one spends the bulk of one's time. Norton, who saw him less often, saw it more quickly.

"It's probably because he's working too hard," I said. "Sometimes he's up all night. He forgets to eat."

"Very likely," Norton said. "Still, don't you think you should have him see a doctor?"

"Why?"

"Well—to be on the safe side."

"Yes, but if I ask him if he's feeling ill, he'll deny that anything's the matter. He'll say he doesn't need a doctor. And even if he's ordered to he won't rest. He's obsessed with his work."

"Obsession with work can lead to a breakdown," Norton said, no doubt recalling his own experience.

We parted in New Court, and I went back to my rooms, where that evening I thought about Ramanujan in a way that I had not done for some time. It was true, a film of gloom seemed always to glaze his studied gentility. So was the trouble, as usual, the weather? The difficulty of finding food he could stomach? Had he not been Ramanujan, I would have asked him what was wrong. Being Ramanujan, however, he would have answered that nothing was wrong, when in fact much was wrong, though I would not learn the details until later.

As I have already mentioned, for many months, though he had received letters from his mother, he had received none from his wife, Janaki. Well, it seems that sometime during the course of that very summer he had, finally, got a letter from Janaki, a very disturbing letter, in which she informed him that she was no longer in Kumbakonam; she was now in Karachi, at the house of her brother. She and her brother would soon be returning to their village, for he was getting married, and could Ramanujan send her some money for a new sari to wear to the wedding? And with what a strange mixture of bitterness and relief did he greet this letter! For finally, after two years, Janaki was acknowledging his existence. But she was acknowledging it only to ask for money. Not a word was said about the many letters he had written to her, and that he presumed her to have ignored, when the truth, as he learned later, was that his mother had intercepted them. The girl's reticence, which in fact owed to her being barely able to write, he interpreted as coldness. Accordingly he sent the money, but grudgingly. Komalatammal, of course, took full advantage of Janaki's flight to advance her case against the girl. The brother's wedding, she told Ramanujan, was merely an excuse. The unhappy truth was that Janaki was a bad girl, a bad daughter-in-law, a bad wife. Possibly Komalatammal implied that there was another man in the picture. Janaki's real motive for running away—to escape her mother-in-law's tyranny, which had driven her to the breaking point—Komalatammal kept hidden or did not see herself.

Oh, that woman! Would that Janaki had only explained all this to Ramanujan! But she did not, perhaps because she saw no necessity to do so; or she did not realize that Komalatammal would distort the facts to bolster her own position; or she assumed that Ramanujan would understand her motives implicitly. Nor did she help her case when, at the end of her "visit" to her brother, she elected to remain at her parents' house rather than return to her mother-in-law's. This "abandonment" gave Komalatammal the ammunition that she needed. Yet for all her supposed occult powers, she did not possess enough in the way of psychological insight to see that her subterfuge would threaten Ramanujan's relationship with herself more than with his wife. For he must have felt, even at such a distance, Komalatammal's clawing efforts to interpose herself between him and Janaki, and whereas before he had written to her every week, now he wrote to her only once a month, and then once every two months, and then not at all.

So you see, he had worries of which I was hardly cognizant. If I am to be honest, even if he had confided in me some of these worries, the likelihood is that I would have paid them scant heed. Like him, I had most of my attention focused on mathematics. What little remained the Russell affair consumed. Not that I forced work upon him. Ramanujan and I were united in our devotion to a task in the presence of which the need to eat, even the need to love, fell away. I'm tempted to say that our intimacy was all the stronger for the many emotions it disallowed, for when we were working, the queer mixture of compassion and irritation and awe and perplexity that the *idea* of him stirred up in me grew fleecy and insubstantial and fell away. I suspect that whatever I was to him fell away, too. In such an atmosphere, anything that threatened to impinge upon the work I resented. And yet we worked together, at most, four hours a day. This left twenty during which we were apart.

Mrs. Neville was wrong to accuse me of ignoring, ultimately to his peril, Ramanujan's unhappiness. Were she more subtle or more intelligent, she might have made the proper accusation: namely, that I failed to *respect* his unhappiness. Of his disappearances, his bad moods, his periods of obstinacy, I was merely tolerant. I did not bother to think what lay behind them. Or if I did think what lay behind them, I did so in frustration, when his behavior interfered with our work.

For instance, that fall, at long last, he got his B.A. I wrote to Madras a glowing report of his progress. I even read one of his papers aloud to the Cambridge Philosophical Society, though he did not come to the meeting. Did I invite him? Probably not. Probably I assumed he would be too shy to want to attend.

And yet the B.A. did not, as I hoped it would, placate him or assuage his need for approbation. On the contrary, the attainment of this emblem of success—two letters that he could now put behind his name—only seemed to exacerbate his hunger for further trophies. And what was the next trophy to be sought? It seemed that Barnes, who had in the meantime left Cambridge, had, before his departure, told Ramanujan that he could count upon being elected to a Trinity fellowship in the fall of 1917. I was not so certain. His reputation was very much bound up with my own, and I was hardly in good odor right then at Trinity. On top of that, there had never before been an Indian fellow. None of this I felt like explaining to him, though. I did not want to give him cause for further worry. At the same time, I could hardly second the assurances that Barnes had given him, and as it was Ramanujan's habit, when faced with uncertainty, to pester, he began to bring up the matter of the fellowship on an almost daily basis, just as before he had brought up the Smith's Prize.

Please understand, his ambition in and of itself did not trouble me. I understood and appreciated that ambition, as I suffered from it myself. For in those days there was a sequence that guaranteed, as it were, a mathematician's authenticity: Smith's Prize led to fellow of Trinity, fellow of Trinity led to fellow of the Royal Society. Had I myself failed to obtain any of these honors—all of which, in my case, came in their due course, "on schedule"—I would have been thrown into a paroxysm of self-doubt and rage. So why did I begrudge Ramanujan the same need for affirmation? I suppose because I sensed that in his case no prize, no matter how grandiose, would be sufficient to quell the longing. But what exactly was it a longing for? Let us define it, then, *reductio ad absurdum*, by imagining that it did not exist. Could years of having doors shut in your face leave you a happy man? Or would those years necessarily leave as their legacy a hunger no quantity of medals would sate? No wonder I could not reconcile that hunger with Ramanujan's putative spirituality, that crucible in which, he claimed, his discoveries were kindled into life! There were two different questions: one had to do with origins and the other with consequences.

Now that I am older, I have a more dispassionate attitude toward these matters. At Cambridge we were taught to view our lives as train journeys along appointed routes, station following upon station until at last we arrived at some glorious last stop, the end of the line which was really the beginning of things. From then on we would bask in a glow of rest and ease, of comfort institutionally sanctioned. Or so we thought. For in truth, how many ways there are to go off the rails! How frequently the timetable is changed, and the guards go on strike! How easy it is to fall asleep and wake up only to discover that you have missed the station where you were supposed to change trains, or that you've been riding the wrong train all along! The worry it cost us . . . yet of course, all that worry is futile, because this is the cruelest secret of all: all the trains go to the same place. At some point Ramanujan must have begun to realize it.

In any case, the morning after the auction, he came to me as always. Now I looked him up and down, and was alarmed to see that, though his body had retained its stoutness, his cheeks were sunken. Fleshy half-moons, lighter than the dark skin around them, puffed out from under his eyes. Contradicting what I had told Norton, I asked him if he was feeling all right; if he needed a doctor. But as I guessed he might, he brushed off the question. "I have not been sleeping well," he said. "I was thinking about . . ." Who knows what? Probably some detail in the partitions theorem. And then we were off.

I have never been a man inclined to dig deeply into motives and processes. Mathematics, for me, has always been like this: you are looking at a mountainous landscape. Peak A you can see clearly, peak B you can barely discern amid the clouds. Then you find the ridge that leads from peak A to peak B, at which point you can move on to further, more distant peaks. All very pretty, this analogy—I used it in a lecture I gave in 1928—and yet what it fails to address is whether, in making this exploration, you should rely only on your binoculars, or actually strike out on foot. In the latter case, you no longer regard the peaks from a distance; you delve into them. And this is a much more dangerous game. For now there are risks that you do not face standing safely at a distance, gazing through your binoculars: frostbite, weariness, losing your way. You may lose your footing, too, fall from the surface you are scaling into the abyss. Yes, the abyss is always there. We cope with the risk of falling in different ways. I coped with it by not looking, by pretending there was no abyss. But Ramanujan, I think, was always staring down into it. Guarding himself. Or preparing to jump.

And what is the abyss? This is where language starts to fail me. It is the place where all the pieces, all the symbols, all the Greek and German letters, fly about and meld and mate in the most preposterous, arbitrary ways. Sometimes miracles are born, more often grotesqueries, creatures for a sideshow . . . Later, when he was sick, Ramanujan told me that during periods of fever he attributed a pain in his stomach to the spike where the zeta function, when drawn on a graph, takes the value of 1 and soars off into infinity. The spike, he said, was gouging his abdomen. By then, of course, he was living in the abyss.

Looking back, the only thing that surprises me about those years is that, with the exception of Thayer, no new players entered the scene. Instead the players were merely rearranged, repositioned. Russell, who should have been in Cambridge, was in Wales. Littlewood was in Woolwich. Alice Neville, strangest of all, was in my London flat. To these reconfigurations I adjusted with what seems to me, in retrospect, remarkable sangfroid. I got used to seeing Alice's hat on the coatrack in Pimlico, to receiving letters from Littlewood on military stationery. Nor did the letters from mothers, telling me that this or that former student was dead, stir up in me the shock that they once had. Hard as it is to say, I grew inured to them. And yet there was one from whom I longed to receive a letter, and did not.

Where was Thayer? Was he dead? I had no idea. Since that dreadful afternoon when he had arrived at the flat and I had turned him out, I had heard not a word from him. It would be unseemly, I think, to describe here the mortifications to which I subjected myself, the hours I spent reenacting the scene, this time treating Thayer, if only in my imagination, with the respect that he deserved, and that he rightly despised me for having withheld. I would have liked to put it in a letter, and yet I doubted some don's pornographic description of the orgies of self-flagellation in which, for purposes of atonement, he indulged in the private safety of his rooms, would mean much to a lad fighting at the front. I wrote him, of course, but they were inadequate letters: again I was the great-aunt expressing her hope that her nephew would call on her for tea the next time he was on leave. Somehow I could find no means of voicing, even in language sufficiently coded to confound the censors, my hope that he would forgive me. Nor, apparently, were my efforts to melt his outrage close to sufficient, for he never replied. Either he was dead or he had concluded that I was not worth the trouble. And really, selfish and terrible as this may sound, I hoped that he was dead. For if he was dead, at least there was a possibility that before dying, if only in his own mind, he had forgiven me.

What I could not do, hard as I tried, was forget him. At least once a week I visited the hospital on the cricket grounds, ostensibly to offer words of support and reassurance to the injured soldiers, really to see if by some miracle Thayer might show up, once again, in one of the wards. Things had changed in the intervening year. In addition to the sisters, uniformed members of the Medical Unit of the Officers Training Corps paced among the beds. They were surgical dressers or clerks. As I moved through the vast expanse of the hospital, I would pretend to a purely academic interest, ask them to explain the treatment methods they were testing out, when in fact all I wanted was to find Thayer. But he was never there.

Occasionally I might strike up conversations with some of the other lads. With surprising frequency these took a flirtatious turn. But I could not muster enough enthusiasm to follow up on the leads I was offered. For Thayer had claimed me. I suppose I must have been in love with him. I wanted no one else.

Under the best of circumstances, hope has a short life span. During wartime its life span is shorter still. At midnight on New Year's Eve,

1917, I raised my glass to the sky (I was alone in Cranleigh, Gertrude and Mother asleep) and declared valiantly that I had given up on Thayer. It was a new year, and I would move on.

Two weeks later the letter came, and when it did, the almost giddy joy I felt upon seeing his handwriting nearly brought me to my knees. It wasn't even a real letter, just one of those forms which, before the fracas, I had become accustomed to receiving from him whenever he was anticipating a leave. I have the form still. At the top there is the usual warning:

> NOTHING is to be written on this side except the date and signature of the sender. Sentences not required may be erased. If anything else is added the postcard will be destroyed.

And then, below, the various lines to be checked off:

I am quite well.

I have been admitted into hospital
$\begin{cases} \text{sick} \\ \text{wounded} \end{cases}$ and am going on well.
          and hope to be discharged soon.

I am being sent down to base.

I have received your
$\begin{cases} \text{letter dated _____} \\ \text{telegram '' _____} \\ \text{parcel '' _____} \end{cases}$

Letters follow at first opportunity.

I have received no letter from you
$\begin{cases} \text{lately} \\ \text{for a long time.} \end{cases}$

Signature $\big\}$
only
Date _____

338

Before, Thayer had always ticked only the line that read "Letters follow at first opportunity." This time, however, he had also ticked "wounded." He did not tick "and hope to be discharged soon."

The real letter arrived the next day. It gave only the name of a military hospital, this one outside Oxford.

I took the first train I could catch, and arrived early in the afternoon. As the hospital was smaller than the one at Cambridge, and was housed, in fact, in an actual building, a girl's school requisitioned for the duration, finding him took almost no time at all.

He was lying quietly in his bed, much as he had been lying quietly in his bed the first time I had spoken with him. His face was intact. Much to my relief, he smiled when he saw me.

"So you got my note," he said.

"I did," I said. "This morning. I came as soon as I could."

I sat down, made a fist and landed it, softly, in the flesh of his shoulder. He did not laugh.

"So what's happened to you?"

"They got the other leg this time. See?" He pulled back the sheet, exposing the leg in its dressings, bandages to just above the knee. "So—two legs down, one arm down, one arm to go."

"What happened to your arm?"

"Oh, that was weeks ago. A bullet. It didn't do much damage—just enough so that I'll never be able to raise it all the way again."

"And this time?"

"A big hunk of shrapnel. But I won't lose the leg. They told me that. And there's pain. Lord, is there pain. That's a good sign."

"Will you be discharged?"

"Doubtful. I don't seem to be lucky enough to get shot up enough for that. I'd probably have to lose the leg to get a discharge, and frankly—" He lowered his voice. "But the truth is I don't want to come back. You know, to England. Not until it's all over. It's hard to explain. Out there in the trenches—you're wretched but you're alive. And then you come back, and everything's going along like it's a normal world. And you sort of—you feel dead. And everyone else seems dead. And you look forward to getting back because you don't like being around all those dead people." He frowned. "You know what I mean?"

"Yes, I do."

"I don't know. I don't know anything anymore."

A few beats of silence passed, and then I said, "I'm glad you wrote to me."

"Yes, I meant to before, only the last few leaves—you see, my sister's going to have a baby, and so I've been up in Birmingham quite a bit. I was in Birmingham with the arm. I never did make it down to London."

Was he going to mention what had happened in Pimlico? Or did he expect me to bring it up? Or had he decided to pretend it had never happened?

"So how long will you be in hospital?"

"A week or so more. Then I'm free for a while." He looked up shyly. "Is that lady, that friend of your sister's, still in your flat?"

"Only during the week. Not on the weekends." I took in my breath. "We get along better now. She leaves me sandwiches. I suppose you wouldn't be free some Saturday, would you?"

He smiled. "To come to tea?"

"Exactly."

"I think I could manage that," he said.

And he did. Two Saturdays later. He managed it as well the next time he had leave. This time they had got the other arm. "Two arms, two legs," he said. "What's next?"

"I hope not this," I said, grabbing him in a crude way, which was what he wanted.

And the amazing thing was that they never let him go. They would break him, and send him home for repair, and break him again. In much the same way, I realized later, we broke Ramanujan, and patched him together again, and broke him again, until we had squeezed all the use we could out of him. Until he could manage no more.

Only then did we let him go home.

PART SEVEN

The Infinite Train

I

GERTRUDE WAITS, while the fire gutters, for her brother to come. Pitch dark at five in the afternoon, and she's reading something Alice gave her, a novel set in Italy. "What a ridiculous country this is!" the heroine tells her lover. "Nearly midnight, and so warm I don't need my wrap!" Words don't melt frost, though, unless you throw them into the fire, and Gertrude is too much of a worshipper of books—even bad books—to burn them. So she puts the novel down and summons her fox terrier, Daisy, from where she sleeps by the hearth. Daisy has improbably good taste: she chewed up Ouida but left D. H. Lawrence alone. Now Gertrude holds the book out—*One Tuscan Summer*—and Daisy sniffs it; licks the spine; turns away and returns to her nest. Indifference. Gertrude laughs. Church bells sound, waking her mother in the next room.

"Margaret?"

"It's all right, Mother," she calls.

"Isaac?"

"Everything's fine. It was just the church bells."

Sophia Hardy (her real name, Euphemia, she has never used) moans and turns in her bed. Lately she converses more with the dead than with the living. She seems to be journeying, as she has countless times before, to the edge of an unknown world. The question is, this time will she cross over? Gertrude hopes she will cross over. The doctor thinks she will cross over. According to him, the situation is dire enough to necessitate Harold being summoned from Cambridge. For he'll want to say goodbye to his mother, won't he? But Harold, she knows, is skeptical. He has made the same journey, for the same motive, one too many times.

Another moan—this time deeper—and Gertrude, with a heave of boredom, gets up again and walks to the drawing room, her mother's bedroom for the duration. Despite her Italian name, Mrs. Hardy is even more a northern creature than her daughter, so pale you can see the fine tracery of veins on her face, frail as a nymph, but a nymph of winter, of icy forests of silver birch. And thin. Gertrude remembers her boasting, on her seventieth birthday, that she could still get into her wedding dress. Then she tried it on and waltzed into the dining room, immemorial, a latter-day Miss Havisham. They thought she was losing it that time. But she came back. She has always come back.

Old age, Gertrude often thinks, can look like second childhood. Certainly it's easy to lapse into the habit of treating the elderly as children, the way the sisters treat her retired colleagues at the Home for Distressed Gentlewomen, leading them in orgies of tatting and sewing and painting watercolors, these women who twenty years before taught chemistry, mathematics, Shakespeare . . . At the Home for Distressed Gentlewomen the year is marked off by holidays, mistletoe through the New Year, hearts until St. Valentine's Day, green for St. Patrick's Day, lambs and eggs until Easter. "It's so they don't forget time," the matron explained when Gertrude visited the first time; when she was still thinking her mother might live there, and she herself might change her work, and move full-time to London. But it wasn't to be.

"Mother, are you all right?" Gertrude fluffs her pillows.

"Would you rub my legs?" Mrs. Hardy asks.

"Very well." Sitting down, Gertrude untucks the blankets from the foot of the bed and lifts them back; reaches inside her mother's nightdress and begins the steady, rhythmic rubbing, thigh to stockinged ankle, from which, for reasons Gertrude can't quite fathom, Mrs. Hardy seems to derive such comfort. Back and forth; skin and bone. There's so little left of her! No flesh, no heft. Whatever's wrong, she recognizes, is something very bad. The doctor doesn't say and Gertrude doesn't ask. She only knows that twice now the pain has got so severe as to require morphine. For the moment, though, Mrs. Hardy is tranquil. She lies back, emitting little hisses of air. "Margaret, bring the flowers into the kitchen," she says. And: "Shell the peas." And: "Do you have your eye in?"

Gertrude flinches. Mrs. Hardy gives out a little cry.

"I'm sorry."

"Even if no one sees," Mrs. Hardy says, "someone is watching. Remember that."

"Yes, Mother."

"You need to marry. But she's a homely girl."

"Who?"

"Margaret."

"Who is Margaret?"

"She taught with me. At the training college."

"And she was homely?"

"Oh no. Pretty as a picture."

"Then who was homely?" But she knows the answer, and keeps rubbing. It doesn't bother her particularly. No niceties in this house anymore, not now that the daughter, with a brisk efficiency that surprises even her, washes twice weekly those parts of her mother from which, decades before, she herself sprang. "Loins." What a word! She washes her mother's loins, her mother's pudendum (another word she loves), more or less bald now. Like an old man's head.

There is a rattling at the door. No one but Gertrude to answer. Maisie, who cleans for them, has gone home.

"I'm coming!" she calls, and removes her hands, gently, from under Mrs. Hardy's nightdress; rolls back the blankets.

"I'm just going now, Mother, to get the door. It's Harold."

"Harold's here?"

"Yes, he's come to see you."

"But I look a fright!"

Gertrude rises. Daisy has beaten her to the door; she leaps and barks at the handle. "Get down," Gertrude says halfheartedly, for she knows her brother doesn't like dogs. It was the principal reason she acquired Daisy.

She opens the door, and Hardy steps inside, shaking his umbrella. "What weather!" he says, and kisses her on the cheek.

"How was your journey?"

"Tiring. It takes hours to get anywhere these days. Oh, yes—" Daisy is leaping at his hands. "Yes, I know you're glad to see me. Yes. Now please get down."

"Sorry," Gertrude says, picking Daisy up.

Hardy hangs his coat on the peg. "So how is she? Is it bad?"

"Come and see for yourself."

"I'd rather not quite yet. I'd like to settle in first."

"Harold, is that you?"

"Yes, it's me, Mother."

"Come and say hello."

He glowers at Gertrude, as if their mother's insistent tone is her fault. Then he smoothes back his hair, and they go in together. Mrs. Hardy smiles. Suddenly she is lucid, garrulous. She wants to be propped up. She wants a hot water bottle. "A game of Vint, perhaps?" she asks. "How long will you stay?"

"I'm not sure. I have to be in London on Monday. I've got some business with the Mathematical Society."

"Good, you can go in for the day and come back."

"We'll see."

But she won't take no for an answer. She wants to chat, she wants to play Vint, she wants Harold to promise he will stay. She is like a child who refuses to go to bed, who has to be talked into recognizing her own fatigue.

Finally, after much cosseting and bargaining ("Go to sleep now, Mother, and we'll have a game of Vint in the morning"), much protesting ("But I'm not in the least sleepy!"), at last, without warning, Mrs. Hardy falls asleep. Now Gertrude and Hardy can retire, as is their wont, to the kitchen. Gertrude makes eggs, laid by the hens she keeps. They drink tea.

"Well, that was easier than usual," Gertrude says.

"Easier!"

"She knows what time it is. Yesterday she woke me at two in the morning wanting her lunch. But at least she read the clock right." Gertrude stabs her egg, so that the yolk runs. "Well, even if you do have to go to London on Monday, I'm glad you'll be staying the weekend. I need to go into town tomorrow and do some shopping."

"What does that have to do with me?"

"Someone has to watch her."

"What about Maisie?"

"Maisie's sixteen. She can hardly be trusted. Anyway, it's not difficult, Harold, all you have to do is bring her meals and make sure she's comfortable."

"But what if she needs the toilet?"

"Maisie will deal with that."

"But I'm supposed to meet a friend for tea tomorrow—in town."

"What friend?"

"No one you know."

"Can't you change it?"

Hardy puts down his cup. "You've got me down here under false pretenses," he says. "You told me she was dying—"

"The doctor said she was dying—"

"—you told me she was dying when the truth is you just want to go shopping."

"I've got to have underwear, don't I?"

He winces at the mention of the underwear.

"I'm a busy man, I can't just pack up and leave every time—"

"All right," Gertrude says. "You go. Go to London, meet your friend, and I'll stay here, just like I do every Saturday, watching and waiting. And when she calls, I'll go to her. And the same on Sunday. And then Monday, teaching. And then in the evening sitting with her, again."

"I know it must be difficult."

"Do you? Do you have any idea?"

"Of course I do. Look, I'm not spending all my time throwing tea parties these days. I don't go to London for my health, you know, I've got two secretaryships, then there's the Mathematical Society, the Royal Society. And at Cambridge my lectures, and this Russell business—"

"But at least you get to leave. You're not in Cranleigh week in, week out."

"No, I'm in Cambridge week in, week out."

"Have you any idea how long it's been since I've had a chance to escape this place? To just do a few normal things, have lunch in a restaurant, go to some shops?"

Hardy says nothing. He puts his fingers to the bridge of his nose.

"You get irritated with me because I summon you down and she looks like she's all right. But the doctor said she was dying. What am I supposed to do, tell you not to bother? And then if she does die—"

"Yes, I understand."

"And if I've got to buy underwear . . . I'm sorry, but a woman needs . . ."

"Yes, I know. All right, I'll stay tomorrow—or part of tomorrow. Perhaps if you were back by three—"

"You never asked me why I told Alice Neville she could let my room in the flat, did you? It was because I never bloody have the chance to go anymore—"

"Yes, Gertrude."

"Well, I don't." She blows her nose. "I'm sorry, I'm a bit short-tempered these days."

"No need to apologize. I am too. Things are very bad at Trinity. And now I've had to enter the fray again, because a Newnham girl—this shit called Ridgway won't let her into his lecture because she's a member of the U.D.C. He took advantage of the fact that women aren't officially enrolled, therefore he can throw them out of the lectures without cause. He couldn't do that with a male student."

"You're turning into quite a feminist, aren't you?" Gertrude says—but he misses the irony in her voice.

"It isn't really about that. Ridgway says that if he could, he'd keep male students out too, if they were in the U.D.C. It's all a tactic. The truth is, he's punishing the girl because she said something in the Newnham Hall that was construed to be pro-Russell. I'm working on a piece about it. Possibly a flysheet. We haven't given up on getting Russell reinstated, you know—after the war."

"It's really quite admirable, the lengths to which you'll go to help other people."

"I do what I can."

"Of course you do."

He coughs; gets up. "Well, I'm a bit tired," he says. "I think I'll go to bed early if you don't mind."

"Why would I mind?"

"And you? Are you going to bed?"

"Hardly, considering it's only half past six."

"Yes, well, as I said, the journey . . ." He leans toward her, palms on the table. "Gertrude, about tomorrow . . . This appointment I have really is rather important, so if you don't mind, perhaps you could go into town early, and I'll plan to leave around two. That way Mother will be alone with Maisie, what, two hours?"

She doesn't say, "But I do mind." It's not her way. It's her way to concentrate her bitterness, to let it spin in the centrifuge of her spirit, until only its essence remains, unspoken and ineradicable.

"As you wish, Harold."

"And if anything goes wrong, if . . . You can telephone me and I'll be on the first train."

"As you wish."

He turns away. She does not get up. Through the kitchen door, she hears Daisy jumping, Daisy sniffing . . . "Yes, fine, goodnight, dog," he says, which brings a faint smile to her lips. In a minute, she knows, she will have to rise from her chair, pile the dishes on the counter for Maisie to wash in the morning: something else her brother would never think to do. But that can wait. These days, moments of solitude are so rare for her she has learned to treasure them. For now she simply sits, listening to the silence, looking at the dark.

2

"EXCUSE ME, SIR, but she's asking after you."
He wakes to the smell of coffee mixed with chicory, the vision of a face at the door: youthful, pallid, fat.

"Who?"

"Your mother."

"Oh, yes." He sits up in bed. This must be Maisie.

"You weren't here last summer, were you?"

"No, sir, I started just before Christmas." A cry issues from downstairs. "Excuse me, sir, but like I said, she's asking after you. She's been ever so grumpy this morning."

"Fine, I'll be there in a minute."

"Very good, sir."

"And close the door!"

"Sorry, sir." It clicks shut. A house of women. He gets out of bed, puts on his clothes, is just finishing combing his hair when he hears the voice again. "Mr. Hardy—"

"Yes?"

"I'm very sorry, sir, but she's got quite ill-tempered. She won't have her breakfast, wants you to go down."

"Very well. I'm coming, Mother!" he shouts, and hurries downstairs, his shirt still half-unbuttoned. His dying mother. Why does it all feel like a stage comedy?

On the bed that has been dragged into the drawing room for her to die on, Mrs. Hardy lies on her back, gazing up at the ceiling. Her gray hair is tied with a bow. Maisie sits at her side, lifting a spoon from a bowl.

"Well, Mother, I'm here," he says.

"Harold," she says weakly. "Sit down. Sit down next to me."

Obligingly Maisie gets up. She hands him the bowl; the spoon. "See if you can get her to eat," she says, then strides off with the brisk vigor of youth to the kitchen.

His mother smiles up at him. He smiles back.

"Well," he says. "And how about some breakfast?"

"Dear Harold. I was speaking of you today with your father."

"Oh yes?"

"He was just back for dinner—from the—the boys were . . ."

"Where, Mother?"

"And then we were shelling peas."

"But what about father?"

"Don't bother to ask," Maisie says, returning with a cup of coffee, which she hands to him. "She'll never follow anything to the end." And Maisie's right. Mrs. Hardy's conversation, if you can call it that, is all sentences that stroll and meander and collapse into themselves; infinite regresses, like Russell's barber. Things he recognizes from the past are mixed up with references to people he's never heard of, as if she's half slipped into someone else's life.

"Won't you rub my legs?"

"Your legs?"

"They're so sore."

"I'll just call Maisie," he says, but before he can stand, she grabs hold of his wrist. Her grip is stronger than he would have guessed.

"No, not the girl," she says. "You."

"Mother, I . . . Maisie!"

The girl comes in, wiping her wet hands on her apron.

"Maisie, will you rub her legs?"

"I'm not rubbing her legs, the last time I tried she nearly bit my hands off. She only lets Miss Hardy do it."

"Rub my legs, Harold."

"You'd better do it, sir. I'll show you how. There now, Mrs. Hardy, I'm not going to touch you, I'm just lifting up the blankets . . ."

"Mother, perhaps you should wait until—"

"There." The blankets are lifted back, exposing his mother's fragile torso in its nightdress, the stockinged feet. He remembers Lawrence describing, with horror and relish, the sight of Keynes in his striped pyjamas. "Now I'll just pull back your nightdress—"

"Don't!"

"All right, Mrs. Hardy, don't worry!" Maisie backs away. "You do it," she says to Hardy. "Come on."

Hesitantly Hardy bends toward his mother; touches his hands to the hem of the nightdress.

"How far back?"

"Halfway above the knees."

But halfway to what? Halfway between the knees and what?

Gingerly he pulls; she lifts her legs obligingly; she's not afraid of *him* touching her. Almost coquettish, her smile, until the nightdress is partway up, exposing the lined and spotted skin, the pronounced knees, the calves with their mottling of bruises.

"Maisie, how did she get these bruises?"

"She bruises easily, sir."

"But Mother, it might hurt you if—"

"Please rub my legs."

"All right." And he touches the skin, which is warm, the consistency of paper. He moves his hands up and down. "Is that all right?"

She closes her eyes.

"Well, I'll just be getting back to the kitchen," Maisie says.

"You know this building used to be a school."

"Did it?"

"The governesses would get very cross. The girls used to cry. The other day in town I ran into . . . I ran into . . . Florence Turtle and she . . . With the loveliest violets . . ." She seems to be gasping, as much for her thought as for air. "That's what gives it its atmosphere," she concludes.

"Well, Mother, and what do you think of Gertrude's new dog?"

"The dog whelped outside the kitchen . . . We had to drown the pups . . . The girls—Margaret said they shouldn't see, but I . . . and the school." Suddenly she looks up at him. "You should marry. I fear for you, dear."

He looks away. "Mother—"

"The eye worries you, I know. But you can be discreet. So long as you never let him see you with it out . . ."

"Oh, yes." He keeps rubbing, harder now, so that he feels the bones through the dry flesh. It strikes him that in her ravings (what else is there to call them?) a common theme keeps emerging. She speaks of school. And why not? All her life she has spent in schools. Both she

352

and his father. From Ramanujan's perspective, there must be little difference between him and Littlewood, him and Russell. All are children of affluence to him. And how can he be expected to recognize what separates Hardy from the others? For Littlewood comes from a Cambridge family; Russell is an aristocrat. Whereas Hardy is merely the child of teachers. Not born, as Russell was, with any guarantees. No private income. Easy enough for Russell to declare that if Trinity doesn't want him, he'll simply teach on his own in London. He can afford to. But Hardy is dependent on Trinity, just as his father was dependent on Cranleigh, his mother on the Training College, his sister on St. Catherine's. The only difference is one of prestige. Without the support of munificent institutions, all of them would be lost. He is more like Mercer than Littlewood.

After she has fallen asleep, and he has tucked her in again, he goes into the sitting room. He wants to have a word with Gertrude—about something, he's not sure what—but of course, the plan is for him to leave before Gertrude returns. And if he's to be on time for his appointment—at the prospect of which he flushes with pleasure and a slight revulsion, to think that these hands, which so lately rubbed his mother's legs, will soon be touching Thayer's; one set old, the other maimed—if he's to be on time, he'll have to leave soon.

So he leaves. He has his rendezvous with Thayer. He spends the night in London, at the flat. But on Sunday he returns to Cranleigh. Gertrude seems only mildly surprised to see him there.

"How was your day in town?" he asks.

"Adequate," she says. "I treated myself to tea at Fortnum's. Rather a limited spread, given the rationing."

"It's even got to Cambridge. At Trinity it's fish and potatoes but no meat on Tuesdays and Fridays, meat but no potatoes the rest of the week. No vegetables to speak of."

"One wonders how Ramanujan survives."

"One does." He looks away from her, at the fire, next to which Daisy sleeps. Then he says, "Gertrude, I want to talk to you about Mother."

"Oh?"

"She's got very demanding. The whole time you were gone she insisted that I sit with her and that I rub her legs."

"Yes, it seems to soothe her."

"My impression is that you coddle her. And then, because you rub her legs, I must rub her legs, else the sky will fall."

"An interesting point," she says. "Given how infrequently you're here, it hasn't seemed much of a problem until now."

"Well, but if I am here . . . in the summer and such . . ."

"So I'm to refuse our dying mother's wish that I rub her legs in order that you, on the rare occasions when you happen to visit, won't be burdened? Is that what you mean?"

"No, it's not what I mean. What I mean is—it can't be good for her."

"No, we mustn't spoil the child, else she'll grow up rotten."

"Oh, for God's sake, Gertrude. Look, just because you're willing to give up everything—"

"Yes, I've chosen to do that. I could have chosen differently. I could have just left and then you would have been it."

"So I'm to be punished because I have the life I have?"

He sits down; rests his chin on his hand. How helpless he looks! Helpless enough, Gertrude thinks, to melt anger. To inspire tenderness. And to think that he thinks himself a feminist!

She's tempted to touch his shoulder. To help him out of the hole into which he's dug himself. To give him an out. She almost feels kindly enough. But not quite. Not quite.

354

3

I T IS A BURDEN to know the fate of a man who does not know
his own fate.

Across the gloaming of the chamber in which the London
Mathematical Society holds its meetings, Hardy looks at Neville.
Neville's glasses hang low on his nose. He's staring into his hands,
twisting what appears to be a piece of string around his right ring
finger. Tightly, so that the flesh bulges. Hardy can make that out, even
from a distance, because unlike Neville, he is blessed with superb
eyesight, as well as an instinctive capacity to recognize the fiddling
stratagems of anxiety. Knuckles cracked, spectacles wiped repeatedly,
a loose button worried until it falls off. And though he wishes he could
go up to Neville right now, provide him with the relief he craves, tell
him, "Your fellowship's been renewed," the sad fact is, his fellowship
has not been renewed, and Hardy knows this already, and Neville
does not, though he must suspect. So Hardy says nothing. In Neville's
face there is worry shot through still with faint hope. Hope against
hope. Neville looks up, and for an instant their eyes meet. He nods.
Hardy nods back. But not to give anything away. At the very least he
doesn't want to be accused of peddling *false* hope.

It takes him about an hour to read the partitions paper. About ten
minutes in, Littlewood arrives, in uniform and looking the worse for
wear. He sits near the back, then pulls a pencil and what appears to be
a postcard from his rucksack and begins taking furious notes. Indeed,
every time Hardy looks up, he's taking notes—and always on the same
postcard, which he keeps turning, presumably in order to find another
cranny he can fill with figures. It's his usual maniacal style—vexing to
Hardy, who believes in penmanship, in cream-colored eighty-pound
paper, in legibility. Should Hardy make a mistake when he is writing
something, he will not cross it out; no, he'll start again with a fresh

sheet. Littlewood, by contrast, seems to take a peculiar satisfaction in the very messiness of the page, as if somehow, from amid that morass of symbols and equations and blots, a vision will coalesce.

Neville takes no notes. He neither blinks nor moves. His hands are coiled on his lap.

Hardy has very strong opinions about how one should read a paper aloud. Some of his colleagues, when they stand before a group of listeners, become amateur actors; they dash off witticisms, use their pointers as if they were épées, indulge themselves in the crudest flourishes. Hardy, on the other hand, believes that the work should take center stage, and therefore tries to speak, today, in as uninflected a voice as he can manage, with the result that two or three of the older members of the audience fall asleep. When he finishes, the weakest of applause greets him. No one understands the paper's importance. He takes two questions, one from Littlewood, the other from Barnes, both technical, after which the meeting breaks up, and he finds himself surrounded by a group of predatory dons from obscure universities, all with narrow little inquiries to make, the sort of inquiries that seem designed to lead him into a trap, or to catch him out in an error. Such feeble efforts, however, he deflects easily, and his persecutors leave disappointed, unrewarded.

The circle breaks up, revealing Neville, who takes Hardy's right hand in both of his. "Very well done," he says. "It does my heart good to see all Ramanujan's managed since he's been here."

"Indeed."

"A pity he couldn't make it."

"Oh, you know Ramanujan, this isn't really his sort of thing."

"But you did ask him."

"No, I—he hasn't been feeling well."

"I'm sorry to hear that." Then Neville smiles, and gazes into Hardy's eyes, as if searching for clues, for a sign. Something. From this searching Hardy turns away. For he can't bring himself to say, as he'd like to say, Neville, it's as you fear. They're throwing you out, ostensibly because they think you're just a mediocre talent (an assessment with which, by the way, I would be inclined to agree), but really to punish you for your pacifism, for being a member of the U.D.C., for defending Russell . . . It's horrible, it's unjust, but there it is. You're not famous enough to fight for. You're not Russell. We're casting you loose. And suddenly, just for an instant, he wonders if he *should* tell Neville, if it might soften the blow to hear it from Hardy instead of Butler. Only it's not his place. He takes on too much as it is.

"And will you be seeing Alice while you're in town?"

Neville laughs. "No," he says. "She's far too busy with her translating to see me. I'm going back to Cambridge right after this. Alice will come down tomorrow." He lowers his voice. "Funny thing, her staying in your flat. If I didn't know you so well, I'd say, 'Hands off the wife!'"

With a laugh, Neville punches him softly on the shoulder.

"Well, there's nothing to be concerned about on that front," Hardy says, "because the fact is, I never see her. I don't use the flat during the week, only on weekends."

"I know. I'm just joking. Hello, Littlewood."

"Neville," Littlewood says. "Hardy."

"Littlewood." Hardy can smell beer on his breath.

"Well, I must be off," Neville says. But he hesitates. "Hardy—" No response. "Well, it's nothing. See you."

With a wave, he disappears through the great dark doors.

Littlewood gazes after him. "Poor devil," he says.

"I know."

"I wonder what Ramanujan will think."

"Littlewood, should I have asked Ramanujan to come up today?"

"I assumed you did."

"No, I—that is, I assumed that even if I did ask him, he wouldn't come."

"It might have been a kind gesture. After all, he's the coauthor. Oh dear, looks like we're being given the heave-ho," he says, for by now the room has emptied out, and a char stands by the doors, impatient to tidy up. He and Hardy move toward the doors. "Sorry to have kept you, darling," Littlewood says, winking at the char, so that she smiles at them.

They stroll out into the corridor, down the stairs, into the dusk light on Piccadilly.

"Shall we walk a bit?"

"As you like. Where are you heading?"

"Back to bloody Woolwich. The end of a very short leave, the bulk of which I spent, I'm sorry to say, engaging in activities of a most insalubrious nature."

With or without Mrs. Chase? Hardy wonders. But he doesn't ask—not, as before, because he knows not to, but because he doesn't know how.

"And have you seen Ramanujan's friend Winnie lately?"

"I haven't been by the zoo in ages." They stop in front of Hatchards, gaze through the window at a display of novels all of which advertise their capacity to take readers far from London, far from the war. "I say, Hardy," Littlewood says, "you wouldn't be willing to let me use the bath at your flat, would you? I'm filthy, and the chances of my getting a decent bath at Woolwich are close to nil this late in the day."

"A bath?" Hardy focuses his attention on one of the novels: *One Tuscan Summer*. A bath! But Littlewood's never even been to his flat, on top of which there's the matter of Alice Neville, on top of which . . . yet how can he refuse a bath to an old friend when it's so obvious how badly he could use one? And a shave. Not to mention some sleep. For though in Littlewood's face he can recognize still—if just barely—the youth who used to stride naked to the Cam each morning, layers of worry and fatigue seem to smother him.

"Of course you can have a bath," Hardy says. "We'll take the tube, shall we?"

"Thanks." And they descend. From the ticket hall, a moving stairway carries them down, effortlessly, into the earth. Hardy hears the rumble of the mechanism; looks at the tired faces of the men and women on the other side of the partition, rising as he and Littlewood fall.

"You know I saw you once climbing a tree?" Hardy says.

"What? When?"

"Just before you took the tripos. I remember that it struck me as particularly odd, that you should be climbing a tree when all the other would-be wranglers were off practicing problems against the clock."

"I have no memory of ever engaging in any such activity. That said, I did try to maintain a lighthearted attitude toward the tripos. I took things as they came."

"Unlike Mercer."

"Poor Mercer. He took it all very seriously. Too seriously."

They step onto the platform just as the train pulls in. The station smells of bakeries. The carriage is crowded. Not far off from where they stand, holding straps to keep their balance, a woman tries to quiet a weeping baby. When Littlewood looks at her, his face breaks a little, and Hardy, to avoid a scene, says, "If these air raids don't let up, I expect we'll all be living in the Underground."

"I'd feel safer," says the woman with the baby.

"But they have let up lately," Littlewood says.

"Men in the sky in big balloons," the woman says. "It isn't natural. It isn't meant to be."

Hardy does not want to have a conversation with this woman. Yet Littlewood—it is his way—always manages to bring strangers into the fold. "How old is your baby?"

"Three months. His name's Oscar."

"Poor fellow, he must not like the crowds. I'm a father myself."

"Are you now!"

"Yes, just a few months. A girl."

"What's her name?"

"Elizabeth."

"Elizabeth. What a lovely name. Now my sister, she's just had a baby girl, and she's insisted on burdening the poor thing with Lucretia. I said, please, give the child a chance, let her be Gladys, Ida. But no. My sister's always put on airs. And how's your wife? Sometimes after birth women become a bit touched—"

"Well, actually . . ." But this must be stopped, Hardy decides, so he leans into Littlewood, and asks in a low voice, a voice meant to exclude, "Do you think there'll be a revolution in Russia?"

"Russell does."

"Oh, have you seen Russell lately?"

"We dined together last week."

"How is he?"

"In fine fettle. He says he wrote a biting piece about rich men deriving pleasure from the deaths of their sons, but Ottoline wouldn't let him publish it."

"Wise of her, I suspect. You know why they're dismissing Neville, don't you?"

"I have my suspicions."

Now the train has arrived at Charing Cross station. Littlewood tips his hat to Oscar and his mother, and they get off; switch onto the

District and ride to Victoria. The sun has set in the meantime and when they step into the gloom of Hardy's flat, he switches on the electric light, revealing Alice's chattels spread about the place, underwear hung to dry in the kitchen, books and newspapers strewn across the table. He was telling the truth when he said he never stays here during the week—even when he's had meetings of the Mathematical Society, he's stayed at a hotel or with friends—and now he sees for the first time how Alice lives when he's away, for on Friday she always cleans everything up; leaves the place immaculate.

"What's all this?"

"Didn't you know? Mrs. Neville stays here during the week. She's working for Mrs. Buxton. The foreign press stuff."

"But what about you?"

"Well, tonight I was planning to go back to Cranleigh. My mother, you know—"

"So you only came here with me so that I could have a bath?"

"It's not a bother."

"That's very kind of you, Hardy," Littlewood says. Then he takes off his hat and coat and heads into the bathroom. Left alone, Hardy inspects Alice's leavings. There is a newspaper article in German—he cannot make out much except that it concerns a Zeppelin attack on Paris—and next to it, half-finished, the translation: ". . . they have made ~~forays~~ raids on open towns, like Stuttgart and Karlsruhe, and have even made a target of the ~~palaces~~ castles of these unfortified cities, wherein the life of the Queen of Sweden was endangered . . ." Next to that, lying open on the table, the same novel he saw in the window display at Hatchards: *One Tuscan Summer*. Across the way, on the divan, a coat and—how irresistible—what appears to be Alice's diary, which he opens to the last page of the most recent entry:

skin that forms over warm milk. Why can't people be honest? Mrs. Chase for inst. insisting that the baby is her husband's, or Hardy who imagines that no one knows he's queer. Yet we persist in thinking that lying is the proper thing to do, hobbled by our inbred attitudes, shutting the windows on the sun and saying, "What a pity the rain makes it

Hardy drops the diary, as if it's bitten him. From the bathroom, he hears Littlewood singing:

> Private Perks went a-marching into Flanders,
> With his smile, his funny smile.
> He was loved by the privates and commanders
> For his smile, his funny smile . . .

It suddenly occurs to Hardy that there are no towels in the bathroom. So he fetches one from the closet and knocks on the door. "Yes?" Littlewood calls.

"I've brought you a towel."

"Come in, then."

Hesitantly Hardy enters. Steam rises from the tub, within which Littlewood, naked and immodest as ever, is smoking and scrubbing himself with a big old-fashioned brush that Hardy doesn't recognize. It must belong to Alice. "I'll just hang this on the hook here."

"Thanks." Littlewood lifts his left arm to soap his armpit. And how odd! Here in the bath he might once again be the young man who climbed the tree just before the tripos, as if he's scrubbed away not just the grime of a debauched night, but time and worry and age. To Hardy, his head looks too old for his body, as if, in a child's game, the mustached face of a middle-aged man has been set atop the neck and torso of a youth: thin shoulders, visible ribs, the flat nipples pink against the white flesh. Littlewood has his arm in the air, and for a moment Hardy is transfixed by the sight of his armpit hair; a whirlpool, black water whitened with flecks of foam.

> Pack up your troubles in your old kit bag
> And smile, smile, smile . . .

"Thank you, Hardy."

"You're welcome," Hardy says—and is about to leave when, exactly on cue, the tumblers click in the lock; the door to the flat creaks open. "Mrs. Neville!" he cries, and dashes out of the bathroom, shutting the door behind him.

From where she stands next to the umbrella stand, Alice gazes at him. She blinks.

"Mr. Hardy."

"Don't worry, I'm not staying."

What's the use of worrying?
It never was worthwhile . . .

"No need to be alarmed, it's just Littlewood. We were at the meeting of the Mathematical Society. He needed a bath, so I said . . ."

"Oh, of course." She hangs up her coat. "If you'd like, I could leave."

"No need, no need. As soon as Littlewood's finished, we'll be on our way."

Both of them look at the divan, on which the diary lies open. If Alice recognizes that it's angled slightly farther to the right than it had been, however, she doesn't say so. And in any case both of them are too preoccupied with the niceties, with the question of which of them can be said, on this Thursday evening in the winter of 1917, to be the actual tenant of the flat, and therefore responsible for asking the other to sit down, to think about the diary.

Finally they both sit at the same time. "And how is your mother, Mr. Hardy?" Alice asks. "I gather she's not been well."

"No, not well. I'm heading back there this evening, as a matter of fact."

"I see. And Mr. Littlewood?"

"He seems to be doing fine."

At that moment Littlewood comes out of the bathroom, adjusting the cuffs of his uniform jacket and looking rather humid. "Hello, Mrs. Neville."

She rises. "Mr. Littlewood."

"We saw your husband at the meeting," Hardy says.

"Yes, he told me he was coming up."

"A pity he couldn't stay."

"His lectures." Alice sits again. "And I saw your friend Mrs. Chase this afternoon."

"Anne? Really? Where?"

"At the Buxtons'. She comes up once a week or so to bring her translations."

"Oh, I see."

"She seems very well since the baby was born."

"I'm glad." Littlewood puts on his hat. "Well, I'm afraid I must be going. Due back at base. Very good to see you, Mrs. Neville."

"And you."

"I shall accompany you," Hardy says.

She sees them out the door. Silently they descend the stairs until they emerge into the smoky darkness on St. George's Square.

"Which way are you heading?"

"Waterloo."

"Same direction. Share a cab?"

"Why not?"

They hail one and climb in. As they ride, Hardy contemplates the vastness of London, the wilderness of streets and places and mewses through which the driver conducts them. All this complication he must memorize. It's his own tripos.

"The Knowledge, they call it," he says to Littlewood.

"What?"

"What cabdrivers have to learn before they can get their license. The streets of London. They call it the Knowledge."

"Oh, yes." But Littlewood's far away from the scenes he's gazing at, brick and stone façades, clung with moss, wet with mist and rain. Hardy can guess what he's thinking. He wonders if Alice meant to be cruel—possibly she did—and wishes he could say something to comfort his friend. But he can speak to Littlewood no more easily than he can to Neville, and that's the devil of it. He doesn't have the Knowledge. He has no idea where to begin.

4

"**I**S THIS SEAT TAKEN?" Alice asks.

A woman with a face like a Pekingese dog looks up at her from her knitting. Her mouth moves, her hands continue the knitting in the way that an animal's legs sometimes kick after it's dead. But she says nothing. Is she ill? Foreign?

"Is this seat taken?"

Now the woman's eyes widen. She seems to rear back against the wall of the compartment, as if seeking protection. Meanwhile the man who is sitting across from her has stood up. He has a mustache that reminds Alice of her grandfather's, and approaches with a look of protective authority. "I'm afraid the lady doesn't speak your language," he says. "Now what seems to be the trouble?"

She almost laughs. So she'd asked the question in German! Mrs. Buxton warned her this might happen; one of the occupational hazards of being a translator, of spending one's life in the disputed border territories that divide language from language. Sometimes words migrate from one side to the other. At the dress shop, you ask if a skirt can be *ausgetaken*. Or walking along St. George's Square, you tell a neighbor that her Scottish terrier is "a very jolie dog."

"I'm terribly sorry," Alice says in careful English. "I was just wondering if the seat was taken, as there's a handbag—"

"No, it's my handbag," says the woman, and quickly snatches it away.

"Thank you." Alice sits. The man from across the compartment, his brow furrowed with anxiety and disapproval, sits too. And what must they think of her? Speaking German . . . A spy? An escapee from an internment camp? As Alice opens her own handbag, the woman with the pinched face shrinks away. The train pulls out of the station. Alice swallows hard so as not to laugh. It's Friday afternoon, and she's on her way back to Cambridge, to Eric, to Chesterton Road. A depressing prospect. Still, it must be done, not for Eric's sake so much as because it's part of her agreement with Gertrude. Not that Hardy comes very much, now that their mother is so ill.

She takes out the *Cambridge Review*. But she can't concentrate, not today, because she's too conscious of what awaits her at the end of this short ride: Eric in the sitting room, beaming with pleasure at her return; Ethel in the kitchen, no doubt having prepared some special supper. Even with the rationing, she manages to turn out miracles on Friday nights. But never a curry, or a vegetarian goose. Ramanujan's name is not mentioned, either. So have they guessed? Eric couldn't possibly. But Ethel might.

It still surprises her, how much she loves her London life. Were she a character in a novel, she'd be having an affair there. She's not, of course. What she savors is solitude. Arriving at the flat each Sunday evening, she breathes in the scent of damp and mothballs with relish. Monday morning she's still delighting in the narrowness of Gertrude's spinsterish bed. By Monday night she's feeling a little melancholy, yes, but even that melancholy is interesting, because it's so fresh; she's never had the time to indulge in it before. By Wednesday solitude has become her natural condition. By Thursday she is starting to dread the return to Cambridge. By Friday her stomach is clenched; she feels ill. And then, on the train, to the quotidian anxiety is now added this weird sensation of being taken for someone she is not. Her heart is racing. She has to work to keep herself from laughing. So she closes her eyes; tries to recall, as she often does when she needs to calm down, a conversation she had with Eric early in their marriage, before he gave up on trying to explain mathematics to her. That time he was trying to make her understand infinity, and he used the analogy of a train. Imagine a train, he said, with an infinite number of seats, numbered from 1 to infinity. Then Little Alice gets on the train—this was what he called her in those days: Little Alice—and there's not a seat to be had. Every seat from 1 to infinity is taken. What's Little Alice to do? But wait—it's an infinite train, so there's no need to worry. All you do is move the passenger in seat 1 to seat 2, the passenger in seat 2 to seat 3, the passenger in seat 3 to seat 4, and so on. And now, lo and behold, seat 1 is free.

But how is this possible? Every seat from 1 to infinity is taken.

Well, that's just it. It's an infinite train. And in fact you can make room for an infinite number of new passengers, because if you move the passenger in seat 1 to seat 2, the passenger in seat 2 to seat 4, the passenger in seat 3 to seat 6, and so on, then all the odd-numbered seats will be free.

But how is this possible? Every seat from 1 to infinity is taken.

It's an infinite train.

The guard comes by. Alice hands him her ticket. She wonders if the Pekingese-faced woman's going to say anything to him, or the man across the way. To be denounced as a German spy would be amusing. No one says anything, though, and the guard moves on.

Is this seat free?

Seat 1 to seat 2, seat 2 to seat 4 . . .

They talked the other day about the infinite train, she and Anne, when they were having lunch in Mrs. Buxton's kitchen. Anne was up from Treen to pick up some articles to translate, and had left the baby with her nurse. "Jack told me the same thing," she said, "only in his version it was a hotel with infinite rooms. And a guest arrives, and wants a room."

"I don't get it. I can't visualize it. Probably I'm stupid."

"You're not supposed to get it. It's a paradox. All of mathematics is built on paradoxes. That's the biggest paradox of all—all this orderliness, and at the heart, impossibility. Contradiction. Heaven built on the foundations of hell."

Alice took a bite from her sandwich. She looked up to Anne as, at another moment in her life, she might have to a more experienced older girl at school. Gertrude, on the other hand, she now looked down upon, and had ever since she had seduced her into taking out her eye. For once Gertrude had taken out her eye, she no longer had anything on Alice, whereas Anne ruled Alice, because unlike poor scrawny Gertrude she, too, was a mathematician's wife (sort of). She was *saftig*. Fertile. And she knew things about sex.

"Eric wants me to have a baby," Alice said.

"Well, why don't you?" Anne asked.

"Because then I'd have to go back to Cambridge. I'd have to be a wife."

"That doesn't sound so terrible to me," Anne said. And Alice hoped she wouldn't mention, as her mother so often mentioned, the glass of water that was half full but also half empty. *Imagine an infinite glass of water* . . . Yet it was true, she had adored Eric once. What had happened?

"I've already made compromises. I haven't seen him or spoken to him in a year."

"What happens when the war ends?"

"He'll go back to India. I expect."

"To his wife."

"Yes. Funny, he hardly knows her. She's just a child."

"And you? What will you do?"

"I have no idea. I suppose there won't be any more *Notes from the Foreign Press*, will there?"

"There probably won't be a *Cambridge Magazine*."

"Then I suppose . . . I suppose I shall just go back to Cambridge, resume my wifely duties, and have a baby. What choice do I have?" The anger in her own voice surprised her.

"You might find that changes everything," Anne said. And taking a pad out of her handbag, she wrote herself a note. "Just a translation thought."

Odd—she carried herself with such assurance! Yet her life, when you thought about it, was put together with glue and sticks: a husband she did not love but would not leave, children by different fathers, Littlewood mournful in Woolwich. Even so, Anne remained serene, as if Littlewood's suffering was merely something to be borne until he "saw sense"; she spoke of him as a mother would a pouting child who has turned his face to the wall and refuses to turn around again until she gives him a sweet. You can't give in. He'll come around soon. And because Alice adored and feared Anne, she did not say that she felt for Jack Littlewood, felt his suffering, his need to have his marriage (what else was it?) legitimized; his fatherhood legitimized. No, she wouldn't dare say that to Anne.

The guard's voice opens her eyes. The train is pulling into Cambridge station. The woman with the Pekingese face is gathering her coat and her knitting. *But wouldn't an infinite train need an infinite track?* Well, nothing to do but get up, get off, hail a cab, and ride from the station up Magdalene Street, past Thompson's Lane. By the time she arrives at the house, her heart is in her throat. She opens the door, bracing herself for Eric's leap, for the shout of "Darling!"

and the scurry to collect her bag. Every weekend it's the same. There's that lurch at the beginning, and then, how quickly she adjusts! For this is home. The Voysey furniture and the piano and the table on which Ramanujan did his puzzle. And of course the chair in which Eric reads, content merely to have her there; demanding nothing of her but her proximity. And Ethel, stumbling through with cups and saucers, evidence of how much more malleable is the human spirit than most of us guess. For Ethel's son has been in France for months, yet she seems to have moved past terror into a sort of euphoria of uncertainty. Yes, she's learned the trick by which so many get by: misery can be wonderfully comfortable. You can ease yourself into it as into a very soft chair. Why, it's happening to Alice now, as she stands in the hallway and takes off her coat. She feels it, the lure of the very soft chair. And every weekend it's the same. By Sunday, she knows, she'll have half a mind to stay. The cup half full . . .

What's odd, tonight, is that no one comes to greet her, though she smells cooking. "Ethel?" she calls. "Eric?" No answer. She walks into the sitting room, and finds Eric in his usual chair. The lights are off. He's gazing into the shadows gathering around the piano.

"Eric? Are you all right?"

Dimly he turns. "Oh, hello, Alice."

"Where's Ethel?"

"Making supper, I suspect."

"Eric, is something wrong?"

He says nothing. She goes to him, gets on her knees next to him, and sees the tears on his face.

"Eric, what's happened?"

"They're throwing me out."

"Who is?"

"Trinity. They're not renewing my fellowship."

Alice reels back. She tries to maintain her composure. She says to herself: do not be shocked. You knew this was possible. More than possible, likely. And yet shock is what she feels—selfish shock—because if Eric is to leave Cambridge, what is to become of them? What is to become of her life in London? And then the old question, suppressed for more than a year now: will she ever see Ramanujan again?

"It's not the end of the world," she says, almost automatically. "You'll find another position."

"Of course I will."

"It's because of your pacifism," she adds, in a tone the accusatory edge of which she cannot quite suppress.

"What are you suggesting? That I should have lied?"

"It's the glass half full versus the glass half empty."

"I can't believe you're saying this. I thought you believed in the same things I did. I expected you'd at least offer me some comfort."

"You could have kept quieter. There's nothing wrong with being circumspect. Look at Hardy." And she stands. The venom rising in her thrills and horrifies her. She does not want to be saying these things, she wants to be on her knees again, caressing his face, promising him everything will be fine . . . But everything will not be fine. And this anger—how free it makes her feel!

"I don't see why you care so much. You're never here these days anyway."

"What do you mean?"

"Well, you more or less live in London, don't you? I'd think you'd be glad to be shed of this place."

"This is still my home."

Eric stands and steps closer to her. She does not back away. She is calmer now. Shock, she realizes, isn't really an emotion: it's what happens when two emotions clash, dread storming quotidian contentment or quotidian sorrow. And when opposing forces rub together like that—well, the current surges, jolting the inner core of the body and then rippling outward, leaving in its wake a tingling numbness. And in this numbness possibilities open. You could flee. You could castigate. You could give in.

"There is one thought I had," Eric says. "It might solve everything."

"What?"

"We could move to London. Over the summer. Live there until— well, until I've got a new position sorted out." He tries to take her chin in his hands but she pulls away. "It could be lovely, Alice. You could go on with your work. And you wouldn't have to stay in Hardy's flat. We'd have our own flat."

At first she wants to laugh—at his ignorance, his innocence. Is it

369

possible, after all this time, that he hasn't seen? Or is he having her on, trying to win her sympathy by pretending to be a child?

Well, maybe she should just say it, what she's never dared to say before: *It's you I want to get away from* . . . But something holds her back.

His eyes. She looks into them. No, he's feigning nothing. He's actually innocent, not just of disloyalty, but of psychology. He loves her, and he wants her to stay with him, and he wants to make her happy, and he wants to cling to his ideals, and he wants to stay at Trinity . . . He wants everything, he wants things that don't fit. Only he doesn't understand that. And somehow the look in his eyes, the simplicity of his longing and his sorrow, cools her rage. She can't hurt him anymore. Not so long as he doesn't understand the source of his own pain.

She lets her expression soften. "Yes, all right," she says. "We'll move to London. But is there enough money to live on?"

"There's what I get from my grandfather. And my brother will help. He can find us a place near him, in High Barnet."

"No, I don't want to be in High Barnet. It'll have to be somewhere more central. Bloomsbury, perhaps."

"As you like."

"And what we can't fit in the flat, we'll leave with my parents until we're settled somewhere else."

"Yes, of course."

"And you'll show them, Eric. Perhaps you can go to Oxford. That would show them."

"I doubt I could get a position at Oxford."

"Well, then, anywhere." She touches his face. He starts to cry again. "Darling—"

"Shall we have a baby?" she asks.

"Yes, let's." And they kiss. Simple as that, he's happy! So much easier than to make Ramanujan, or Gertrude, or Littlewood happy. And if she can make at least one person happy, that's something, isn't it? Something to be proud of. She releases him, and lets herself sink into that very soft chair.

PART EIGHT

Lightning Fells a Tree

I

MAHALANOBIS COMES TO Hardy's rooms to tell him that Ramanujan has been taken ill. He is in a nursing hostel that caters to Trinity men, on Thompson's Lane.

"A nursing hostel!" Hardy says. "But why?"

"We were with him last night," Mahalanobis says. "Ananda Rao and I. He had asked us over to share his meal. We were eating *rasam*, and discussing the work of Mr. Oliver Lodge—"

"Oliver Lodge?"

"And in the middle of the conversation poor Ramanujan keeled over with a terrible sharp pain in his stomach."

"Why didn't you call me?"

"He insisted we not trouble you. We fetched the porter, and the porter fetched a doctor. And the doctor said he must go in the nursing hostel."

"But I saw him just yesterday morning and he seemed fine."

"My impression," Mahalanobis says, "is that he has been hiding the severity of his symptoms for some time now."

Hardy puts on his coat, and they walk together to the nursing hostel. It is early in the spring, the season when you veer to the sunny rather than the shady side of the street, when despite the chill—ice crystals still hang from awnings—you can feel incipient warmth on your head. Ramanujan in a hospital: although he wouldn't say so to Mahalanobis, Hardy feels as annoyed as he is alarmed. Either God has once again vexed him, or Ramanujan is acting out of sheer perversity, as he did the night he left his own dinner party and went to Oxford. For he has managed to get sick not just as spring is beginning but just as they are completing their big paper on the partitions function—and this is something Hardy would never allow himself to do. Even if he did get sick, he wouldn't let it stop him from working. He'd keep working.

No, no. Unreasonable. A man can't help what happens to his stomach. You can't expect him to ignore pain. Also, for all Hardy knows, Ramanujan may be working even now, writing out formulae in his bed.

When they arrive at the nursing hostel, a matron wearing a severe and elaborate hat leads them up to Ramanujan's room. Although it is a room designed to hold two inmates, he is alone in it. The furniture consists of two iron bedsteads, two side tables, two chairs, and a dresser. No pictures on the chalky white walls, just the one window, which looks out on the Cam. The scent of Dettol permeates the air.

Ramanujan is lying in the bed closer to the window, gazing with pallid indifference at the river.

No pad, no pencil.

"Ramanujan," Hardy says, and he turns; smiles faintly.

Hardy pulls up a chair and sits next to him. His appearance is alarming. Perhaps it's the glaring hospital light that does it, revealing a haggardness and a leanness that the gloaming of Trinity disguised. Or is the truth that anyone would look sick in such a light? Hardy as well? He wishes there was a mirror in the room.

"So I gather you were taken ill," he says.

Ramanujan's lips, when he speaks, are parched. "I had a pain in my stomach," he says. "Perhaps some curd I ate."

"Where exactly does it hurt?"

"Here. The right side."

"Is it a sharp pain or a dull pain?"

"It is not a continuous pain. I seem to be feeling fine, and then there are . . . stabs, shall we call them?"

"And have you seen the doctor?"

"Dr. Wingate will be in later this morning, sir," says the matron, who's pouring water from a jug into a basin. "He'll examine the patient then."

"Of course."

"The trouble is, he won't eat his breakfast."

"Mr. Ramanujan is a Hindu. He has a very strict diet."

"It was only porridge."

"I have no appetite, thank you," Ramanujan says, glaring at Mahalanobis, who looks away. Is he angry, Hardy wonders, that

Mahalanobis disobeyed his instructions and told Hardy that he was in the nursing hostel?

"Did you bring the book?"

"I shall bring it this afternoon," Mahalanobis says.

"What book? I can bring you books," Hardy says.

"It doesn't matter."

"But I assure you—"

"It doesn't matter."

Mahalanobis looks away. And now Hardy understands, or thinks he does: the book in question must be one Ramanujan doesn't want Hardy to know that he wants. Perhaps a cheap novel. Or something by Oliver Lodge?

Then the doctor comes in, all swagger and flourish, sweeping into the room when in Hardy's view a doctor ought to step in mildly, just as a lecturer ought to speak with minimal inflection. Like a character in a Shakespeare play, he enters from stage left, carrying a pad, followed by a retinue of assistants and a nurse. He is in his early fifties, with raisin-shaped eyes and pockmarks on his cheeks. "Hello, there!" he says, and the matron motions to Hardy to get up from his chair. "Well, now, Mister—what's his name?"

"Ramanujan," Ramanujan says.

"I won't try to pronounce it. So what seems to be the trouble?"

"A pain in his stomach, doctor."

"Shall we let the man speak for himself?" Dr. Wingate puts his hand on Ramanujan's head. "Any fever?"

"None this morning, doctor. Last night 99.5."

"And where exactly is the pain? You do speak English."

"Yes." Ramanujan points to the right side of his abdomen.

"I see. May I?" The doctor holds out his hand and flexes his fingers. "Now I won't press too hard. Just tell me when you feel the pain. Here? Here?" Ramanujan waggles his head. "What's that supposed to mean?"

"Pain now and again," Hardy says.

"Here?"

Ramanujan winces and cries out. "There's the trouble spot," Dr. Wingate says with triumph, and writes something on the pad. "And what brings you to Trinity, young man? What are you studying?"

"Mathematics."

"How interesting. I once had a mathematician as a patient. I said, 'Sir, you have a distinctly odd sense of humor,' and he said, 'How do you mean odd? 3, 5, 7?'"

Ramanujan looks at the window.

"Yes, to the same gentleman I said, 'Even if you're feeling better, you must finish your medicine.' And he said, 'How do you mean even?'"

"When may I go home?"

"Not any time soon."

"But my work—"

"You're not in any shape to be working. Intermittent fever, a severe, undiagnosed pain." Dr. Wingate puts the pad under his arm. "No, you'll need to stay where we can watch you, at least until we can work out what's wrong with you. Who are you, by the way?" He is speaking to Hardy.

"G. H. Hardy."

"And what's your relationship to the patient?"

He stumbles. No one's ever asked him this question before. And how *is* he supposed to describe his relationship to Ramanujan?

"Mr. Hardy is a don at Trinity," Mahalanobis says. "Mr. Ramanujan is his pupil."

"I see. A word, if you don't mind?" And he motions for Hardy to follow him into the hall. "Now don't quote me on this," he says in a low voice, "but ten to one, he's suffering from gastric ulcer. Has he been under any strain lately?"

"I don't know . . . He's been working hard. But no harder than usual."

"Anxieties over the war? Family troubles?"

"Not that I . . . He hasn't mentioned anything."

"Well, we'll keep an eye on him. If it is gastric ulcer, he'll need to be on a special diet."

"He's already on a special diet. He cooks all his own food. He's a strict vegetarian."

"That may be the problem. Not much in the way of fresh vegetables to be had these days." Dr. Wingate holds out his hand. "A mathematics don, eh? Beastly stuff, mathematics. My brother was better at it than me, he was a senior optime in—1898, I believe."

"Yes, I remember a Wingate."

"Do you? He's with the home office now. Well, good day, Hardy."

"Good day."

Then the doctor, followed by his retinue, exits stage right. Hardy goes back into Ramanujan's room. The matron is fussing with a white enameled ewer and basin. Mahalanobis, who is now sitting on the chair by the bed, jumps up as soon as he sees Hardy.

"It's all right," Hardy says. "Stay where you are."

"No, please," Mahalanobis says, offering the chair with the obsequiousness of a waiter.

"But I don't want to sit."

"What did the doctor say?" Ramanujan asks.

"He thinks you may be suffering from gastric ulcer."

"What does that mean?"

"I don't know exactly. I only know that it's caused by strain. So you'll have to relax."

"Probably it's something you ate," Mahalanobis says. "Or didn't eat."

"The curd, I think."

"You have to take better care of yourself, Jam! You cannot be too careful with curd."

"I have not had time to think about cooking. I have been busy."

Hardy looks at his watch. "Well, I must be going," he says. "I have to give a lecture. Mahalanobis, will you be coming or staying?"

"I must go as well," Mahalanobis says. "I shall come back this afternoon."

Ramanujan says nothing. Instead he rests his head against the pillow and turns, once again, to look at the river. And Hardy wonders: from his starting place, from the *pial* at twilight, could he have traveled further?

2

"I DIDN'T KNOW Ramanujan was interested in Oliver Lodge,"
Hardy says to Mahalanobis as they cross Bridge Street.
"Oh yes," Mahalanobis says. "We all are."

"I assume you mean his work with radio waves?"

"No, we are interested in his writings on psychical phenomena. You
know that Mr. Lodge is president of the Society for Psychical Research."

"So I've been told."

"Ramanujan in particular is interested in psychical phenomena.
Dowsing rods, poltergeists, automatic writing. Hauntings."

"Ramanujan?"

"Yes."

"It probably won't surprise you to learn that in my view it's all
nonsense."

"No, I am not surprised. Nor would Lodge be surprised. He
anticipates scorn, and accepts it as inevitable."

"Then why does he go on?"

"Because he believes that supernatural phenomena merit investiga-
tion."

"But these phenomena aren't real. They're in people's imagina-
tions."

"Who can say? Have you never experienced the supernatural, Mr.
Hardy?"

Hardy thinks of Gaye; his occasional, if unwelcome, visits. How
disconcerting those sudden entrances could be! Yet he dreamed them
all—didn't he?

"No, I never have. Have you, Mr. Mahalanobis?"

"In India," Mahalanobis says, "these things are regarded as . . .
shall we say, part of ordinary life. My grandmother often claimed to

have psychic visions. Once she received a message from the flames in her fire. A voice warned her not to visit a neighbor's house. She obeyed, and that very day, in the neighbor's house, there was an outbreak of typhoid."

"Could have been coincidence. Or your grandmother might have *believed* she'd had the vision, after the fact."

"As for me, they say certain rooms in King's are haunted by dead fellows. Last winter I put a scarf on the bedstead one night before I went to sleep. In the morning it was gone. I turned the room upside down looking for it. I assumed that my memory was faulty, that I had left it in Hall or on the train. And then, the next winter, the first cold day, it turned up again, perfectly folded, in my drawer."

"Well, you could have put it in the drawer and forgot."

"I open that drawer every day. No, I suspect the ghost needed the scarf."

"I don't think ghosts are supposed to feel the cold."

"That would be the kind of question Sir Oliver would have us look into."

Hardy laughs. "And this is what you talk about, while you have your supper?"

"At first Ananda Rao and I were skeptical. Ramanujan, however, convinced us. You see, he too has had certain . . . experiences."

"Such as?"

"I doubt you will believe him."

"Try me."

Mahalanobis looks away for a moment, as if trying to decide whether telling Hardy will amount to a breach of confidence. Then he says, "All right. This was in Kumbakonam, before he came to England. One night he had a dream. He was standing in a house he did not know, and under one of the pillars on the verandah he saw a distant relative. The relative was dead, and his people were in mourning. Then the dream passed, and he forgot it, until some time later he had occasion to visit the same relative, who was then living in a town far from Kumbakonam. Imagine his surprise when he discovered that the house was the same house he had seen in his dream—and not only that, but that there was a patient undergoing medical treatment staying in the house. Later he saw the man lying on a mattress under the same pillar that he had seen in his dream. And the man died there."

Hardy raises his eyebrows. "But in the vision it was his relative who died," he says. "Not a stranger in the relative's house."

"Yes. An inconsistency. Perhaps a sort of . . . mistranslation, or miscommunication. Sir Oliver makes the point that the messages received during séances cannot always be taken literally."

"Hedging his bets."

"Perhaps. Still, why not investigate these matters? Scientifically, of course. Controlled experiments."

"But how can we investigate them? What tools would we employ?"

"Dowsing rods, the board . . . There are tools for those willing to use them."

They have arrived at the gates of Trinity. With great formality, Mahalanobis bows. "Well, I shall leave you now. I must return to my own college. Good day, Mr. Hardy."

"Good day, Mr. Mahalanobis." And they shake hands. All very odd, Hardy thinks as he steps into the porter's lodge. If only Gaye would appear right now, spit out some of his acid wisdom, and in so doing help Hardy to burn through the morass of Mahalanobis's words! And yet if Gaye appeared, that would count as a psychical phenomenon. In which case Lodge would be proven right.

Hardy approaches the porter's desk. The porter is writing figures on a ledger. "Good afternoon, sir," he says. "Been to visit Mr. Ramanujan?"

"Indeed."

"He looked quite poorly last night. I hope he's feeling better."

"Better, yes. He asked me to bring him a book. Might I borrow the key to his room?"

"Of course, sir." And the porter extracts an enormous ring, hung with dozens of keys, from a hook under his counter. With astonishing speed he rifles through them before detaching one and handing it to Hardy.

"You know all those keys by heart?" he asks—noticing, for the first time, something he's always seen but ignored.

"Yes, sir."

"But that's extraordinary."

The porter points a finger to his own skull. "Just part of the job."

"I see. Well, thank you. I'll bring this back later." And he heads out into Great Court, full of wonder and vexation. Nothing makes sense today. Climbing the stairs in Bishop's Hostel, he feels that he must move stealthily, like a thief. And why? He's no thief. Still, when he opens Ramanujan's door, and the hinges creak loudly, he winces. Stepping inside, he pulls the door to more slowly than he opened it, but this only prolongs the creak. Just as slowly he shuts it until it catches.

There. He's in. No one, so far as he knows, has seen him.

He looks around himself. It's the first time he's been in Ramanujan's rooms since the infamous dinner party. That evening everything was tidy. Today the room is in disarray. A loose purple garment is thrown over the back of the chair. The bowls from which, presumably, Ramanujan and his friends were eating when he had his attack are piled by the gas ring. Papers are scattered on the desk. Justifying his earlier sense of himself as an intruder, Hardy rifles through them: mathematics mostly, relating to the work they're doing right now on compositeness and the primes. And yet there is one sheet that surprises and tempts him as much as Alice's diary did. The heading is "Theory of Reality." He reads it through twice.

Theory of Reality

o = the Absolute, the *Nirguna-Brahman*, the reality to which no qualities can be attributed, which can never be defined or described in words. (Negation of all attributes.)
∞ = the totality of all possible attributes, *Saguna-Brahman*, and is therefore inexhaustible.
o × ∞ = the set of finite numbers.
Each act of creation is a particular product of o and ∞, from which a particular individual emerges. Thus each individual may be symbolized by the particular finite number that is the product in his case.

Hardy blinks. The hand-writing is Ramanujan's. The neat, fine strokes are unmistakable. He recalls receiving Ramanujan's first letter, the bewilderment he felt when he encountered the equation $1 + 2 + 3 + 4 + \ldots = -\frac{1}{12}$. So is what he's reading now just another example of Ramanujan's peculiar shorthand? Or perhaps the ideas that Ramanujan is trying to express are philosophical rather than mathematical. When, in his heyday, McTaggart lectured the Apostles, Hardy would yawn and look at his watch, while Moore sat riveted, taking in every word. Even today he doesn't know what Moore heard that he didn't. So perhaps Moore could make sense of Ramanujan's "theory of reality."

Hardy puts the sheet of paper down. Two books are sitting propped open on the arm of the armchair. One is written in what he supposes to be Hindi. The other is Oliver Lodge's *Raymond*, and this one he picks up. Though he hasn't read it, he's certainly read *about* the book, which was all over the papers when it was published: how Lodge, two days before his son Raymond's death at Ypres, had a precognition of the event. A message came to him at a séance. Supposedly his account of subsequent communications with Raymond's spirit has brought comfort to thousands of bereaved parents—ludicrous, Hardy thought at the time. But what does Lodge actually say?

He glances through the opening pages; reads:

Raymond was killed near Ypres on 14 September 1915, and we got the news by telegram from the War Office on 17 September. A fallen or falling tree is a frequently used symbol for death; perhaps through misinterpretation of *Eccl.* Xi, 3. To several other classical scholars, I have since put the question I addressed to Mrs. Verrall, and they all referred me to Horace, *Carm.* II. xvii. as the unmistakable reference.

Mrs. Verrall, of course, Hardy knows, or knew. She was the widow of Verrall, one of the elderly Apostles who held sway during his youth, and a classicist herself. She died only the summer before. And now, reading back a few pages, he begins to grasp the sequence of events. At a séance, "Richard Hodgson" (a ghost?) left an obscure message for Lodge that Lodge then passed on to Mrs. Verrall, who interpreted it as a reference to a passage from Horace. The passage from Horace is one Hardy himself remembers from his days at Winchester: it describes how lightning struck a tree that then fell, and would have landed on Horace, had Faunus, guardian of poets, not stopped it. This message Lodge interpreted as meaning that "some blow was going to fall, or was likely to fall, though I didn't know what kind . . ."

A few days later his son died. The eponymous Raymond. Hardy turns to the frontispiece. Is it only because he knows his fate that Hardy sees, in the youth's face, a certain expression of doomed indifference? Raymond is far from handsome, with a pear-shaped head and flat brown hair. The first section of the book is described as its "normal portion," and consists of Raymond's letters from the front and letters from the officers he fought with. Then there is a "supernormal portion" and a section called "Life and Death." Opening to a page at random, Hardy reads:

The hypothesis of continued existence in another set of conditions, and of possible communication across a boundary, is not a gratuitous one made for the sake of comfort and consolation, or because of a dislike to the idea of extinction; it is an hypothesis which has been gradually forced upon the author—as upon many other persons—by the stringent coercion of definite experience. The foundation of the atomic theory in Chemistry is to him no stronger. The evidence is cumulative, and has broken the back of all legitimate and reasonable scepticism.

There is a knock on the door. Hardy jumps, nearly dropping the book.

"Mr. Hardy," he hears a voice call from the corridor.

It is Mahalanobis. Hardy opens the door and lets him in. "You startled me," he says.

"I'm sorry," Mahalanobis says. "The porter told me I would find you here."

"Yes, I thought I'd get Ramanujan that book he wanted."

"I came for the same reason."

"I assume it's this one?" He holds out the copy of *Raymond*. But Mahalanobis shakes his head.

"Oh, I see. Then the one in Hindi?"

"That is the *Panchangam*. An almanac. It is written in Tamil."

"So that's not the one he wants either?"

"No, sir. He asked for Carr."

"Carr?"

"May I?"

"Of course."

Gingerly Mahalanobis steps past him, into the bedroom. He returns a moment later carrying a heavy, worn tome. "*A Synopsis of Results in Pure and Applied Mathematics*," he announces. "This was the first mathematics book Ramanujan was ever given. As a boy he used to read it on his mother's porch."

"I know. But why should he want Carr now? It's obsolete. He's miles beyond it."

"I believe it is a source of comfort to him. I have observed that he often reads through the numbered equations, at night, when he cannot sleep."

"Comfort from Carr?"

"Yes, sir." Mahalanobis adjusts his turban. "Well, I shall be going now. Good day."

"Good day."

Then Mahalanobis leaves, as quietly as he came, so that Hardy is once again alone amid Ramanujan's few possessions; these few signposts to a life about which, he realizes, he knows far less than he thought. The portrait of Leibniz hangs on the wall. From the hearth an elephant-headed figure gazes at him. He has four arms. A rat sits at his feet. From the kitchen the familiar pot of *rasam* gives off a sour smell. Hardy peers into it and sees that the silvering on the inside is wearing away.

He takes *Raymond* with him when he goes. Despite himself he finds that he's become intrigued by the mystery: the séance, the passage from Horace, ghosts and visions. So much he doesn't know! On the stairs he encounters a bedmaker, carrying a mop and a pail. Who supplies her with her mop? And how has the porter managed to memorize all the keys? Yet the world goes on, the tumblers ceaselessly click, the mops ceaselessly slap the floors. And all the while Hardy, blind to nearly everything, cuts his steady, narrow path through the wilderness.

It is only as he enters the porter's lodge that it hits him. Zero and infinity. The things we can never know because they are unknowable and the things we can never know because there are too many of them. An infinitude of them. From this coupling a life is born.

"Did the Indian find you, sir?" the porter asks.

"Yes, he did. Thank you. Here's the key."

"Very good, sir," the porter says, and slips the key back onto his immense ring. How many keys are there? One of them, Hardy knows, opens his own door, while others open the doors of the absent and the dead.

3

ARLY IN THE SUMMER, Sophia Hardy dies. In Cranleigh,
the vicar of Hardy's childhood, now middle-aged and corpu-
lent, pays a call on him and Gertrude. He tells them that he will
pray for their mother, which strikes Hardy as provocative, considering
his own outspoken atheism and Gertrude's indifference to religion.
"You must miss her very much," the vicar says, sounding like Norton,
to which Hardy wants to reply: No. Her dying was tedious. Perhaps
not for her; she had pain to keep her occupied, and plenty of company,
the living and the dead parading in and out of her room in rapid
succession. Men and women they had never heard of, a sibling
drowned in infancy, their father (but rarely). Toward the end, her
hands were always busy. She seemed more engaged by life than she
had in years. She talked constantly, though in the last days they could
make no sense of what she was saying. Until then, every time she had
gone to the brink of death she had come back again, but each time she
was less connected to the world of the living, as if she had left another
piece of herself behind. And then, on a Thursday morning in June, she
actually died. Perhaps it was because Hardy, for once, hadn't got back
in time to give her a reason to revive. He was stuck in Cambridge due
to mysterious railway delays. By the time he arrived in Cranleigh she
had been dead two hours, the divergent series that was her dying—a
half, plus a third, then a fourth—having at last made its crossing into
infinity. When Gertrude told him, he embraced her—not in grief but in
joy. At last it was over for both of them.

Of course they tell the vicar none of this. Their mother was an
observant woman, and out of respect for her, they go through the
formalities required of and by vicars: making arrangements for the
funeral, giving this man, who really knows nothing about their
mother, the information he needs in order to deliver the eulogy. After

half an hour, he announces that he must go, and Hardy sees him to the door. Dusk is just beginning to fall. "I haven't forgotten that conversation we had," he says in the doorway. "Do you remember? We were walking in the fog."

"Yes, I remember," Hardy says, and doesn't say that he's surprised that the vicar remembers. After all, it was years ago. The vicar was at most twenty-five, whereas today he's . . . fifty-four? Is it possible?

"I thought you impudent at the time, though now I see that I should have taken you more seriously. I should have prayed for your salvation. You have grown into a nonbeliever."

"That's true."

"But a peculiar kind of nonbeliever. Always trying to outwit God. Let me give you fair warning, you shall lose in the end."

"Who told you this?"

"A ship bound from Denmark, a gale at sea . . ." The vicar touches Hardy on the shoulder, and he draws back. "Consider the possibility, at least, of grace. Perhaps God wanted you to survive. And perhaps you do believe. Otherwise, why fight so hard?"

"How do you know all this?"

"On another subject, I gather your Indian student is not well. I'm sorry."

"Thank you."

"Please tell him he is in my prayers."

"Why? He's not your religion."

"Prayer may transcend the particularities of faith. It may help him to know that others are thinking of him."

"I'm not sure I'd agree with that. In my experience, when people pray for the dying, they die faster, either because they assume that prayer will do the job and stop taking care of themselves, or because the knowledge that all these people are constantly praying for them makes them feel obliged to get better, and the pressure does them in."

"An interesting theory. In that case you should say nothing to your student, though of course I shall pray for him nonetheless. Well, goodbye, Mr. Hardy." And the vicar holds out his hand. Hardy takes it: limp fingers slide alongside his palm. Then the vicar walks away, leaving Hardy to wonder, once again, who told him about what happened in Esbjerg. Was it Gertrude? It seems unlikely. Their mother, then? But did he send their mother a postcard? He can't remember.

He reenters the house. Gertrude is opening the curtains, letting pale light into a room that has been dark for weeks. He goes to her, and at last they give into a giddiness that has been building for hours. They summon Maisie and together, with euphoric abandon, the three of them move the bed in which Mrs. Hardy died out of the drawing room, return the furniture to its original configuration. Light, light! Gertrude sweeps, brushing away the dust that was once their mother's skin, while Maisie scours the floors. After that they're not sure what to do, so they play a game of chess. Hardy, to his own surprise, loses. This seems to delight his sister, who bursts, once again, into laughter. Then they seem to run out of laughter, and they go to bed, even though it's still early, even though the light hasn't yet drained from the sky.

In the morning they take a walk through the village. Men and women they hardly recognize—shopkeepers, former students of their father's, grown into middle-aged men—salute them and offer condolences. When they get home, Gertrude is agitated. "It's only a matter of time," she says, taking off her gloves. "Mark my words, the undertaker's going to ring up and tell us that Mother's woken up and proposed a game of Vint." She laughs again, and this time her laugh is shrill, slightly mad.

"It seems unlikely," Hardy says. "Though with Mother, you never know."

"What do you call it—the place an undertaker does his . . . whatever he does?"

"I have no idea. Parlor? Studio?"

"Salon?"

"Like a French hairdresser." Suddenly Hardy too is laughing; both of them are laughing like children, the laughter infectious, until they are literally on the floor, with tears in their eyes.

Two days later the vicar presides at the funeral. They manage to get through it without cracking a smile, though Hardy nearly breaks down when, during his eulogy, the vicar refers to their mother as "a crack card player." After that there is a reception, ghostly figures, few of which they recognize, standing about the drawing room holding cups of tea, while Maisie serves sandwiches that no one dares eat. And why is it, Hardy wonders, that eating after a funeral is construed as disrespectful to the dead? As he drinks his tea, he watches the vicar eyeing the sandwiches, observes with pleasure the spiritual battle that is clearly raging in the vicar's soul, between longing and calling, the lure inherent in the demonic sandwiches and the will to resist. And in the end, resistance wins. "He must be so proud of himself," Hardy says to Gertrude after the last of the guests has left and they are gorging themselves on the sandwiches. "No doubt back at the rectory he's making sandwiches for himself right now. Huge sandwiches, the sort that Americans eat." Gertrude laughs so hard she nearly chokes.

Such hilarity! Going to bed that night, Hardy is amazed: he never imagined death could be such a lark. And what comic turns will the next day bring? The next day they have an appointment with their mother's solicitor, the elderly Mr. Fanning, who seems to have stepped out of another century, brought forward by Wells's time machine complete with his fountain pens and his nibs and his hand-written ledgers. Of course this is a much more serious business. The truth is, neither of them knows how much money their mother had. And given that, in all likelihood, Hardy's never going to write his book about Vint, or his murder mystery, he could use some money. So could Gertrude. Thus they listen closely as Mr. Fanning, with great formality, reads out the terms of the will. As expected, both the house and the estate are to be divided equally between the children of the deceased, Godfrey Harold and Gertrude Edith. As for its value . . . Here Mr. Fanning pauses; puts down the will. "Unfortunately," he says, "it appears that in her last years your mother allowed . . . certain debts to accrue."

"What kind of debts?" Hardy asks.

"Most are of the ordinary variety, monies are owed to shopkeepers, for coke and for the delivery of milk. And of course the doctor's bills. But there are other debts—older debts—these she seems to have inherited from your father. He had borrowed some money, many years ago, and with interest the amount owed is now . . . considerable."

"She never mentioned any of this."

"I rather suspect that she hoped that if she simply stuffed the notices in a drawer, they would, as it were, disappear. Such is often the case with elderly persons."

"How much is owed?" Gertrude asks.

"Not so much that the estate cannot pay it. But there will be very little left over."

"Does that include the house?"

"No, the house is safe."

"Thank heavens for that," says Gertrude. "Thank heavens, at least, for that."

Afterward, at home, they are not, for once, laughing. "I wonder why Father was borrowing money," Hardy says. "Do you suppose he had a mistress? Or gambled?"

"Father? Don't be ridiculous."

"You never know. Down, please." It's the terrier again, pawing at Hardy's knees as he takes off his hat. "Well, at least when we sell the house we'll get something."

"Sell the house? What are you talking about?" Gertrude grabs the dog to her breast.

"But I thought you wanted to move to London."

"Perhaps, yes. But even if I did . . . I won't have this house sold. This is where we grew up, Harold. We must keep it in the family."

"I don't think it likely that either of us is going to have children."

"You can't be sure of that."

"What, are you suggesting I might marry?"

"Are you suggesting I never will?"

Suddenly she starts to weep. He is bewildered. "Gertrude," he says, but she won't meet his eye. She's buried her face in the fur of the dog's back, the poor dog, now absolutely still in her arms, as unequal to her mawkishness as he.

"Gertrude, why are you crying?"

"Isn't that obvious? Our mother has just died."

"But yesterday you were glad."

"Not that she was dead. That it was over. It's not the same thing. Are you honestly saying you don't see the difference?"

He says nothing. She puts the dog down. "You must feel it too," she says.

"What?"

"Grief."

But the fact is, he doesn't. Nor can he make sense of the change that has come over his sister. After all, wasn't she insisting, just a few days back, that it was only the burden of having to care for their mother that kept her in Cranleigh? And now the burden has been lifted, and she won't lift a finger to escape. Instead she goes to bed. She takes out her glass eye and settles, as she has all her life, into the narrow bed of her childhood.

Now her attitude toward him changes—subtly but distinctly. For the first time in their lives she appears to regard him as an adversary. Though they never speak of it, the house, and their very different ideas as to what they should do with it, becomes a barrier. The flat in Pimlico is empty; Alice Neville has moved, with her husband, to Bayswater. Yet Gertrude, despite the removal of this last obstacle, won't go into London even for a weekend. "I'm frightened by the air raids," she says; whereas Hardy himself isn't the least frightened by the air raids. On the contrary, he relishes the possibility of being caught in one, seeing the zeppelins passing overhead like great airborne whales. And why? He knows that, were he ever actually to have to endure an air raid, he wouldn't be so flippant. Norton got caught in an air raid, and afterward, for two days, he could not stop shaking. And yet . . . how to explain this secret longing he nurtures for apocalypse? Others share it, he suspects. Catastrophe might shake them all from their anomie. Sometimes late at night, from the window of the flat in Pimlico, he gazes out at the black sky, hoping to witness brilliant illuminations, hear distant roaring. But he never does. It seems that the sky glows orange, that sirens wail, only when he is in Cambridge or Cranleigh. Every day the papers publish lists of the dead, every day he scans them, looking for familiar names. If there are fewer and fewer, it is only because so many of the men he knows have died already. There is not an infinite supply of youth. And though he never sees Thayer's name, this doesn't mean Thayer isn't dead. Meanwhile he waits for a note, and none comes.

For reasons he cannot quite deduce, he starts to spend more time at Cranleigh than he did before his mother died. Gertrude affects indifference not just to his presence but to his efforts to win back her sympathy. One afternoon when they're having lunch outdoors, on the back lawn, he even tries to make friends with her dog. Gertrude seems hardly to notice. "Here Daisy," he calls, and throws an old tennis ball across the lawn. But even though Daisy chases after it and picks it up, she won't bring the ball back to him; instead she runs up to

him and, when he tries to take it from her mouth, darts away; runs up
to him again and darts away again, over and over.

"This is ridiculous," he says, after a few minutes. "You're supposed
to want to chase the ball."

"She's a terrier, not a retriever," Gertrude says. "Probably in a
minute she'll be trying to bury it."

"Then why am I bothering?"

"No one asked you to." His sister smiles over her knitting, some
strange fragment of a sweater that hangs from her needles, its ragged
edges dragging the remnants of the lunch on her plate. "You should
really get yourself another cat."

"I suppose I will someday. Here, Daisy!" And he gets up and runs
after Daisy, which delights her to no end. She drops the ball; nudges it
with her nose; waits until he's reaching to pick it up and then grabs it
away again. "Damn you!" he cries in exasperation, for he's learned
that what she really wants is to torment him. And wouldn't you
know? She keeps leading him back to the spot where, thirty-five years
ago, he swung a cricket bat, heard a cracking noise, reeled back, and
saw his sister splayed out, her skirt blown up over her drawers.
Always that spot. The grass stayed red for weeks, until the spring
came, and the gardener cut it, and it was green again.

Here's the irony. Gertrude doesn't remember any of it. But he does.

Suddenly a butterfly distracts Daisy's attention. It's his moment.
"Got you!" he cries, tackling the dog, who wriggles in his grasp,
escapes, and leaps away, bringing him crashing down onto the lawn.
Gertrude laughs.

He stands up; brushes himself off. "Ridiculous animal," he says to
Daisy, who sits before him, tail wagging, the ball held firmly between
her teeth.

4

A MONTH AFTER his admission, Ramanujan is still in the nursing hostel on Thompson's Lane. Hardy goes to visit him as often as he can. He brings work with him when he goes: scribbling paper, pens, notes on what they've already done. Unfortunately Ramanujan is listless and contributes virtually nothing. No one seems to know exactly what is wrong with him, only that the pain in his stomach has persisted. He describes it now as a dull pain—and for Hardy, dull is exactly the right word for it, especially after so many weeks of listening to Dr. Wingate speculate as to its cause. Gastric ulcer was blamed only until "intermittent pyrexia" set in. "Pyrexia," Hardy soon learned, simply meant "fever." How unbearable doctors are, with their private language, their pomposity! Nonetheless, and much to his own annoyance, he soon finds himself employing the same language. When he arrives in the afternoons to visit, he asks the matron for a report on Ramanujan's pyrexia. "Down a point," she says. Or: "Up half a point at three o'clock." The fever, in other words, is capricious, coming and going at its whim, until in July—for reasons no one seems to be able to determine—it settles down into a routine. Now there is no pyrexia during the day. Instead, every night at ten, his temperature spikes. He shivers and sweats so much the sheets have to be changed, and while they are being changed, the matron tells Hardy, he mutters mysteriously, frightening the nurses. "He's probably just speaking Tamil," Hardy says. "His native language."

"It doesn't sound like any language to me," the matron says. "It sounds like the devil."

No wonder Ramanujan is tired during the day! The nights are an ordeal for him. Examining him one afternoon, Dr. Wingate says, "Tuberculosis seems likely." It sounds like a weather prediction.

"But doesn't tuberculosis affect the lungs?"

"Usually, yes."

"Has he had any lung trouble?"

"His lungs are clear—for now. Even so, Indians in England are always contracting tuberculosis. The change in diet," he adds, waving his fingers about. "Not to mention the cold weather. We need to watch him carefully. The other symptoms should start manifesting themselves soon."

After Dr. Wingate leaves, Hardy returns to Ramanujan's bedside. He hopes that he'll be able to read in his face how his friend has reacted to the news. Will he be relieved, at least, that a diagnosis seems to have been hit upon? At least tuberculosis can be treated, even, on occasion, cured. There are sanatoriums for that. And yet, whether Ramanujan is relieved, or terrified, or grievous, Hardy cannot guess, for his face remains impassive. Tuberculosis! In *One Tuscan Summer* (Hardy has now read it, furtively) another young genius, a pianist, contracts tuberculosis. Shreds of romance cling to the disease. Perhaps Ramanujan is reflecting on the utter idiocy of the doctor's backward reasoning: because many Indians get tuberculosis, it must be tuberculosis. The fact that he shows no symptoms of the illness does not matter. Now they must all just sit back and wait for the coughing and spitting to begin.

But here's the thing: they don't begin. The summer draws to a close, and Ramanujan's lungs remain clear. And this failure of his lungs to do what they're supposed to do appears to puzzle Dr. Wingate as much as it does Hardy. Whether it puzzles Ramanujan himself is uncertain. Most of the times Hardy visits, he lies feebly in his bed, gazing at the river. He continues to show scant interest in mathematics, and consequently work on the partitions and compositeness papers grinds to a halt. Even when Hardy tells him that he's read *Raymond*, and asks his views on the séance, he mumbles only the vaguest reply.

It reaches the point where Hardy wonders whether he should bother continuing to visit. "What good does it do?" he asks Mahalanobis, who looks at him with a pained expression.

"But Mr. Hardy," Mahalanobis says, "every day before you come, he asks if you are coming. He looks forward to your visits more than anything else."

Is this possible? It hardly seems likely. Still, Hardy takes Mahalanobis at his word, and keeps visiting. Sometimes, when he arrives, another patient is lying in the bed next to Ramanujan's, usually an old don with lung trouble or an undergraduate sent back from the front with an infection. Invariably these companions are gone within a matter of days. Ramanujan, from what he can tell, never exchanges so much as a word with any of them. Nor, apparently, do they introduce themselves to him. The situation puts Hardy in mind of a joke he once heard, about two Englishmen stranded on a desert island for thirty years. A ship finally rescues them, and the captain is amazed to learn that they have never spoken to each other. He asks why, and one of the men says, "We haven't been introduced."

And yet, if the man in the next bed knows Hardy, then he'll talk to *him*. Usually they talk about the war. By now, news has reached England of the explosions under the Messines Ridge. For more than a year British miners have been tunneling under the German lines, planting stacks of dynamite all of which were detonated at once, on the same day. The mines blew the top off the ridge. You could hear the explosion in Dublin. Lloyd George claimed he could hear it on Downing Street.

It is a turning point: Hardy is sure of that. At last, after months of leading its men to slaughter, England has done something intelligent. Plumer has taken the Germans by surprise; he has undermined, literally, their complacency, the trenches in which, if rumors are to be believed, their officers slept in comfortable beds, and ate their meat off china, and drank their schnapps from crystal glasses at tables laid with cloths, in bunkers illuminated by electric light. No more of that. A rude awakening: the phrase echoes in Hardy, because the battle of Messines has been an awakening for him, too. Suddenly it is clear to him how inured he has become to living in a state of chronic war. Out in the world, Russell is agitating; miners are tunneling; and in Cambridge, too, they are tunneling, with a mind toward exploding certain foundations, the ones on which the members of the Trinity council rest their large bottoms. Yet how modest is their ambition! It is merely to reinstate a philosopher who is decidedly ambivalent about being reinstated, and even then only once the war is over. But when will that be? And what is Hardy doing to bring the day about? Nothing.

One afternoon he goes to see Ramanujan and finds Henry Jackson lying in the second bed. He has not spoken to Jackson since the meeting in which Jackson said that he hoped the war would continue after his death. Now he lies in the bed next to Ramanujan's with his bandaged left foot outside the covers, the heavy wrinkled lids of his eyes lowered, and Hardy thinks: your wish will come true. Judging from the look of you, the war will outlast you.

Hoping not to wake Jackson, he sits, as is his habit, at Ramanujan's bedside. He asks Ramanujan how he is feeling, and his voice is enough to rouse the somnolent old man; the heavy lids flutter and open, revealing reddened slits of eyes. "Hardy," he says. "And what brings you here?"

"I am visiting Mr. Ramanujan," Hardy says.

"Ah, the Hindu calculator," Jackson says, as if Ramanujan isn't even there. Then he says, "I'm here for my gout. My gout is bad. I'm old, Hardy. Seventy-eight years old. I am nearly deaf, I suffer from rheumatism as well as gout. My life is nothing but pain." Without a hint of embarrassment, he passes wind. "And there is the war. There is always the war."

"I'm sorry you're not feeling well."

"What?" He cups a hand round his ear. "Well, it cheers me no end to see the troops drilling in Nevile's Court."

"You know my views on that, Jackson."

"What?"

"You know my position."

"So many have died. Friends, students. Hardly anyone left here in Cambridge. We are all just spinning in place."

Jackson is right. Stasis—unhappy stasis—is the condition of their lives. The explosions under the Messines Ridge shook things up for a time; but only for a time. "I fear you are right," Hardy says. But Jackson has fallen asleep.

After that the war resumes its halting, grinding immobility. Once again, the badly planned offensives fail, the names of the dead are published in newspapers, the shell-shocked are brought home stuttering, "treated," then sent back to the front. Intermittently there is talk of an armistice; hope shimmers in the distance, then recedes. Soon Hardy learns that he must greet any mention of an armistice with the same skepticism with which he and Gertrude greeted their mother's doctor's assurances that her death was imminent. Take nothing for granted. Assume the worst.

And Ramanujan? He lives in a stasis of his own, his condition neither worsening nor improving. Experts are called in. A host of doctors poke and palpate him. The dull pain, they note, is now constant. Eating and drinking make it neither better nor worse. *Not* typical of tuberculosis. So what *is* he suffering from? Some mysterious Oriental germ, one doctor suggests, but can go no further. Specialists visit Ramanujan, throw up their hands, and recommend other specialists, who in turn throw up their hands and recommend yet more specialists, until it is agreed that Ramanujan must go into London and see Batty Shaw. Yes, Batty Shaw is the man. A lung man. Batty Shaw will be sure to know what to do next.

5

T HEY GET HIM DRESSED, Hardy and Chatterjee. After so
many weeks in bed he is shaky on his legs. His trousers hang
loose on him, even with the belt buckled its tightest—evidence
of how much weight he has lost. "You must eat more," Hardy says
every time he visits. But Ramanujan will not eat. Even when Mahalanobis provides the cook with recipes for dishes to his liking, she
prepares them incorrectly, Ramanujan says. Nor does he trust her not
to fry the potatoes in lard.

They take a taxi to the station, the train to Liverpool Street, another
taxi to Batty Shaw's surgery, which is in Kensington. During the
examination Hardy and Chatterjee sit in the waiting room. Chatterjee
is reading the *Indian Magazine*, his hard cricketer's legs twitching and
agitated within their folds of loose flannel. As for Hardy, he has brought
no book. He feels too tired to read. These last weeks he hasn't been
sleeping well. As soon as he gets into bed, images start flashing before
him: Jackson cupping his hand round his ear, the vicar eating a
sandwich, a postbox on the dock in Esbjerg. Only during the day does
he find himself able to sleep peacefully, and then only at moments like
this one, when prolonged sleep is impossible. Indeed, no sooner has he
felt his eyes starting to close than Batty Shaw's nurse is summoning them.
Chatterjee puts down his magazine; she leads them down a long corridor
into a study full of books, diagrams, maps, dark old paintings. On one
shelf, Hardy notices a scale model of a lung. Not far from it something
murky seethes in formaldehyde. Three chairs face a huge oak desk
behind which a man in his sixties with a flat-topped head and a high,
shiny, furrowed brow reads a medical textbook. Ramanujan sits in one
of the chairs, staring into his hands, which are folded in his lap.

They sit, and Batty Shaw looks up. On his nose hangs the tiniest pair
of spectacles Hardy has ever seen. He stands, offers them his immense,

dry hand to shake, then sits down again. "I have made a thorough examination of Mr. Ramanujan," he says. "Dr. Wingate—and you may correct me if I'm wrong—reports nightly pyrexia, a steady abdominal pain with no apparent link to digestion, weight loss, and a white blood count that is lower than usual, if not strikingly so."

"I didn't know his blood count was taken," Hardy says.

"Standard procedure," Batty Shaw says. "Further examination on my part has revealed an enlargement of the liver, which is tender to the touch. I also observed a jagged scar of about one-and-one-half inches in length running the length of Mr. Ramanujan's scrotum."

Chatterjee coughs.

"When I asked Mr. Ramanujan about this scar, he told me that in India, before his departure for England, he underwent surgery for the treatment of a hydrocele. A swelling of the testicles. Is that correct, Mr. Ramanujan?"

Ramanujan waggles his head.

"Yet incredibly, none of the doctors who examined him took note of the scar, nor did he inform them that he had had such an operation."

"I did not think it pertinent," Ramanujan says.

"I therefore speculate," Batty Shaw says, "that the operation was in fact not for the treatment of a hydrocele, but for the removal of a malignant growth on Mr. Ramanujan's right testicle. For whatever reason, the doctor chose not to inform Mr. Ramanujan of what he found. Subsequently the malignancy spread and now my theory is that Mr. Ramanujan is suffering from metastatic liver cancer."

"Cancer?"

"It would explain all the symptoms, but most crucially the tenderness and enlargement of the liver."

Hardy looks at Ramanujan. His face, as always these days, is without expression. And really, what extraordinary brutes doctors can be! They deliver the grimmest news without even a hint of compassion, as if the patient wasn't even in the room.

"The diagnosis would also be in keeping both with the nightly fevers and the low white blood count," Batty Shaw says.

"But are you sure it's cancer? How can you be sure?"

Batty Shaw removes his tiny glasses. "Nothing is definitive," he says, "though in my many years of experience, it has generally been the case that when the symptoms match a diagnosis, the diagnosis is correct."

"So there's no way to tell for certain? No way to test?"

"Time will be the test." He puts his spectacles back on. "If, as I surmise, Mr. Ramanujan has liver cancer, then within a very few weeks his condition will begin to deteriorate markedly."

"Is there a treatment?"

"Neither treatment nor cure. He will live six months at most." Almost as an afterthought, he adds: "I am very sorry." The curious thing is, he says this to Hardy, not to Ramanujan. He doesn't even look at Ramanujan.

They get up to leave. Batty Shaw follows them through the door that leads into the corridor, Chatterjee with his arm around Ramanujan's shoulder. And what is Chatterjee thinking? Has grief struck him dumb? Or is he raging, as Hardy is, not just at the arrogance, but the sloppiness of doctors? *When the symptoms match a diagnosis, the diagnosis is correct* . . . No student of mathematics would be allowed to get away with such fallacious logic! It seems to Hardy that doctors ought to have to prove their diagnoses, the way that mathematicians prove their theorems. *Reductio ad absurdum*. Let us postulate that indeed Ramanujan has liver cancer. Then . . .

"Sir."

Hardy turns. Batty Shaw is beckoning him.

"I wonder if I might have a word with you in private."

"Of course."

Batty Shaw nudges closed the door to the waiting room, through which the Indians have already passed. "If you don't mind my asking," he says, his voice low, "I was wondering about the bill . . ."

"What about it?"

"To whom should it be addressed?"

"To Mr. Ramanujan, of course."

Batty Shaw raises his eyebrows. "But can he afford the expense?"

"All his medical bills are being paid out of his scholarship. Trinity can guarantee that."

"I see." Suddenly Batty Shaw looks impressed. "He told me nothing about himself, you see. What is he?"

"He is the greatest mathematician of the last hundred years. Possibly the last five hundred."

"Really," Batty Shaw says.

"Really," Hardy says. And without another word, he passes through the door into the waiting room.

6

W HAT THOSE WHO have never experienced it firsthand do not know, Hardy is quickly learning. Illness is boring. For every brief episode of pain or despair, there are hours of inertia to be borne, during which fear quiets. Though fear is always present in the room of an invalid, you can't always hear it. But you feel it. A buzzing or trembling in your veins.

In the wake of Batty Shaw's diagnosis, there is nothing for Hardy and Ramanujan's other friends to do but brace themselves for the worst. Each day they wait for signs of deterioration to manifest themselves, however, and each day Ramanujan remains, so far as they can tell, exactly the same. His weight steadies, the nightly fevers keep to their schedule, the pain neither intensifies nor lessens. During the day he is lucid, if lethargic. Then at night the fevers come and he hallucinates. Ghosts appear before him, voices shout at him. Some nights he sees his own abdomen floating in the air above his bed. "Like a zeppelin?" Hardy asks, and he shakes his head.

"No, it takes the form more of a . . . a sort of mathematical appendage, with points attached to it that I have come to think of, or been told to think of, as 'singularities.' And what define these singularities are precise if mysterious mathematical surges. For example, when the pain is at its most steady and driving, I know that there is a surge at $x = 1$. And then I have to work to bring the pain down, and when it is half as intense, I know that the surge is now at $x = -1$. All night I work, trying to keep track of the surges, and to alleviate the pain by manipulating the singularities, so that by the time morning comes, and the fever has lifted, I am exhausted."

"The Riemann hypothesis," Hardy says. "The zeta function zooming off into infinity at 1."

"Yes," Ramanujan says. "Yes, I suppose that is part of it."

"Perhaps," Hardy suggests, "you may find the proof during one of your hallucinations."

"Perhaps," Ramanujan replies. But his voice is distant and disappointed, and he turns and looks out the window: for the moment, it appears, he is tired of talking.

They haul him back to Batty Shaw. Once again he is examined, once again Hardy (this time accompanied by Mahalanobis) is led by the nurse into the study with the swimming thing in formaldehyde and the model lung. "Well, you're right," Batty Shaw says, wiping his tiny spectacles. "There appears to be no change in his condition."

"Does that alter your diagnosis?"

"Perhaps. It may be too soon to tell. Cancer is not my specialty. We shall have to make an appointment for him to see Dr. Lees, the cancer specialist."

And so, in due course, Ramanujan is taken to see Dr. Lees, the cancer specialist. By now his condition seems actually to have improved a little; that is to say, he manages the train journey more easily than he did the first time, and seems even to take some pleasure in being in London. Unfortunately, Dr. Lees proves to be even less helpful than Batty Shaw. While he agrees that Ramanujan's illness is not following the typical track of liver cancer, he can't say what track it is following. The liver remains enlarged and tender. His white blood cell count has increased only slightly. "A disease brought back from India?" he asks, and Hardy remembers the early proposition of an "Oriental germ." This calls for yet another expert, Dr. Frobisher, specialist in tropical diseases. Unfortunately, so far as Dr. Frobisher can determine, Ramanujan's symptoms do not match the pathology of any known exotic malady. Swabs for malaria have come back negative. "Tuberculosis?" Dr. Frobisher asks, with hesitancy and humor in his voice, as if he is making a guess during a game of Charades. So they are back to tuberculosis! Oh, what a sloppy science is medicine!

It is decided that there is no good reason for Ramanujan to remain at the nursing hostel. From now on he will convalesce in his own rooms at Trinity. Hardy hopes this news will please him, but he greets it with typical indifference. Once again, he is put into his clothes; helped into a taxi. They drive the short distance to Trinity, where the porter awaits them. "Very good to see you again, sir," he says, opening the taxi door and taking Ramanujan's case.

"I am glad to be home," Ramanujan says, and Hardy is struck, even startled, that he should have come to think of Trinity as home.

Then Hardy helps him through Great Court to Bishop's Hostel, and up the stairs to his rooms. The bedmaker appears to have cleaned them in his absence. The bed is tightly made. In the kitchen the dishes have been washed and stacked. She hasn't thrown out the *rasam*, though; it still sits in its pot, a thin veneer of mold on the top. Perhaps she was afraid to touch it.

Almost immediately upon entering the room Ramanujan starts to undress. This surprises Hardy, who always assumed him to be a modest man. Or perhaps the hospital stay was enough to abolish all modesty, for now he throws off his clothes with a recklessness to match Littlewood's. Hardy turns away—but only after catching a glimpse of Ramanujan's light brown body, the distended stomach sloping down toward the genitals, which are small and dark, deeply withdrawn between the legs. He cannot make out a scar in those shadows. And what a vulnerable thing, he thinks, is the male organ of procreation, especially when it is put before a doctor to squeeze or slice into! Most of the day it lies placid in its nest, a tiny, wretched thing, like a baby bird or a baby kangaroo. Then stimuli arouse it, it engorges with blood, doubles or trebles in size, and becomes the great thruster, the great, greedy, penetrating sword of pornography. Only to see it at rest, you would never believe it possible.

In any case, Ramanujan is naked just a few seconds. Soon he has pulled on his pyjamas, loosened the sheets, and climbed into the bed.

Who, now, is to care for him? Had this happened a year earlier, Hardy could have counted on the Nevilles to help. But now the Nevilles are in London, their house on Chesterton Road to let, so the responsibility falls to Hardy himself. The first week, Mahalanobis, Chatterjee, and Ananda Rao take it in turn to sit with the invalid, to inquire about his pain and to make sure he eats. Ananda Rao, to the best of his ability, prepares the meals. Unfortunately, this rotation proves tenable only until the term begins, at which point they are all far too busy, and Hardy must hire a nurse to look in on Ramanujan. Three times a week, she takes his temperature, monitors his stomach, listens to his chest and heart, then sends reports back to Dr. Wingate.

Ananda Rao continues to make Ramanujan's lunch and dinner. Mrs. Bixby takes charge of the sheets, which, due to the night sweats, have to be changed every morning.

For months he has hardly spoken about mathematics. At first this vexed Hardy; then he realized that he had no choice but to rein in his disappointment and focus his attention on work outside the purview of partitions. Since then he has written several papers on his own, and two with Littlewood, who, in his own way, is proving to be a less than reliable collaborator. For Littlewood, by his own account, is as depressed as Ramanujan. He despises his work at Woolwich. He longs to be in Treen with Mrs. Chase, and at the same time he cannot bear the thought of being in Treen with Mrs. Chase, because Mrs. Chase is raising her daughter to believe that Chase, not Littlewood, is her father. Whenever he and Hardy see each other in London, Littlewood wants to go to a pub. He drinks too much—beer and, less often, whisky. Nor is he willing to do much in the way of work on the papers they are writing together. "I leave the gas to you," he tells Hardy—"gas" being their code word for the rhetorical flourishes, the elegantizing, that every good paper requires. Yet he is equally unwilling to do his share of the technical grunt work that every good paper requires just as much as it requires "gas." Grunt work bores him, he says. Ballistics bores him. Too much boredom, and he will break down.

So it is for the time being. Of Hardy's two collaborators, one is ill, the other morose. Neither can be counted on.

As often as he can, he goes to see Ramanujan in the afternoons. He sits with him and tries to persuade him to eat, but just as at the nursing home Ramanujan complained that the cook did not prepare the dishes he required properly, now he complains that Ananda Rao's *rasam* is not to his taste. "It is not sour enough," he says. "I'm sure he is using lemons instead of tamarind."

"Even so, you must eat."

"Did you know," Ramanujan says suddenly, "that I made an important breakthrough in the partitions function while making *rasam*?"

"Did you now?"

"Yes. I was counting lentils. I started dividing them into groups."

It seems an opening, if only a narrow one. "MacMahon and I

continue our investigations, of course," Hardy says. "He asked after you the other day."

"Did he? How is he?"

"As well as any of us, under the circumstances. He sends you his best wishes."

"That is kind of him."

"Of course it goes much more slowly without you."

"Yes, I am afraid I left off the work on partitions when I became ill. I apologize for that."

"You need not apologize."

"And what progress have you and the major made?"

Inadvertently Hardy smiles. Whatever hope he might be feeling right now he knows better than to indulge, as experience has taught him that hope cannot be relied on. And he is right: whatever curiosity he may have sparked in Ramanujan will dissipate within the hour. And yet, for the moment, the hope is real, and he grabs at it. The war has taught him to do this, to grab at what you can while it lasts. He tells Ramanujan what he has been thinking. Ramanujan waggles his head. Hardy takes a pen and some paper from his pocket, and for about half an hour, while Ananda Rao's inadequate *rasam* cools in its pot, they do what they have not done since spring. They work.

7

A T THE TIME, he did not take it very seriously. Or did he? He remembers the gales that day, the small boat docked at the pier in Esbjerg. Does he remember fear? No. It is curious—and perhaps something to be grateful for—that fear, like pain, doesn't last in memory. That is to say, though Hardy can remember, at various times, experiencing fear and pain, he cannot remember feeling fear and pain. Phrases such as "shortness of breath" or "constriction of the stomach" do not in and of themselves bring on shortness of breath or constriction of the stomach, perhaps because the very fact that you are now able to remember means that whatever provoked the fear or pain has been got past. Has been survived. The gales, the waves, the small boat rising and falling. Water splashing on the deck. The postbox nearby.

He was visiting Bohr in Copenhagen. Before the war, he often went to visit Bohr in Copenhagen. Bohr was younger than Hardy—in his mid-twenties—and had been on the Danish national football team when it placed second in the world in 1908. He wasn't exactly handsome: his brown hair, which he kept long, had a tendency to fly straight up, while the thick, downward slanting brows over his large eyes made Hardy think of the *accent grave* and the *accent aigu* in French. Still, there was something distinguished and memorable about his face. He had a lean, upright body. Like Littlewood, he was passionate about women, and noticed them, and took no notice of men.

The visits were always the same. Bohr would welcome Hardy at his apartment on the Stockholmsgade, then lead him straight through the sitting room and into the kitchen, where they would work out an agenda for the visit. The first item was always the same: "Prove the Riemann hypothesis." Then they would take a walk along the moats and bridges of the Østre Aenlag Park, even if it was winter, even if the trees were dusted with fine snow and the paths treacherous. Sometimes men and women would run up to Bohr and ask for his autograph, which he would provide with some embarrassment. For it wasn't the mathematician whose autograph they wanted; it was the football player's. It seemed that it was Bohr's fate always to come in second—later to his physicist brother, Niels; in those early days, to himself.

Once they got back to Bohr's kitchen, they would go to work. Usually they drank coffee. Sometimes they drank beer. It pleased Hardy to gaze across the table at Bohr as he scribbled on a pad, the stein of beer partially blocking his view of the thick hair sprouting from the top of his head.

Yet another brilliant man with hard legs who loved women.

Usually Hardy stayed three days. They never proved the Riemann hypothesis. Bohr always saw him to the station, where he caught the train to Esbjerg; walked to the dock and watched for the boat that was to carry him home. A small boat this time, rocking on big waves. Was it safe? The weather looked grim, a gray, thunderous sky and swooping winds. He sought out the captain and asked if it was safe, and the captain laughed, and pointed at the stormy sky as if it were nothing.

It was then that Hardy noticed the postbox. He thought of God. Later, he would tell himself that he did it only in order to have a good story to tell at Hall. And in fact he dined out on the story for years. Yet at the moment—he will admit it now—he felt real fear. He suffered shortness of breath, constriction of the stomach. He saw the boat capsizing, the passengers flailing in cold waters.

There was a little shop off the dock that sold picture postcards of Esbjerg. He bought a handful of them. He can't remember how many. And on each he wrote, "I have proven the Riemann hypothesis. G. H. Hardy." And then he bought stamps, and carried them to the postbox, and dropped them in.

To whom did he send them? Littlewood, certainly—he remembers Littlewood ragging him about it later on. Possibly Russell. Certainly Bohr himself. And Gertrude. Or was it his mother? Or both? Perhaps he sent the postcard to his mother because he knew she would keep it, even if she didn't understand it. In any case, someone told the vicar.

For the idea, once again, was to outwit God. Were the ferry to sink, and Hardy to die, then the postcards would arrive after his death, and people would believe that he had proven the Riemann hypothesis, and that his proof had gone down with the ship, just as Riemann's proof had been fed to the flames. Hardy would then be remembered as the second man to have proven the Riemann hypothesis and lost his proof—and this God would not stand for. Or so Hardy believed. In order not to be bested by Hardy, God would make sure that he did not die. He would see the ship safely to its destination, and thereby insure that Hardy be denied any undue glory.

Afterward it was a little embarrassing, having to make his explanations. He had an urgent telegram from Bohr which he had to answer. Later Bohr laughed over it. And Littlewood, once he got over the initial shock, laughed too. Perhaps they were disappointed, perhaps relieved. Because at least the Riemann hypothesis remained unproven, which meant that either of them might be the man to prove it. It was still fair game.

All of this, of course, happened long before Ramanujan. It is only an anecdote, and, like most anecdotes, it has lost its power through too much telling. Hardy no longer dined out on it.

And then the vicar brought it up.

What was troubling to Hardy was that the vicar seemed to think he'd gained an advantage over him; discovered a chink in the armature of his atheism. And who was to say he hadn't? For Hardy knew he would sound like an idiot if he pretended it was all just a joke. The anti-God battery—sweaters, papers, Gertrude's immense umbrella—he preserves still, and still puts to use from time to time, just as he still finds himself, sometimes half-consciously, offering up prayers for the opposite of what he wants.

Back in Cranleigh, he watches Gertrude carefully. Far from embracing her newfound freedom, every day she roots herself deeper in the life of the village. Yes, she has entrenched herself, exactly like a soldier, joining the board of several charitable organizations and taking on, in addition to her regular teaching, some private pupils. One of these is with her when Hardy arrives one afternoon in the fall—a churlish, sour-faced girl of fourteen, to whom Gertrude is attempting to explain the conjugation of the French verb *prendre*. This time two fox terriers lie by the fire. Two?

Yes, she has acquired another one, a male. Epée. She hopes that he and Daisy will breed.

"Je prends, tu prends, il prend, vous prendez—"

"Vous *prenez*."

"Vous prenez, nous prendons—"

Hardy slinks to his bedroom. It is all very odd. When they have supper that night, she tells him that she has been working with the vicar on a plan to raise money for the restoration of some stained glass in the church. Working with the vicar! So perhaps Gertrude is the source of the leak. And is she planning to marry the vicar? It seems mad, impossible. In any case, she's playing her cards close to her chest. She cuts her meat furtively, and will not meet his eye. The dogs sit at her feet, hoping for scraps, never going anywhere near Hardy, as if they know better than to try, though in truth he would be more likely to give them his food than Gertrude. Indeed the prospect of undermining her efforts to instill discipline in them rather delights him.

They do not talk about the house. As has been the case every time he's visited since their mother's death, he has arrived determined to bring the subject up, and then lost courage. The dogs themselves seem to bar mention of the subject, sitting as they do on either side of her, like sentries. They sleep in the kitchen, where Hardy, waking in the middle of the night, feeds them leftover slices of cold beef. With satisfaction that he is breaking one of Gertrude's rules, he watches them swallow the beef in single gulps, all the while gazing up at him, nervous tongues licking black lips.

Before he returns to Cambridge, he pays a call on the vicar, who sits before him in his study with his hands clasped on his lap. For some reason the vicar's hands repel Hardy more than any other part of him: more than his clean-shaven jowls, or his smug lips, or his spreading breasts, over which the cross droops. The hands are fat and glossy. There is a ring on one of the fingers. He leans back and smiles at Hardy, content in his minor authority and the good lunch he has just eaten. When Hardy starts to speak, he burps. The fingers woven. "Excuse me," he says.

"I want to speak to you about that postcard," Hardy says. "I am assuming, of course, that you're not at liberty to tell me who shared it with you?"

The vicar says nothing; merely smiles.

"In any case, I thought it important to explain to you my rationale."

"I understand your rationale. You assumed that God would save you out of spite. So that you would not die a famous man."

"I've thought it over very carefully. I believe it was a psychological tactic, a means of contending with the arbitrariness of nature and the universe. I call this arbitrariness God, and I make it into an adversary."

"You mean that this God whom you claim to be your enemy—you don't believe in Him?"

"God is simply a name I give to something . . . without meaning."

"Then why choose the name God?"

"To amuse myself."

"And are you amused?"

Hardy looks away. "I am a rationalist. I told you years ago, when I was a child. A kite cannot fly in a fog."

"Did the boat that day encounter fog? Or only wind?"

"Rain. Heavy wind."

"You feared for your life."

"Yes. Though I felt protected because of the postcards."

"So God protected you."

"No, not God . . ."

"Then what?"

"A talisman. A means to avert fear until we reached England."

"God protected you. He saved you. Perhaps He intends for you to solve the Raymond hypothesis."

"Riemann."

"Excuse me. I am no mathematician."

Hardy leans forward in his chair. "Who told you? It can't have been Mother. She wouldn't have understood so much. It must have been Gertrude."

Again, the vicar does not answer. His smile widens.

"Why would she tell you?"

"Why have you come here?"

"To make sure you know that you haven't won. I still don't believe in God."

"Whether or not you believe in God is one question," the vicar says. "The other is whether God believes in you."

8

A T F I R S T , climbing out of the tube station onto Queensway with her bag of foreign newspapers, she isn't sure it's him: a haggard figure, too small for his clothes, and thinner than she remembers. He is standing outside the station, peering, with a kind of studious fascination, at the map posted there. Then he turns, and it's too late to decide whether she wants to flee, much less to flee. "Mr. Ramanujan," she says.

"Mrs. Neville," he answers. And smiles. "What a pleasant surprise."

She takes his hand. She doesn't want to give away that over the course of a few seconds, all the convictions on which she has depended to survive, these last months, have collapsed. No longer is the past a novel finished and put back on the shelf; no longer is she a different woman than she was, a Londoner, impervious to the pleas of beggars and the banshee-echo of underground trains. For he has returned, and now she is the same Alice who lived on Chesterton Road. She never stopped being in love with him.

What's happened, she realizes as they walk together down Queensway, is that this chance meeting has carried her past the moment she dreaded, the moment at which she would have to acknowledge that awful visit to his rooms. It's as if a wind has picked her up and carried her across that border she would not let herself cross by choice, and now she's here, on the other side. They're walking together toward her flat. She's asked him up for coffee.

Up the stairs to the door. Although the flat is only on the second floor, the climb leaves him winded. "Miss Hardy told me you haven't been well," she says, letting him in. "I'm so sorry."

"I was in the nursing hostel for several months," he says. "But I'm better now. I'm back at Bishop's Hostel." He follows her into the small, square sitting room, into which most of the Cambridge furniture—the piano, the Voysey settee, the two spinsterish chairs—has been stuffed.

"Forgive the crowdedness. The flat is so much smaller than our house."

"It's fine," he says, sitting down on one of the chairs. "Rather like seeing old friends." And he rubs the upholstered arm with what seems to her genuine fondness.

"I'll just get the coffee. I'm afraid we don't have any milk, and only a little sugar, so it can't be a proper Madrasi coffee. The shortages."

"I understand. And how is Mr. Neville?"

"As to be expected," she says from the kitchen. "He's away today, in Reading."

"Oh yes?"

"The university there may offer him a position."

"I hope so."

"Yes, I suppose I do, too. Though it will mean leaving London, and I've only just got used to London." Having put the coffee on, she returns to the sitting room; sits in the second chair. There is so much more she could say—to him, to anybody—about what she has learned in these last months! In a marriage, it is the repetition that kills: the repetition of meals; of conversations; of bickering ("How did you sleep?" "I told you never to ask me that again"); of sex or no sex; of habits (his dribbling urine on the toilet seat, her flatulence); of grief (the long afternoon naps of sorrow); of laundry; of repetition itself (totting up the accounts twice, because Eric's arithmetic, amazingly, is worse than hers); of his obliviousness and her hardness; of his calling her "darling"; of the knowledge that there will always be things in him that she will never understand and things in her that he will never understand; of the knowledge, always, that no matter how far he goes or for how long, he will come back.

Yes, she thinks, in a marriage, it is the repetition that kills. And it is the repetition that saves.

She turns to Ramanujan. Only now does she see how much weight he has lost. His face, bereft of its pudginess, is lean and serious, and she takes in, as if for the first time, its beauty: the black, haunted eyes, the heavy brows, the flared, flat nose. Ramanujan has brilliantined his thick hair, combed it to the left. His collar is open. What firm fat once concealed—the ropy ligaments of his neck—illness has now exposed. Illness, and the open collar. She has never before seen him with an open collar, except that once, in his room.

"I didn't think I'd see you again." She says this without sentiment; a mere statement of fact. "Yet here you are."

"Yes."

"It's odd. So much has changed, yet everything is the same. The same furniture in a different flat."

"It is a pleasure to sit in this chair again. Your house was my first real taste of England."

"If only we could fit everything! But you see, this is only temporary, this flat. Until Eric gets a position. It's ridiculous, the dining table barely fits in the dining room. You can't even pull the chairs out without hitting the wall."

"And how is Ethel?"

"I'm afraid she's not with us anymore. You know her son was killed."

"No, I didn't."

"He ran away from the front. He couldn't bear it. They shot him as a deserter."

"You mean the English?"

Alice nods. "We tried to get her to come with us to London, but she didn't want to be so far from her daughter. I understand, of course. So now we just have a char who comes in twice a week."

"Please give her my regards if you write to her."

"I shall. The war is such a horror, Mr. Ramanujan. But at least I have found a place for myself." And she tells him about her work, about Mrs. Buxton, about the house in Golders Green. She talks and talks—until she realizes that she is leaving him far behind, forgetting him. "I'm so sorry," she says, "I've not even asked what's brought you to London."

"Just a doctor's visit."

"Of course, your illness. And what did the doctor say?"

"So many doctors have said so many things. And now it seems I am to go to a sanatorium. Mendip Hills. Near Wells. The doctor who runs it is Indian. Most of the patients, too."

"But isn't that a sanatorium for tuberculosis?"

"Yes. My symptoms fit no other diagnosis, so by process of elimination, it has been concluded that it must be tuberculosis."

"But you don't cough."

"No lung trouble. Just the pain and the fever. Nothing changes. Every day the same. Illness is really very boring, Mrs. Neville."

"Repetition," Alice says faintly. And suddenly she remembers the coffee; hurries to the kitchen; pours it into cups and brings them back. "I have a little sugar here."

"No need, I shall drink it as it is."

Then they sit, in a small, square room in Bayswater, drinking their dark, bitter coffee. She is thinking that the room is like one of those stalls at the Paris flea market that are set up to look like rooms, but rooms in which no human being could live, because there is no space to move. So it is now: their lives up for sale. What will happen next? Only a few steps separate her from the settee, the table on which Ramanujan did the jigsaw puzzle, the piano. She looks at it, then looks at him.

"Do you ever sing anymore?"

He waggles his head.

"'I am the very model of a Modern Major General . . .' Remember?"

"'I've information vegetable, animal, and mineral . . .'"

"You do remember!"

"Of course."

Then, together:

"'I know the Kings of England, and I quote the fights historical, From Marathon to Waterloo, in order categorical.'"

They finish the song, laughing. "I wouldn't have thought you'd remember the lyrics," she says.

"I remember them all."

Once again, she turns toward the piano. "It needs to be tuned. I don't know how it will sound. It's been months since I've played."

"It doesn't matter."

They get up, and sit together on the bench. She feels the heat of his nearness—in her marrow she feels it. Still, she doesn't touch his arm. She doesn't touch his hand. She arranges the music on the desk.

Late afternoon sun pours through the window. Elsewhere in London, a woman receives a telegram that her missing son is alive. Hardy tries to write a letter to his sister. Russell gives a speech. And on the train from Reading, Eric Neville adjusts his spectacles; opens up a battered copy of *Alice in Wonderland*. He is happy, because Reading will give him a fellowship, and his wife has just told him that she is pregnant.

Fingers on the keys: the simple accompaniment is rendered strange by the out-of-tune piano. As they sing, the past embraces them, and the furniture bears witness.

9

New Lecture Hall, Harvard University

THIS MORNING, walking along the streets of your fair city, this other Cambridge, I had the oddest hallucination. I was standing in Harvard Square, looking in the window of a bookshop, when I happened to notice the reflections of the men and women in the glass superimposed over the books, and suddenly it seemed to me—that is, I was sure I could see it—that one of the women had fish hooks hanging from her flesh. Fish hooks protruded from her cheeks, her arms, her legs and neck. Some of the wounds were fresh and bleeding, while in other places the flesh seemed to have toughened around the hooks; almost to have accepted them. And then, when I turned—as what I am describing is, admittedly, a waking dream, I shall resort to the locutions of Milton—when I turned, methought I saw a man passing by whose flesh was also pierced with fish hooks. And then, behind him, another man, and another woman, until it dawned on me that every passerby on the square this morning had fish hooks hanging from his flesh, some of them dragging shreds of line, while in other cases the line was not cut; the line was being tugged at, so that these men and women jerked in their efforts to escape their captors. Yes, some tried to escape, and still others seemed glad to follow, ran as if willfully with the lines. And then . . . methought I saw, there on Harvard Square, a cat's cradle of fishing line entangling these poor men and women, their feet and bodies. Everyone trapped, hooked, holding reels even as they were being reeled in.

What has this vision to do with Ramanujan? It is true that, as I crossed Harvard Square this morning, I was thinking about my departed friend; rehearsing in my mind the speech I was to give in his memory. So perhaps the Goddess Namagiri supplied me with this vision, as a way of indicating the line (pardon the pun) that Ramanujan, who is no doubt reincarnated today in some superior form, wishes me to take. Or perhaps the hallucination was merely the product of an increasingly elderly and diseased imagination. I don't know. All I can offer is an interpretation: we spend our lives, all of us, trying to hook each other. We hook, and are hooked. Sometimes we fight it, and sometimes we take the hooks gratefully, sink them into our own flesh, and sometimes we try to outwit those who have hooked us by hooking them, as I tried constantly, in my younger years, to hook God.

Ramanujan, in the late months of 1917 and the early months of 1918, was a man from whose body many hooks dangled. Of these, at the time at least, I could only see some. There was the hook that connected him to me, to my ambition for him, which he felt obliged to meet, and to my fear of him, which he felt obliged to allay; and there was the hook of his illness, obliging him to rely on the care of doctors; and the hooks of duty and love connecting him to his three friends, Chatterjee, Rao, and Mahalanobis; and the predatory hook (this one particularly sharp and menacing) plunged into him at an early age by his mother; and the hook of responsibility and desire that linked him to his wife across the ocean; and the hook of the war, embedded in everyone's flesh in those years; and finally the hook of his own ambition, which of course he had driven into himself.

Do you see, now, what it was like for him? Do you see in what a complication of duties, hopes, and terrors he was enmeshed? I hope you do, because I didn't, at least at the time. After all, there was so much of which I wasn't aware, and about which I didn't think to ask. By now he was out of the nursing hostel and living, once again, at Trinity. His health had improved only to the extent that he was no longer bedridden. He could once again dress and wash himself, and come to see me in the mornings, and on occasion he even felt well enough to travel up to London, where he stayed with his beloved Mrs. Peterson, whose heart he would soon break. And yet he was not in any sense recovered. The pain in his stomach persisted, as did the fever. Illness must have made him vulnerable, and perhaps this is why, in those months, he found himself thinking more than ever before of his wife, Janaki, the girl with whom, back in India, he had been able to spend so little time, as his mother (I learned this later) had kept them from sleeping in the same bed, using his surgery as an excuse. Yes, I can imagine that in his solitude and confusion—separated from his homeland by the war, deprived (again, by the war) of all but the most rudimentary foods, facing another gloomy, cold Cambridge winter— he might well have started dreaming of that young girl to whom he referred, in the Indian fashion, as his "house." (It was during these weeks that he told Chatterjee, "My house has not written to me," and that Chatterjee replied, "Houses don't write.") And yet it would be a mistake to imagine that he dreamed of her with undiluted longing. There was great bitterness in Ramanujan, as I soon learned from an unlikely source.

What happened was this. Early in the fall I received a letter from a childhood friend of his, an engineering student named Subramanian, who told me that he had gone to visit Ramanujan's mother and that she and his blind father and his brothers were in a state of agitation because for months Ramanujan had not written to them. Naturally when Ramanujan came to see me that morning, I told him about the letter. "Is it true," I asked, "that you are not writing to your people?"

"They hardly write to me," he replied.

"But why is that?"

Then he told me, for the first time, about Janaki's flight from Kumbakonam to her brother's house in Karachi. "Now I do not even know where she is," he said. "She has written me only a few very formal letters, asking for money. And my mother—she wrote that she believes I have hidden my wife away in some secret place in India, that I have hidden Janaki away *from her* and that Janaki is writing to me against my mother, waiting for me to come and join her, in that secret place, without my mother's knowledge, and that I am always listening to her."

"But she's your wife. It's natural that you should listen to her."

"My mother was offended when Janaki ran away. But what she does not understand is that Janaki offends me too, for she writes me only these formal letters."

The mother's jealousy seemed obscene to me. I suggested that perhaps it was her unreasonable attitude that had driven Janaki away, and Ramanujan shook his head no. It was a firm no—not his usual ambivalent waggle. Clearly both fish hooks were smarting.

In the end, I persuaded him, at least, to write to them and assure them that he was all right. At least I think I did. For just as, at the mention of Subramanian's letter, Ramanujan had suddenly opened himself to me, now that we were back to the question of letter writing, he withdrew. It was fascinating to watch, this withdrawal, like the infolding of one of those flowers that close their petals at night. "You may tell Subramanian that you have got me to promise to write to my people," he said. A very careful instruction which, you will note, contains no promise. I put it into my reply word for word. Whether he did write to them I have no idea.

It was now October. For a while he disappeared. He went to a sanatorium called Hill Grove, near Wells, in the Mendip Hills. This institution was run by a Dr. Chowry-Muthu, whom Ramanujan had met when he had come to England from India; it catered mostly to Indian patients suffering from tuberculosis. But Ramanujan did not like it there, and when Chatterjee and Ananda Rao went to visit him, he had only complaints to voice. It seemed that Dr. Chowry-Muthu employed curious treatment methods, one of which was to make his patients wear masklike inhalers containing germicides. He compelled them to take part in singing exercises and to saw wood in a workshop. The "chalets" in which they lived were rustic shacks. Nor had Ramanujan anything good to say about the food or the beds. To make matters worse, he was in a state of great agitation, Ananda Rao told me, because he knew that very soon, at Trinity, it would be decided whether he would be elected to a fellowship. As I mentioned earlier, since the spring of 1916 he had been trying to get me to reassure him that his election would be, as Barnes had foolishly asserted, a fait accompli. But now Barnes was gone, and I was left with the responsibility of trying to put the election through. The trouble was, I suspected—rightly, as it turned out—that, despite what Barnes had said, Ramanujan would not be voted in.

In retrospect, I see that much of what happened was my own fault. I should not have been the one to put him up for election. To say the least, I was unpopular at Trinity just then, due to my militancy on Russell's behalf. Especially among the old guard, there were men who would have fought *any* nomination I'd put forward, no matter how worthy. Nor can we underestimate the irrational distrust, even hatred, that the mere sight of dark skin can unleash in white men. Walking with him on the street, I had on occasion heard boys, with perfect equanimity, call Ramanujan a "nigger." And then, at the meeting to decide the fellowships, Jackson—with the same equanimity—vowed that so long as he was alive, Trinity would have no "nigger fellows." His was the ranting of a tyrant, and Herman, to his credit, rebuked him. But in the end, when it came down to the vote, Ramanujan lost.

Now I wonder: did he feel it happening at Hill Grove—a tug on a line that crossed the countryside, crossed valleys and rivers, to connect a sick Indian in a sanatorium to that Trinity chamber in which dons had gathered to decide his fate? In that same chamber, only a few months before, Neville's banishment had been assured. And surely Ramanujan must have been thinking about Neville that afternoon, as he sat on one of Hill Grove's porches, wrapped in blankets, the hated mask over his mouth. He was waiting—hoping—for a telegram. But none came. I could not tell him, as I wanted to, that he was now a fellow, and so I told him nothing.

The next day he left the sanatorium. He took a bus from Wells to Bristol, where he caught the train to Paddington. Probably there were delays: the train service was constantly being disrupted just then, as more and more cars were requisitioned for use in the war. But finally he arrived, and from Paddington he went immediately—two stops on the Bakerloo—to Mrs. Peterson's boardinghouse in Maida Vale. This was one of about a dozen more or less identical establishments ranged around a narrow rectangle of garden behind Maida Vale Station. Any of you who have done time in London will be familiar with the layout of such places: the hall with its coat rack and telephone stand, the formal front parlor, the carpeted stairs leading up to the tenants' rooms, the doors marked "Dining Room" and "Private" and "Kitchen." All that made Mrs. Peterson's boardinghouse unique was that its clientele consisted entirely of Indians. This was nothing she had planned, she explained when I went to see her in 1921; her husband having been killed in a tram accident, she'd had to find a way to make a living, so she'd opened the boardinghouse and, as it happened, the first lodger to knock on her door was an Indian. "Mr. Mukherjee," she said. "He was studying economics. He still writes to me. From Poona. And he liked the place, so he told his friends, and word got round."

It was a rainy April afternoon when Mrs. Peterson told me this. We were sitting in her tragic front parlor, with its stiff little chairs and

Meissen figurines and floral wallpaper; a room grown stale from its own protection, from its having been reserved, for so long, for some ceremonial occasion that would never take place: a visit from royalty or the viewing of a coffin. Every now and then, I suppose, someone must have come to see her whom she felt obliged to entertain somewhere other than in the kitchen, at which point the curtains would be flung open, the floors mopped, and fresh flowers put on the table, with the result that the room's spirits lifted a little. A fat young woman whom I assumed to be Mrs. Peterson's daughter brought the inevitable tea. Mrs. Peterson herself was not fat; she was a small, elegantly proportioned woman in her mid-sixties who had known much loss: two sons dead in the war, in addition to the husband. "After Mr. Mukherjee there was Mr. Bannerjee, and Mr. Singh, and two Mr. Raos." I nodded, as an Indian in a checked suit and turban quietly took off his coat in the front hall, hung it on the rack, and padded up the stairs.

We spoke about Ramanujan. Tears came to Mrs. Peterson's eyes as she told me of his first visits, his shyness with her, the quiet gratitude he expressed when she served him his supper and he saw that the dishes were familiar ones. "For you see, I had to learn to cook Indian, for the sake of my gentlemen," she said. "Mr. Mukherjee, he taught me how to make the things he liked. He showed me the shops where I could get the ingredients. And since I wanted him to be comfortable, I went along, though the food seemed strange to me at first. I'm a fairly quick learner in the kitchen." She put down her teacup. "I only ever wanted to make my gentlemen happy. That's the sad part. I was so very fond of Mr. Ramanujan. He seemed so alone in England. Those last times he came to me, when he was visiting the doctors, he looked so unwell. There was a room he preferred, a small room on the top floor, and I tried to always put him in it."

I asked if I could see the room. "Of course," Mrs. Peterson said, and led me up the stairs—past the first floor, where the permanent lodgers lived in larger suites, to the attic with its low ceilings and constricting walls. Once, these had been servants' quarters. The room that she showed me was under the eaves, cozy and neat, with a small desk by the window and the bed pushed into a corner beneath the angled wall. The view was of other roofs. The wallpaper, of climbing roses, clashed with the carpet, which was dark brown and patterned with interlocking hexagons. Still, it was an appealing room, a warm room: I would have liked sleeping there myself.

"Mr. Ramanujan was happy here," Mrs. Peterson said, as she led me back downstairs. "I know he was happy." And I thought: yes, you are the sort of person who can know such things. I am not. "That was why it took me so by surprise, what happened. I never expected it. You see, I'm always very careful what I give my gentlemen. I even keep a separate set of pots and pans to cook the meals in, for the ones who don't eat meat. It never occurred to me to look at the label on the Ovaltine tin."

"Rest assured, no one imagines that you meant any harm," I said. "And Ramanujan was—shall we say, rather highly strung at that point."

"Still, I regret it. I remember it as if it was yesterday—him sitting at the table in the kitchen and me stirring the glass. I thought it would be a treat for him before retiring. 'Have a glass of this Ovaltine, Mr. Ramanujan,' says I, 'it's a flavoring for milk,' and he takes the glass and drinks it down. 'Did you like that, Mr. Ramanujan?' says I. 'I do indeed, Mrs. Peterson,' says he. 'Well, here's the tin so you can write down the name,' says I, 'then you can buy some for yourself for when you're in Cambridge.' 'Thank you,' says he, and starts to read the label . . ."

She quieted. Tears again sprang to her eyes. "You needn't go on," I said, for I knew the next part of the story already from Ramanujan's friends: how, upon examining the tin, he happened to glance at the list of ingredients, and saw that one of them was powdered egg. Eggs, of course, were forbidden to him. To eat eggs was as polluting as to eat meat.

Then, I think, he must have gone a little mad. Springing to his feet, he cried out, "Eggs, eggs!" and threw the tin at Mrs. Peterson as if he couldn't bear even to touch it. When she read the word *egg*, she was aghast. "I chased after him," she told me, "I said I wouldn't have dreamt of giving him egg, and I was ever so sorry, but he wouldn't listen to me. To tell the truth, I don't know that he heard me. He went up to his room, and whilst I stood there at the door apologizing and trying to calm him, he packed his case. I followed him down the stairs. He tried to give me money, but I wouldn't take it. 'Mr. Ramanujan!' I called from the front door as he went down the path—he was running, which can't have been good for him—'Mr. Ramanujan, where will you go?' You see, it was nine in the evening by then. But he didn't answer." She wiped her eyes. "That was the last I saw of him."

Mrs. Peterson put down her cup. She looked over my head, at the mantelpiece with its careful arrangement of figurines. "It's not your fault," I said. "Remember, he was very ill, and probably a bit off his head." To which I might have added: given so many months of illness, and his not having been elected to a fellowship, and the war, and his troubles at home, who could blame him? A man from whom dozens of hooks hung, like a great fish that has escaped capture again and again, careering across Baker Street with poison on his lips. Where was he heading? Liverpool Street Station, he told me later. He wanted to get back to Cambridge. It was the night of October 19th, 1917, and London was calm. It had been so long since there had been an air raid that when the fleet of zeppelins wafted across the channel and started dropping their cargo, no one was prepared. The response was strangely blasé; at two theaters, performances were interrupted, the audience were told they could leave if they wished, but once the raid was over, the plays would go on. Meanwhile bombs crashed down onto roadways, windows shattered, some people were killed outside Swan & Edgar's. But as so often seemed to be the case in those days, most of the dead were poor children, asleep in workmen's cottages.

And what of Ramanujan? From what he told me later, he was just coming out of the tube when he heard the explosions. Because he knew that Liverpool Street had been a favored target of the Germans in the past, he did not go into the station. Instead he ran in the opposite direction. He looked up, but could not see the zeppelins. They were too high and obscured by smoke. Had it been me, I would have wondered what the pilot was thinking, as he looked down from that immense floating tablet upon the abstract flames. What does carnage sound like from on high? What does it look like? Soon he would turn around, he would churn across the quiet channel, peacefully aloft among the stars, only to be shot down himself over France. But Ramanujan was not thinking about the pilot. He had only one thought in his mind: the powdered egg. The taint on his tongue. He had done the unforgivable, and now the gods were unleashing their punishment. The air raid was not meant for London: it was meant for him. And so he ducked, and wept, and begged for mercy, if not in this life, then in the next.

This, at least, is what he claimed. Later he wrote a letter to Mrs. Peterson describing what had happened. She showed me the letter. As I read it, I wondered how much I should believe. For I had tired the poor lady out quite enough for one day; nor did I see any point in interrogating her on the matter of Ramanujan's religious scruples. Instead I rose and bid her goodbye, and just as, a few years before, she had watched Ramanujan hurry away, now she watched me walk toward the tube station. When I looked over my shoulder she was on the doorstep still. The sun was setting. Another Indian came up the path, and she made room for him to pass, before she turned and shut the door behind her.

PART NINE
Twilight

I

HARDY DESPISES TELEPHONES. He always has. For the first year that they shared the flat in Pimlico, he and Gertrude did not have a telephone. But then their mother became ill and Gertrude insisted on putting one in so that the servant could find her in an emergency. Nor, after their mother died, did she have the thing removed, even though there was no longer any good reason to keep it. Now it sits in the hall on its own little table—ridiculous, Hardy thinks, that a piece of furniture should have been invented purely for the purpose of supporting such an apparatus. Although it never rings, it seems forever eager to do so. He has given the number to no one except Thayer, who has never used it.

And so when the black mechanism suddenly starts shrilling at him that Tuesday afternoon in October, Hardy's first thought is that some sort of siren or alarm is sounding: perhaps an air raid is about to take place. Once he identifies the source of the noise, it occurs to him that until this moment no one has ever rung him up in the flat. He's never before heard the thing's terrible little voice, so frantic in its urgency. Hurrying into the hall, he regards the machine. It is impassioned as a cat in heat. It vibrates. If for no other reason than to shut it up, he picks up the receiver.

The voice on the other end is male, hoarse, shouting. Hardy can barely understand what's being said. Whole words fail to come through. "Professor Hardy? This is (inaudible) Scotland Yard." But why should Scotland Yard be calling him? "(Inaudible) your sister."

"My sister?"

"Trinity College (inaudible) your sister and your sister gave us this number. I'm sorry to say (inaudible) in custody."

"What?"

The voice repeats the mangled word. He repeats it again. Only after

429

he has repeated it a third time does Hardy realize what the voice is saying, or trying to say: "Ramanujan."

"In custody. Why?"

"I'm not (inaudible) over the telephone, sir. Very respectfully I must request that you come to Scotland Yard as (inaudible) has given your name and (inaudible)."

"Has he been arrested?"

Hardy cannot make out the reply. He drops the receiver, pulls on his coat and hat, and heads downstairs to hail a cab. What on earth can have happened? he wonders, as the cab carries him past the swarms hurrying into Victoria Station. The last he heard, Ramanujan was in a sanatorium in the countryside. So what is he doing in London? And what could he have done to get himself picked up by the police? Importuning—that's the first thought that enters Hardy's mind. Suddenly he imagines Ramanujan in one of the notorious public toilets near Piccadilly Circus, the ones Norton has told him about, but which he's never dared visit. Is it only because his own longing has drawn him, time and again, to walk past those urinals that he sees Ramanujan standing at one, reaching out his hand to touch the trousers of a plainclothes officer? But no. That's the wrong plot. So what else might it have been? Ramanujan has run away before, most notably after the dinner party in his rooms. Could the sanatorium have sent out a bulletin? Is he a fugitive? Do laws forbid flight from such places? Or perhaps he left of his own accord, ran out of money, and was picked up for vagrancy. Or got in a fight—over what? Highly composite numbers?

He glances out the window. A light snow has started falling. On Parliament Square, a woman takes off her hat and turns her face to it. She smiles at him—he smiles back—and then she is gone, the cab turning onto Bridge Street, then Victoria Embankment, where it pulls up in front of the headquarters of Scotland Yard. It is really too warm for snow; the featherlike flakes melt as soon as they hit the ground. Still, he pulls his collar up, and having paid the driver, hurries inside the brick fortification with its turrets and medieval fripperies. The corridors are wide and echoing and ablaze with electric light. He tells a female officer why he's there, and she points him toward an enormous waiting room. Here he sees a rouged tart and a drunken soldier. There are men who fidget and men who stare silently into their laps. There are upright, proud women who look like the servants of his childhood, wives and mothers no doubt summoned to fetch wastrel husbands and sons. One of the fidgeting men talks to himself. The rouged tart talks to everyone. The air smells of beer and rotten fruit, and in the distance he can hear someone coughing.

What a place! Ever fearful of germs, he wipes his seat before sitting down; keeps his coat collar pulled up to his mouth. He wonders at the strange course his life has taken these last years: that a letter he might easily have ignored, that others ignored, should have led him from the safety of his rooms in Trinity to this place.

He waits. An hour passes. No one calls his name. To make the time pass, he listens to the tart's monologue, which is oddly compelling: ornate and subtle and full of references to men and women with whom she assumes everyone else in the room is familiar. The ingredients are those of a novel: a jealous sister, a cheating husband, a married lover. " 'You keep it to yourself, Jack,' I tell him, 'I don't want nothing to do with it.' But will he listen? No. He's just like Annie, always has been, has to have his own way . . ."

The story is just reaching its climax when the female officer strides in and shouts out a name. "Hold your horses," the tart says, and, having adjusted her various accoutrements—stockings, handbag, necklaces—she stumbles away on loud heels. And how quiet the room is suddenly! Aside from the coughing, all he can hear is the muttered monologue of the man who fidgets. And what is he saying? Hardy strains his ear, catches a single word—"butter"—then his own name. He looks up. "Please come with me," the female officer says, and he stands and follows her down a long corridor into a windowless office where two chairs face a desk at which no one sits. "Please wait here," she says. "The inspector will be with you shortly."

She shuts the door behind her. He looks around. The walls are bare except for a calendar and a clock with a loud tick. (*Tick, tic.*) Why didn't he bring something to read? Where is the toilet? It suddenly occurs to her that the officer might have locked the door, locked him in. He panics at the prospect. *Dear God, let the door be locked so that the tart will not molest me.* Then he gets up and walks to the door and tries the handle. To his great relief, it opens. He closes it again and sits down.

Ten minutes later two policemen come into the office, both huge and mustached, one in his sixties and the other, at most, twenty-five. "Sorry to keep you waiting," the older one says. "I'm Inspector Callahan. This is Officer Richards." Hardy shakes their enormous hands. Then the inspector sits at the desk and the officer takes the third seat, the one next to Hardy's. "Tried to jump under a train," the inspector says, opening a ledger.

"What?"

"The Indian. Tried to jump under a train at Marble Arch station."

"Oh my God." Hardy shuts his mouth. God is not someone whose name he wants these men to hear him utter. "But why? Jumped? He didn't fall?"

"There were witnesses. The station was crowded. A woman screamed, 'Don't jump!' and he jumped."

"Is he all right?"

"He's all right," the younger officer says, the one called Richards. "I was the officer called to the scene. From what the witnesses tell me, sir, the stationmaster, seeing him jump, turned off the switch, and the train came to a stop just a few feet in front of him. It was a miracle, was what one woman said. I had to climb down onto the tracks and help him up, which was difficult, as he'd done considerable injury to his legs."

"Where is he? Can I see him?"

"He's in a holding cell," the inspector says. "We had him bandaged up. Normally in a case like this he'd be kept under guard in a hospital. But there aren't enough beds. Bloody war." The inspector lights a cigarette. "I'll be honest with you, I've no patience with these suicides. Attention's all they want. They're just like spoilt children. And when you consider all the young men dying at the front . . . It's a crime, you know, attempted suicide. No magistrate's going to look kindly on it, especially these days."

"But he's not well."

"Has his behavior been at all odd lately?" asks the younger officer.

"I couldn't say. I haven't seen him. He's been at a sanatorium. He's very sick."

"What is he, a mathematics student?"

"He's the greatest mathematician alive today. And an F.R.S.— Fellow of the Royal Society."

What, Hardy will wonder later, made him say that? It is a lie.

Ramanujan is *not* a Fellow of the Royal Society. Nor, until that moment, had it occurred to Hardy that perhaps he *ought* to be; that Hardy ought to put him up for membership. Had Hardy thought before he spoke, he might later have claimed that he was making a gambit, hoping that the inspector would be sufficiently impressed by the idea that Ramanujan was an F.R.S. that he would let him go. And, as it turned out, the inspector *was* impressed, as was his lieutenant. But that was sheer luck. "An F.R.S.," he said, and you could see it in his face: a stepping back, in deference to intellectual superiority as sanctioned by a respected body. "I didn't realize. All he told us was he was at Cambridge. Well, well."

"As I said, he's not been well lately. And geniuses do tend to be . . . temperamental."

"Of course, if he's put before a magistrate, charges will be brought."

"Is that absolutely necessary? It would be highly embarrassing . . . not just to him but to the college. And it could be disastrous for his future. A criminal record." Hardy leans in confidentially. "I'll ask you to keep this between us, because it's not something we want to get round—the newspapers and such—but Mr. Ramanujan is on the brink of making what most would agree is the single most important breakthrough in the history of mathematics."

"Is he now? Well, let's see what's to be done. I'll need to speak to the chief, of course."

The inspector leaves, slamming the door behind him.

"Would you care for a cup of tea?" Richards asks.

"Thank you, yes," Hardy says.

"I'll just ask Florence to fetch some for us. Florence!" And he shouts through the open door for the female officer with whom Hardy first spoke. She slinks in, looking resentful in her bowlerish hat, her long black skirt and thin tie. An officer of the law, requisitioned for tea-making.

"Fetch us some tea, will you, darling?"

She says nothing; disappears down the corridor. Richards pushes the door half shut. It's the first time Hardy's had the chance to get a good look at him. The mustache is a pity, in that it conceals his lips, which are thin and wet. His brown eyes are open and curious beneath narrow brows and a block of dark, thick hair. Smiling, he takes his seat; says to Hardy, "This breakthrough you mentioned—I wouldn't half mind knowing what it is. I've always been keen on science. And you can trust me to keep quiet about it."

Hardy leans in for a confidence. And really, he thinks, Richards is young. So why isn't he in France? An injury? Good connections? Or is he just lucky—kept out of the war to patrol the streets of London?

"Mr. Ramanujan is on the brink of proving the Riemann hypothesis," Hardy says.

"The Riemann . . ."

"It has to do with the prime numbers. You see, for hundreds of years, mathematicians have wondered about the mystery of the primes and their distribution." Like the lecture he gave to the girls at St. Catherine's. Only Richards listens more carefully than the girls did. He gets irritated when Florence interrupts with the tea, stops Hardy intermittently to ask questions, and seems just on the brink of grasping the essentials when the inspector's voice booms again in the corridor.

Instantly, at the first click of the door handle, Richards pulls back, as if to put a safe distance between himself and Hardy. And how immense, ungainly, interruptive is the inspector's presence! His, Hardy recognizes dimly, was the barking voice on the telephone. "Well, I've had a talk with the chief," he says, taking his place at the desk, "and he is of the opinion, as am I, that attempted suicide is a very serious offense. Mind you, if he did it once, he might do it again. There's a reason it's a crime in this country, you know, and that's to protect the public and protect a man from himself who's liable to off himself at any moment." The inspector rubs his nose, so that his mustache quivers. "Still, the chief appreciates the delicacy of the situation, and so, given the gentleman's reputation and his status as an F.R.S. and so forth, we are willing to forgo bringing criminal charges *provided* he enters a hospital straightaway and stays there for at least a year. You say he's not well, he's been in a sanatorium."

"Yes. Tuberculosis."

"Well, get him back to the sanatorium. And make sure he doesn't run off. Because if we catch him walking the streets of London or standing on the edge of platforms in tube stations, there'll be no leniency."

"I understand. May I see him now?"

"Richards, go and fetch him."

"Yes, sir." Richards hops up and leaves.

434

"Cigar, Mr. Hardy?" the inspector asks. Hardy declines. "Well, I don't mind if I do myself." And he lights the cigar, stretching his legs out in front of him under the desk. "So, a mathematician," he says.

"That's right."

"Myself, I was bloody awful at maths. As a lad I could barely add two and two. Still can't. My wife won't even let me near the accounts book." He laughs. "Of course I suppose you could tot up fifty figures in your head in half a minute."

"No, like most professional mathematicians, I am abysmally bad at what you call 'totting up.' But Ramanujan could."

"Could he now?"

"He's well known for his feats of mental arithmetic. We had a contest once, between him and a Major MacMahon, to see which one could break down a prime number in the shortest time."

"A what?"

"A prime number. A number that—" But before Hardy can complete his explanation, the door opens, and Richards ushers in Ramanujan, who is limping badly. Both his legs are bandaged. Richards has his right arm around his waist.

"Ramanujan!" Hardy says, leaping up from his chair. But Ramanujan doesn't answer. He won't meet Hardy's gaze. And suddenly Hardy understands that all this jollity—explaining the Riemann hypothesis to the good-looking Richards, talking about calculation contests with the less good-looking Inspector Callahan—has only been a caesura; a respite. For now Ramanujan is standing before him, and in his eyes there are no tears. There is no rage. No grief. Nothing. This is a man who just tried to die.

"Here you are. Mr. Hardy," Richards says. "That's right." And he hands Ramanujan over like a package. An arm loosed, another arm put around the shoulders. Ramanujan can barely stand; for a moment Hardy staggers under the weight until his feet find purchase. He smells, very faintly, of blood; of sand; of the grit and exhaust that puffs up from Underground stations.

"All right, my friend, you're safe now," Hardy says. "We'll get you in a taxi and get you home." And he leads Ramanujan toward the door, praying the whole while that Ramanujan will say or do something mad—cry out, "I want to die!" or hurl himself against a wall—

something to jeopardize this tenuous probation that Hardy has negotiated. But Ramanujan says nothing.

"Remember the terms," the inspector calls from the door. And Hardy says that yes, he will remember the terms. Then he and Ramanujan leave, followed by Richards, who helps them down the steps and into a cab, and stands by as the cab pulls away.

2

I T'S ONLY ONCE they're in the taxi, moving the wrong way along Victoria Embankment, that Hardy realizes he has nowhere to take Ramanujan except to his own flat. It's too late to catch a train to Cambridge. Nor, under the circumstances, can Hardy quite imagine dropping Ramanujan off at Mrs. Peterson's boardinghouse.

The whole journey, Ramanujan is silent. The snow has started to stick a little more. Hardy watches it as it falls on women in bus conductor's uniforms and macintoshes, on businessmen in bowler hats, on soldiers on leave and the tart who was in the waiting room at Scotland Yard, now sheltered by an umbrella held up by a shadowy keeper. These days London is especially frantic at dusk, its citizens scrambling to get home before the lights go out, and it becomes a different world. "Once I was in Venice," he says, and Ramanujan turns; looks at him dimly. "Yes, and it was quite terrifying. You see, the city's so lively during the day, and then at night—not a soul. I got lost trying to get back to my hotel. It was like walking through a city of the dead."

Is this the wrong thing to say? Probably. For how is Ramanujan, who has never been to Venice, supposed to respond? And what is Hardy supposed to say to him next, as the cab ride attenuates, the traffic thickening and thinning, like soup that needs to be stirred? If only St. George's Square would arrive, then at least Hardy could busy himself with making arrangements for the night! And then he looks at Ramanujan, heaped in his corner of the cab, and he realizes that it makes no difference. Ramanujan is not requiring talk of him. On the contrary, he seems to want silence.

At last the cab pulls up to the curb. Hardy helps Ramanujan out, and is mildly surprised that he makes no effort to run away, until he looks down and sees, once again, the bandaged legs, and realizes that, even if he wanted to, Ramanujan couldn't. Not now. "You've banged yourself up pretty well," he says, as he eases Ramanujan through the door and up the stairs.

"I fell onto the rails," Ramanujan says. "They tore the flesh of my legs."

"That must have hurt."

"There were no broken bones, though." Is there disappointment in his voice?

One landing, then another. "Here we are then." And they step inside the flat. The light is still on from when Hardy left, the book he was reading flung open on the chair, the receiver of the telephone dangling to the floor of the corridor. He returns it to its cradle. "Do sit down." Ramanujan sits gingerly, breathes out very loudly. "You've never been here before, have you? My flat."

"No."

"Or rather, I should say, the flat I share with my sister. Miss Hardy."

"Yes."

"So there's a spare room. My sister's room. You can sleep there tonight and tomorrow we'll take the train to Cambridge."

"What is to become of me? Am I to be sent back to Hill Grove?"

"I don't see why not, assuming you were happy there."

"I was not happy there. I could not bear the place. I left four days ago."

"So you came to London?"

Ramanujan nods. He has picked up English habits of certainty. "At first I stayed at Mrs. Peterson's but then there was . . . an incident. I left, and was caught up in the bombing raid. I could not get a train back to Cambridge so I found a hotel. I stayed there until I had no money left." He grows suddenly quiet. And how is Hardy supposed to nudge him on? Is he supposed to nudge him on? So far as the human psyche is concerned—he would be the first to admit it—he is as inept a student as has ever been born. Mathematicians live in abstract realms for a reason. But Ramanujan, too, is a mathematician. That was what brought them together. So why shouldn't they be able to speak to each other?

"Of course you don't have to talk about this if you don't want to,"

Hardy says, "but . . . well, needless to say, I was very alarmed when the inspector told me . . . Is it true that you jumped?"

Ramanujan gazes into his lap for several seconds. Then he says, "It does not matter."

"Why?"

"I shall die soon anyway."

"You don't know that."

"At Hill Grove there was an old man in the next hut. They called it a chalet but it was a hut. This old man came from a village not far from my own. Not far from Kumbakonam. He had bathed in the river every day, as I did, before he came to England. For many years he had a restaurant in Notting Hill, and then his sons took over the restaurant. They quarreled, and it was sold. He was made sick from their quarreling, and they sent him to Hill Grove. And every day he coughed up blood, and in the end the noise coming from his hut was frightful."

"I'm sorry."

"It does not matter. His fate is mine, only in my case it will come sooner. Since I was a child I have known I would die young. It doesn't matter how."

"But that's nonsense. There's no reason you can't live to be eighty. And you've so much left to achieve! We've work to do, Ramanujan, the partitions theorem, the Riemann hypothesis still to prove."

He smiles thinly. "Yes, I have been thinking, a little, about the Riemann hypothesis."

"Have you? Tell me."

"But I am very tired."

"Of course you are. I'm sorry." Hardy stands, then walks into the corridor off which the bedroom doors open. He opens the door to Gertrude's room. "You should find everything you need here," he says. "I'm afraid the bed hasn't been slept in for a while, though. The sheets may be musty."

"I don't mind."

"Oh, but I haven't offered you anything. Wouldn't you like something to eat? Or to drink? Some tea?"

"No. I only want sleep."

"Fine, then. You don't want to bathe?"

Another distinct shake of the head: no. And then he shuffles through the door to Gertrude's room; pulls off his clothes until he is wearing just his drawers. Only then does Hardy see how badly he's been hurt. The bandages cover his legs from the ankles to just above the knees, and are bloody in places.

"Those will have to be changed."

"Tomorrow." Ramanujan climbs into the bed. "You see?" he says, pulling the blankets to his chin. "I've learned. When I first arrived, I didn't understand your beds. I slept on top of the covers, and piled myself with sweaters and overcoats to keep away cold. Then Chatterjee explained . . . you had to get *into* the bed, like a letter into an envelope." He laughs. "To think I was so ignorant!"

"But how long was it before you learned?"

"Oh, months. At least until November of that first year."

"But that's terrible. You must have been frozen!" And without thinking, Hardy laughs, too. They laugh together.

"It was long ago."

"Of course. Well, I'll leave you then. Goodnight." And he moves to shut the door. But Ramanujan says, "Wait."

"What?"

"Would you mind leaving the door open?"

"Of course. Of course I'll leave the door open."

"And the door to your bedroom . . . Would you leave that open, too?"

"Of course. Well, sleep tight."

"Sleep tight?"

"An expression. Goodnight again."

"Goodnight again."

Hardy turns, and is halfway across the corridor, halfway to his own room, when a thought comes into his head, and he stops.

"Ramanujan."

"Yes?"

"You're not going to try it again, are you?"

"No."

"Good. Well, goodnight yet again."

"Goodnight yet again."

Outside the window, the city is dark. He pads into his own bedroom, being careful to leave the door ajar; takes off his clothes; lingers, for a moment, naked in the dark, before starting to put on his pyjamas. Then he flings them away. Now currents of air connect him to

Ramanujan, over which any sound would carry, the groans of intimacy as much as of pain; the thrashings of loneliness; his own snoring. Sleep claims the sufferer, the same oblivion that will elude, tonight, his putative savior. Hardy hears rumblings in the distance, and revels in the unfamiliar sensation of the draft from the corridor brushing against his bare skin.

3

"**WELL, WELL, WELL.**"

He starts at the voice, the sensation of weight pulling the blankets taut. Gaye, in formal coat and tie, sits on the edge of his bed. He holds Hermione in his lap. To his surprise, Hardy is happy to see them.

"It's been so long since you've visited me," he says.

"Busy, busy, busy," Gaye says. "Every week is May week here. Balls and balls and balls. And what a long way you've come, Harold, since last I saw you!"

"How do you mean?"

"Yet another suicide to your credit."

"Suicide attempt. And it wasn't my—"

"I stand corrected. Attempt." Gaye strokes Hermione's neck, so that she purrs. "Mine worked, of course. But then again I never intended it not to. You know if you look carefully you can nearly always tell the difference between the ones who really mean it and the ones who just want some attention. It's rarely ambiguous."

"It wasn't ambiguous in your case."

"No, I meant to die. You see, I'm methodical. I thought it all out very carefully in advance, I made a list of all the possible methods, correlating the likelihood of success with the degree of pain. Unluckily for me, I'm afraid of pain. Some people aren't. Hermione, for instance. You were a brave girl, even through the death agonies, weren't you?" And he picks her up, so that her tiny pink nose touches his. "But where was I? Oh yes. So I wrote out the options. It was in early February that I started planning, just as it was becoming clear you wanted nothing more to do with me—"

"I never—"

"First tablets . . . Now tablets, Harold, are very good in that they

442

won't cause much pain, but then again they're not necessarily guaranteed to take. If you choose the wrong ones, you'll just vomit, and even if you choose the right ones, there's every chance someone's going to barge in and find you sprawled out on the floor and drag you to hospital. So tablets—out. Next knives—but here the pain factor is very high, and besides, it's so easy to cut in the wrong place and just maim yourself, so I scratched that off the list. No pun intended."

"Please stop."

"Then I thought of jumping out a window—that's pretty much a safe bet, if you can get high enough. Unfortunately, at Trinity there's every chance you'll land on a bush, or fall just hard enough to break your neck and be paralyzed the rest of your life and then, once you're paralyzed, you'll have to ask someone else to help you do it, and humans being the skittish creatures they are, they're going to be afraid, no matter how sympathetic they feel, because it's murder, isn't it, and who wants to go to prison? You, for instance, would never have helped me. Hermione, yes—if she could have. Cats are not sentimentalists."

"Why are you doing this?"

"Which leaves guns. Now here are the advantages of a gun. First of all, assuming you put it in your mouth, it's instantaneous, so there's no pain. Second of all, the effect after the fact is really quite impressive. You know, the handsome young man lying atop his bed with his brains splattered all over his pillow. And on Easter Sunday to boot! The only pity was that it was the bedmaker who found me."

"You didn't want her to find you?"

"Of course not! I had nothing against that bedmaker. Poor woman, I gave her the fright of her life."

"God, how you must have hated me."

"No, you're wrong there, dear. I loved you." Gaye nods toward the open door. "Now that one . . . I'm not sure, but my guess is, he does too. So bravo to you, Harold. That's two you've driven to it."

"I haven't driven anyone to anything. I want to make this perfectly clear, you both have free will. *You* put a gun in your mouth, *he* jumped—"

"Ah, but I never said you killed anyone, I said you drove us to it. Consider my situation for starters. I loved you and you stopped loving me. I said I couldn't live without you and I proved it. And in his case . . ."

"He doesn't love me."

"He owes you everything. You brought him to England, you gave him a chance when no one else would. 'The Hindoo Calculator.' Only the trade-off is that he's sick. And now, to cap things off, Trinity doesn't want him."

"That's not my doing."

"Who said it was? And it wouldn't necessarily have made things better. Some are born for fame. I was. It was my calling. I had the hunger for it, not to mention the equipment to cope with it. But alas, I didn't have the goods. The talent. Such an irony . . . Those who can cope with it never get it, whereas those who get it can't cope with it."

"So is that why he did it? Because he couldn't cope with fame?"

"There's never just one reason. Trinity dropped me, too, remember, thanks to Barnes—"

"Barnes had nothing to do with it."

"Whether he did or not, I lost my fellowship. And then what was I supposed to do? Move back in with the family? Get a job as a master at some dreary second-rate public school? You can't know, it never happened to you. You work like a fiend, then someone decides he doesn't like you, and that's it, mate."

"I can assure you that Barnes had nothing to do with your losing your fellowship, Russell."

"Well, there are other routes to fame. So I finished the Aristotle translation, signed my name to it, and left instructions for a copy to be sent to you. I assume you received it."

"Yes."

"But you didn't come to the funeral."

"I couldn't face your family."

"Bravery was never your strong suit."

"Russell—"

"The point is, there comes a moment when things add up, and one day, you're there in the station and you're looking at that line, you know, the one you're never supposed to cross, because if you cross it, you'll be too close to the tracks. And you just think, why in bloody hell shouldn't I? Because it's so easy to step across that line . . . Like one of your asymptotic formulae, Harold, half an inch closer, then a quarter of an inch, then an eighth, a sixteenth, a thirty-second . . . And the closer you get, the more obvious it becomes that no one's going to reach out and stop you, because no one's paying you the slightest attention. They're all thinking about themselves. And even though you don't know what you'll find on the other side of the line, at least you know it'll be something different to this. And this is hell, isn't it? So you just . . . move your feet . . . and cross it."

"I've never been tempted to cross it."

"No, not yet."

"What's that supposed to mean?"

Gaye laughs. "You should know. You're the one who's got Oliver Lodge by your bedside. When the dead come to visit from the other side, they usually bring warnings, right? Foreshadowings, precognitions. Well, I wouldn't want to disappoint you. So write this down on your tongue. Beware a man in black. Beware the hour of twilight. There may be an accident in your future. And don't imagine that you, too, won't one day try to cross the line . . ."

"Try?"

"Ah!" Gaye throws his hands into the air. "But the spirit has departed! A candle goes out, the medium drops her turbaned head to the table, exhausted from her labors."

"It's not fair. I only ever wanted to help."

"No, you wanted to save. There's a difference."

"Oh God."

"Exactly. Why do you think I chose Easter Sunday?"

"Bertie told Norton I vampired you. That was the word he used: 'Vampired.'"

"Now Bertie—there's a man who knows how to handle fame. He got his chance, he planted the seed, he cultivated it. Now look where he is! Whereas you, Harold, you're one of those who'll never make anything of what you've been given." Gaye smiles. "Poor Harold." And he lays a hand on Hardy's cheek, a hand Hardy feels. It is cold and dry—how he welcomes it! But when he tries to put his own hand over Gaye's, Gaye withdraws. He stands from the bed and holds Hermione up in the air. "I'm flying! I'm flying!" he says, pretending to be her. "Remember, Harold? Remember how we used to make her fly?"

"I remember."

"And now she flies all the time. You're an angel cat, aren't you, Hermione?"

As if in answer, she wriggles out of his grasp, scuttles across the floor, and starts to sharpen her claws on the curtains. Gaye follows her. "Bad girl," he says, bending down and detaching her claws, which rake the silk.

"Don't leave," Hardy says, but he already feels the severing, smells the smoke of the guttered candle.

He climbs out of bed; switches on the lamp. The room is empty. And though he knows before he tries that he'll feel no striations or rips in the silk, still, he kneels before the curtain and fingers the hem. In the deep silence he hears no voices, only Ramanujan's breathing across the corridor. And this Hardy holds on to as tightly as he does the curtain's edge. Its steady rise and fall is like a railing to him, something to guide him through to morning. This one he loves also, and this one, he reminds himself, is still alive.

4

New Lecture Hall, Harvard University

ONE AFTERNOON NEAR the end of 1917 (Hardy said in that lecture he never gave), Littlewood and I sat down together to solve what we had come to think of as "the Ramanujan Problem." "Problem," I now believe, is a word that should never be applied to matters of the human spirit. It belongs to mathematics, as in *Waring's Problem*: for any natural number k, does there exist an associated positive integer s such that every natural number is the sum of at most s k^{th} powers of natural numbers? (Toward the solution of this problem, incidentally, Ramanujan made an interesting if little-known contribution.) Human situations, on the other hand, are complex and multiform. To understand them you must take into account not only misunderstandings, occasions, circumstances, but the mystery of human nature, which is as rife with contradictions as the foundational landscape of mathematics. And the thing is, no one ever does. We didn't. Instead, when Littlewood and I sat down together—in the same London café where he had told me of Mrs. Chase's pregnancy—we laid the situation out in front of us and looked for a reason, one reason, why Ramanujan might be depressed. And we decided that he was depressed because Trinity had failed to elect him to a fellowship. Ergo, in order to keep him going until next October, when we could once again put him up for a fellowship, we would have to replenish his self-esteem. Ergo we would have to arrange for honorifics to rain down on him. As we saw it, powerful institutions would be induced to affirm his worth, his spirits would revive, and he would go back to work. Then the "problem" would be solved.

Now, of course, I see that our approach was hopelessly naïve—and

I think, in our hearts, we knew it. Both of us disdained honorifics. We admitted as much, even as we acknowledged that ours was the luxurious disdain of those who, having won the prize, can afford to dismiss it. Nor can we have failed to recognize the likely futility of a "cure" that fixated on one cause of the malady while ignoring all the others.

Nonetheless we set ourselves, with alacrity, to the task at hand. First we got Ramanujan elected to the London Mathematical Society. Then we proposed his name to the Cambridge Philosophical Society. The first election went through quickly, in December. I wired him—he was in another sanatorium by then—and his response, while enthusiastic, was muted. For though these elections, we knew, would bolster our case when we brought his name up at the fellowship meeting next October, we also knew that neither was sufficient to haul our friend out of his torpor. If we were to solve the Ramanujan problem, a more substantial change would have to be brought about, and this would be to have him elected an F.R.S.

Let me try to give you some idea of what it means, in England, to be named an F.R.S. For any kind of scientist, it is the highest honor in the land. Each year over a hundred candidates are put up, in all disciplines, of which at most fifteen are elected. Rarely is a man elected who is under thirty. When I was elected, I was thirty-three. So was Littlewood.

We considered Ramanujan's chances. What he had going for him was his obvious, indisputable genius. What he had going against him was his youth—he was just twenty-nine—and the fact that he was Indian. In its history the Royal Society had only ever had one Indian member. In all probability, we reasoned, he would not be elected. Still, we decided to float his name. After all, if we failed, he need never know we had made the effort. And if we succeeded, it might be just the thing to save him.

Just then, the president of the Royal Society was the physicist Thomson. He was the discoverer of the electron (hence his nickname, "Atom"), and in a few months he would succeed Butler as the Master of Trinity. I knew him well enough that I could write to him on Ramanujan's behalf. In my letter, I tried to impress upon him the tenuousness of Ramanujan's situation. While I believed that he would probably be alive in a year's time, I could not guarantee it. And though

I felt hesitant about rushing a fellowship for which, under ordinary circumstances, he would have been considered too young; the fragility of his health and of his spirit, in my view, argued for an exception to be made. Of his merit there was no doubt; he was vastly more qualified than any other mathematical candidate.

Much to my relief, the tactic worked. In February 1918, Ramanujan was simultaneously elected a fellow of the Cambridge Philosophical Society and an F.R.S. The coincidence of the two elections led to some confusion, for when I sent him a telegram informing him of the latter, which he did not expect, he confused it with the former, which he did. Indeed, he told me later, he had to read the telegram three times before he understood what it actually said. And even then, until I verified the news for him, he did not believe it.

By this point, Ramanujan was no longer in Cambridge. Instead he was living in a tuberculosis sanatorium called Matlock House in Derbyshire. Why he had settled, in the end, on this particular institution I am not sure. It might have been because Dr. Ram, who worked there, was Indian, or because the cook was supposedly willing to prepare dishes to the tastes of the individual inmates. In any case, his decision came as a relief to me, as it meant that I could go along with the conditions imposed by Scotland Yard without revealing to anyone that Ramanujan had tried to kill himself. All I had to do was to inform the doctors, on whom I supposed I could count for discretion. In November of 1917, then, Ramanujan went by rail to Matlock and stayed there for most of the following year.

Matlock was distinguished, among other things, by its remoteness and difficulty of access; during the war it could be reached only by one train that arrived at eight in the morning. I will not pretend that I liked the place. The structure itself was unforgiving, and had the look of one of those punishing schools to which children in Victorian novels are sent to languish. Back in the last century, it had begun its life as a hydropathic institution, which explained the plethora of disused equipment—various forms of tubing and emptied pools—that littered the grounds. The bathtubs were enormous. A staggered brick wall divided the house from the sloping road that ran alongside it, giving it the look of a prison, which was apposite. It *was* a prison. Let me say this once, clearly and for the record. Ramanujan was not there to be treated for tuberculosis. He was there for the convenience of his friends and to satisfy an informal sentence handed down by a chief inspector at Scotland Yard. And he knew it. He must have known it.

From the beginning of his tenancy, he was unhappy. Dr. Ram, as it turned out, was a bullying sort, who wielded the power I had unwittingly put in his hands with relish. Using as his weapon that authority with which medical men naturally endow themselves, he made it immediately clear that under no circumstance should Ramanujan imagine that he would be allowed to escape Matlock. So long as his doctors declared that he was unwell, he had no freedom, no rights. Nor would he be allowed under *any* circumstances, even an improvement in health, to leave sooner than twelve months from the date of his arrival. Whether Dr. Ram elucidated, or Ramanujan guessed, the true source of this sentence I cannot say. I know only that Ramanujan, much to my perplexity, appears to have accepted Dr. Ram's word as law. At Hill Grove he had rebelled; at Matlock he submitted.

How can I impress upon you the peculiarity of his situation in those months? Let me describe the two visits that I made to him at Matlock. The first took place in January of 1918, the second in July. On the first occasion, I went with Littlewood, who managed to borrow a motor from his brother so that we might avoid any difficulty with the trains. It was a very cold day—snow had fallen the night before—and as we drove through the gates I was startled by the sight of tuberculosis patients sitting outdoors at tables and in chaises longues, swaddled in wool blankets. Ramanujan himself we found inside, but in a room without windows: a sort of verandah that must have served, during Matlock's hydropathic heyday, as a sun room. Although he too was swathed in blankets, he was shivering from the cold, and his teeth were chattering. We had not wired to alert him to our arrival, and when he saw us striding toward him he looked, at first, taken aback. Then he smiled, threw off his blankets, and stood to greet us.

He had lost even more weight, and his face was haggard. We shook hands, and he immediately took us on a tour of the place, which he conducted with that combination of indifference, disgust, and pride that a schoolboy exhibits when performing the same office for his parents. First he showed us his bedroom—bare of any decoration, and, again, freezing—and then the dining room with its long refectory tables and jugs of cold milk, and then a sort of sitting room cum library, the shelves of which were stocked almost entirely with detective thrillers. Finally he introduced us to Dr. Kincaid, the director of the place, a mild-seeming man in his fifties who greeted us with the bored cheerfulness of a headmaster. At Dr. Kincaid's suggestion we returned to the open verandah and had tea. By now Littlewood and I were both extremely cold, even though we had on coats and gloves, and we drank the hot tea fast. Other patients were also lying about on the verandah; they stared at us, and our tea, with envy.

Having first congratulated him on his being named an F.R.S., we asked Ramanujan how he was faring. I will admit that I hoped he would answer by declaring brightly that his health had improved, or, better yet, pull from his pocket some sheets of paper scrawled with mathematical figures. Instead he began to complain. First he complained about the cold. When he had arrived at Matlock, he said, he had been allowed to sit for a few hours before what the staff called a "welcome fire." Since then, however, he had been allowed no fires at all. Even when he asked Dr. Kincaid to provide him with a fire for an hour or two each day, so that he might work on his mathematics, Dr. Kincaid refused. His fingers got so cold he could not hold a pencil.

Next was the food. Despite what he had been promised, the cook had *not* proven amenable to his dietary requirements. She had spoiled the pappadums that one of his friends had sent him, and claimed that she had no butter in which to fry potatoes for him. Mostly he subsisted on bread and milk. Every day the nurses tried to impose oatmeal and porridge on him, both of which he despised. An effort at curried rice had been disastrous, as the rice had arrived so undercooked as to be inedible. Even plain boiled rice the cook could not make properly.

Even in the best of circumstances, there is something pathetic about the grumblings of the invalid, in that they reveal the bereftness of his world, the degree to which his life has been systematically reduced to a ceaseless pursuit of the most basic comforts. And in Ramanujan's case, illness was even less a factor than in most. For if his efforts to satisfy his needs for warmth and for food now consumed his attention, it was mostly because Matlock House deprived him deliberately of those necessities for no good reason. Cold weather and cold milk might benefit the tubercular patient, but they did not benefit Ramanujan, whose condition, in any case, remained the same, and who still showed no symptoms of the disease.

What disturbed me most was his sour, scowling tone. After all, this was the same man who had laughed at *Was It the Lobster?*, who had sat on the *pial* of his mother's house and deduced, entirely without instruction, the Prime Number Theorem. He was an F.R.S.! And now here he sat on another sort of *pial*, and all he could talk about was his dislike of macaroni custard. If there was some cheese in it, he said, it might be tolerable. But the cook *claimed* she could find no cheese, just as she *claimed* she could find no bananas. Whereas Chatterjee had written to him the other day that in Cambridge he could still buy bananas for 4d. each. Well, if you could get bananas in Cambridge, why couldn't you get bananas in Matlock? Littlewood promised that as soon as he got back to London he would arrange for some bananas to be sent on.

After a suitable pause we asked him how his work was going. At this Ramanujan leaned in close, as if to deliver a confidence. "I have discovered," he said, "that there is one room in the place that is always kept very warm, and that is the bathroom. And so every afternoon I go into the bathroom with my notebook and pencil and lock the door. Then, for a short while, I am able to do some work."

"And what work are you doing?"

"Still partitions." And he started talking. As he did—Littlewood told me later that he noticed it as well—his face changed entirely. I have no recollection at all what he said—I suppose it must have been some quite trivial point he was making, the sort to which, at Cambridge, I would have responded with a raised eyebrow or a comic yawn, or not responded at all. Only we were not at Cambridge—Littlewood and I knew perfectly well what our function was—and so we reacted with the sort of exaggerated enthusiasm one usually reserves for shy children who need to be "brought out." We opened our eyes wide, we opened our mouths and raised our hands into the air and begged him to go on. And as he did, much to our surprise and regret, his spirits, rather than rising, sank. I suppose he must have recognized the ruse. "If only I could have more time in the bathroom!" he lamented. "But there is a lady called Mrs. Ripon, and it seems that she is out to bedevil me. Every time I go in there, and get settled, she starts banging on the door, wanting her bath. Oh, I wish she would leave, or die! She had a terrible coughing fit last week, so I was hopeful . . ."

We left soon after. On the way back to London we did not speak much. Each of us had private troubles to contemplate. Much else was wrong in our lives besides the poor Indian trapped in a dismal hydro in Derbyshire. Others rode in that car too, a woman who lived in Treen and a soldier who might very well have been dead.

That spring, the Russell affair erupted again. In February, Russell published his notorious article in the *Tribunal*, in which he wrote that whether or not the American garrison, then en route to Europe, proved "efficient against the Germans," they would "no doubt be capable of intimidating strikers, an occupation to which the American Army is accustomed at home." This reckless sentence resulted in a visit to his flat by two detectives, his subsequent arrest on the charge of making "certain statements likely to prejudice His Majesty's relations with the United States of America," his conviction on that charge, and a sentence of six months in Brixton prison, at the gates of which he arrived early in May in a taxi. Prison life seemed to suit him. The sameness of the days, he said, made him wonder if his true vocation was to be a monk in a contemplative order, and he got a lot of philosophical writing done. In the meantime, at Trinity, Thomson was inducted as the new master, and while we hoped his arrival (and Butler's departure) would help our case, we didn't bank on it.

So far as the war went, the tide appeared to be turning against Germany. For any Englishman who was alive then—even a pacifist like me—it is still a humiliating thing to admit that this was entirely due to the arrival of you Americans. Yet the fact is, your troops made a huge difference, and the day that news drifted back to Cambridge of your victory at Cantigny is one I shall never forget. It was the end of May—what should have been the season of balls—and while I recall working hard to hold back in myself any emotion as reckless as optimism, I also recall thinking, "Yes, the war will end. There will once again be life without war." Make no mistake, our troubles continued. Young men kept dying, while at Cambridge a perfectly benign librarian named Dingwall was fired for his antiwar views. And yet the charge in the air was as distinct as the smell of the summer stealing back into England and brushing away the last dirty snow piles that have survived the spring. This, I recognized, was what it felt like to be on the winning side, and though I didn't give up my pacifist stance, secretly I reveled in the sensation.

In June I returned to Cranleigh, to Gertrude, whose passive stubbornness had proven effective: I had given up any hope of persuading her to sell the house. We were friends again, and resumed our usual summer habits, even the games of Vint with Mrs. Chern, whose niece Emily made a redoubtable fourth. Miss Chern, whose mother was American, was reading mathematics at Newnham—she kept a newspaper photograph of Philippa Fawcett, the woman who had beaten the senior wrangler, over her desk—and asked often after Ramanujan, whom she looked upon as a kind of mysterious prophet. Indeed, many people looked upon him this way. Clippings of articles about him periodically came my way, courtesy of friends in America and Germany and India, articles misrepresenting his achievements and offering somewhat romanticized versions of his story. From reading them, you might have thought he spent his days parading about Cambridge performing feats of mental arithmetic while a retinue of admirers strewed flowers in his wake, when in fact he remained under lock and key at Matlock.

I wondered if he had any idea that he was becoming a famous man, or if sending him some of the articles would contribute to his improvement. For he was improving, if only a little. As Littlewood and I had hoped, the news that he had been elected an F.R.S. boosted his spirits to some degree. Unfortunately, my efforts to persuade Dr. Ram to lift the ban on travel and allow him to go to London for the induction ceremony proved unsuccessful, and he had to write to the Society to ask if the ceremony might be postponed. I don't know that it mattered to him much. The worst of the winter weather had passed, resolving, at least temporarily, the crisis of cold, and though the crisis of food persisted, at least he was working. Indeed, he had entered into a new period of productivity, sending out from the bathrooms of Matlock all sorts of new contributions to partitions theory, including the famous set of identities that you know today as the Rogers-Ramanujan identities.

And that was the least of it. During May and June of 1918 it seemed that every week I would receive at least two or three letters from him, most concerning a paper we were writing together on the expansions of elliptic modular functions, some concerning partitions, still others offering, almost as afterthoughts, those odd, seemingly random arithmetical observations of which he made a specialty. It may seem strange to a non-mathematician that when I remember Ramanujan, I remember, in addition to his barking laugh and his black eyes and his scent, the fact that in a letter from Matlock he once threw off, almost as an aside, the following remarkable equation:

$$\left(1+\tfrac{1}{7}\right)\left(1+\tfrac{1}{11}\right)\left(1+\tfrac{1}{19}\right) = \sqrt{2\left(1-\tfrac{1}{3^2}\right)\left(1-\tfrac{1}{7^2}\right)\left(1-\tfrac{1}{11^2}\right)\left(1-\tfrac{1}{19^2}\right)}$$

And yet it was just such identities upon which his imagination, in its wanderings, would stumble; that he would pick up like curious pieces of fauna to study and preserve and then later, with an ingenuity that always took me by surprise, pull out of his sleeve and reveal to be the missing pieces in complex proofs to which, on the surface at least, they bore no connection. Since he had become ill, I had missed his habit of arriving in my rooms in the mornings bearing the fruits of his nightly labors, the messages that he claimed the goddess had written on his tongue. Now those messages came in the form of letters, and though I lamented his remoteness, nonetheless I was glad to see that he was back on form.

In July, I went to see him, once again, at Matlock. As a treat, I brought along Gertrude and young Emily Chern, who undertook the expedition with the noble gravity of a disciple. Summer weather had remade Matlock, which no longer looked like a resort out of season. The trees were in flower, and the verandah on which we had discovered Ramanujan freezing the January before now provided an amenable and comparatively warm oasis.

He was not alone. With him was a young Indian who stood to greet us almost as soon as we walked through the door. "Mr. Hardy, what an honor," the Indian said, taking my hand. "I am Ram—A. S. Ram, not to be mistaken for Mr. Ramanujan's doctor, who is L. Ram. You may call me S. Ram if you think that will help to avoid confusion."

"How do you do," I said. And I introduced him to Gertrude and Miss Chern, whose hand he kissed.

We sat down. He was a good-looking youth, not tall, with hair at once curlier and finer than most of his countrymen's. As he rapidly explained, he had met Ramanujan back in 1914, when Ramanujan had just arrived in England and both of them were staying at the Indian Students' Hostel on Cromwell Road in London. "We struck up a friendship," he told us, "though very quickly circumstances and the war divided us. Mr. Ramanujan went to Cambridge, and I took a position as an assistant engineer on the North Staffordshire Railway. I have neglected to mention that I come from Cuddalore, near Madras, and have a degree in Civil Engineering from King's College, not the famous King's College of Cambridge but the one at University of London. In any case, when the war broke out, I joined His Majesty's forces, and after sixteen months with the army, a small part of which I spent with the Indian contingent, I was released to work on munitions at Messieurs Palmers Shipbuilding and Iron Company in Jarrow. I continue to be employed there—but you are probably wondering how I came to be back in contact with Mr. Ramanujan and what I am doing here today!" And here he laughed—his laugh high, shrill, distinctly out of tune with his speaking voice, which, though swift, was deep.

He paused, took a breath. Gertrude was staring at him in amazement. I suppose in those gloomy days we were not used to talkers of this vintage.

He went on. As he spoke I glanced at Ramanujan, who was in turn gazing at his own lap. I had hoped he would look healthier than he did; in fact he looked much the same as he had in January—if anything a bit gaunter. In some ways, though, gauntness suited him; brought out his beauty. He was wearing a yellow jumper that contrasted garishly with his skin, and Miss Chern was gazing at him with the sort of adoration that young girls usually reserve for cinema stars. It was obvious that she was not listening to a word that S. Ram was saying.

As for this S. Ram, it was becoming rapidly clear to Gertrude and me what he was: an admirer, a "fan," if you will, who had taken it upon himself to oversee Ramanujan's rehabilitation. And like most "fans," he was really much more interested in exhibiting his own virtue and selflessness than in contributing to the well-being of the friend on whose behalf, he was telling us, he had just taken a "most beastly journey, all night long, the train stopping all the time." For S. Ram, it seemed, had arrived at Matlock two days previously and been put up in an empty room there. "You see," he said, "since the rationing scheme took effect here in England, my good people back in Cuddalore have worried, it seems to me, rather excessively about my condition, and thinking I must be starving they have made it their habit to send me by post parcel after parcel of eatables, so much that it remains a problem how I am to dispose of these and I have had to send a cable home saying 'Stop pause Sending pause Food pause Ram.' I should put in here that while I am a vegetarian, I am not of the same caste as Mr. Ramanujan, thus I have not been, since my arrival here in England, a vegetarian staunch and strict. For instance, I take eggs on occasion, as well as beef tea and sometimes Bovril. You see, I am determined to keep up my health, as lately I have had a bit of luck and, on condition that I pass a test in horse riding in Woolwich at the end of this month, I have been promised release by the army so that I may sail for home on or about the end of September next in order to take up a civilian service position in the Indian Public Works department. So I have of late been eating eggs to keep up my strength in order that I can stick to my work at Palmers and also have some riding practice at Newcastle-Upon-Tyne." Again he paused. Through this whole monologue, it seemed, he had not taken a breath. Would he go on like this all afternoon? I looked to Gertrude for help, which, to my relief, she provided. (As she later explained to me, in her work at St. Catherine's she had become accustomed to dealing with men and women of this stripe, inveterate talkers whose fondness for their own voices was in fact symptomatic of a mental disorder called logorrhea. "Many teachers are logorrheacs," she said.)

Now she turned her steady, prim gaze on S. Ram and said, "Quite fascinating. And tell me, how did you come to renew your acquaintance with Mr. Ramanujan?"

Across the table, S. Ram looked at her with a kind of gratitude; it seemed that he appreciated being brought back to the subject at hand. "You see," he said, "it was the food," and proceeded to explain to us how, upon finding himself with a surplus of "eatables" sent over by his parents, he remembered Ramanujan and his fondness for Madrasi-style dishes. "It was at this point," he said, "that I wrote to you—though you may not recollect it, Mr. Hardy."

"You wrote to me?"

"Yes," S. Ram said. "I wrote inquiring after Mr. Ramanujan's health and to see if he would share some of these foodstuffs with me. And you replied giving me his address as Matlock House, Matlock, Derbyshire."

"Did I? Oh, of course I did."

"And so I began a correspondence with Ramanujan, and in response to his request for some ghee—this is Indian clarified butter, Miss Hardy—I forwarded to him intact two parcels containing three bottles, two of ghee and one of gingelly oil for frying purposes, as well as a small quantity of Madras pickle. As you are no doubt aware of the difficulty and bother involved in sending bottles by post, you can well imagine that it was most convenient merely to send on the packages prepared by my people, already sealed."

"Much more convenient," I said.

"And of course they had sent much more than I could possibly consume. I then proposed a visit. Owing to changes in my schedule I was unable to postpone my holidays to July thirty-first to suit my riding examination, and had no choice but to take the previous fortnight. With nothing particular to do during this holiday I wrote to Ramanujan . . . and now I am here." He smiled. Ramanujan continued to gaze into his lap.

"And I'm sure," Gertrude said, "that Mr. Ramanujan has been grateful for your company. Haven't you, Mr. Ramanujan?"

"Oh yes," Ramanujan said.

"Yes, we have been talking all the time," S. Ram said. "We have discussed all sorts of topics, personal, political, war, Indian social customs, Christian missions, marriage, the university, the Hindu question, and I can say without question that at no time did Mr. Ramanujan seem to me at all to have 'gone off the rails.'"

"Really."

"I have also carefully observed his temperature whenever the nurse takes it and written up charts of his temperature, his eating habits, and his bowel movements. Here, let me show you." And he removed from his jacket pocket three sheets of paper, which he proceeded to unfold on the table. "As you can see, for breakfast yesterday Mr. Ramanujan took scrambled eggs, toast, and tea."

"He ate eggs?"

"Yes. I too was surprised. In our religion, Mr. Hardy, eggs are, shall we say, a gray area. For instance, neither of my parents take eggs, though my brother does. My sister does not, nor does she allow her children to take eggs. I would normally not take eggs were I not in England and needing to keep up my strength for horse riding, but then again I am not of the same caste as Mr. Ramanujan, and thus less scrupulous in the practice of vegetarianism—"

"But you were telling us what he had eaten."

"Yes, of course. Lunch was plain boiled rice with chilies and mustard seeds fried in butter—I should add that there is a new cook at Matlock, much better, Mr. Ramanujan tells me, than her predecessor. Then for tea more or less a repetition of breakfast, and dinner more or less a repetition of lunch with a glass of milk added. Obviously this is not a very toothsome menu, and, in the interest of improving Mr. Ramanujan's situation, I consulted with Dr. L. Ram as to whether he should be prohibited for reasons of health from eating pungent stuff like curry. Dr. L. Ram said that he could eat anything that he liked. But this contradicts what I have been told by friends at Jarrow, namely that chilies and pickles and other pungent items should be avoided by consumptive patients, and in any case the cook here is no expert at Indian cookery. I then asked the matron if I might be allowed to cook something myself for Ramanujan and she was most rude with me, refusing to let me go into the kitchen though she did allow me to write out a recipe to give to the cook. Unfortunately when the cook tried out this recipe—it was for a very simple Madrasi soup, called *rasam*—she botched it."

"How unfortunate."

"Yes. I had hoped to make more of an impression on her in the three days that I was here. And yet I do feel that my presence has been a benefit to Mr. Ramanujan—so much so that I am considering extending my stay for several more days."

"No, Ram, there's no need for that," Ramanujan said.

"Of course not. You must have your holiday," Gertrude added.

"No, I have made up my mind," S. Ram said. "My duty is here. So long as I am free, before I return to India, I shall pledge myself to assisting Mr. Ramanujan and improving his material conditions so that he can continue to bestow upon the world his wonderful capabilities."

Ramanujan put his hand to his forehead. "Are you feeling all right?" I asked, and he waggled his head, and said he hoped we wouldn't mind if he took a short nap; he would meet us again for lunch. Time was not pressing, I assured him; we had taken rooms for the night at an inn in Matlock. So he slunk off, leaving the three of us alone, this time, with the indefatigable Mr. A. S. Ram.

Actually, in lampooning Ram this way, it occurs to me that I am being unfair to him. Gertrude would certainly say I was. For though, it is true, his "logorrhea" could be fatiguing, he meant well, and may have done more actually to help Ramanujan than anyone else who came into his orbit during the years he spent in England, including myself. For instance, as was becoming quickly clear, he took a different—and decidedly more Indian—view of Ramanujan's case to mine and Littlewood's; that is to say, where we saw the solution to "the Ramanujan problem" in terms of approbation, he saw it in terms of food. "I have been a bit harsh with him," he told us, "and tried to impress upon him that he must cease to be cranky and headstrong. More important, he must choose between controlling his palate or killing himself. So what that he does not like porridge or oatmeal? I do not like porridge or oatmeal. Yet I have learned to stomach porridge and oatmeal because I want to be strong in order to pass my test in horse riding. And he must learn to stomach them too. He cannot live on pickles and chilies and rice. He must drink more milk. The other day we heard Dr. Ram tell a patient, 'You must take milk or you will go to hell!' "

"Really."

"Indeed. And though I can help him to a certain degree—I shall seek out for him tinned maize, which is very hard to get but healthy, and, if I can, desiccated coconut, as opposed the moist coconut kernel from which most coconut cakes and biscuits are made . . . this is very different from what we are used to in South India, where a dish that I grew up eating—and Ramanujan too, I suspect—was a delicious coconut chutney. We would eat this with *sambar*. Do you know *sambar*? It is a stew of vegetables spiced with—"

"You were saying how you might help him?"

"Oh yes. Well, I can get him some cashew kernels too, and of course I shall share with him the provisions sent by my people, but in the end how he fares is up to him. He must eat plenty of porridge, tomatoes, bananas if he can get them, macaroni and cream. But unless I am here to force him, I fear he will continue to take only boiled rice with chilies. So I have thought that it would be best if he were to leave Matlock for another institution."

"An interesting idea," I said. "Unfortunately his friends at Cambridge sought in vain, last year, for a sanatorium that served vegetarian food."

"They are correct. There is none. And here the cook is mostly unhelpful. For instance, a friend sent him some—*aplams*, we call them, they are more often called pappadum—they are good for him to eat, not too pungent or acidic or sour. They simply want frying in oil, exactly like chips, but when I arrived I discovered that Ramanujan was eating these, along with some dried vegetables, raw, and the bottles of ghee and gingelly oil that I had sent him were unopened. He says he prefers to eat these things raw, but this is just to protect the cook. No, he must go elsewhere. I have three proposals to make."

"What are they?"

"The first is sending him to Southern France or Italy. If this is permitted he can be moved in a Red Cross carriage and a hospital ship. The climate of Italy would no doubt help him."

"I don't think that would be practical before the war ends."

"The second is that we obtain him an Indian soldier to act as his cook. I think we could propose this to the military, and while it might be argued that requisitioning a soldier to act as a cook would be misusing soldiers, it is worth pointing out how many soldiers are now on munitions like myself, in effect doing civilian jobs. I daresay I could probably get a hold of one or two *lascars*—colored workers on merchant marine ships—there are many knocking about in Newcastle, but these are highly unreliable, even though some are quite good cooks, and they would likely desert Ramanujan as swiftly as they desert their ships."

"What is the third alternative?"

"To move him to an institution in London. My sense is that he is pretty keen to be in London, as there he could easily obtain Indian condiments and dishes. Of course I am not entirely convinced that is a good idea—he might do irreparable harm to his stomach, gorging on spicy foods and sweetmeats. And yet if he would be happier in London . . . I don't know if this is pertinent, but in the course of my military training, I passed the second year's examination in ambulance and first aid work, and for Ramanujan's sake, I would not mind taking the qualifying exam in sick nursing, in which case I might put off my departure—"

"No, I don't think that will be necessary," I said. "We don't want you to jeopardize your career. Still, we might look into your suggestion of finding a place for him in London." After all, though Scotland

Yard had demanded that Ramanujan must spend a year in an institution, they had not specified that it be a particular institution.

"But would London be the best place for his stomach?"

"There are occasions," Gertrude put in, "when the condition of a man's heart must be put ahead of the condition of his stomach."

This point was not one against which S. Ram seemed able to muster an argument, and he agreed to help us. As I subsequently learned, he left Matlock the next morning for London (Ramanujan was greatly relieved), where he proceeded to make a tour of every nursing home and private hospital in the city and, based on his findings, drew up a list of what he considered the ten most likely to suit Ramanujan's needs. Of these, the one he preferred, for its food and the quality of its beds, as much as for the medical attentions it promised, was a hospital called Fitzroy House. And so it was to Fitzroy House, early in August, that we moved Ramanujan, carrying him in Miss Chern's cousin's motor car in order to insure him a comfortable ride.

Fitzroy House was located on Fitzroy Square, off Euston Road, and within walking distance of Regent's park and Ramanujan's beloved zoo. In contrast to Matlock, the severe façade of which suggested a public school or an orphanage, it had a shabby, genteel air about it. The rooms, with their Persian carpets and chintz curtains, reminded me of the ones in Mrs. Chern's house. Ramanujan's was crowded with furniture, including an elaborately frilled lamp hanging from its ceiling, a bureau with an attached mirror, and a sort of mechanical armchair, covered in brocade, that stretched out into a chaise longue when you pushed a button. In this last contraption he seemed to take particular pleasure. On more than one occasion when I came to visit him, I found him spread out on the thing, or opening and closing it in an effort to deduce the mechanism by which it operated.

Yet the differences between Fitzroy and Matlock were more than decorative; they were intrinsic. For whereas Matlock was a sanatorium specializing in the treatment of tuberculosis, Fitzroy was simply a hospital catering to the wealthy. It had no doctors on its staff; the patients brought their own. The nurses wore aprons that made them look like maids. All told it was a gentle and indifferent place. Not here would a doctor be likely to tell a patient that if he did not drink his milk, he would go to hell. Instead the patients ate and drank what they liked. Most of his meals Ramanujan ordered from a nearby Indian restaurant, which sent the dishes over in a peculiar stacked arrangement of round tin boxes fitted with a handle that he called a "tiffin bell." First he would unpack the boxes and then range round him his tray. One contained rice, one pickle, one some variety of curried vegetables, and the fourth a peculiar whole wheat flat bread in which he would wrap mixtures of the other three. If he was having this meal during the day, he would refer to it as his "tiffin." If he was having it in the evening (which was more rare), he would call it his "dinner." If I happened to be visiting, I would sometimes watch him eat, or even share the meals with him, and wonder what S. Ram would think, to learn that Ramanujan was partaking of such "pungent eatables." No matter what damage it might have been doing to his stomach, however, the food seemed to lift his spirits, and this was the thing that mattered.

He began to work again. When the weather grew cold—as it did, sometimes, even in September—he would be given a fire in his room. No longer was exposure to the elements part of his treatment. For by now, I think, it had become obvious to all of us who knew him that Ramanujan was not, in fact, suffering from tuberculosis at all, and that the regimen imposed upon him at Matlock, far from doing him any good, might have been doing him harm. Now his mood was brighter, but his physical condition had deteriorated. The feverish attacks, after a long period of leveling off, began to increase in both frequency and intensity. He complained of rheumatic pains, and continued to lose weight, though he was eating more, and better.

Once again, a fleet of doctors was called in. The old warhorses, gastric ulcer and liver cancer, were trotted out and dismissed, the mysterious "Eastern germ" was again invoked; and a doctor named Bolton declared that both Ramanujan's fever and his rheumatic pains were due to his teeth and could be cured by extraction. Fortunately the dentist who was supposed to perform the extraction couldn't come, saving Ramanujan's teeth, and paving the way for yet another doctor to propose yet another theory, that Ramanujan was suffering from lead poisoning, which might have made sense had there been any evidence that he had been consuming lead. Theory after theory . . . and all of them Ramanujan greeted with a kind of placid indifference. The truth was, I think he had become habituated to his illness. He sought neither cause nor cure. He was preparing to die.

One afternoon in September I took him to the zoo. The American air assault had just begun, and in London there was a feeling of optimism in the air that no one seemed quite sure how to exploit. Bus conductors (women, most of them) and nurses and mathematics professors handled it gingerly, the way an old bachelor might handle a baby. Ramanujan was waiting in the sitting room of Fitzroy House when I arrived, dressed in one of his old suits. The jacket hung off him, and I realized how rarely, in recent weeks, I had seen him wearing anything but pyjamas. As a surprise, I had brought Littlewood along. He was in uniform, which made a great impression on Ramanujan, and we headed off together jovially—on foot, at Ramanujan's insistence, though I made him promise to alert me if he flagged so that I could hail a cab. He did not flag, though, and twenty minutes later we were walking through the zoo.

It was a warm afternoon. Mothers were out with children, and a man was selling balloons. It occurred to me that it had been a long time since I'd seen a balloon, and this reflection made me recognize the degree to which, for years, we had been deliberately draining our daily lives of color and light. Today, though, there were balloons everywhere, reds and greens and bright oranges. Children were running down the corridors between the cages, the colored balls were colliding in the sky like the bombers over France. I looked at Ramanujan, wondering if all that color would remind him of home, of that more vivid landscape of which he sometimes spoke, all hot pinks and gilt and silver thread. To my surprise, though, he seemed not even to notice the balloons. Instead his attention was fixed on the animals, some of whom he greeted by name. Though he had not seen them for years, he remembered them, in particular an elderly giraffe and a lion named Geraldine. Yet there was one animal he was particularly keen to visit, and to this creature's cage Littlewood led him with the expertise of a jungle guide. Like children, they stood with their hands on the bars, and Ramanujan, his face open with simple astonishment, smiled and said, "Winnie, how big you've got!"

It was true. The cub he had known was now a huge black bear, and was sitting in a corner of her cage picking nits out of her fur. If she remembered Ramanujan, she did not show it. She did not even acknowledge him. Instead she focused on her nits, occasionally letting out a grumble that sounded like a belch. And still Ramanujan smiled. "I remember the first time I saw her," he said. "She was just so—" And he held his hand at the level of the abdomen where his pain resided.

Afterward, we went and took tea I tried to remember the last time the three of us had been alone together, and realized that it must have been before the war started, during Ramanujan's brief summer of happiness, his "Indian summer"—the words came to my lips almost before they came to my mind. "Remember your Indian summer, Ramanujan?" I asked. And to my relief, he laughed, and said that he did: the balls, and the tripos results being posted, and *Was It the Lobster?* Then, for an hour or so, until Littlewood had to return to his post, we talked about the zeta function. We talked about Mrs. Bixby, and Ethel, and Ananda Rao. I told Littlewood about S. Ram—"Rarely in my life have I met anyone who talked quite that much," I said—and Ramanujan, with great enthusiasm, said, "But I just got a letter from him!"

"Is he back in India?"

"Yes, he arrived two weeks ago."

"Thank goodness. How long is the letter?"

"It is twenty-seven pages long. Almost the entirety of it consists of advice about food—what I should take, what I should not. It seems he has been consulting doctors in Madras about my case."

"What a funny man he is."

"Yes. At the end of the letter he wrote, 'Now then hurry up and begin eating and devouring plenty and get fat. That is a good boy.'" Ramanujan sipped from his teacup. "You know he wanted to take me to India with him. He promised he would care for me on the voyage. It was all I could do to stop him from buying me a ticket."

"Did you ever consider going with him?" Littlewood asked.

"I would have had to jump off the boat."

We laughed. A silence fell. Then Littlewood said, "Well, take his advice. Get well, get fat, come back to Trinity. We've much work to do. We still haven't proven the Riemann hypothesis."

"Yet, but I think I must return to India when the war ends," Ramanujan said. "At least to see my wife . . ."

"Of course," I said. "A long visit."

"A long visit," Littlewood repeated.

And Ramanujan stared into the dregs of his tea.

In October, we put him up a second time for a Trinity fellowship. It was a tricky business. Given what had happened the year before,

Littlewood thought there would be a greater likelihood of Ramanujan being elected if he, rather than I, proposed him. As it happened, Littlewood was in Cambridge himself right then, recuperating from a concussion he had suffered when, he claimed, a box of bullets had fallen on his head; my guess was that in fact he had got drunk and fallen, and then dreamed up the box of bullets to excuse the injury.

We had our work cut out for us. There was at the time a cabal of Trinity fellows who considered it their duty to oppose Ramanujan's candidacy on racial grounds. As it happened, Littlewood had a spy in the enemy camp, his old tutor Herman, who also opposed Ramanujan but was too naïve to dissemble. From him we learned the worst. R. V. Laurence, for instance, had said that he would sooner resign than see a black man made a fellow of Trinity. His allies, seizing on rumors of the suicide attempt, pointed to a statute prohibiting the "medically insane" from being named to fellowships. Even Ramanujan's status as an F.R.S. these swines managed to pervert into a "dirty trick" perpetrated by Littlewood and me purely to put pressure on Trinity. As if we had the power to manipulate the Royal Society for our own ends . . . And yet I have learned over the years that prejudices are bred in the bone. Neither logic nor pleading will ever prevail over them. Such an enemy you can only fight on his own dirty terms.

Thanks to Herman, we had one advantage: we knew what tactics would be brought to bear, and this meant that we could, at the very least, arm ourselves. Accordingly Littlewood obtained certificates from two doctors declaring that Ramanujan's mental state was sound—certificates that, in the end, didn't even have to be read. For the vote, much to my surprise and relief, went in our favor, despite Littlewood's absence from the meeting on the grounds that he was "indisposed." Or perhaps his absence helped. Herman, as Littlewood's representative, read out a report that he had prepared, detailing Ramanujan's achievements and culminating in his election as an F.R.S. His being an F.R.S. did the trick, I think, not because the title in and of itself impressed the fellows, but because they foresaw the bad publicity that might ensue should an F.R.S. be voted down. Thus Ramanujan became the first Indian to be elected a fellow of Trinity.

Littlewood brought me the news. Afterward, as I was hurrying to send a telegram to Ramanujan, I ran into McTaggart, creeping as usual along a wall. "It is the thin end of the wedge," he said; then, before I could answer, he slunk away to where he had parked his tricycle.

I sent the telegram. The next day a letter arrived from Fitzroy House, asking me to thank Littlewood and Major MacMahon on Ramanujan's behalf. All told, his response was more muted than I might have hoped, and certainly less resonant with joy than it would have been had he been elected a year earlier. "I heard that in some colleges there are two kinds of fellowships," he wrote, "one lasting for two to three years and the other for five or six years. If that is so in Trinity, is mine the first or the second kind?" As it happened, the fellowship was for six years, as I immediately told him. At the time I assumed that he wanted the assurance because he hoped to stay at Trinity as long as he could, though now I wonder if, already, he was thinking of his family and what might become of them after he died.

The most interesting part of the letter was mathematical. Ramanujan, as we suspected, was working again—and working on partitions. He had come up, he said, with some new ideas about what he called "congruences" in the number of partitions for integers ending in 4 and 9. As he explained, if you start with the number 4, the partition number for every 5th integer will be divisible by 5. For instance, $p(n)$ for 4 is 5, $p(n)$ for 9 is 30, and $p(n)$ for 14 is 135. Likewise if you start with 5, $p(n)$ for every 7th integer will be divisible by 7. And though Ramanujan had not considered the case of 11 "due to tediousness," his hunch was that, if you start with 6, $p(n)$ for every 11th integer thereafter will be divisible by 11. As, indeed, turned out to be the case. The next number to test, of course, would be 7, after which, according to Ramanujan's theory, every 13th integer would be divisible by 13. Unfortunately the theory broke apart at 7, as the partition number for 20 (7 + 13) is 627 and the prime factors of 627 are 19, 11, and 3. Once again, mathematics had tantalized us with a pattern, only to snatch it away. Really, it was rather like dealing with God.

How the story speeds up as it nears its end! Have you noticed the way the first days of a holiday pass so much more slowly than the last? That was how it felt in the autumn of 1918. True, some diehards continued to brood, murmuring of a German plot to unleash a secret weapon, some monstrosity so powerful that none could imagine its destructive potential. Instead the Germans folded. Austria sent a peace note to Woodrow Wilson, Ludendorff resigned, and it was over. I was in Cambridge at the time. I remember hearing, from my rooms, a distant roaring in which I felt I had no right to take part, not only because I had opposed the war from the beginning but also because I did not much feel like roaring. A horrific fire finally put out, a flow of blood finally staunched: are these really things to cheer about? I don't think so. So I stayed in my rooms, and at midnight, when I went to bed, I fell into a sleep so deep it seemed to pass in a minute. By the time I woke, the sun was coming through the curtains, it was ten o'clock in the morning, and for the first time in four years I didn't feel tired.

That afternoon Miss Chern came to see me. She had heard the news of Ramanujan's fellowship and wondered how she might best congratulate him. I gave her tea, and she showed me her album of newspaper clippings, most of them collected in America, where she had spent much of her girlhood. There was an article from the *New York Times*—an old one, given her by her father—in which a friend of Philippa Fawcett provided an intimate account of her victory in the Tripos. A second from the *New York Times*—provided by the Marconi Transatlantic Wireless Telegraph—announced Ramanujan's arrival in Cambridge in April of 1914 and included an interview with me that I had no memory of giving. Two others—from the *Washington Post* and the *Christian Science Monitor*—also announced Ramanujan's arrival in England, yet what was curious about these articles was that they laid emphasis less on his work in number theory than on his ability to perform lightning-quick calculations. The first compared him to a Tamil boy named Arumogan of whom I had never heard, and who had been the subject of a specially convened meeting of the Royal Asiatic Society. "Multiply 45,989 by 864,726," the second began.

Well, that problem wouldn't flabbergast S. Ramanujan, a young Hindu, who last year left India and entered Cambridge University. It would take him only a few seconds to multiply 45,989 by 864,726. In less time than that he could add 8,396,497,713,826 and 96,268,393. In the time it would take the average schoolboy to divide 31,021 by 12, Ramanujan could find the fifth root of 69,343,957, or give the correct answer to the problem: What weight of water is there in a room flooded 2 feet deep, the room being 18 feet 9 inches by 13 feet 4 inches, and a cubic foot of water weighing 62 ½ pounds?

This article concluded by comparing Ramanujan to an American "boy calculator" known as "Marvelous Griffith." "Could Ramanujan really perform those calculations?" Miss Chern asked, and I laughed. It seemed to me unlikely; more to the point, it seemed to me beside the point. And I wondered, not for the last time, if this was how my friend would end up being remembered: not as a genius of the first rank, but as a circus sideshow attraction, the freak at whom members of the audience throw numbers like fish for him to gobble, only to watch as, without recourse to pen and paper, he spits out the sums.

I was not getting into London very often. Still, we wrote to each other at least twice weekly. It seemed that Ramanujan had entered into another one of those spells of productivity that punctuated his list-lessness, and was working on a dozen things at once: partitions, Waring's problem for fourth powers, theta functions. Once again he raised the possibility of his returning to India—as the war was over, there was no longer any risk (at least any non-spiritual risk) in crossing the ocean—and with his permission I wrote to Madras on his behalf. As I saw it, there was no reason for him to stay if he wanted to leave. His fellowship did not require him to be in residence at Trinity, nor did it bind him to any particular obligations. And while he continued to refer to the impending trip as "a visit," I think I knew, even then, that he was going to die.

He gained a little weight. The fevers, he said, had ceased to be irregular. He no longer suffered rheumatic pains. Perhaps for this reason, in November he left Fitzroy House and moved into a nursing hostel called Colinette House in Putney. This was an altogether more modest (and cheaper) affair than Fitzroy—a stalwart brick house with eight bedrooms, fully detached and indistinguishable from most of the others that lined Colinette Road until you stepped inside and saw the array of medical equipment piled in the sitting room. An impressive staircase led to the first floor, and to Ramanujan's room, which had a bow window and overlooked the front garden. The ceilings were high and the moldings elaborate. At the time of his stay, he was one of only three residents, the others being a retired colonel whose dementia led him to believe that he was still in Mangalore and an elderly widow named Mrs. Featherstonehaugh who took a curious liking to Rama-nujan and amused him when she explained that her name was pronounced "Fanshawe."

Because I could get there quickly from Pimlico, I visited Ramanujan more often at Colinette House than I had at Fitzroy Square. Usually I took a taxi. His health had stabilized by then, if only into an unvarying routine of sickness; much as during the months he'd spent on Thompson's Lane, feverish nights gave way to peaceful, tired days. And yet he was less irritable and obstinate than he had been at Matlock. Every morning he ate eggs for breakfast, and when one morning I interrupted him in the middle of his meal—I had come to help him sort through some financial details—he looked up at me from his plate and waggled his head in the old way, as if to say: yes, I have given up. It doesn't matter so much anymore. Eggs no longer matter.

Then his health, with the onset of the cold weather, started to decline. At least he was allowed a fire. When I arrived one morning in January, I was surprised to find him still in bed. He greeted me with a wave, and told me that he had received a letter from the University of Madras—the same university that had once shut its doors in his face—offering him an income of £250 per annum upon his return to India—this on top of the same sum from Trinity. "But Ramanujan, that's marvelous!" I said, taking my coat off and sitting down. "Five hundred pounds a year will be a fortune in India. You'll be a rich man."

"Yes, that is the trouble," he replied.

"How so?" I said.

"I don't know what I will do with so much money. It is too much."

"But you need not spend it all on yourself. You may have children. And whatever's left over you can give to charities."

"Yes, that is exactly what I was thinking," he said. "Tell me, Hardy, would you mind writing out a letter for me? I feel too weak to hold a pencil."

"Of course." I took some stationery from the table. "To whom is the letter to be addressed?"

"To Dewsbury, the registrar at Madras."

"Ramanujan, you're not going to—"

"Please, will you write it?"

"But you'd be a fool to tell them to lower the offer—"

"Please do as I ask."

I heaved a sigh—loud enough, I hoped, to signal my disapproval. Then I said, "All right," and took out a pencil. "I'm ready. Go."

"Dear Mr. Dewsbury," he dictated, "I beg to acknowledge the receipt of your letter of 9th December 1918, and gratefully accept the very generous help which the University offers me."

"Very good," I said.

"I feel, however, that after my return to India, which I expect to happen as soon as arrangements can be made, the total amount of money to which I shall be entitled will be much more than I shall require. I should hope that, after my expenses in England have been paid, £50 a year will be paid to my parents and that the surplus, after my necessary expenses are met, should be used for some educational purpose, such in particular as the reduction of school fees for poor boys and orphans and provision of books in school."

"Very generous, but wouldn't you like to control how the money is disbursed?"

"No doubt it will be possible to make an arrangement about this after my return. I feel very sorry that, as I have not been well, I have not been able to do so much mathematics during the last two years as before. I hope that I shall soon be able to do more and will certainly do my best to deserve the help that has been given me. I beg to remain, sir, your most obedient servant, etc., etc."

"Etc., etc.," I repeated, handing him the letter to sign.

"Are you sure about this?" I asked, putting it into the envelope.

"I am sure," he said.

Obviously he was determined to keep the money out of his parents' hands.

I suppose now I might as well tell the anecdote. I don't much like to tell it these days. It's been told too much; it feels as if it no longer belongs to me.

Any speculation, mathematical or otherwise, as to what might have lain behind Ramanujan's answer I leave to you to ferret out.

I had gone to see him in Putney. I suppose this must have been in February, a month or so before he boarded the ship for home. And he must have been feeling poorly, because the curtains were drawn, and he only kept the curtains drawn on bad days.

He was in bed, and I sat in the chair up next to his bed. He said nothing, and I had nothing particular to tell him. No special motive lay behind my visit. Still, I felt the need to break the silence. So I said, "The taxi I took from Pimlico today had the number 1729. It seemed to me a rather dull number."

Then Ramanujan smiled. "No, Hardy," he said. "It is a very interesting number. It is the smallest number expressible as the sum of two cubes in two different ways."

You may do the maths now if you like. You will see that he is right. 1729 can be written as $12^3 + 1^3$. But it can also be written as $10^3 + 9^3$.

If only the *Christian Science Monitor* had been present!

Here Ramanujan's story ceases to be mine. Of what remained of his life—a little over a year—I can tell you almost nothing, because he lived these months out in India, while I remained in England.

What I know I picked up secondhand. It seems that instead of getting better upon his return to India, as he was supposed to, he got worse. The university authorities put him up in great luxury, in a series of splendid villas loaned to him for the duration, with a break in the summer during which he was whisked away from the city to the banks of the River Cauvery, on which he had played as a child. Thence back to Madras. What Komalatammal, used to living in a shack with mud walls, must have made of the splendid Raj villa in which her son spent his final months I cannot guess. I have seen a picture of the place. The stairway, its banister carved from teak, descends to a vast sitting room with carved moldings and a granite floor. "Gometra," the house is called, in the suburb of Chetput, which Ramanujan called "Chetpat": in Tamil, "It will happen soon."

Soon enough Janaki arrived with her brother. It will not surprise you to learn that Komalatammal was not remotely glad to see her. She even tried to bar Janaki from the house, but Ramanujan insisted that his wife stay with him, and in deference to his condition, I suppose, his mother held back, or at the very least made a show of having reached an accord with her daughter-in-law. (With what rancid remarks she showered the girl in private I can but guess.) All told, the situation was fraught with tension, and Ramanujan must have felt the unease ricocheting between the two women as they competed for the coveted spot by his bedside. No doubt concern as to who would benefit most from his legacy intensified this frantic contest to see which of the women he would allow to nurse him, to change his sweat-soaked pyjamas, to feed him milk from a spoon.

Now there were no longer those spells of improved health that in England punctuated the long torpor of his sickness. The atlas of his life centered on a mattress low down on the cool granite floor, from which he rose only when the sheets had to be changed. And yet, despite his declining health, he still had intermittent bursts of productivity. During one of these he came up with an idea that I suspect will prove to be among his most fruitful, that of the "mock theta function." This was the subject of his last letter to me, a letter that he wrote in bed, and that consisted entirely of mathematics.

I am told that upon his return, India greeted him as a hero, and that India wept at the news of his demise. Quite an ending to a story that began so modestly, and would in all likelihood still be going on, modestly, had I not intervened.

Had Ramanujan stayed in India—had he survived—he would now be on the brink of fifty. Instead he died at thirty-three.

Tuberculosis was given as the cause.

And what of the others?

With the conclusion of the war, Littlewood reconciled with Mrs. Chase. Another child has been born. I assume it is his.

My sister, dear devoted Gertrude, remains on the faculty of St. Catherine's School to this day.

Daisy and Epée have given rise to several generations of fox terriers.

The Nevilles are in Reading.

Miss Chern is a tutor at Newnham.

Russell was reinstated at Trinity.

True to my word, in 1920 I left Cambridge for Oxford, taught there happily until 1931, then returned, drawn like the proverbial moth to the flame that will singe his wings, to the college where I had begun my career, the college that had perpetually betrayed and bullied me, the college on whose grounds I am fated to end my days.

I still collaborate with Littlewood.

The hospital on the cricket grounds was dismantled.

Thayer I never saw or heard of again.

There is only one story left to share.

Earlier this year—it was April, I believe—I was taking a stroll through Piccadilly Circus. It was late afternoon, a light rain was falling, and as I stepped off the curb onto Coventry Street, a motor-cycle hit me.

Let me admit right now that the accident was entirely my own fault, and not the cyclist's. I wasn't looking where I was going. No doubt my mind, as it is so often these days, was on the Riemann hypothesis.

The next thing I remember I was lying on the pavement a full thirty feet from where I'd been walking. The motorcycle had dragged me that far. And now the cyclist, a fair-haired youth, was gazing anxiously into my eyes. "Are you all right, sir?" he asked. And then his face was gone, replaced by that of a bobby. "Are you all right, sir?" the bobby asked.

"I'm fine," I said.

"There, there," the bobby said, "give the gentleman room, move on, move on."

Then the bobby lifted me, in one motion, onto my feet.

"I think I'm fine," I said. "Just had the wind knocked out of me." No sooner had I said this, though, than my knees crumpled under me, and the bobby had to stop my fall.

A crowd had formed. "Step out of the way," he ordered, and then he led me across the street, out of the rain, until we were standing under the arches of the Prince of Wales Theatre.

"Thank you," I said.

"You ought to look where you're going, sir," he said, propping me up and dusting me off, as if I were a child.

"Yes, I ought to."

"There you are." He stepped back; took off his helmet. "It's Mr. Hardy, isn't it?"

"Yes," I said. "How do you know me?"

"You don't remember me, do you, sir?"

"Should I?" And I looked at his face: the brown eyes, the thick mustache.

Then I did remember.

"Richards."

His mouth broadened into a smile. "That's right, sir. It was me that was there when you came in to fetch Mr. Ramanujan—how long ago was it?"

"I can't think . . . twenty years?"

"A bit less. The autumn of 1917, before the war ended."

"Yes. And what a happy coincidence. I'm glad to see you. I've often wished I'd looked you up, back then."

"Did you now? I wish you had, too. A pity. Still, better late than never, my wife says."

"You're married then?"

"Indeed I am, sir, with three daughters. Funny, though, I always knew I'd run into you one day. I just knew. And now look where we are."

"Yes. In front of the Prince of Wales Theatre."

He smiled. I smiled. Then suddenly his face grew stern. "A sad thing about Mr. Ramanujan, sir. Of course we could see back then he wasn't well. And then I read the obituaries, and I thought, well, now it all makes sense."

"Yes, I suppose it does."

"And to think that he wasn't made an F.R.S. until 1918."

"1918, yes."

"But when you came in, sir, you told us he was already an F.R.S., and that was 1917."

"Oh, did I say that?" And I smiled again—less because I'd been caught out in a lie than because the lie in which I'd been caught out was one that, until that moment, I'd forgotten.

"Well, he was almost an F.R.S."

"So you admit you lied."

"I don't see why it matters."

"Are you suggesting the law doesn't matter, sir?" Richards frowned. "It's a serious business, lying to Scotland Yard, sir. Perjury. I could have you sent up for it."

"Oh, bosh. It was years ago! And besides"—I gestured vaguely toward Coventry Street—"I've just been hit by a motorcycle."

Then Richards laughed. He laughed and laughed. "Had you there, didn't I?" he said.

"Yes, you did," I said.

And then the most extraordinary thing happened. Perhaps it was a hallucination brought on by the shock of the accident—to this day I'm still not sure—but it seemed as if he pushed down on my shoulders. And whether it was because I wanted to, or because I was weak, I sank to my knees.

Suddenly all the noises of the street drained away. I could see the last rays of the sun broadening across a pool of puddled water. I could see, in the distance, umbrellas closing as the rain let up.

Very calmly he put his hands on my head, dug his nails into my scalp, and pulled my face deep into the woolly, animal blackness of his uniform trousers.

Only for a moment. Then he let me go.

"Come on, get up." I stood, still wobbly on my feet. "You'll be wanting to get home now, sir," he said, and, turning me around, he pointed me into the street, the claxons blaring, wet faces smudged in the dusk.

"Thank you," I said. By way of reply, he gave me a gentle push, tipping me over the edge of the pavement onto Coventry Street, toward the stairs that led to the Underground.

5

HARDY STEPPED BACK from the podium. The applause that filled the room was like the sound of rain against the roofs of cars.

Suddenly he was surrounded. Hands shook his, mouths came intolerably close to his face, murmuring congratulations and asking questions. The questions he answered with the voice he had used to deliver the lecture, while inside him the other voice, the secret voice, recalled that night in Pimlico when Gaye's spirit, summoned or conjured from the ether, depending on one's point of view, sat on the edge of his bed and warned him to beware a man in black and the hour of twilight.

As it happened, it was the hour of twilight. Voices to which he could not attach names asked if he wished to rest before dinner, and he said that he would. Others offered to escort him to his hotel, and he waved them away. No, he would go on his own. The walk would do him good. And so, released at last into solitude, he hurried out of New Lecture Hall into the vesperal air; walked fast across commons and amid the shadows of red brick buildings, paying no attention to where he was going. For the point was not to arrive anywhere; it was to put as much distance between himself and the ghosts he had summoned as he could.

Soon he found himself in Harvard Yard. The sight of two undergraduates wearing leather gloves and throwing a ball back and forth arrested his attention. Ever since his first trip to "the States," American baseball had fascinated him. Now he stood on the cement path that cut a diagonal swath across the yard and watched the young men play, his gaze transfixed by the bent posture each assumed as he reached back to throw the ball; the arc that the ball described over the green grass; the satisfying thump when the hard white leather of the ball's surface hit the soft brown leather of the glove. It did not matter that the sun would soon be setting; he knew these young men would play until the last light was drained from the sky, until the twilight was drunk down to its lees.

Why should it still surprise him that he knew so little of Ramanujan? He was too old to believe any longer that he had touched more than a fragment of that vast, infernal mind. None of them had—not Littlewood, not Eric or Alice. Ramanujan had come into their world, and for a time their lives had revolved around him, much as distant planets revolve around a star of which they can discern only the weakest penumbra. And yet that star, for all its remoteness, governs their orbits and regulates their gravity. Even now, dreams of Ramanujan pulled Hardy from sleep each morning. And when he went to bed, a darting radiance suffused his dreams, like the light reflected off a varnished cricket bat, or a Gurkha's raised sword.

SOURCES AND ACKNOWLEDGMENTS

While researching and writing *The Indian Clerk*, I consulted hundreds of sources—and I owe a debt of gratitude to the many historians, archivists, mathematicians, and librarians whose patient work brought these sources to light.

That said, this is a novel based on real events, and—like most novels based on real events—it takes liberties with historical truth, mingles fact and invention, and transforms historical figures into fictional characters. What follows is a brief narrative account of some of the reading that I undertook and where it led.

It is my hope that, after finishing *The Indian Clerk*, some readers may want to learn more about the three remarkable men around whose lives the novel revolves. The best starting place is Robert Kanigel's masterful biography *The Man Who Knew Infinity: A Life of the Genius Ramanujan* (Crown, 1991), which provides not just a lucid and detailed account of Ramanujan's life but of Hardy's as well.

Fortunately for me, by the time I came to write *The Indian Clerk*, most of the primary sources I needed to consult—letters, reminiscences, photographs, documents—had already been brought together in a series of omnibus volumes. Of these, the earliest, published in 1967 (six years after India issued a stamp in Ramanujan's memory), were S. K. Ranganathan's *Ramanujan: The Man and the Mathematician* (Asia Publishing House) and P. K. Srinivasan's two-volume *Ramanujan Memorial Number* (Muthialpet High School), consisting of *Ramanujan: Letters and Reminiscences* and *Ramanujan: An Inspiration*. In 1995 the authoritative *Ramanujan: Letters and Commentary* came out, followed in 2001 by *Ramanujan: Essays and Surveys*. Both were edited (superbly) by Bruce C. Berndt and Robert A. Rankin and published jointly by the London Mathematical Society and the American Mathematical Society.

My account of Ramanujan's illness takes into consideration the exhaustive research on the subject conducted by Robert A. Rankin and Dr. A. B. Young. Their articles—"Ramanujan as a Patient" and "Ramanujan's Illness"—can both be found in *Ramanujan: Essays and Surveys*. I hold with Dr. Young in suspecting that Ramanujan did not, in fact, suffer from tuberculosis, and have based my account of his suicide attempt and its aftermath, in part, on Dr. Young's very interesting detective work.

No lesser writer than Graham Greene praised Hardy's remarkable 1940 memoir, *A Mathematician's Apology*, which remains in print from Cambridge University Press. This volume also contains a moving recollection of Hardy by his friend the novelist C. P. Snow.

Ramanujan: Twelve Lectures on Subjects Suggested by His Life and Work—the text of the lectures that Hardy gave at Harvard in 1936—is available in a reprint edition from AMS Chelsea Publishing, as is *Collected Papers of Srinivasa Ramanujan*, edited by G. H. Hardy, P. V. Seshu Aiyar, and B. M. Wilson. Hardy's collected papers (Oxford University Press, seven volumes) can be found at most university libraries. Of his mathematical texts, the most famous is probably *A Course of Pure Mathematics*, which Cambridge University Press has kept in print all these years.

The best account of the Bertrand Russell affair at Trinity College remains Hardy's own *Bertrand Russell & Trinity*, privately published but available in a reprint edition from Cambridge University Press. Three articles published in *Russell: The Journal of the Bertrand Russell Archives* deepened my understanding of the relationship between Russell and Hardy: Jack Pitt's "Russell and the Cambridge Moral Sciences Club" (New Series, vol. 1, no. 2, winter 1981–82); Paul Delaney's "Russell's Dismissal from Trinity: A Study in High Table Politics" (New Series, vol. 6, no. 1, summer 1986); and I. Grattan-Guinness's "Russell and G. H. Hardy: A Study of Their Relationship" (New Series, vol. 11, no. 2, winter 1991). In addition, I read letters culled from Russell's voluminous correspondence, some of them published by Routledge in *The Selected Letters of Bertrand Russell* (in two volumes, edited by Nicholas Griffin), others, including several from Hardy, made available to me through the generosity of the staff of the Bertrand Russell Archives at McMaster University.

Not surprisingly, given Russell's penchant for wanting to control his intellectual legacy, his autobiography (Atlantic Monthly Press, 1967) tells us less about his dismissal from Trinity than do Ray Monk's *Bertrand Russell: The Spirit of Solitude, 1872–1921* (Free Press, 1996) and Ronald W. Clark's *The Life of Bertrand Russell* (Alfred A. Knopf, 1976).

In researching the Cambridge Apostles, I relied on Paul Levy's deeply considered *Moore: G. E. Moore and the Cambridge Apostles* (Oxford University Press, 1981) and, to a lesser extent, on Richard Deacon's informative but contentious and intermittently homophobic *The Cambridge Apostles: A History of Cambridge University's Elite Intellectual Secret Society* (Farrar, Straus & Giroux, 1985). W. C. Lubenow's *The Cambridge Apostles, 1820–1914* (Cambridge University Press, 1998) also proved to be an invaluable resource. (I am grateful to Professor Lubenow personally for helping me to clarify the murk surrounding the question of whether Hardy did or did not "attest" during World War I.)

Through the letters of the Brethren—in particular Russell, Lytton Strachey, James Strachey, and Rupert Brooke—I gained a sense of what the Society's meetings felt and sounded and smelled like. Many of Lytton Strachey's letters about the Apostles are included in *The Letters of Lytton Strachey*, selected and edited by Paul Levy (Viking, 2005), while Brooke's correspondence with the younger Strachey can be found in *Friends and Apostles: The Correspondence of Rupert Brooke and James Strachey, 1905–1914*, edited by Keith Hale (Yale University Press, 1998). Paul Delaney's *The Neo-Pagans: Rupert Brooke and the Ordeal of Youth* (Free Press, 1987) sheds light not just on Brooke but on his Hungarian rival, Ference Békássy, while Michael Holroyd's magisterial *Lytton Strachey: The New Biography* (W. W. Norton, 2005) merits reading as much because it is an exemplar of the art of the biography as because it offers such a penetrating portrait of its subject. Finally, John Maynard Keynes's memoir "My Early Beliefs," included in *Two Memoirs* (Rupert Hart-Davis, 1949), articulates with pathos and wit G. E. Moore's profound philosophical and moral influence on the Apostles.

In researching J. E. Littlewood, I turned to his own book of memoirs and essays, *A Mathematician's Miscellany* (Methuen, 1953), and Béla Bollobás's *Littlewood's Miscellany* (Cambridge University Press,

1986), which brings the contents of the first book together with other writings by Littlewood and a fascinating recollection of the man by Bollobás himself.

The account of Russell Kerr Gaye's suicide (and its effect on Hardy) derives from Lytton and James Strachey's letters on the subject and, to a lesser extent, from Gaye's obituary in the *Times*, while the story of their cat's illness and the circus lady who caught rats with her teeth comes from Leonard Woolf's memoir *Sowing* (Harcourt, Brace & Co., 1960).

Gertrude Hardy's poem "Lines Written Under Provocation" was published in October 1933 (about thirty years after I attribute it to her in the novel) in *St. Catherine's School Magazine*. Robert Kanigel includes this remarkably spirited piece of satire in *The Man Who Knew Infinity*. Kanigel is also the source for a number of details from Hardy's life that I dramatize in the novel: among them, the "Indian bazaar," the performance of *Twelfth Night*, the conversation with the vicar about the kite, and the tragic story behind Gertrude's glass eye. Kanigel also tracked down the exact puzzle from the *Strand* magazine that Ramanujan solved so quickly.

For those seeking a broad understanding of the world into which Hardy was born (and the war it gave rise to), I cannot recommend highly enough Samuel Hynes's *The Edwardian Turn of Mind* (Princeton University Press, 1968); its lesser-known sequel, *A War Imagined: The First World War and English Culture* (Atheneum, 1990); and Paul Fussell's *The Great War and Modern Memory* (Oxford University Press, twenty-fifth-anniversary edition, 2000).

The attitudes that obtained toward homosexuality in the England of those years are shrewdly interrogated by Graham Robb in *Strangers: Homosexual Love in the Nineteenth Century* (W. W. Norton, 2004) and by Matt Houlbrook in *Queer London: Perils and Pleasures in the Sexual Metropolis, 1918–1957* (University of Chicago Press, 2005). Yet it was from a sequence of novels—Pat Barker's *Regeneration* trilogy (*Regeneration*, *The Eye in the Door*, and *The Ghost Road*, all published by Plume)—that I got the most vivid sense of the ways in which homosexual love was expressed, exploited, and manipulated in England during the Great War.

Luckily for lay readers, four very good books on the Riemann hypothesis have come out in the last four years. Of these, the ones I would recommend most strongly are Marcus du Sautoy's *The Music of the Primes* (HarperCollins, 2003) and Dan Rockmore's *Stalking the Riemann Hypothesis* (Pantheon, 2005). Hardy and Ramanujan make appearances as well in Paul Hoffman's entertaining biography of the mathematician Paul Erdös, *The Man Who Loved Only Numbers* (Hyperion, 1998).

My research on the history of the mathematical tripos and Hardy's battle to abolish it focused on primary sources, including letters to the *Times*, items from that same paper's "University Intelligence" column, and obituaries. I also read—and learned much from—Jeremy Gray's "Mathematics in Cambridge and Beyond," in *Cambridge Minds*, edited by Richard Mason (Cambridge University Press, 1994) and several of the personal essays collected in the three-volume omnibus *Mathematics: People, Problems, Results*, edited by Douglas M. Campbell and John C. Higgins (Wadsworth, 1984): A. R. Forsyth's "Old Tripos Days at Cambridge"; Leonard Roth's "Old Cambridge Days"; J. C. Burkill's "John Edensor Littlewood"; L. J. Mordell's "Hardy's *A Mathematician's Apology*"; and George Pólya's "Some Mathematicians I Have Known."

Speaking of Pólya, the entertaining *Pólya Picture Album: Encounters of a Mathematician* (Birkhäuser, 1987) contains the largest selection of photographs I have found yet of the famously photophobic Hardy.

The story of Philippa Fawcett's victory in the mathematical tripos was mentioned only in passing in the *Times* of London but made much of by the *New York Times*. I am grateful to Jill Lamberton for sharing with me an 1890 letter in which Helen Gladstone described the event to Mary Gladstone Drew.

Much of what D. H. Lawrence says to Hardy in the novel derives from letters that he wrote to David Garnett and Bertrand Russell, before and after his disastrous visit to Cambridge. These can be found in *The Letters of D. H. Lawrence*, volume II, June 1913–1916, edited by George J. Zytaruk and James T. Boulton (Cambridge University Press, 1981). That Lawrence "had a long and friendly discussion" with Hardy during the visit, and that he appears to have liked Hardy uniquely among the many dons he met, is confirmed in a number of sources, including Edward Nehls's

D. H. Lawrence: A Composite Biography (University of Wisconsin Press, 1957–59).

Most of the vegetarian dishes to which I refer really could be found in vegetarian cookbooks of the period. For those interested in exploring this fascinating subject, I would strongly recommend Colin Spencer's *Vegetarianism: A History* (Four Walls Eight Windows, 2002).

Now on to inventions and half-truths:

While my account of Ludwig Wittgenstein's induction into the Apostles is by and large accurate, I moved the event forward three months to accommodate the novel's chronology.

Eric Neville really did have a wife named Alice, whose kindness toward Ramanujan, and concern for his well-being, Ranganathan warmly recalled. That said, there is no reason to suspect that Alice Neville spoke Swedish, fell in love with Ramanujan, worked for Dorothy Buxton, sang Gilbert and Sullivan, or read Israfel.

Israfel did exist; the passages quoted are from her book *Ivory Apes & Peacocks* (At the Sign of the Unicorn, 1899). Dorothy Buxton existed too, and—after devoting the entirety of the First World War to publishing her "Notes from the Foreign Press" in the *Cambridge Magazine*—went on to found the Save the Children Fund with her sister, Eglantyne Jebb.

While Ramanujan's Indian friends at Cambridge included men named Chatterjee, Mahalanobis, and Ananda Rao, there is no reason to suspect that they in any way resemble the fictional characters to whom I have given their names. And though Ramanujan did run away from the dinner he gave in honor of Chatterjee and his fiancée, Ila Rudra, no source suggests that Hardy was present. (Miss Chattopadhyaya was.)

"S. Ram" was, astonishingly enough, a real person. His monologues are derived from the long letters that he wrote to Ramanujan and Hardy.

Although entirely a fiction, Anne Chase is based loosely on "Mrs. Streatfeild," a married resident of Treen with whom Littlewood had a long affair and at least one child. However, the real Littlewood, from what I gather, did not meet Mrs. Streatfeild until after Ramanujan's death.

Thayer is entirely an invention, as is Richards.

I am solely responsible for any other lapses, ornamentations, or imaginative swoons that come to light. The muse of history will probably not forgive them; I hope that the reader will.

For help and support of many kinds, I wish to thank Krishnaswami Alladi of the University of Florida Department of Mathematics; George Andrews; Amy Andrews Alznauer; Liz Calder; Dick Chapman; Vikram Doctor; Maggie Evans; Michael Fishwick; Sunil Mukhi; K. Srinivasa Rao; John Van Hook of the University of Florida Libraries; Greg Villepique; and the generous faculty of Sastra University, Kumbakonam, Tamil Nadu.

For their careful editing of this novel, I am immensely grateful to Colin Dickerman and Beena Kamlani. I am likewise grateful to Prabhakar Ragde for giving the novel such a careful and considerate reading and for correcting some of my more egregious mathematical errors.

I owe a special debt of thanks to the indefatigable R. Balusubramanian ("Balu") of the Institute of Mathematical Sciences, Chennai, who took me for a ride on an electric rickshaw through Triplicane, let me hold Ramanujan's original notebooks in my hands, and introduced me to Janaki's adopted son.

As always, I thank my agents, Jin Auh, Tracy Bohan, and Andrew Wylie, for their unceasing support and encouragement.

Addendum to the paperback edition:

Since the publication of the first edition of *The Indian Clerk*, numerous readers have written to alert me to a variety of small errors—mathematical, grammatical, punctuational, and historical—in the original text. I have made every effort to correct these errors in the paperback edition. These readers have my heartfelt thanks.

A NOTE ON THE AUTHOR

David Leavitt is the author of several novels, including *The Body of Jonah Boyd*, *While England Sleeps*, and *Equal Affections*. A recipient of fellowships from both the John Simon Guggenheim Foundation and the National Endowment for the Arts, he teaches at the University of Florida in Gainesville.

A NOTE ON THE TYPE

The text of this book is set in Linotype Sabon, named after the type founder Jacques Sabon. It was designed by Jan Tschichold and jointly developed by Linotype, Monotype, and Stempel, in response to a need for a typeface to be available in identical form for mechanical hot metal composition and hand composition using foundry type.

Tschichold based his design for Sabon roman on a font engraved by Garamond, and Sabon italic on a font by Granjon. It was first used in 1966 and has proved an enduring modern classic.

B L O O M S B U R Y

Also available by David Leavitt

The Body of Jonah Boyd

It's 1969 and Denny is on her way to the annual Thanksgiving dinner at the Wrights' plush campus house. Denny is more nervous than usual because she has recently begun an affair with Dr Ernest Wright, a psychology professor who happens to be her boss. Needless to say, Ernest's wife Nancy doesn't suspect dowdy Denny of seducing her husband and continues to treat her more like a servant than a friend. To add to the tension, the Wrights' only daughter is having a secret affair with Ernest's protégé, and their youngest son, Ben, is as delicate and insufferable as only a poetry-writing fifteen-year-old can be. Then there are the guests, Nancy's best friend Anne and her new husband, the celebrated novelist Jonah Boyd. Their arrival will spark a chain of events that will change the family's lives forever.

'One of his generation's most gifted authors' *New York Times*

'Clever and funny . . . He gleefully details the pretensions of the aspirational middle classes, with their cheese balls, kaftans and affected radicalism, and he's perceptive about the lies and self-deceptions practised by family members' *Independent on Sunday*

'[A] modern comedy of bad manners' *Scotland on Sunday*

ISBN: 9 780 7475 6828 5/ Paperback / £7.99